OUT OF IRELAND

OUT
OF
IRELAND

A Novel

MARIAN O'SHEA WERNICKE

She Writes Press

Published 2023
Printed in the United States of America
Print ISBN: 978-1-64742-399-5
E-ISBN: 978-1-64742-421-3
Library of Congress Control Number: 2022915860

For information, address:
She Writes Press
1569 Solano Ave #546
Berkeley, CA 94707

Interior Design by Tabitha Lahr

She Writes Press is a division of SparkPoint Studio, LLC.

In honor of my maternal great-grandmother,
Ellen Hickey Sullivan Jewett,
And all her descendants in the Ward,
Bender, and O'Shea families.

Out of Ireland have we come.
Great hatred, little room,
Maimed us at the start.
I carry from my mother's womb
A fanatic heart.

—WILLIAM BUTLER YEATS
"Remorse for Intemperate Speech"

Barrett Street, St. Louis, Missouri, 1935

....

It's a dark February afternoon. Maggie's fingers are frozen as she reaches the front door of the big house on Barrett Street. Tall and slim, she looks more like a high school girl than she does an eighth-grader at Holy Name Catholic School. In the foyer, she pulls off the too-thin gloves. Glancing up, she notices her mother standing very still on the shadowy landing.

"Mom, what is it?"

"Oh, Maggie. I didn't hear you come in. It's your grand-mother. She's very bad today. Can you go in and see her for a minute?"

"Sure, Mom." Maggie groans inside. She dreads entering that bedroom these days. It's hard seeing her beloved Grand-mother Eileen and friend—the one who's been her refuge in a house full of loud, growing brothers—as she lies there in bed with sunken eyes, and hands grasping restlessly at the quilt, moaning in pain.

Maggie examines her own image in the mirror above the coat rack. She smooths her dark hair and bends to tug off her rubber boots, caked with dirty snow and ashes from the street. She grabs her scarf and dries the tracks puddling on the polished hardwood floor before Mother sees them. Then she runs up the stairs and gently pushes open the door of her grandmother's bedroom.

Light streams weakly between the slats in the blinds of the two windows facing the street. The smells hit her: a mixture of camphor, cold tea, sachets of lavender, and the musty scent of old age. Pearl rosary beads gleam on the night table next to the bed, beads Maggie loves to wind through her own fingers as she's seen her grandmother do.

Maggie tiptoes toward the slight figure in the bed. The old woman's head turns back and forth on the white pillowcase. Its crocheted edges frame her face, and her long gray hair spills out like a fan.

"Hi, Grandma. It's me, Maggie, home from school." Eileen's eyes shift in her direction, gray and opaque, unseeing. She murmurs, but Maggie catches fragments only: "Black bread and fish . . . the sea is rough today. . ."

Maggie sinks onto the bed, feeling her grandmother's thin body beneath the quilt. She takes the brown-speckled hand in her own small, white one and begins to chatter about her day at school, how Sister Rose Margaret shocked them all during arithmetic by making a joke about bottles of beer. At last, her grandmother quiets, drifting into a doze.

Tears run down Maggie's cheeks. Whom will she turn to when her grandmother dies? Her older brothers tease her with their rough play and their jokes that she never quite seems to understand. Her father is a distant figure, much older than her mother, and when he comes home from the painting company he owns, all he wants is his hot supper, a bucket of beer from the bootlegger across the street, and some peace and quiet while he smokes his cigar and reads the *St. Louis Post Dispatch*. She adores her mother, but Nell is busy running the house, always in the kitchen or supervising Miss Annie who comes to help her clean and wash and iron.

It is her mother's mother, Eileen, who has been her confidante and defense since she was little. Even though Maggie had been a big girl of seven when her sister Helen left to get married, she often lay trembling at night in the lonely room they'd shared. On stormy nights with the crack of thunder, the winds howling through the tall trees surrounding the house, Maggie would dash into her grandmother's room, leap into bed beside her, and burrow into her side with her eyes closed. Her grandmother would pull her close, and they would whisper to each other long into the night. Eileen told her the stories of her own childhood in Bantry, living near the sea, then the trip over on the boat, and finally, meeting the love of her life here in St. Louis.

Now Maggie grabs the rosary and slumps to the floor beside the bed. "Hail, Mary, full of grace. . ." She gazes at her grand-mother. So, this is death coming, this gradual withdrawal from every bright bit of the world around you. She decides she never wants to die herself.

Her grandmother snores softly. Maggie wanders over to her dresser, examining the old woman's treasures. She picks up a faded blue stuffed horse, its seams still tightly sewn. Why had her grandmother kept this old toy? She uncorks the bottle of Blue Grass perfume, a gift she had given her grandmother two Christmases ago. It smells spicy, fresh. Next to it, coiled in a porcelain cup, is a tarnished silver chain, with one bright pearl gleaming in the faint light.

Then she examines the picture she loves: a man and a woman, her grandparents when young, with her mother Nell, then a fair-haired little girl of about three, her arm thrown lovingly across her father's leg. A young Eileen, tall, her hair pulled back, with tiny curls carefully arranged on her forehead, stares out, calm and almost smiling. The bodice of her dress is fitted with a row of tiny buttons down the front, and a long, full taffeta skirt. She carries a parasol in her right hand. The young man is seated, handsome, with long legs stretched out in front of him, showing his highly-polished boots. His eyes look out fearlessly, his posture erect. The little girl's bonnet hangs on the back of her father's chair. The blond child is dreamy, serious, and probably tired of the long process of making a formal portrait. Visible at the bottom is the printed name, *Fischer*, and an address, *Cor. Ninth and Franklin Ave., St. Louis, MO*. Her grandmother would gaze at the picture, and with a sly smile, say, "Ah, he was the one, the love of my life."

Maggie stands still, her heart beating steadily. *What will my life be? Will I find the love of my life?*

Part 1

························

BANTRY BAY,
IRELAND, 1867

CHAPTER ONE

....

"For God's sake! Get down from that tree this instant, Mary Eileen O'Donovan! Sure, aren't you sixteen years old?"

From her perch in the great oak tree, Eileen saw her mother standing there, hands on hips, with her hair pulled back in a bun, and the wind from the sea whipping her skirts. Pretending not to hear, Eileen watched storm clouds scudding across the bay and the sky darkening to purple, melding with the gray of the sea. She was free up here, the place she could be alone and dream in peace. But she'd better obey. She sighed as fat raindrops fell, gathering her skirt and picking her way, branch by branch, to the ground. Suddenly a crack of thunder sent her sprinting toward the house.

After the light of the afternoon, the house was dark. Eileen glanced at the oval picture of the Sacred Heart of Jesus on the mantel. She touched the flaming heart with its crown of thorns and smoothed her hair, tucking the wild curls into her headband.

Her mother's back was toward her as, with both hands, she lifted the kettle from the fire in the wide kitchen hearth and poured water into the teapot, and the steam rose to her face. Eileen cut the bread, arranging it on the blue and white china plate she knew her mother loved, one of the few things left from her wedding gifts. Neither of them spoke.

Finally, the girl felt her mother's gaze taking in her wind-blown hair and her unbuttoned collar, showing a bit of the linen shift she wore beneath her blouse. She waited. Her mother cleared her throat, and when she spoke, Eileen was surprised at her calm, measured tone. She had expected a scolding.

"Eileen, dear, you know that things have been hard for us lately. Your brothers work themselves to death all day on our land, then at the Big House. But the price of grain has fallen, and we still owe the money for the seed we bought last year." She sipped her tea then, her eyes never leaving Eileen's face.

Eileen nodded, adding a spoonful of honey to her tea, stirring it slowly, trying to ward off what she knew was coming.

"Mother, I know. But I'm studying hard so I might have a chance for a place at the Teacher's College in Cork City. That would mean one less mouth to feed, and soon I'd be earning a salary for us all, something we could depend on, year in and year out." She paused, muttering under her breath, "Not like this stupid farm." Eileen looked down at her hands then so she wouldn't see the hurt in her mother's eyes.

Her mother stood. "Eileen, you know well that this house and this land are your father's legacy to us, the thing he was most proud of after the famine years, the thing he slaved away on so that he and I could marry, and then you little ones would have something to call your own and not have to be dependent on a landlord!"

Eileen had heard it all before: how her father, Martin O'Donovan, one of the smartest boys in Bantry Town, quit school at the age of ten to help his widowed mother and his five brothers and sisters. How they had come through the horror of the famine years, begging and scraping for every last bit of food, until finally, ingratiating himself with the Earl, Martin was hired to work at Blackthorn House. Then after several years of hard work, he was given this cottage and parcel of land—rent-free—on condition that part of each harvest was paid to the Earl.

But to Eileen these were only stories. She had no memory of this father. All she knew was that when she was three, her brother Martin had found their father lying dead in the field on a hot summer day, his head cradled in the grass near the shovel he'd been wielding before he was "felled by the bursting of his great heart," as her mother always said.

Her mother's voice was firmer now: "Eileen, your brother Martin and I have decided that it's time for you to marry like your cousin Kathleen. John Sullivan is a widower, and Martin tells me he's looking for a wife."

Heart hammering, Eileen stared at her mother. "No! Mother, how can you? I'm just sixteen! I've never even walked out with anyone."

Her mother avoided her gaze and fussed with the tea things. Eileen shoved her chair away from the table, grabbing a shawl hanging beside the hearth. "You can't make me, Mother! I'll run away. I'll go to the Presentation nuns in Cork City." She ran to the door, flinging it open onto the trees thrashing in the spring squall, and sobbing, raced out into the darkening yard, down the path toward the sea. She rushed on blindly with the wind and rain lashing her face.

They can't make me, they can't! She pictured cousin Kathleen, with two babies in three years, her husband a man already balding at the age of thirty-eight. Eileen knew about sex. She'd been raised on a farm, so she'd seen the savage way bulls mounted the poor dumb cows as they moaned in fright. She'd seen the bloody birth of a foal, and the way her dog Queenie had pushed away the puppies trying to nurse every time they'd get the chance. No! She could not picture being a mother herself.

Working at Blackthorn House had set her imagining another life, a life like the lives she read about in novels. She wanted to have adventures, and fall in love, but there was no lad in Bantry who could make her dream. Huddled beneath the oak tree, she pictured the Big House and its hushed solemn rooms, above all, she thought of the library. How often she'd dusted and swept that room, lingering over the mahogany desk with its pens and marble ink stand, and brushing her hands over the rows of tall volumes with gilt lettering. Lady Mary caught her in there one day with a book in her hands. Eileen's face flushed as she stammered, "Pardon me, Ma'am, but the books seemed a bit dusty."

"Yes, Eileen, I expect they are, as no one ever reads them anymore." There'd been a hint of a smile on her mistress's long face. "If you would like to borrow a book now and then, I'm sure the Earl wouldn't mind."

"Oh, thanks so much! I promise I will take good care of anything I borrow."

"Well, just write down the title and leave it here on the Earl's desk," Lady Mary said as she handed Eileen a piece of stationery with the Earl's crest. It was fine paper, paper Eileen wanted to keep and copy poems on. She'd tucked it in the pocket of her apron and gathered up her rags. Next time she'd choose a book and wrap it in her shawl to take home.

Since that day, she had read *Jane Eyre*, thrilling to the story of the poor orphaned cousin Jane, cast out to an orphanage by her aunt and the evil clergyman, but who ends up with the love of the darkly handsome Mr. Rochester, and an inheritance to boot! And how she loved the poems of Mr. Keats, especially "The Eve of St. Agnes." Brilliant, it was.

Now she thought bitterly of those books. A married woman had no time for books; she'd spend her days keeping house, working in the fields, and tending babies, one after another. She was to be traded off, like some cow on market day. Soaked and chilled to the bone, Eileen gazed out at the roiling bay before she turned back toward home. She'd talk to Michael. Surely, he'd be on her side.

CHAPTER TWO

....

"Michael, for God's sake wait till the storm has passed." In the dusky shed, three men huddled near the door, watching as Michael pulled his coat on, jamming his cap on his head.

"No, boys, I'm off home. Mammy will be waiting tea for me."

As he pushed open the door, he heard O'Brien sneer, "Ah sure, he's quite the revolutionary."

Two weeks had passed since Michael O'Donovan and three other local boys had been part of the failed uprising of the Fenians. In Cork, they were among the four thousand men who'd gathered at Fair Hill and marched to the train junction in Limerick, burning several police barracks in their wake, the four men gathered here in Bantry among them. Their membership in the Irish Republican Brotherhood was a secret, at least as far as they knew, and they needed to keep it that way. No one in Bantry knew where they'd been on the night of March 5th, but there were rumors in the town already that several local men had been in on the Rising. Now rebels of the failed attempt at independence were being hunted down, not only by the British Army, but also by the hated Irish Constabulary. Someone might rat them out at any minute. Time to lie low.

Michael walked fast, head down, with hunger gnawing at his stomach. What a fool he'd been! For months they'd drilled secretly at night after long days of work in the fields. They'd had such hope, but the Rising had been a disaster, the British Army brutally putting it down with their numbers and firepower.

As he trudged through the muddy fields, Michael felt despair creep in like the cold rain running down his back through his thin jacket. He was sick of working for the Earl, sick of no prospects for a future, sick of Ireland. He'd begun to think of America, of escape. It would mean leaving his mother, but he reasoned to himself, she had Martin around to help. The one he'd miss was Eileen. Only two years younger, his sister had been his playmate and friend, the only one in the family who knew about his secret Fenian activities. He'd persuaded her to cover up his late-night escapades, hinting to the family that he had a girl he was seeing. His only girl lately, the one he'd been fighting for, was Kathleen Ni Houlihan, Ireland herself!

As the rain slacked off, Michael gazed out at the sea. If he left Bantry, would he miss this small town on the edge of the restless Atlantic? And the sea with its constant roar as it clashed on the rocks of the bay, the green fields, and the smell of peat fires? He had few skills, he knew, but he could read and write well, and he knew how to care for sheep and cows, how to plant and plow. But was that how he wanted to spend his life? What could he do in America?

By now he had reached their cottage, smelling the smoke rising from the chimney. He found his mother and Martin sitting at the table, not speaking. Their old sheep dog, Queenie, lifted her head and thumped her tail on the hearth in greeting. Michael bent to run his hands over her thin frame, murmuring softly to her in Gaelic.

His mother looked up, frowning at his dripping coat and hat. "Michael, go and change and then sit down and have your tea. I want to talk to you."

Michael paused, his worn boots squeaking with water. Did she know about his activities? Did Martin? His older brother watched him, unsmiling. Michael headed for the ladder that led to the loft the brothers shared. Soon he was back at the table, wolfing down two thick pieces of black bread, smeared with his mother's currant preserves. The tea was hot and strong, just the way he liked it. He leaned back in his chair. "So, what's up with yous? Is it a wake we're having?"

"Don't say yous," his mother said absentmindedly. She folded her hands on the table and leaned forward. "I've just told Eileen that we want her to be married. Martin has spoken with John Sullivan. He's been widowed two years now, his farm is doing well, and he would be a good match for Eileen."

Michael sat back, his eyes and the set of his mouth betraying a brief flash of relief and then shock. "How could you?" He looked at Martin. "The girl is barely sixteen, and Sullivan is at least forty, and an old sour forty at that! My God, you people!" He stood up, shoving his chair away from the table. "You know she wants to study; the girl lives for books. You'd sell her to that old man, let her bear his kids year after year before she is even twenty? No, Mammy, don't do it." He looked pleadingly at his mother.

Mamie O'Donovan, practical, brisk, cleared the table without meeting his eyes. Michael sensed he was her favorite from the way she touched his hair sometimes as she passed the back of his chair while he was eating. Her eyes laughed when he told stories or went on and on about the bloody British. And she hadn't questioned too closely his absences at night over the past few months. But now as he glared at her, she looked away.

"No, Michael, it's time for that one to settle down. She's gotten way beyond herself, working up at the Big House, her head always in the books, even late at night. We need the help that Sullivan can provide," she said, looking down, and Michael knew she was ashamed.

His brother pushed back his chair roughly, bringing his face close to Michael's. "It's all arranged, Michael, so just shut up about it now and try to persuade Eileen to be reasonable. We've invited Sullivan over for tea on Sunday." They gazed at each other, and Michael's blue eyes were ice as he stared back at his older brother.

"You know, Martin, I'm sick of you bossing me around. You are not my father. I'm a grown man earning my keep and more, as you well know."

"No, what I do know is that you've gotten mixed up with the Fenians, the crazy bastards, and that you could bring ruin down on our house if you keep this up." Martin's face flushed.

Shocked, Michael looked at his mother who turned away from him. So, they did know what he was involved in. He felt a chill. His family was against him. They had little sympathy for the cause of Irish freedom, seemingly content to go on living as they and their ancestors had for two hundred years under British domination, barely scraping a living from the land and the sea, owing everything to the Earl's capricious will. And now his sister, with all her hopes, was to be the latest sacrificial lamb to their lack of courage. Well, at least now he could see his way clearly. And that way would lead to America, when and how he could not imagine, but Ireland was finished for him.

He leaned down and kissed his mother's cheek, saying softly, "Good night, mother. I hope you can sleep knowing what you are doing to your daughter."

Eileen, in bed in the room she shared with her mother, overheard the whole exchange. The pillowcase was damp from her tears, so she turned it over, pretending to be asleep as she heard her mother put out the lamp and throw ashes on the fire in the hearth. In the dark room, the moonlight shone in from the one window as her mother entered the tiny bedroom. She crossed over to the other side of the bed and began to undress slowly. She undid her corset, her strong, full figure outlined against the window. She sighed heavily as she slipped the coarse muslin nightgown on, and then Eileen heard the creak of the bed springs as her mother knelt to say her prayers. She'd grabbed her rosary from the bedpost and was mumbling the Hail Marys when Eileen felt her own eyes closing, unable to resist the lure of forgetfulness.

When she opened her eyes again it was dark, but she'd heard a faint whistle from outside. She pushed back the covers, gasping as her bare feet hit the cold floor. She crept noiselessly to grab her skirt and shawl and headed to the door, watching her mother's form rising and falling evenly. Gently, Eileen pulled the bedroom door shut and dressed hurriedly by the ashes of the hearth. She grabbed her clogs by the door and carried them outside. By now the moon had set, and the outlines of the trees and bushes were etched black against the faint gray fields in the distance.

"Halt!"

She whirled around to see her brother Michael, his white teeth gleaming in the gray light as he grabbed her and put his hand over her mouth. "Not a word, now, until we're farther from the house." She followed him down the lane until they stood beneath her favorite tree, still dripping from the afternoon storm.

"Oh Michael," she began, "what can I do? I don't even know this man. I swear I'll run away!"

"No, you won't, alannah. We'll think of something." He began stripping bark from the tree, frowning. "Maybe we could ask Cousin Kathleen to talk to Mammy. She understands now what it is to be a wife and mother."

"Oh, Kathleen! No, she's always been the obedient girl, the girl who couldn't wait to be out of school and set up in her own little place." Eileen stared at the tree above them, looking up through the branches to search for the stars. She knew her cousin would have no pity for her, even if she did seem overwhelmed when Eileen visited her, the wet nappies hanging from the rafters in their cramped cabin on rainy days, and the baby fussing as she nursed him, while her toddlers banged spoons on a dented pot. Although, she thought, Kathleen had been lucky in her husband, a shy, quiet fellow who never raised his voice to her and who seemed overwhelmed at his good fortune to have such a beautiful girl for his wife.

In the gray mist, Michael paced back and forth. "I don't like it either. Sullivan is too old, and one for the drink too. People say he used to beat his wife, the poor thing."

Eileen had heard her brother Martin, who worked for the widower at times, talk about Sullivan, how his infant son had died shortly after birth, and by the following year his wife was dead too, carried off by pneumonia, they said, but more likely by heartbreak.

"Wait!" he whipped around to face Eileen. "You'll tell them you're going to confession on Saturday. Then you can talk to Father Gleason in secret; surely it's against the Church to force a woman to marry against her will." He smiled in the gloom. "You might even hint that you'd been thinking of studying, maybe even of becoming a nun."

Eileen gasped, "Michael, now how could I be lying in church, in the very confessional?" She shook her head at the wild brother in front of her. But she realized that Father Hugh Gleason was the one person in Bantry her mother and older brother would listen to.

Ever since he had replaced Monsignor McCarthy, who retired to the old priests' home in Cork City, the people of Bantry had grown to respect and even love the new priest. Somewhere in his forties, he was a big man, broad of chest, with a crooked nose in a wide face. He reminded Eileen of a prize-fighter. When he gave her the Body of Christ in communion, his hands were rough and strong, not the soft hands of a city priest. There were even rumors in town that Father Gleason secretly supported the Fenians, although the bishops of Ireland claimed to be against the movement.

As Eileen gazed at the hills to the east, dawn was tracing pink and violet smudges across the sky. She too, like Ireland, was caught in a trap of being ruled by others when all she wanted was to learn and become whoever it was she was supposed to be, not some old man's unwilling second wife!

"Well, I'll go to confession on Saturday then. Surely our mother won't object to that," she said, linking arms with Michael. As they made their way back to the house, the rough sleeve of his shirt with its odor of cigarettes and sweat was a comfort in the cold dawn.

CHAPTER THREE

....

Saturday in the O'Donovan cottage was baking day. Eileen did not work at Blackthorn House on Saturday, instead spending it with her mother—and sometimes Kathleen—baking soda bread, apple cake, and scones for the week. At Blackthorn House, Mamie O'Donovan was known as the best baker around, and Lady Mary often requested her services when giving a large weekend party at the Big House. But today, to Eileen's relief, it was just she and her mother, aprons tied around their waists, their sleeves rolled up, with flour, sugar, eggs, apples, currants, and precious jars of cloves, nutmeg, and cinnamon laid out on the rough kitchen table.

Mother worked quietly, speaking only to direct Eileen in preparing the fire and greasing the pans, and leaving the tricky business of the actual mixing to herself. The girl watched as her mother patted the dough, tenderly shaped it, and then patted it gently again. Soon, Eileen shoved several trays of scones into the wide hearth, and the kitchen filled with the scent of cloves, cinnamon, and baking dough. But Eileen found that today she had little appetite. She still had not broached the subject of confession to her mother, nor had her mother said anything more about the marriage. She knew that the widower was to come to the house for tea on Sunday afternoon. She fought down the nausea that threatened to rise at the thought of the suitor.

"In two weeks it will be Easter," her mother sighed, "and then we'll start the planting again. I only hope the crops will be better this year." She frowned, brushing back her graying hair from her face as she glanced at Eileen.

"Yes, and I was thinking I'd like to go to St. Finbarr's this afternoon for confession, if you don't need me." Eileen kept her eyes on the scones.

"Confession! Why, what need do you have to go to confession?" Eileen felt her mother's gaze on her now.

"Mother, you know it is the Easter duty to go to confession and communion. Don't worry. There probably won't be a long line." She smiled at her mother then, washing her hands and slipping out of her apron.

Her mother nodded and bent to take the scones out of the deep hearth. "Well, run along then, and when you come home you can bring me a bit of gossip; you can tell me who else was in line." She smiled again at her daughter, and Eileen felt a pang of guilt at her maneuver. But they couldn't force her to marry. It wasn't right, so she had to fight with the only tool she had, cunning.

As Eileen set out for St. Finbarr's parish church, her heart lifted. She pulled the white shawl from her head and swung it as she walked. The sun glinted on the bay; the sky looked a blue so deep she could drown in it. All traces of yesterday's storm had passed, leaving the air clean and cool. She loved climbing the steps to the gray stone church and entering the dusky coolness. She loved the scent of the incense lingering there and the red votive lights flickering in the gloom. At the far end was the golden tabernacle where, she knew from the candle glowing in the scarlet sanctuary lamp swinging above the altar, Christ in the host rested night and day.

Unlike her friends who often giggled and whispered during Mass on Sundays, Eileen felt exalted as she watched Father Gleason in his silk chasuble bowing before the altar, holding the gilt-edged missal high before reading the gospel, first in Latin and then in Gaelic. Hearing the notes of the silver bell as the host was held high for all to see, Eileen felt that the world itself, the sea, the trees, the hills, were being drawn up to God along with all the poor sufferers on earth.

As she walked to confession, she rehearsed what she would say to Father. She'd tell him her sins, her gossiping with her friends, her impure thoughts, mostly arising from her reading, her disobedience. Then she'd ask him about obedience. She'd pour out her heart to him, maybe even shed a few tears, and beg him to save her from marriage to a man she scarcely knew. Father Gleason knew she loved studying. She'd tell him of her desire to be a teacher and help her family that way.

Entering St. Finbarr's, she reached for the holy water font and blessed herself. Her eyes adjusted to the dim light. Only a handful of people knelt near the confessional, mostly old ladies. She watched as Patch O'Kelly stumbled out of the confessional, wheezing and coughing, and Mrs. Halloran slipped into the other side. Eileen stood at a little distance, waiting her turn, trying not to hear the murmurs of the woman and Fr. Gleason. Suddenly she felt afraid, and she whispered to herself, "Mary, dear Mother of God, help me in my hour of need."

Finally, it was her turn. Father slid back the little wooden panel, and through the grate she could make out his rugged profile.

"Bless me, Father, for I have sinned. It's about a month since my last confession. I have gossiped with my friends, telling tales about other people. I have impure thoughts sometimes when I am reading novels. I have disobeyed my mother and my older brother many times." She stopped.

"Go on, my child. Is that all?"

She thought she heard the priest yawn. Now she whispered, "No, Father. I need your help. It's Eileen O'Donovan, Father. My mother is trying to force me to marry an older man, a widower. I am barely sixteen, Father! I want to study, be a teacher. Can you please come and speak to my mother and brother? God can't want me to marry someone I don't even know, can He?"

There was silence for a few long minutes. "Who is it, Eileen?"

"John Sullivan," she said, her voice trembling.

Father Gleason sighed and shifted in the hard wooden chair. She thought she heard him say a curse word. Then he whispered, "Eileen, have you ever felt called to become a nun? I could make a much better case to your mother if you wanted to dedicate your life to our Lord that way. After all, you like to study, so you could become a Presentation nun in Cork City, not too far from here. Then you could become a teacher." His voice rose in hope as he finished.

Eileen was silent. Oh, how she wished she could go along with the priest's plan. But the thought of shutting herself up in a convent, all those hours of praying, putting on a veil and long black habit, never having a fellow to walk out with on soft summer evenings as she had imagined so often, everything inside her rose up against the idea.

"No, Father," she said mournfully. "I'm afraid I don't have a vocation."

"Well then, young lady, I will see what I can do. Now for your penance, say three Our Fathers and three Hail Marys. *Ego te absolvo....*"

Eileen recited the Act of Contrition in a rush so she wouldn't forget it. Father slid the wooden panel closed, and she pushed the dark red velvet curtain aside, walking quickly to a pew in front. She bowed her head as she said her penance. Then she looked up at the altar with the image of the crucified Christ suspended above: the crown of thorns, the matted hair, his gaunt face, and the nails in his white hands and feet.

"I'm sorry for Your troubles, Lord," she whispered. As she rose to go, she felt suddenly ashamed of her own cowardice. Maybe she should sacrifice everything to help her family. Who did she think she was, anyway? But Father Gleason had not said this. He said he would help her.

As she walked home, she felt the wind from the sea in her hair, and she broke into a run. She'd be free, she thought, she'd never give in to this marriage.

On Saturday, Michael headed up to the Big House to see if he was needed to drive the carriages or fetch packages from town for the family and the cook, while carrying his mother's freshly baked apple cake for the Earl and his family. Through the linen towel, he felt the warmth, and the smell of apples and cinnamon made his mouth water. It had been hours since his breakfast, and that had been only bread and tea with a little grease from the bacon jar spread on the bread.

As he came to the long driveway, he saw Caroline, the young daughter of the house, astride her black filly, Maeve. Caroline rode well; her long black riding habit set off the slender grace of her figure. Her honey-blond hair was tucked into a bun, but as she cantered toward him, some wisps escaped. Her eyes shone when she pulled up in front of him.

"Well, if it isn't young Michael on this fine morning," she grinned, her teasing just on the edge of flirtatiousness.

Michael always tried not to stare at her, hiding the gleam of desire she might read in his eyes. She was not for him, he knew. Rich, Protestant, and a world above him, she enjoyed exercising her power over any man in her path. Several times lately when he'd helped her onto her horse and felt the supple waist under his hands, he'd been sorely tempted to crush her to him. He might have tried it, he knew, but he sensed something cold and calculating as she ran her eyes over him every time they met.

She was bad business for the likes of him. He lifted his cap in an exaggerated motion and bowed.

"Good morning to you, Miss." As he turned to go, he felt her riding crop on his shoulder. He looked up at her.

"Michael, why don't you ride with me sometime? We could race over to the Sheridans."

"Ah, many thanks Miss, but I've duties to fulfill."

"Well, maybe I could be one of those duties."

He stared at her as a faint blush rose on her cheeks. For once he could think of nothing to say. With a laugh, she wheeled her horse around and took off, scattering mud from yesterday's storm on his boots. Michael swore and followed her with his eyes. To her he was just a plaything, a puppy to be fondled and petted and then cast aside.

For years now he'd struggled with "temptations of the flesh," as Father Gleason called them. And it would be years until he could afford to marry, if ever. What was he supposed to do with desire? Fumble under the covers at night, holding his breath so that his brother Martin wouldn't hear, fantasizing about Caroline coming toward him through the woods in a flowing white gown that outlined the curves of her body, his heart beating like mad, her scent of roses and spice overwhelming him as took her in his arms and buried his face in her hair. *He was mad.*

He kicked every stone in the driveway with a vicious pleasure. Another reason to flee to America. He'd heard the girls fell all over you in the States, and in New York there'd be no gossiping villagers around every corner.

He entered Blackthorn House at the back door as Mrs. Hanrahan was just taking a ham from the oven. Its smell overwhelmed him. She gave him a quick glance and saw the towel-wrapped cake under his arm.

"Oh, God be praised," she sighed. "Michael, your mother is a saint, she is! I haven't had time to make a dessert this morning and Lady Mary will be cross if I give them fruit again."

Michael put the cake down on the wooden table, and Mrs. Hanrahan slid it onto a crystal cake plate. He could not keep his eyes off the steaming ham, and finally, the cook relented. Silently, she sliced a large chunk from the ham and wrapped it in brown paper, tying it with string. She shoved it inside Michael's jacket with a wink. "Sure, now they won't miss it, with the ladies on a diet and Sir John already hitting the port."

"Thanks, Mrs. H., this will be great with our tea this after-noon." He could hardly wait to get out of the kitchen. Ham was something they had only at Christmas, and the smell over-powered him. By the time he got home, the piece of ham would have shrunk, he knew. He felt ashamed somehow of his hunger and of the sly way he had wheedled the gift from the cook, a gift that was not hers to give. It was a damn shame to live in a country in which a man had to shuffle and grovel, hiding his real feelings at every turn.

Outside, beneath his favorite beech tree, he took a bite of the ham and watched the sun filtering through tender new leaves. He forced himself to wrap the ham again and save the rest for the family. He spent the day in the barn turning the last of autumn's hay in the loft. He worked until sweat stained his shirt, conscious always of the ham nestled there.

By five-thirty the sun's rays gleamed on the bay in the fading evening light, and Michael, wiping his face, hung up his tools carefully before shutting and latching the barn door. As he started down the gravel drive toward the great iron gates of Blackthorn House, he heard a whistle from the edge of the woods surrounding the house. A flash of a red handkerchief meant one of the boys of the Rising was waiting for him. Look-ing around, he walked slowly toward the copse and entered the shady woods on the edge of the avenue.

"Well, if it isn't the hard-working lad of the Big House," said John O'Brien as he stepped out from a tree. He was a short, stocky man, older than Michael, with a sarcastic twist to his mouth. He raised a flask to his mouth and took a long drink. "Sure, you must enjoy being around the gentry, especially the fair Lady Caroline," he smirked as he wiped his mouth on his sleeve.

"O'Brien, you know how I feel about the landowners. You're not the only one who wants to see the backs of them when they leave."

"And that's just what I've come all this way to see you about, my boy. The IRB is not finished in spite of all the dirty informers who sold us out. There are plans afoot to start more actions closer to home, like raiding the army's barracks for guns. These will be stealth raids at night, not open warfare. We'll be in and out before anyone even knows we've been there."

Michael felt his stomach lurch. He'd relished the action in Cork a few weeks ago, taking on the British Army alongside hundreds of armed Irishmen, as well as seasoned Irish American veterans of their own civil war, all in the name of freeing Ireland. Somehow that attempt, although unsuccessful, had seemed a fair and above-board type of warfare. But to raid the army's barracks only a few miles from Bantry, with just a handful of poorly trained country lads, sounded a hell of a lot more dangerous.

"So, the boys and me will be waiting for you in Paddy's hut on Sunday night to talk over the plans," O'Brien said, taking another swig from the flask. "We can count on you, Michael now, can't we?"

"I'll be there," Michael muttered. He stared at O'Brien as the man turned away, melting into the deep woods. Damn! His loyalty would be suspect now, and his family too might become a target for the IRB if they suspected him of less than enthusiastic support for the cause. He felt for the chunk of ham beneath his coat and turned down the great drive toward home.

CHAPTER FOUR

······················

Eileen woke suddenly, hearing her mother bustling around the kitchen; her heart sank as she remembered. It was Sunday. She lay still and squeezed her eyes shut, willing herself to go back to sleep. Rain beat against the high window of the bedroom. She pulled the covers over her head and grabbed the rosary she had clung to last night to lull herself to sleep. Surely Father Gleason would think of something.

Later, in the kitchen, her mother, dressed for Sunday Mass in her best long black skirt and cotton blouse, turned to look at her. "Get dressed, girl! We're going to the eight o'clock Mass, so I'll have plenty of time to get ready for tea this afternoon." She laid a white linen tablecloth with a blue border on the old wooden table. She avoided Eileen's eyes. "Wear your good dress, and carry your shoes, so they don't get ruined in the wet," she called after Eileen as the girl disappeared into the bedroom without a word.

The two women walked down the hill toward the church in silence, speaking only when they passed their neighbors on the way to early Mass. Her serene mother had a smile and a greeting for all she met. The rain slacked, and Eileen stepped carefully over the puddles on the road, carrying her good shoes beneath her shawl, her stocking feet soaked in her clogs.

As they entered the church, Eileen stared. All the statues and the crucifix over the altar were shrouded in purple. Even the altar itself was draped in purple. It was Passion Sunday, the beginning of the final two weeks of Lent, leading up to the sorrowful mysteries of Holy Week and then the burst of joy on Easter Sunday.

Eileen thought bitterly of Easter. *"Please, dear Lord,"* she prayed as the two women knelt on the hard kneelers, *"make my mother's heart soften. I'm not ready to be married."*

Father Gleason, clad in the purple vestment of the Passion, ascended to the pulpit for the sermon. She raised her face to him. The priest, towering over the lectern, cleared his throat and stared out at the congregation. He paused, and all the shuffling and coughing quieted.

"This morning we have read the Gospel of St. John, in which our blessed Lord and the Pharisees are locked in a tense confrontation. They accuse Him of having a devil! But Jesus replies, 'I have not a devil; but I honor my Father and ye have dishonored Me. But I seek not my own glory; there is one who seeketh and judgeth. Amen, amen, I say to you, if any man keep my word, he shall not see death forever.'" The priest paused and looked around the congregation.

"Now what could Our Lord have meant about honoring His Father? The Pharisees did not at first understand that he was referring to God, but when it finally dawned on those hard-hearted, self-righteous men, they accused Him of blasphemy for equating Himself with God." Closing the missal with a loud thump, the priest looked out at the upturned faces.

He began softly, "And how do we honor our Lord? By being smug and self-righteous like the Pharisees? The fourth commandment tells us to honor our father and our mother. But what about parents? Should they not also honor the children God has given them? Do fathers have the right to beat their sons? Do mothers have the right to force their daughters into marriages they do not wish? Let each and every one of us look into our hearts this morning and ask ourselves if we are truly honoring our Father in heaven when we dishonor His children on earth."

No one breathed. The air in the church grew tense as people wondered what in the world Father was on about. Eileen glanced sideways at her mother. Mamie O'Donovan's eyes were closed as she passed her rosary beads through her fingers. She did not seem to be listening to the words of the sermon, but Eileen knew, from the grim set of her mouth, that she had heard every word and knew full well for whom his words were meant. Eileen's heart thudded.

On the swift walk back home, once out of sight of the villagers, Eileen's mother gripped her arm hard, digging her fingers into it. "I will not have that priest in my house again, I swear by my husband's grave. He can keep his nose out of our affairs. And how did he know anyway?" She stared at Eileen, striding faster, "What does he know about feeding a family on nothing, living in fear of the crops failing, losing the house we have only been granted by the whim of a landlord that may flit back to England at any time?" She paused for breath, her face white and stony.

Then she turned to look into Eileen's eyes. "Alannah, I know you are afraid of marrying Sullivan. But you will learn to love and respect your husband in time. And then the babies will come, and you will be so busy and happy. . . " Here her voice trailed off. With a shock, Eileen saw lines of worry and sorrow carved into her mother's strong face. She looked old for the first time to Eileen, an old woman.

Her mother's voice softened as she went on, "Eileen, I grew to love your father, a man my father chose for me. I pray it will happen for you too." She reached up, and with her shawl wiped the tears from Eileen's cheeks. Stung by this unaccustomed tenderness, Eileen followed her mother home. The rain had stopped, but the day was gray and dull. As her clogs crunched on the gravel road out of town, they chanted, "No hope, no hope."

By four o'clock the cottage was ready for the visitor. Three chairs were set around the kitchen table and the fireside seat was pulled up for two more. The men would take a glass of Spanish sherry from the bottle Mamie had kept hidden, a gift from the Earl last Christmas. A platter of soda bread slathered with butter and the thinnest slivers of the ham Michael had brought home from the Big House was on the table, an apple cake fresh from the oven next to it. Five rose-bordered cups and saucers were set out for the tea, with five starched white napkins folded neatly beside them. A blue pitcher, stuffed with the first snowdrops to appear around the cottage, made the centerpiece.

Martin and Michael wore freshly ironed white shirts, their hair plastered back with the marks of the comb still evident. Mamie, still in her linen blouse and long black skirt, was hurriedly removing her apron. She called to Eileen, "Well now, come on out, and show yourself, my girl. Let's see the bride-to-be," she called with a forced note of gaiety.

Just then Queenie began barking, and they saw the widower approaching the house. Martin opened the door to receive him. Sullivan bent his head as he entered mumbling, "May God bless all within this house." He bowed to Mamie and shook hands with the two men.

They stood around stiffly until the bedroom door opened and Eileen appeared in the doorway. Her face was white, her light brown hair pulled back by a black ribbon at the nape of her neck. Her dress, her only good one, was green, with sprigs of white blossoms, and she plucked nervously at the lace cuffs. With her head high, she walked over to John Sullivan and held out her hand. He took it in his, and Eileen felt the hard calloused hand swallow hers. He bowed his head, and mumbled, "John Sullivan, at your service." She looked into his eyes and said clearly, "Mary Eileen O' Donovan, sir."

With much scraping of chairs, the men settled down while the women served the glasses of sherry and heated the water for tea. Eileen sat next to Michael, his eyes bright as he gave her a sly wink. Martin began, "So now, John, how have you been keeping on your farm all alone in that house?

"Well, you know that times are hard, Martin. I'm hoping to put in two fields of oats this spring." He gripped his sherry glass as he gazed at Eileen. The talk flowed over her as she tried not to stare at his thinning hair, hooded eyes, his broad red nose, and the stubble on his face. His coat was worn but mended neatly, and his boots were clean. He said little, his speech halting, but when he smiled, she saw the big, bashful boy he had been. She felt a sudden pity for him, forced to be inspected just as she was.

He noticed her watching him and turned to her, "I hear that you have been working at the Big House these days."

"Yes, I go up when needed, to dust and sweep and help Mrs. Hanrahan in the kitchen."

"Oh, and Eileen is becoming a fine cook these days," prodded Mamie. "Isn't she now, boys?"

Michael grinned and sat back, reaching for another glass of sherry despite his mother's warning look. "I don't know if I'd say that. In truth she likes keeping her nose in the books while the baking burns. The girl loves to study, you see, John, and has always wanted to be a teacher." Michael's eyes blazed as he looked at Sullivan to be sure he got the message, ignoring the stares of his mother and brother.

Sullivan shook his head. "Not much time on a farm to be reading books," he said, looking at Mrs. O'Donovan. She jumped up to pour the tea.

Michael reached for his jacket and cap, saying hastily, "Sorry to miss this, but I'm off. I've urgent business in town." He avoided Eileen's eyes, and as he passed her on his way out, she hissed under her breath, "Coward!"

Eileen thought the visit would never end as the conversation, in fits and starts, circled awkwardly around the crops, the weather, and the gossip of the town, with Sullivan stealing shy looks at

Eileen without ever addressing her. Finally, as he stood up to go, he asked Mamie, "Would it be all right, Mrs. O'Donovan, if I call on Eileen next Sunday to go walking?"

"Certainly, you may," her mother said brightly, "and you must stay for tea when you come."

Once more, Sullivan grasped Eileen's hand, murmuring, "Happy to meet you, Miss." She forced herself to look into his eyes. They were dark and unreadable as he pressed her hand hard in farewell.

Michael walked swiftly, the evening, wet and windy, darkening around him. He had to get out of that house with his mother and brother fawning over John Sullivan, his usually bold sister so pale and subdued, the lump of that man, tongue-tied and morose as he'd gazed hungrily at Eileen. He himself had eaten nothing, not wanting to give his mother the satisfaction of seeing her brood united around the table as they prepared to sell his sister to the highest bidder! God damn them! The worst of it was that he could do nothing to save her.

Well, now a great thirst was upon him as he hurried through the gloom toward the meeting with the lads at Paddy's cabin deep in the hills. There'd be strong poteen he knew, and he quickened his steps, almost able to taste the burn as it slid down his throat. To his left, far below, the sea roared in its infernal restlessness, echoing the tumult of his mind. He was not looking forward to the gathering, knowing the cock-eyed plot O'Brien had let slip.

In the distance a light flickered, and as he neared the hovel, a dog ran out, baring his teeth as he jumped at Michael. He was tempted to give the dog a swift kick, but he refrained, ashamed. He entered the dark, smoky room, barely able to see the group huddled around the hearth, their caps pulled down over their faces. Paddy, a stocky old man, rose to greet him.

"Welcome to you, Michael O'Donovan," he said in the high, fawning voice he assumed with the Irish Republican Brotherhood men. Michael didn't trust Paddy. He was a hanger-on, good for the poteen and the place to meet, but not really one of the Brotherhood. If trouble came, he wasn't sure that Paddy wouldn't sell them out to the Royal Irish Constabulary. The others looked up and murmured their greetings, shoving aside so that he could sit close to the fire. Paddy put a mug into his hand, and Michael took a long drag, gasping as he wiped his mouth on the rough sleeve of his jacket. As the men's murmurs began again, Michael glanced around the hut. O'Brien was there along with Mick Quigley and Johnny Fagin, all boys he had grown up with in the parish, boys who had trained with him for the aborted Rising this past year.

In the center stood a stranger, gray-haired with a close-cropped head. In the flickering firelight, the stranger's eyes shone a deep, cold blue. Michael took another drag of the drink and turned to listen to him.

"You boys are too young to remember Wolfe Tone, but your grandfathers would. In '98, he came from France with a fleet of forty-three ships to these very shores. The damned Irish weather beat them back. Tone was a Protestant, lads, but a Dublin man convinced of the need for Ireland to be free forever from the bloody British. He'd talked the French into helping Ireland, even going to parlay with old Boney!" The stranger's voice was low but ardent as he spoke. When he stopped and looked around at each man, they raised their mugs and toasted the French. Michael kept his eyes on the stranger, stirred by the passion in his voice.

"Tone came back again, but this time with a pitifully small fleet of Frenchmen. Our people rose up with pitchforks to help, but were quashed by thirty thousand English troops. The French soldiers were considered prisoners of war and were shipped home. But what happened to the Irish men and women who fought?" Here he looked around the group who sat silent, willing him to go on. "They were shot, every man and woman, their houses burned to the ground, the fires lighting up the night all over the countryside." He stopped, and the men took a long drink. Michael noticed that the stranger was not drinking.

"What happened to Tone?" asked Michael. For the first time he felt the blue eyes trained on him.

The stranger glanced at Michael and continued, "He was arrested, brought to Dublin and court-martialed, then condemned to death by hanging. They found him the morning he was to be hanged with a knife wound to his throat. He died eight days later." He looked around at each of the men. "Today, boys, the English occupy our country with more of their soldiers than they have in the whole continent of India. So, you see, the English will do anything it takes to keep us a subject nation. Your parents saw that in the famine, with food being shipped every day to England while they and your grandparents went hungry, forced from their miserable homes out onto the road with their babies to starve in the hedges. And as they left, those huts were burned to the ground." He smiled, and Michael thought he would never like to face that particular smile.

The stranger's voice rose in the stuffy room, "But now a great force of Irishmen has arisen. We are eighty thousand Fenians in this island right now! And in America, there are twice that number supporting us, sending money and even men here who have fought in America's Civil War. We can do no less!"

The group cheered, heartened by the strength of the movement. The stranger continued in a steely voice, "So lads, the IRB has decided that what we need now are guns, lots of guns. This will mean stealth raids here around Bantry on both army barracks and Irish Constabulary barracks, with roadside attacks on convoys of soldiers as we pick up the fight once more. Can we count on you brave Bantry boys?"

O'Brien spoke first after the silence grew heavy. "I, for one, am in, Captain!" He looked around, swaying a bit on his stool.

One by one they murmured their assent until finally all eyes were on Michael. The stranger looked at Michael. "I see, someone has doubts about up-close warfare," he said quietly.

"It's not safe for those of us who live here," Michael said, struggling to keep his voice steady. "Already there's talk here in Bantry that some of us were involved in this past March's troubles. Surely, we'd be better off going somewhere nobody knows us."

The stranger stood up, not looking at Michael. "Well lads, I've told you the plan. Before Good Friday I want O'Brien to give me the names of all who are in. The leaders of the IRB in Dublin have now proclaimed an official Provisional Government. So, each of you needs to take the oath of fealty to the new government. You will be notified of a time and place. Anyone not on board is henceforth excluded from any gathering of the Brotherhood and will be under surveillance by the IRB. Understood?"

He rose, and Michael was surprised at what a slight figure the stranger cut in the light of the fire. The man turned up the collar of his jacket and tugged a tweed cap down low over his face. Like a cat, he slipped from the room, leaving the men to their drink and their talk. The atmosphere lightened, but Michael felt dizzy with smoke and fear.

"Who the hell was that?" he whispered to Quigley.

"He calls himself MacDonogh, but I suspect that's not his real name. He's an officer of the IRB from somewhere around Waterford." He peered at Michael. "Say, O'Donovan, you're not going soft on us now, are you?"

"I don't fancy strangers coming in here and telling us what will be done," Michael whispered. "He doesn't know Bantry and wasn't willing to listen to us. Bantry is a small town, and everyone has known us here since we were running around in nappies. Who's to say we wouldn't be ratted out by people who think the Fenians are crazy?"

Quigley, quite drunk by now, slapped him on the back and got up to refill his jar. Michael rose to leave, tipping his cap to the others as he threw a few coins in Paddy's dish by the door. As he left, he heard laughter and felt that he was now suspect, as the captain had said.

The walk home in the dark steadied Michael after the tense, over-heated air in the cabin. He cursed softly to himself for not having drunk more deeply. The stranger had been mesmerizing with his recital of the sins of the Brits, the hard edge of fury in his voice all the more thrilling for being so soft and contained.

Why had he opened his mouth? Was it fear for his life that held him back? He hadn't been afraid during the Rising last month when the guns blazed around him, just angry and aroused as he'd fired aimlessly into the darkness toward the garrison of the Brits, surrounded by hundreds of armed IRB soldiers. And still they had failed, betrayed by informers within the ranks of the Fenians. Hundreds of men languished now in British hell-hole prisons. Even more chancy would it be to attack a local garrison or ambush a convoy with local members of the Royal Irish Constabulary, people he knew, and who knew him.

Jesus! He *was* getting soft, just as Quigley had said. He'd take the damn oath with O'Brien. He'd go to the meeting, he'd listen to the plan and hope he could convince this MacDonogh, or whatever his name was, that they'd be better to go further afield, maybe even past Cork where they were not known.

He looked up at the stars gleaming in the cold spring night and thought with a pang of America, under those same stars. He was trapped, he and his sister, his ancestors, all of them caught in a doomed land unable to escape the tidal pull of their history, their sorrow. Ireland was a cruel mistress unwilling to let anyone leave her without guilt.

CHAPTER FIVE

....

Easter came and went as Eileen walked like a specter through the days. Planting began, with the men hard at work in the fields all day, the women going out to them morning and afternoon to bring them tea and sandwiches. Her moments of pleasure came only on days like today when she was walking up the tree-lined avenue that led to the circular entrance of Blackthorn House, with the blue bay glittering off to the right. Wisps of smoke rose from each chimney, for the mornings were still cool now at the end of April.

She entered the kitchen through the trade entrance and said good morning to Mrs. Hanrahan, who looked up from her chopping to greet her. Then she headed with her dust cloths and polish upstairs to the two drawing rooms, pulling back the rose velvet drapes to the sight that never failed to delight in every season: the bay, sparkling as now on a perfect spring day, or even on a stormy day when it became an angry gray, tossing the sailboats like match boxes, or on a clear winter day when frost glittered on the terraces and the bay gleamed blue and still all the way to Whiddy Island and the Caha Mountains beyond.

Today she dawdled over the dusting and sweeping, poking the fire, and making sure the logs were hissing in the brass grate of the marble fireplace. As she left the drawing room, she turned and gazed at the perfection of the long room, with its tufted couches, silken peach-covered chairs, the blue and white vases she feared she might break as she dusted them, and, on the center table, the tall crystal vase with pussy willow and forsythia branches. Who had gone out so early to cut them? Today she pretended that she was the daughter of the Earl, and she swayed and lifted her arms to a dashing figure who bowed over her hand as he asked her to dance.

As if summoned by her fantasy, Lady Caroline appeared at the door, dressed in her riding habit.

"A beautiful morning, Miss," breathed Eileen with a little bob of her head.

"Oh! It's you then," Caroline glanced her way. "I thought I heard my mother in here. Eileen, when you get to my room, be sure to gather up the things that need to be washed and take them downstairs to the laundry. I'm afraid I've left them strewn all over. I'm in a hurry to get in a ride before the rain starts up once more." She had already turned to go, so didn't see the way Eileen lifted her chin and the flash of something like ice glinting in her blue-green eyes.

Eileen had a hard time with the young miss, a girl she had known ever since they were both small. Once, years before, they had played together under the oak tree on the great swing that Eileen's father painstakingly carved and hung for the Earl's only child. Eileen had walked up to the House with her mother to deliver some baked treats, and when she'd spied the lacy petticoat of the child swinging higher and higher, she bolted from the kitchen door and stood shyly in front of her. Caroline stared at her gravely as she let the swing slow down, and with a gesture of her little hand, invited Eileen to sit beside her. Side by side, they swung higher and higher, with Eileen pumping vigorously until their feet, hers bare and Caroline's shod in patent leather slippers, almost touched the branches of the oak. They shrieked with joy. Suddenly a window from the second floor was flung open, and Lady Mary leaned out.

"Caroline," her voice rose silvery but firm, "It's time for your lessons. Mademoiselle is waiting in the library." Without a word to Eileen, Lady Mary closed the window, and somehow in that moment Eileen understood that she was not to be the playmate of this child and that she would never sit in a library and have her lessons from Mademoiselle.

Now, relieved that Caroline was gone, she crept silently into the library. She'd dusted it just the other day so had no business being in here. If Mrs. Grogan, the elderly housekeeper, saw her, she'd be suspicious, the old bat! But Eileen knew her days in the House were few now that she was to be married. No more would she be able to choose a book, and feel its soft leather cover like silk in her hand, or see its gilt-edged pages gleaming. Never again would she sign the paper on the desk with her name and the title, and then at night in her bed read and read, burning the candle until it guttered out and her mother sighed to her to put down the blessed book and get some rest.

Well, she was here now, and this time she was not going to sign the book's title nor her name on the page. On the desk was a book she had not seen before, *Wuthering Heights*, by Emily Brontë. Eileen had loved *Jane Eyre* by Charlotte Brontë. Could this book be by her sister? She slipped the fat volume into her apron pocket and stuffed some rags on top of it. This would be a keepsake. She knew she'd have to confess the theft to the priest, and then, somehow, she'd have to return the book, but right now the Earl and his wife owed her this book, these people who had stolen her ancestors' land.

With her chores done and making sure the coast was clear, she made her way down the wide staircase, past the portraits of the Earl's ancestors with their stiff, long Anglo-Irish faces gazing down on her as she caressed the warm wood of the banister for one last time, her footsteps silent on the thick carpet.

In the kitchen Mrs. Hanrahan was sitting at the table sipping her tea. She smiled at Eileen when she noticed her standing still in the doorway. Eileen spoke softly, trying to hide her sadness. "I'll be off now, Mrs. Hanrahan, as soon as I wash out these rags."

"Oh, sit down, lass," the cook motioned to her, "and have some tea while you tell me all about your wedding." The woman's eyes were kind as she gazed at Eileen.

Eileen sat and poured herself a cup of tea. She found she could not speak and looked mutely at Mrs. Hanrahan. At last, she heard herself say, "It's to be the first Sunday in June after the banns have been called three times," she whispered.

"Ah, so soon?" the woman laughed. "You know the old saying, 'Marry in haste, repent at leisure.'"

"I've already repented, a thousand times," Eileen said and burst into tears. Mrs. Hanrahan put down her cup and came over to Eileen, lifting the girl's face to look into her eyes.

"Now then, alannah, no need for tears. John Sullivan will make you a good husband and you will have your own cottage and pretty soon some babies to fill your days. You are young, it's true, but strong and smart. You will be able to get round him in a thousand ways and he will end up doing your bidding, I should wager. As long as you keep him fed and happy in bed, you should get your way." She brushed the tears from Eileen's face and then busied herself with wrapping a loaf of bread for Eileen to take home with her.

The cook, bent from her years of serving in the kitchen, walked with Eileen to the door of the kitchen and together they looked out into the garden beyond. Bees buzzed in the wisteria and a golden haze hung over the garden. Eileen thanked her with a shaky smile, picked up the pile of rags that hid the stolen book, and walked slowly through the garden maze, feeling the eyes of Mrs. Hanrahan on her until she turned the corner to the driveway. She did not look back.

Michael had given O'Brien his name reluctantly, hoping he could still talk MacDonogh into attacking a convoy or a barracks in some other county, far from Bantry. The meeting of the newly formed unit of the IRB in Bantry was set for this night, the first Saturday in May, and once again would be held in Paddy's cabin in the hills above the town. Michael left home after their tea and the rosary, during which his mumbled Hail Marys were a strange prelude to the evening's business. His mother was worried about him, he knew. Martin had become the steady one now, while Michael's secret comings and goings at night, and his refusal to go to communion on Sundays, instead slouching in the back of the church during Mass and bolting out the door after the last blessing before Father had even left the altar, all pointed to something dangerous that was luring him away from family.

The May night smelled of freshly mown grass, cow dung, and the sea. Michael climbed up into the hills overlooking the bay. The new moon and a few stars gleamed in the blue, fast-falling dusk. He thought grimly that he should be courting a beautiful girl on a night like this, not stepping into a trap that could lead to his death or imprisonment. An image rose, the black hair and blue eyes of Caroline, the way she sat on her horse, wielding the whip lightly but expertly as she galloped over the treacherous hills leading out of Bantry. What in hell was he doing?

The cabin rose out of the darkness. Michael was surprised when he entered not to see Paddy. He glanced at O'Brien and lifted his brows questioningly.

"Paddy's been sent on an errand. Captain doesn't trust him," O'Brien muttered to Michael. This time there was no drink either.

MacDonogh stood in front of the skimpy fire in the hearth, warming his hands. He looked steadily at Michael and reached out his hand. "Glad you are joining us," he said with no smile. "I like a man who does not take this action lightly."

Michael nodded as he shook his hand and took his place on a stool away from the fire. He looked around. The number was smaller than he'd expected, with Quigley nowhere to be seen. O'Brien was there along with Fagin, his companions in the aborted rising. But there were only seven others, mostly young single men from the parish, boys really, whom Michael had watched grow up.

They looked at one another, shuffling their feet and mumbling softly in the cabin's gloom. MacDonogh wasted no time. They stood in silence as each man, his hand on a Bible, took the oath, one by one. Michael, despite his doubts, felt thrilled as he repeated the words after the captain:

"I, Michael O'Donovan, in the presence of Almighty God, do solemnly swear that I will do my utmost, at every risk, while life lasts, to make Ireland an independent Democratic Republic; that I will yield implicit obedience, in all things not contrary to the law of God, to the commands of my superior officers; and that I shall preserve inviolable secrecy regarding all the affairs of this secret society that may be confided in me. So help me God! Amen."

MacDonogh rose after the last man recited the pledge. "So, boys, this is our group. Not quite the twelve apostles, but ten of us can cause some troubles in these parts, troubles that will surely bring down the wrath of the Brits. The first task will be to scout out the movements of the Royal Irish Constabulary in Bantry, find out what days they patrol, how many men are in the barracks at different times during the day, that sort of thing. We'll divide into five pairs, so as not to cause suspicion, each pair the same four hours every day for two weeks. Watch the barracks, take notes on how many men are in there each hour, when they eat and sleep, when they patrol, then report back here in two weeks with your notes. I assume you all know how to write?"

He looked around, but only a few nodded. He then called out the names, assigned them a partner and the hours they would be on watch, leaving finally only Michael and himself.

"Michael, you will come with me, and we'll take the shift from 9 p.m. until 1 a.m." Michael nodded.

"One more thing," said MacDonogh, "each pair will have one gun." He picked up a leather satchel, scuffed but of fine quality, and withdrew five RIC Webley pistols. He handed one to Michael. Michael felt the gun in his hand, shocked at how natural it felt, smooth and cold, fitting his hand perfectly. He'd carried a rifle in the Rising, but this was finer, easy to hide, and deadly at close range.

MacDonogh watched them. "Well, boys, we'll meet two weeks from tonight and each pair will report on what you have learned. The sooner we start the better, as I have my doubts about Paddy. Any questions?"

The room was silent, with the men looking stunned at the quickness of the plan's unfolding. MacDonogh looked around as he said, "Be sure to hide the guns in a safe place. I hope we'll not need them, but if they were discovered the whole thing would unravel."

He looked over at Michael as one by one, the men filed out. "Can you get away Tuesday night after sunset, O'Donovan?"

"Yes. Where should I meet you?"

"Take the road south from the Big House and listen for a whistle from the woods by the old mill. We'll make our way to the barracks outside town." MacDonogh smiled, his blue eyes bright in the firelight.

Michael was ashamed of the flood of pleasure he felt at being singled out to partner with the captain. It wasn't until later, on the long walk back home, that he realized he may have been picked to go with the chief because the man didn't quite trust him.

He could not take the gun home, he knew. His mother or brother would be sure to discover it. As he passed the entrance to Blackthorn House, he knew what he would do. He strode up the long drive and veered left toward the stables. The moon had set by now, and clouds covered the stars. A breeze was picking up, and he could smell rain.

Softly he unlatched the gate and headed toward the last stall where Caroline kept her black filly, Maeve. He was the only one who cleaned these stables. The mare knew him, came to his outstretched hand, putting her head down happily as he petted the shining coat. He fumbled for a piece of apple he kept in his jacket pocket, whispering to Maeve as he fed her the apple and slipped into the stall. She peered at him as he went to the pile of fresh straw he had put down that very morning and fumbled deep beneath it. Then he reached overhead for the rag he had used to dry Maeve off after her outing with Caroline, and wrapped the pistol in the rag, tying the ends securely to make a pouch. He stuffed the parcel beneath the layers of straw, sneezing as he did so.

Maeve skittered, startled by the sound, and let out a soft whinny. He gentled her, murmuring in Irish the love words he had never used on a girl. Latching the stall door behind him, he moved stealthily to the door of the stables and stood still for a moment to listen for any dogs he might have alerted. All was quiet, wind whistling through the newly budding branches of the trees. Under the arching, swaying trees, Michael ran silently down the driveway toward home.

Michael's turn to spy on the barracks finally arrived. He met MacDonogh a mile south of Bantry on the evening they'd arranged. They would head toward Ballydebob where a lone barracks stood, a distance of about three miles from Bantry. The walk in the dark took more than an hour as the two kept to the side of the road, trying to avoid the bright moonlight suffusing the countryside with a silvery glow. When they reached the barracks, Michael examined the small, dark building, surrounded by a few scraggly bushes, out in the middle of nowhere. Why in the world had the British stationed the RIC in this lonely place? He looked questioningly at MacDonogh, and started to whisper, but the man held his finger to his lips and shook his head no. All was still. The men crept toward the building and circled around the back. Michael held his breath, expecting a vicious dog to charge out barking furiously, alerting the men inside. Nothing. Through a smudged window on the side of the building, a dim light flickered.

MacDonogh crouched down and motioned for Michael to check the window. Making his way noiselessly step by step, careful to avoid stepping on any branches that might give him away, Michael reached the window, and slowly lifted himself up to peer inside. A constable sat at a table, reading. His cigarette glowed in the dim room. For a minute Michael admired how deeply absorbed in his book the constable was. When the man coughed and turned slightly toward the window, Michael gasped. By God, if it wasn't Tim O'Connor!

O'Connor had been his father's childhood chum, according to his mother, who had a special gleam in her eye on Sunday mornings after Mass when Constable O'Connor would bow and take her hand in greeting. The youngest son in a large family, the fellow had joined the Irish Constabulary much to the derision of his old pals. Michael's heart raced at the thought of facing this man at the point of a gun. He scanned the room for any other figures but was unable to see much beyond the lamp and the reading man. Carefully he made his way back to the captain, stumbling once in the dark. He held up one finger, and shook his head no as MacDonogh, his eyes almost invisible, looked at him questioningly.

The two men sat and waited, their backs resting against the trees within fifty feet of the barracks. The hours ticked by, with rustlings from the woods the only sounds that broke the silence of the night. MacDonogh checked his watch often, and once Michael awoke with a start, realizing he had fallen asleep. By now the darkness was complete as the moon had set. Finally, MacDonogh crept silently over to the window and peered in. When he crawled back to Michael, he pointed at his watch and mouthed, "Let's go. The next watch isn't due until three."

As they made their way back toward Bantry, MacDonogh lit a cigarette. "The constable was asleep, and I could not see into the room. I have a feeling that there are only two men on duty at night."

"What a bloody waste of time," Michael grumbled.

MacDonogh turned to look at him. "O'Donovan, what do you think is inside those barracks?"

"You mean besides a sleepy constable reading quietly?"

"Guns, man, guns we need desperately, and here they are, oiled and ready, with only two men to guard them in the midst of nowhere. This is the perfect place for us to begin. With a team of five masked men, we can create a diversion, say a small brush fire nearby, and when they rush out to check, we'll have them bound and gagged while we gather the arms." MacDonogh took a drag of his cigarette.

"So how do we make it back to Bantry, with five of us carrying guns and ammunition?" Michael tried to keep the doubt out of his voice.

"We'll have a wagon piled with straw and crates of potatoes hidden at a certain spot down the road, and the guns can be hidden there. Then we all split up and head for Bantry. It's doable." They walked on in silence for a while until MacDonogh looked at him closely, "I know you have doubts about attacking barracks so close to home. Where do you see yourself in action as a member of the IRB?'

Michael returned his look, trying to see if this sudden personal talk was a trap or not. "Well, to tell you the truth, I've been thinking of trying my luck in America these last few weeks." The older man nodded, indicating that Michael should go on. "Since the fiasco of the Rising in March, I am under suspicion around here. My brother Martin will inherit our farm, so for me there is little left here in Bantry."

They'd walked in silence for a while. MacDonogh lit another cigarette, its glow the only light on the now moonless night.

"There's plenty to do in America, lad. The boys there are raising money and shipping arms through Germany to us. But perhaps you could do more good in London for the Cause."

"London?" Michael raised his eyebrows, wondering why he would want to go into the lion's mouth.

"London is full of Fenians," said MacDonogh. "And it's easy to get lost in that city and much harder for the British to know who's who over there." He took a drag of his cigarette. "I'm only saying that just in case things get too hot for you here in Bantry, you have alternatives. That is, if you are heart and soul in the Cause."

Michael didn't know the answer to the unspoken question. He was disgusted with Ireland's subservience, its impotence. He wanted to clear the British out. But did he want it enough to risk his life which had barely begun? And did he have the stomach for attacking men he had known since he was a child?

MacDonogh spoke softly, "You know, I come from Sligo, and there're rumors that one of my ancestors was with Wolfe Tone in '98, one Andrew MacDonogh. My life is given over one hundred percent to the Cause. It's my bride, my family, and will lead one day to my death. But at least I will know that I can hold my head high and did not buckle under to the heavy foot of the British Empire on our necks."

He then looked at Michael, his gaze steely. Michael knew he was waiting for a response, but for once in his life Michael was speechless. They walked back to Bantry in uneasy silence until MacDonogh melted away at the edge of town and Michael headed for home, the sky in the east just beginning to glow with the dawn.

CHAPTER SIX

....

Eileen awoke on Sunday morning to bright sunshine and groaned. Sullivan was coming to visit today, the third time they'd go out walking. She'd been hoping for rain as that would mean a short visit by the hearth surrounded by others, rather than a long walk up into the hills around Bantry. She dressed quickly, hearing her mother and brothers talking in the kitchen.

Her brothers stood around the table, dressed in white shirts and clean pants for Sunday Mass. Her mother looked her over carefully as they set off for the eight o'clock Mass at St. Finbarr's Church.

The banns were read for the second time as Father Gleason, in a grim voice, announced the coming wedding of "John Sullivan, widower, to Mary Eileen O'Donovan on Saturday, the first of June, the year of our Lord 1867."

Eileen felt the eyes of the congregation on her back as she stood to recite the Creed.

"Confiteor Deo," Father intoned.

Eileen bowed her head in silence, hardly able to profess her faith in a God who was letting this happen. She glanced over at the statue of the Virgin, whose hands extended out from the blue cloak, as if reaching for something, Mary's small bare foot stepped delicately on the head of the serpent coiled into the marble. *So will you be helping me or not?* she wondered. At communion she noticed that Michael did not approach the altar, and she peeked toward the back of the church to see him leaning against a pillar and then slipping out the door without taking holy water to bless himself.

John Sullivan appeared at their cottage promptly at three. With quick greetings to her mother and Martin, he took Eileen's arm and ushered her out into the spring afternoon. They walked in silence through the fields. "So how are you getting on, girl?" he asked without looking at her, huffing as they climbed the hill out of town.

"Oh, all right, I suppose. Last week was my last day at the Big House."

"Hmm." He drew on his pipe. "Well, you won't be needing to work there anymore. There'll be plenty of work at my farm."

She saw herself mucking out the barn, scrubbing the floors, hauling in the potatoes in rain and wind and mud. They said no more, climbing steadily until they reached the crest of the hill and turned to look back down. In the distance the blue haze of the Caha Mountains enveloped the bay. The water shimmered in the slanting rays of the sun, and the roof of Blackthorn House rose to the left of Bantry itself. She wondered what Mrs. Hanrahan was preparing for dinner and wished she could be in the library, sunk in one of the armchairs with the copy of *Wuthering Heights.*

Suddenly Sullivan grabbed her to him and crushed her mouth with a kiss. He smelled of tobacco, whiskey, and sweat. She pushed him away, trying to laugh as she turned and headed back toward home.

His face reddened, and he growled, "Now you can be coy, lass, but soon you'll be doing your duty in my bed." Behind her she heard the crunch of his boots and dread filled her until she tasted it, like metal, in her mouth.

The day before, she'd taken an apple cake over to her cousin Kathleen. For once the babies were asleep on their cot, and the kitchen was snug and quiet as Kathleen made them a fresh pot of tea. "So now you've had your sixteenth birthday, you're ready to be a married woman, I guess?" Kathleen smiled, a tired but heartfelt smile as she gazed at Eileen.

Eileen looked around the cabin, the diapers hanging in front of the fire, the mending piled high in her basket by the hearth, the pot of soup congealing on the stove, and finally at her cousin's rough, chapped hands.

"Not at all! I'm not ready, cousin. The man is old, has no fun in him, not even any talk. I'm going to hate it, I know." She wasn't sad anymore, just angry. They'd all let her down, her mother, her brothers, even Father Gleason had done nothing to stop this farce.

Kathleen stared at Eileen over the rim of her cup. After a minute, she put down her cup and took Eileen's hand in her own. "Has your mother talked to you about what will happen on your wedding night?"

Eileen looked up, her eyes wide. "No, not a word. But I guess I can imagine the scene well enough."

"No, you can't," said Kathleen. "I loved Brian so much when we married, but I wasn't prepared for what it felt like to have him climb on top of me that first night and grunt and groan as he put his thing in me, hurting me so I had to stuff my hand in my mouth to stifle the scream. It's just like that the first time or two, is what I'm saying, but it gets better when things slow down and he takes his time, kissing and fondling. . . ." She broke off suddenly and rose from the table to gaze at her sleeping babies. She sighed as she covered up their bare legs, and soft as air, brushed their heads with her hand. "These little ones will make it all worth it," she smiled over at Eileen, who joined her looking down at the infants, so rosy and warm.

Eileen had walked back home slowly, gazing out over the bay in the fading light, smelling the smoke of the peat fires in the cabins dotting the hills, wanting time to stop, to stay just as she was, happy in her mother's house, reading her book by candlelight at night when her mother'd gone to sleep, and dreaming of someone young and handsome whose kisses would be tender but insistent, and into whom she would melt with fierce desire. Now that would be a wedding night!

The celebration of the wedding was to be a modest affair, but something the whole town could join in later in the day. Father Gleason would celebrate the nuptial Mass at nine in the morning, with a breakfast at the O'Donovans' house afterward. In the evening there would be dancing and drink and food at the old barn on Sullivan's property.

Mamie O'Donovan was in high gear, bustling around all day cooking, sewing the lace on Eileen's light blue dress, and visiting the neighbors to invite them and secure offers of food for the party. "After all," she said, "it isn't every day that your only daughter gets married." Eileen felt as if she were in a play. This could not be real.

Her mother cast worried glances at her but kept silent. Martin teased her sometimes, ignoring the flush that rose on her face at his coarse jokes. She saw little of Michael now, as he seemed always to be hurrying off to work, or so he said. Many nights he did not come home, but no one commented on his absence. The house was filling with secrets like some gray fog.

On the day of the wedding, a burst of thunder woke Eileen. She lay in bed listening to the rain beat on the roof, her mother's place in the bed empty. *The last time,* she kept saying over and over to herself, *the last time I will lie in my mother's house. If only I could flee over the hills and hide somewhere like Catherine in Wuthering Heights.*

She pulled on a shawl over her nightgown and entered the kitchen to find a fresh pot of tea and loaves of her mother's soda bread laid out on the table for the breakfast later. But then she remembered. She had to be fasting if she wanted to receive communion at Mass. She looked longingly at the bread and tea. Not even water should pass her lips.

From the window in the parlor, she spied her mother and brother walking toward the cottage, their heads bent against the rain. As her mother entered, she sang out, "Rain before seven, clear before eleven!" and came over and kissed Eileen lightly on the cheek.

"Well, let's hope so or we'll all be drowning in mud on our way to the church. But isn't there something about happy the bride the sun shines on?" Martin asked as he emptied the sack of potatoes they'd gathered that morning into the big pan on the hearth.

Their mother covered the potatoes in water, placed the kettle over the fire, and poked the fire in the hearth to boil them. With her sleeves rolled back and her skirt tied up, she was a figure of strength, and in spite of her resentment, Eileen felt a rush of love for this woman who had fought on so bravely alone after her young husband's death. She hoped on this day she would have such strength not to disgrace her family in front of everyone.

She lifted her chin, "I'll start packing my things now before I get dressed." Her voice was firm and both Martin and her mother exchanged glances of relief. Eileen suspected they'd both been afraid she'd be running away or at least breaking down in front of the whole town.

She had little to pack, just her two muslin nightgowns, her chemises, underwear, stockings, her old shoes for the farm, her red skirt, her good dress, her hairbrush, mirror, a few hair ribbons, a locket with her father's picture in it, clean rags for her monthlies, her old shawl, and wrapped in it, the book she had stolen from the library of the Big House. For the wedding she would carry the leather prayer book that the nuns at the Mercy Convent had given her when she left school at age twelve.

When the rain slacked off, she would go outside and pick some lilac that grew by the shed and tie it with a ribbon around the prayer book. On the cupboard door of the bedroom hung the blue wedding dress, its square, low-cut bodice trimmed with lace. Her new cloak, scarlet wool, was spread out in the parlor on the chair by the fireplace with soft black slippers beneath it.

She stared into the mirror by the washstand as she rinsed her face. Her brown, sun-streaked hair was pulled back, the curls struggling to be released, her eyes gray-blue in the dim light. She was pale, pale as death. She pinched her cheeks and rubbed her lips for color. She stripped to her waist to wash, and looked at her breasts in the mirror, so high and small, their nipples like pink buds. *Oh God, please help me through this day and this night.*

She looked around the room before she closed the valise her mother had given her, to see what she had forgotten. Then she saw a small package wrapped in what looked like green paper. It had been tucked beside her mirror under the linen scarf on the washstand. When she picked it up, she saw the wrapping was a large leaf, not paper, and it was tied with a willowy stem instead of string. As she unwrapped it, a note fell out before her, but first she reached for the silver chain with a single pearl. She had never had anything so fine. She opened the note:

> *Alannah,*
> *It is with great sorrow that I will watch you walk down the aisle this morning of June in the church as a bride. You are my dear sister and friend of my heart, so never forget I am always at your side in any trouble or sorrow. May God keep you safe, Eileen.*
> *Your loving brother,*
> *Michael*

She felt the sting of tears. How in the world had her brother afforded such a gift? Michael had been so distant lately; she'd wondered if he was angry at her for giving in to their mother and brother. Was it true that he would always be nearby? But her heart lifted at his gift and his words.

Suddenly, she heard her cousin Kathleen's voice from the kitchen. With a loud knock on the bedroom door, Kathleen peeked in, her bright reddish hair and laughing eyes a welcome sight. "So, how is the bride on this fine spring morning?" she chirped. "I thought you might need some help getting ready. I knew your mother would be busy, so I left the wee ones with their daddy for the morning. Let's see what a mess they will be when he brings them to church!"

She chattered on happily as she squeezed the modest valise shut and turned to Eileen. "So, it's time to get you dressed," she said firmly. "No more dawdling!"

She picked up the gleaming white underwear, the linen chemise with a white silk ribbon drawn through the bodice and helped Eileen into each piece. Then she slipped the blue muslin dress over her head, pulling the bodice low and tying the sash firmly around the girl's slender waist. Eileen was tall, so Kathleen had to stand on tiptoe to button the long row of silk-covered buttons down the back.

"My, my," gasped Kathleen, "your mother has certainly gone all out with this dress."

Eileen tried to smile, "She went to Cork to buy the fabric and picked up a pattern there in a shop. She found the buttons here in Bantry but had to cover each of them with silk remnants. She sewed it herself, you know." Eileen stepped back and watched in the mirror as Kathleen brushed her long hair, letting it fall freely down her back. Then she picked up the silver chain, handing it to her cousin to fasten around her neck. "Michael's gift," she said.

With that, her mother entered the room and stopped when she saw the bride. She said nothing, just gazed at the tall slim girl, now transformed into a young woman, poised, even regal, in the blue dress.

"It looks. . . no, you look beautiful, alannah," she murmured, studying the girl, the fragility of her waist, and her slender neck, now bared by the gown. The mother cleared her throat, "It's time to be walking to church now. Let's save your new slippers. I'll carry them while you put on your old shoes."

As the little party stepped outside, the sky was clearing, the sun breaking through heavy silver clouds over the bay. Eileen, clad in her scarlet cloak, picked two branches of lilac, but her hands were trembling so badly she had to ask Kathleen to attach them to her prayer book. Martin and her mother led the way, Eileen stepping carefully, holding up her skirt from the mud, Kathleen trailing behind, carrying the prayer book and flowers.

They came to the steps of St. Finbarr's where a small group of folks from the town gathered to watch the proceedings. Eileen nodded, trying to smile as they cheered her. She mounted the stairs slowly, Kathleen at her side.

When they reached the great doors, she spied John Sullivan in the vestibule, standing alone. In the gloom, he cut a dim figure in his black suit and high white cravat, and a tall black beaver hat on his head. His mustache had been trimmed and stood out starkly against his white face. He loomed above her and said nothing, just stared at her looking as frightened as she herself felt.

Her mother stepped forward. "Go on with you now, John Sullivan! Sure, it's bad luck for you to see the bride before she walks down the aisle." Mrs. O'Donovan took him by the arm and pushed him into the church, where, a lonely figure with no one beside him, he approached the altar by the side aisle.

"Jesus," Eileen's mother sighed. "Doesn't that man have anyone who could have accompanied him today?" Eileen saw Martin scowl, and she turned to see her brother Michael running up the steps of the church. He grinned, "Not too late, am I, darling?"

Eileen met his eyes, touching the pearl at her neck. "Thank you, Michael. It's beautiful," she whispered.

"And so are you this day, Eileen," he said, staring into her eyes.

"Well thanks be to God you showed up," said his mother. "I never know when you will honor us with your presence these days." She gazed at her son, trying to hide her smile.

Martin muttered, "Oh, Michael has better things to do these days than work with us in the fields."

Michael stared at him, unsmiling. Martin then stood beside Eileen and put her arm in his. Michael went to her other side and grabbed her other arm, "Oh no you don't, Martin. We'll both walk the girl down the aisle."

As they started the long walk, Eileen felt her knees buckle, but her brothers held her tightly, and Michael whispered, "Don't let them see you falter, girl."

Light streamed in through the stained-glass windows of the sanctuary, drawing her on over the black and white marble-tiled floor up to the red carpet where Father Gleason and Sullivan awaited her. She heard the voices swirling around her, gave the responses, but it was as if someone else were in her body, seeing and hearing all, even speaking, but that she herself was mute and helpless, trapped inside this calm-seeming girl.

After the Mass ended, she and Sullivan turned to walk back out of the church to the smiles and nods of the congregation, and she felt her new husband's large hand squeezing her arm above her elbow, gripping her to him as he proudly nodded to one and all.

The breakfast was served in their crowded cottage, with people filling their plates with the abundance of eggs, loaves of soda bread with homemade butter, blackberry jam, pints of ale for the men, and hot tea for everyone. Thanks to Lady Mary's gifts from the Big House, her mother had nothing to be ashamed of in the spread she provided. The Earl's wife had also sent bouquets of flowers from their garden that morning, and the scent of the rain-spattered roses and hollyhocks mingled with the smells of breakfast.

Eileen watched her mother, dressed in her best black, moving among her friends and neighbors, laughing, and pouring the tea, secure in her daughter's new status as the wife of the widower Sullivan. Would her mother even miss her? She tried eating a crust of bread and choking it down with a cup of steaming strong tea. Next to her, John Sullivan devoured his food, chewing loudly and glancing shyly at her now and then over the rim of his jar of ale.

Finally, the newlyweds stood at the door of the cottage to shake hands and receive the good wishes of all as they left. Sullivan had hired a jaunting car to take them out of town to his farm, and when Eileen appeared at the door with her valise, the people crowded around the cart and began to throw rice at the couple as they climbed aboard. Sullivan flicked the whip at the horse, and the cart rattled down the lane into the noonday brightness. The sun had shone on the bride after all.

Eileen had never been to Sullivan's place, and her heart sank as they came up the road to a small, weathered house with a thatched roof and a sagging front door. It was a barren place, with no trees or flowers in sight. Behind the house was a barn in slightly better condition than the house, and in the distance sheep and cows grazed on the hillside. Eileen's brothers helped out at harvest time on Sullivan's land, and somehow, she had imagined it to be a fine, prosperous farm.

When Sullivan helped her down from the cart, he grinned and pulled her to him in a crushing embrace. "Welcome, Mrs. Sullivan, to your new home," he said, pulling her face to his and kissing her fully and suddenly on the mouth. He smelled of beer, and his face felt rough even though he had shaved for the day, trimming his heavy black mustache. She felt nothing at his kiss.

Scattering a few chickens pecking in the yard, he held open the door for her and she entered a small, dark room with the hearth at one end, a kettle hanging over the fire, and two straight-backed chairs pulled up next to it. There was a broad oak table, with two more chairs, some blackened pots and pans, and a dresser with dishes and a faded picture of the Sacred Heart of Jesus hanging over it. He led her into the only other room, where the marriage bed was spread with a dark green quilt. Then she spied a tiny crib in a corner of the room. She walked over to it, fingering the knitted white blanket folded neatly on the bare mattress. She turned to look at her husband.

His head was bowed, and he answered her look softly, "It was, you know, our baby's crib. He died after a month of the cough, and my wife followed him within the year. I could not bear to get rid of the crib. And now," he looked at her directly, "maybe soon it will be useful again."

Eileen turned away, "I'm sorry," she said quietly, "it must have been terrible for you."

"You can put your things in the wardrobe there," he nodded, "while I go out to look after a sick cow I have in the barn."

Relieved, she busied herself with arranging her few things and hiding the book she had filched in her old nightgown. She glanced in the mirror she had brought and looked for somewhere to hang it. Inside the door of the musty wardrobe was a hook, so she hung her mirror there and closed the door. She'd look for some lavender in the fields to dry and store there to freshen the smell. She stood up straight and headed out to see the barn which would be the scene of the wedding celebration that night.

The long June evening was sliding into dusk when the Straw-boys arrived. By now everyone had eaten and drunk, and some of the men with rosy faces were having trouble walking straight. From outside came the sounds of flutes and drums, and soon the scarecrow-like figures were snaking around the two long tables, straw masks hiding their faces. They played their flutes, some banging away with sticks and drums, shouting, and laughing as they struck the guests lightly on the back and shoulders. At the sounds of the fiddles and harps, the dancing began, with Sullivan and Eileen sitting stiffly at the table watching the fun.

Eileen had drunk a few swallows of ale, and her cheeks were aflame in the heat and the dust the dancers raised. Sullivan beside her had been drinking for hours, and now he swayed back and forth to the beat of the bodhráns. Two fiddlers, the Conroy boys, were playing "The Minstrel Boy," and even her mother jumped up to be swept off by old Paddy to the dance floor. The music beat on as the dancers swirled around in a frenzy of laughter and shouting. Eileen looked around for Michael, and in the distance saw her brother Martin talking to their cousin Kathleen and her husband.

One of the Straw-boys approached Eileen, bowed, and pulled her up roughly to join the dance. Next, they were whirling around the room, and Eileen, dizzy and laughing, felt her body yield to the music and drink, oblivious of anything but the strong arm of the strange figure before her holding her around the waist. When he spoke, she knew.

"Michael!"

He laughed and spun her again, nearly stepping on the hem of her wedding dress. "It's a fine husband you have there, sitting all morose by himself, Mary Eileen O'Donovan!"

She looked into his eyes, bright with love for her, and felt tears. "Oh Michael, I don't know how I shall stand it."

"Stand it you will, my girl. You are stronger than you think, alannah. Visit Mammy when you can. She'll be missing you more than she knows." With that he twirled her one more time and led her to her place.

Sullivan stood up suddenly and grabbed her arm. With that, Father Gleason rose from the table and motioned for quiet. He held up his glass, clearing his throat, and called out, "The newlyweds have had a long day, so we will let them go in peace. But before they leave, let us bow our heads for a prayer." Silence fell upon the barn, with even the youngsters standing still after running around all evening.

The priest raised his arm, still holding his glass, to give the blessing. "May God be with you and bless you. May you see your children's children. May you be poor in misfortune and rich in blessings. May you know nothing but happiness from this day forward."

Eileen met Father's eyes as he glanced her way and saw with satisfaction that he smiled sadly at her and bowed. Wordless and unsmiling, she took her husband's proffered hand and, gathering her skirts, her eyes straight ahead, she walked slowly and deliberately out of the barn into the darkening evening. When the couple left, the music resumed, echoing over the hills of Bantry, out over the bay glittering in the summer moonlight.

CHAPTER SEVEN

....

Once out of the barn, Sullivan lost his grip on Eileen's arm and stumbled up the path toward the cottage. She followed, her steps lagging, breathing in the fragrance of the summer night, a mixture of sea air and damp earth. At the cottage, the fire in the hearth was dying, with only a few bits of turf still smoldering. Sullivan lit the lamp and motioned her toward the bedroom. Without a word he began peeling off his clothes, and they fell to the floor in a heap beside him.

Eileen stepped behind the door of the wardrobe. With shaking fingers, she undid the long strand of buttons on the back of her dress, thinking of her mother sitting so patiently by the fire of an evening as she sewed the blue silk over each one. Yes, but it was her mother who had brought her to this night, she thought bitterly. She stepped out of her dress as she heard the bed creak with her husband's weight.

"Girl, come on to bed now. I've had enough of your fine ways. . . ." he trailed off, laughing softly. She knew he was drunk and prayed that sleep would overtake him. Carefully, she hung up her dress, stepped out of her knickers, pulling the new chemise over her head. In the dim light she glimpsed her face in the mirror, her eyes wide. She pulled the new nightgown over her head, untangling her hair from the collar and tying the silk drawstring neatly below her chin.

Finally, able to delay no longer, she slipped into bed beside him, turning on her side, clinging to the edge of the bed. In a flash he was on her, pawing at her gown, sliding his hands up her legs, grabbing and pinching her hard, his fingers reaching inside her. She stiffened and tried not to scream. Then her gown was over her head, and she struggled to breathe. She felt his mouth on her breast, and then he was nipping at her like a puppy, moaning and whining. Soon she felt his full weight on her and his swollen great penis was pushing into her, tearing at her flesh. She felt she would suffocate. She bit her bunched-up gown to stifle her cry, determined to endure the pain when suddenly he gasped and moaned, and it stopped. With a huge sigh, he rolled over to his side of the bed, and after a few minutes, terrified, holding her breath, she heard his snoring.

She turned away from him now, and the tears seeped through her tightly shut lids, dampening the coarse pillowcase. Then she felt something sticky and wet between her legs and reached down to wipe herself with her gown.

So, this is what all the poems and songs were about! This terrible tussle in a dark room, with no words, no wooing? How did the Church condone this, even encourage it? She longed for a bath to cleanse herself from his assault. In the darkness, Eileen tried to pray a Hail Mary, but she knew now that no one, not even the Virgin Mary, was coming to save her.

Michael slipped away from the celebration shortly after the bride and groom, suspecting that among the Straw-boys were two or three of his cronies in the IRB, whom he did not wish to meet. He was hurrying back to the Big House. In the middle of the festivities, a twelve-year old boy he'd seen around the Big House had stuffed a note in his hand. Back at the table under pretense of refreshing his drink, Michael turned his back on the dancers and read the note. It was on fine paper in a strange hand he did not recognize, but his eyes went quickly to the signature, a finely wrought C. *Meet me this night in the stables, my friend, as I have a surprise for you. C.*

Finally, he thought, she's going to make good on all those coy ways she has of luring me on. But what could have possessed her to take such a chance? His blood pounded in his veins. He was crazy, he knew, for trusting this invitation, but the drink, the dancing, the despair of thinking about what awaited his sister that night, above all his desire for the little minx all drew him out the door of the barn and into the coolness of the night.

The walk back to the Big House was long. He ran, relishing the wind in his face and the rhythmic beat of his footsteps pounding the grass. He tripped once and fell headlong, not seeing a hole in the hillside. He stood, panting, and brushed off his pants and shirt, now drenched with sweat. A fine figure of a lover he'd cut this night, he jeered to himself, all smelling of drink, sweat, and even manure!

Finally, the entrance to Blackthorn House was before him. He walked stealthily up the gravel path, turning left at the stables. He guessed it was almost eleven and stopped for a moment to listen. In the distance an owl's call faded in the deep woods. Silence. He moved in the shadows of the stable, heading toward Maeve's stall.

In the dark, a slight form rose before him, and Caroline stepped out of the stall. Her voice was low and warm. "There you are, Michael! I was sure you'd come." Her arm was outstretched toward him, and it was then that he saw in the dimness the pistol in her hand. She smiled, "And what have we here, my boy?"

Frozen, Michael cursed himself for a fool. How could he have thought she wanted him? Something fierce arose in him then. He said coldly, "Put the gun down, Caroline. It's not a toy."

She laughed. "Oh, I know that well, Michael lad. But the question is what is the stable boy doing with a British Army officer's gun? The only thing I can think of is that somehow you have been stupid enough to join the Fenians."

Michael faced her, walking slowly toward her still out-stretched arm. "So, it's the stable boy I am, after all. How pitiful that the lovely young lady of the house has no one else to play with on this beautiful spring night than a stable boy."

She took a step back. Now he was close enough to see the fear in her eyes, and he made a sudden lunge for the gun in her hand. She struggled mightily, but at last he wrenched it from her as she cried out in pain. He tossed the gun onto the ground and grabbed her to him, tilting her head back so he could look into her eyes. "You are playing with dangerous toys this night, my lady." Then he bent to kiss her with rage that turned quickly into yearning. She did not resist.

Finally, he thrust her from him, wiping the taste of her from his mouth. "Unfortunately, I find I cannot trust you. I've known you all your life, Caroline. And it's a spoiled, selfish girl you are. You would be wise to keep this little scene a secret, my girl. After all, I have your compromising note. You wouldn't want it to be known all over the county that the young lady of the house was reduced to seducing the stable boy now, would you?"

She stared at him, her eyes wide, panicked. He picked up the gun then, trying to hide the shaking of his hands. He bowed, turning his back on her and forced himself to slow his steps, his heart racing. As he left the stable, he heard the filly Maeve whinny.

Away! Running, running, all down the long drive. *You've done it now. You're finished here!* She'd have the RIC after him before dawn for sure. He'd humiliated her above all by not making love to her. Oh, he'd wanted to, maddened by anger and lust, but something cool inside had held him back. He kept seeing her form with the gun pointed straight at him, her crooked smile disfiguring that lovely face.

His footsteps pounded down the gravel drive. He could not go home. That's the first place they would look for him. No, he'd head out of town this night and somehow get word to Mac-Donogh. He'd be no use to the lads now. Then he remembered. The gun! He veered off the driveway into the woods. He could see nothing at first, then gradually his eyes adjusted to the shifting murky light, and he stumbled deeper and deeper into the trees, branches clawing at his face and clothes. Finally, he saw a tree with a gash at eye level. His hands were shaking as he stuffed the gun into the gash, then grabbing dirt and leaves from the forest floor, he thrust them on top of the gun until it disappeared. He swore softly to himself as he ran silently down the drive and away from Blackthorn House into the night.

CHAPTER EIGHT

....

In the weeks after the wedding, the long summer days dragged for Eileen. The loneliness of living with a stranger who seldom spoke overwhelmed Eileen at night as she lay quietly next to her snoring husband. She missed the bustle of her mother's house and longed once more to flit up the stairs of Blackthorn House and enter the sun-filled library with its musty books.

Hard work was her escape, so she scrubbed and swept the rooms from ceiling to floor, spending whole days washing the bedding, and hanging it on fine days to dry and air in the summer sunshine. Near the barn she'd dug up a small patch for a vegetable garden, hoping for turnips, parsnips, potatoes, and even some lettuce if the rabbits didn't find it first. On rainy mornings she mended and patched John's pants and shirts. Once a day she went out to the fields to bring him sandwiches and a jar of hot tea.

John was gruff with her at times, often correcting her, complaining about the way she cooked his food or prepared his tea. He was a silent man, so she learned to sit with him in the evenings by the hearth while he smoked a pipe and she sewed. On Saturdays, he went down to the pub in the village, and it was on those nights that she dreaded his homecoming, knowing what it meant for her in bed at his return. That she would never get used to. The only good thing was that his pleasure came quickly, and he did not seem to expect any participation from her. She felt revulsion when she thought of the things he did to her in bed. Was this to be her life?

It was a shock to her in November when she realized her monthly period hadn't come for the second time. Her breasts were sore too. When she undressed that morning, she ran her hands over her belly but felt no swelling there. She needed to visit her mother.

At breakfast she looked carefully at her husband. "John, I'd like to go see my mother today and bring her some bread I've made, if that is all right with you. It's been a while since I've seen her."

He looked up from his porridge, nodding, "If you wait until this evening, I can come with you."

"Ah, no need for you to trouble yourself when you've all that work getting the hay into the barn. I thought Martin was coming to help you today," she smiled at him, "and really, I don't mind the walk." Eileen hoped she didn't sound too eager. She took his grunt for consent and busied herself with wrapping two loaves of bread in a towel, thanking her mother silently for having taught her to bake.

Within the hour, Eileen was walking down the lane, feeling the warmth of the sun on her face, and admiring the hay bales rounded and tied in the fields, ready to be stored before rain. Martin appeared around the first bend, his pitchfork slung over his shoulder. She was surprised at the pleasure she felt at the sight of him although he had always been the bossy big brother and was, she suspected, the person most responsible for her marriage.

"And where are you off to, young missus?" he called out.

She cuffed him lightly as they passed one another. "I'm off to see our Mammy and bring her some bread I've made."

"Ah, any excuse to escape your duties as a good farm wife, I see," he said as he mockingly raised his cap to her, and she laughed, thinking it was only too true.

Alone, she felt herself, free and young, and now the thought of the secret within her made her pulse quicken. The sky arched above her, blue as the Virgin's mantle, with only a few wispy clouds racing across it. The trees were golden, shimmering, their dried leaves rustling and showering down in her path. She pressed the loaves to her breast, imagining a tiny baby there.

As she entered the house, the familiar smell of her mother's baking mixed with the smoke from the hearth gave her a pang. She'd been homesick. She called out, but no answer. When she walked outside, she spied her mother coming slowly uphill from the barn carrying two pails of milk, her back bent with the weight.

Eileen ran toward her, grabbing the pails. "Mammy, that's too much for you. Let me carry them." Mamie's eyes lit up briefly as she touched her daughter's face. Eileen was shocked at the sadness she saw there, in spite of her mother's attempt to smile. Her mother had aged since Michael had gone away, her hair now all white, and her shoulders slumped.

In the kitchen her mother sat at the table and let Eileen pour her a cup of tea. "Alannah, it's glad I am to see you today," she sighed, looking closely at her daughter.

"Still no word from Michael?"

"No." They sipped their tea in silence. Eileen tried being cheerful. "Mammy, I've told you he is probably fine. But ever since the barracks was attacked, the RIC has been hunting the Fenians. Michael probably felt that he had to run to avoid suspicion. In Bantry they say that O'Brien and Quigley have fled also, so I'm sure Michael is with them. "

"Eileen, you know that Michael disappeared the night of your wedding, well before the attack on the barracks. And the people at the Big House have been so strange lately." Her hands moved restlessly over the table, picking at the blue tablecloth.

"Strange. How?"

"I don't know. Something's changed. Lady Caroline left for London suddenly, the day after your wedding. Mrs. Hanrahan said that Lady Mary had come down to the kitchen twice to ask why Michael was not helping with the crops lately. I had to go over and explain that we hadn't a clue where Michael was, that he'd run off with no word. Then old Conlan told Martin that his services were no longer needed about the place. Now none of us are up in the Big House these days except for when I take them some baked goods."

Her mother stood and moved slowly to the hearth to get the kettle. She sighed heavily. "It feels strange to me now, not to be welcome in a place I've worked all my life. Martin and I are on our own now, the only two left to plant and harvest the land."

Eileen watched her mother, her slumped shoulders, and the lack of steel in her spine. Perhaps her news of a grandchild would cheer her.

"Well, Mammy, I've come to ask your advice," Eileen said. "My monthly has not come for two months now, and my breasts are so tender lately. Do you think. . . ?" She raised her eyes to her mother's, letting the question hang in the air.

"Jesus, Mary, and Joseph, you're expecting!" Mamie stared at her daughter, and a look of fear passed over her face.

Eileen laughed in spite of herself. What did her mother think would happen to her youngest child when she'd married her off at sixteen! Well, now that a baby was on the way, she had to make the best of this marriage. John Sullivan was not a cruel man, just morose and silent. He worked hard all week, got drunk on Saturday nights at the pub, and let her alone the other nights.

To her surprise, the thought of the baby growing inside her brought a queer new joy. She felt pity for the tiny creature, soon to be thrust out into the world, a world of hard work, a cold harsh world of wind and storms, but also, she knew, a beautiful world of green fields, the sea around them at all times, the softness of a summer night, the smell of hay, and the taste of warm bread. Fiercely, she longed for the child, hoping though that it would be a boy, a boy free to go his own way, to study and learn, free to marry whoever he wanted or even not at all. Yes, the child would be her joy, a reward for having done her duty, as her mother had put it before her marriage.

Now her mother pushed herself back from the table and came around to Eileen, putting her hands on the girl's shoulders. "I am very happy, alannah, that you will be giving me my first grandchild. I'm only sorry this came so fast, even before your next birthday." She searched her daughter's face and asked, twisting her wedding ring round and round, "And is Sullivan good to you, my girl?"

"Good enough, Mammy. Good enough." She rose and embraced her mother, startled to feel the boniness of her mother's back, this strong, brave mother who was aging before her eyes. They walked together out into the yard as the sun was beginning its descent into the sea, the air already cooling in the autumn afternoon. The town beneath them was spread out like a toy village, the steeple of St. Finbarr's gleaming in the sun. As Eileen kissed her mother goodbye, she decided she would visit Father Gleason after confession on Saturday to see if he knew anything about Michael. Worry was pushing her mother into an early grave, and she cursed her brother softly under her breath as she began the walk back to her duty.

The line for confession on Saturday was not long. Eileen decided not to confess herself, for after all, what sins did she have? She waited in the last pew behind a pillar, watching the sun light up the stained-glass window with St. Patrick, his green vestment gleaming like a jewel, his halo a thin gold band hovering above the thick brown curls of his head. Finally, old Mrs. Mulcahy hobbled out and knelt stiffly to say her penance. Eileen wondered what she could have confessed, probably gossip, as that was the chief entertainment of the women of

Bantry. Then she crossed herself and asked God to forgive her for uncharitable thoughts. That was one of her sins!

Suddenly, Father banged open the door of the confessional, pulling off the purple stole as he strode down the side aisle. He stopped when he saw her. "Ah, were you wanting to confess, Eileen?"

"No, Father. Thanks. But I wonder if you have a minute to talk." The tall priest's eyes softened as he gazed at her. He smiled, "Sure, I have all the time in the world. But let's walk outside. The air in here is damp."

They walked together down the steep steps, turning right onto the grass of the cemetery. Ancient gray monuments with dates and names carved into each one told the stories of babies dying, young mothers carried off by disease and childbirth, and old married people lying peacefully side by side for eternity. It was a friendly place, Eileen thought, where someone could visit her loved one any time she wished. Her father's grave was in the far-left corner, and she led the priest to it. The inscription was brief:

MARTIN O'DONOVAN
1820-1854
BELOVED HUSBAND AND FATHER

"I was only three when he died," Eileen said softly.

"Oh, I am sorry I did not know him, but your mother has told me what a fine man he was, working so hard all through the famine to keep a roof over your heads." Father sighed and looked over at her. "Eileen, are you still angry at me for not having helped you avoid this marriage? Is John treating you badly?"

Eileen did not meet his eyes but kept gazing at her father's grave. Finally, she looked up, and said, "I'm thinking this day that my own father would have saved me from marrying a man I hardly knew." She went on, "But it's Michael I've come to talk to you about. Mammy is worrying herself into old age since Michael disappeared with no word to any of us. I thought maybe you would have heard some news in Bantry these last few months."

Father looked away, gazing out over the hills in the distance. His big hands tugged at the cincture at his waist. "You know the barracks on the road south of Bantry was attacked in July, and everyone knows it was the Fenians. I suspect Michael may have had something to do with that."

"But Father, he disappeared the night of my wedding, weeks before the attack."

The priest shook his head. "Sure now, the lads had been planning things for months. I know there've been Fenian meetings up at old Paddy's. To tell you the truth, at times I've been sorely tempted myself to join them." He laughed harshly at the look on Eileen's face.

"You never thought your priest sympathized with the struggle for Ireland's freedom? Many of us have had our fill with the bishops' ranting against the Fenians. It's we priests in these villages who must watch the poverty and misery of our people, the harsh rotten treatment of the landlords and overseers. The bishops are high and dry in their palaces, with the best of food and drink, only seeing their people at Confirmations and never walking through the villages on a Saturday night with drunken farmers spilling out of pubs and alleys drowning their sorrows—ah, sorry I am to be going on like this, Eileen."

His face flushed, and he tugged at his high white collar. "I'll try to find out about Michael. We have our methods of getting information, you know," he said, smiling.

"Thank you, Father." She clasped his hand.

"And Eileen, if ever John Sullivan hurts you in any way, you come to me." She nodded, and together they walked back to the front of the church. Eileen felt the priest's eyes following her as she ran down the steps and headed back to the farm.

CHAPTER NINE

....

A dvent with its purple vestments and altar coverings arrived, and as the weeks slipped by, Eileen knew she would soon have to tell John about the baby. She was haunted by the baby crib in the bedroom and so was he, she suspected.

Christmas Eve came on a Tuesday that year. Eileen had been inside all day, plucking a goose for the next day and baking pies. The weather was cold and wet, and at night the wind moaned. John was quieter than usual these early winter evenings, and loneliness crept inside Eileen like the cold and damp itself. She was starved for company.

She was looking forward to going to midnight Mass and then to her mother's house for a hot drink and some gossip and laughter with the neighbors. Their farm here was so isolated. She had only the one stolen book to read, sneaking it at odd times when her husband was out. Saturday nights when he went for hours to the pub were the best for reading. *Wuthering Heights*, though, was not a cheerful tale. She kept getting the characters mixed up and decided she didn't like any of them! Even Kathy was a spoiled brat, fickle and vain. It didn't feel like a love story at all.

When John entered the cottage at dusk he was soaked. He called her to help him take off his muddy boots, and she knelt before him to tug them off. Suddenly she looked up at him, and with an intake of breath that sounded like a sigh, she said, "I'm pretty sure I'm going to have a baby."

He stared at her for a long moment, then got up, peeling off his wet clothes. He said nothing, just waited quietly for her to fill the tub with hot water for his bath. She was shaking as she did so, and then, while he bathed in front of the hearth, busied herself getting their dinner on the table: a soup made of turnips and potatoes with bits of bacon she had saved. She sliced several pieces of bread and put a blue cotton napkin beside each place. They ate in silence.

After dinner, John lit his pipe and pushed his chair in front of the hearth. Finally, he turned to her. "Eileen, I thought I'd be happy to hear those words. But when you said that, a cold chill went down my spine. When we lost Thomas," his voice trembled as he said the name, "I was heart-stricken. I never wanted to go through that again. Maybe that's why I waited so long to marry once more." He stared into the fire.

Eileen came and sat across from him. It was the first time he had spoken of the death.

He went on without looking at her. "After the child's death, I slept in the barn, afraid to put my wife through that and afraid even more to put myself through it. We had a bad time of it; I drank too much and got angry all the time. And then in the spring, she was gone too."

"I'm sorry," Eileen said softly, unable to think of any comforting words.

His dark eyes stared into hers as he murmured, "I know you didn't want to marry me. You are too young. And now you might die too," his voice trailed off in a snarl.

"I'll do my best not to die," she answered with a half-smile. She rose and touched him lightly on the shoulder. "Aren't we going to church soon? I must change my dress and pack up the things I want to take to Mammy."

The steps leading up to St. Finbarr's were slick with rain as people hurried into the church, lit from within, glowing in the dark night. The scent of pine and cedar filled the church, the windows draped with fresh-cut greenery. To the left of the altar was the crèche: a rugged barn hewed from the local ash trees sheltered the Holy Family, small porcelain figurines from Italy, their garments painted in bright colors.

As children, Eileen and her brothers had loved coming up to look at them, especially at the sheep and cows and the exotic strangers from the East in garish, gold-trimmed robes. Now Eileen thought bitterly of her scattered family: Michael, God knows where; Martin grown old and sour before his time; and their mother, sick with worry for them all. She knelt beside John, burying her face in her hands.

Suddenly she felt a warm arm pressed against her own and looked up to see her mother kneeling next to her. She stole her arm around her mother's waist.

"Where's Martin?" Eileen whispered.

"Sure he's in the back, so he can leave early to smoke," her mother muttered as she pulled her shawl up over her head, raindrops glistening in her gray hair. "Are you coming to the house after Mass?"

Eileen nodded as Father Gleason and the servers clanged the bell and processed to the altar in luminous white vestments. *Adeste Fidelis* rang out in Latin as one and all joined in to welcome the Holy Child on this rainy wet night in the year of our Lord 1867. What would the new year bring, Eileen wondered? She would become a mother. She asked the Virgin Mary to bless and protect her baby and to keep Michael safe, wherever he was.

London on Christmas Eve was rainy too. Michael shivered in his thin jacket, pulling it tightly around his throat. *If only I had a scarf*, he thought. He'd had a few pints with the boys from the docks after they'd been paid, and a shot of whiskey warmed him for a while, but he'd had nothing to eat since noon. He passed lighted houses on the edge of St. James Park, with carriages rolling up to splendidly lit doorways, spilling fur-clad ladies and gentlemen up the porch stairs and into wide, welcoming doorways. He kept to the park side of the street, away from the light. He almost laughed at his plight, all alone in London on Christmas Eve, hiding from anyone the fact that he was Irish and on the run.

The Irish were hated even more in London now. There'd been a terrible mistake by the Fenians these past days. On the thirteenth of December, a group of Fenians bombed the prison at Clerkenwell House of Detention, trying to free the two men who had led the Manchester Prison breakout. The fools had wheeled a barrel up to the prison trying to light a fuse, but the damn gunpowder hadn't gone off. The second attempt the next day was only too successful: the newspaper reported that the explosion had leveled sixty feet of the prison wall, as well as many houses in the poor surrounding neighborhood. Twelve people dead, and many more injured. The paper even claimed that twenty babies in the womb were murdered also. The English were furious. The Fenians were hunted as terrorists. Fear and suspicion of anyone Irish spread like wildfire. And to top it all off, the two men they were trying to free were not even in the exercise yard at the time! The whole plot was a disaster.

Michael had been trying to lie low in London, working as a day laborer on the docks, and using his wages to share a room with two other Irishmen, taking turns in the bed each night. He could not go back to Bantry after his encounter with Caroline in the barn, and he did not trust the post in Bantry to get a letter safely to his mother. Surely the RIC was on the lookout for him. MacDonogh and the Irish Republican Brotherhood would be hunting him, too, since he'd disappeared without a word to anyone. He knew too much; they'd think he was now a spy.

When he spoke to anyone in the shops, he tried to sound English but knew he probably fooled no one. So, this night when he heard footsteps behind him on a dark patch of the road, he pulled up his collar and glanced over his shoulder. A young boy ran past him, and he found himself pitying any child out alone on Christmas Eve in the wet and the cold. The wind picked up and Michael's steps did too. He thought of home, his mother baking, the fire burning brightly in the hearth, and his dog Queenie. How was Eileen? Were they all at Midnight Mass in St. Finbarr's? He looked up to the heavens, wondering if God was still with him, even here in godforsaken London.

Suddenly the rain changed to thick heavy snowflakes. By the time he reached his lodgings in Bloomsbury, his cap and the shoulders of his jacket were covered with the quick-melting flakes. He climbed the steps in the darkness, trying not to stumble at each curve. The room was empty! What luck. The others must have been out celebrating or maybe even at Mass. He tugged off his boots and put them under the one window to dry. He hung his jacket, shirt, and pants over the chair next to the bed and used the chamber pot, which for once was empty. He dove into bed, pulling the one cover up to his chin. He lay on his back, hands behind his head. There was no pillow.

He had to get word to his people in Bantry. They'd be worried to death, he knew. Suddenly he thought of Father Gleason. He'd send an official-seeming letter to the priest, and on the envelope, he'd print "Private, conscience matter." Even the RIC would not read letters addressed to a priest. After Christmas he'd go to the British Museum. There were places he'd discovered on Sunday afternoons where you could roam freely to look at the treasures. He'd spend a few shillings on paper and an envelope. There he'd compose his letter to Father Hugh Gleason, Parish Priest at St. Finbarr's Catholic Church, Bantry, County Cork. As the snow fell like so many feathers on the streets of London, Michael sank into a blessed sleep.

CHAPTER TEN

·······················

The months after Christmas crawled by for Eileen. John was underfoot all day when the winter storms hurled themselves against the cottage like beasts, raging and snarling. She sewed baby clothes when she had a few minutes in between the cooking and washing, and the mucking out of the barn. After a late April snowfall, the sun glinting like silver on the blankets of snow covering the fields and the barn, the weather softened, and bits of green could be seen in the fields and yard. Eileen felt awkward and restless with her belly huge, and the baby tumbling and punching like mad when she lay down at night.

In the first week of May, Eileen felt sharp pangs as she was coming back from the barn at mid-morning, carrying a pail of milk to the house. The pains felt like mild cramps at first, so she beat back her panic, smoothing her hand over her swollen belly, trying to reassure the little creature inside. John had arranged for the midwife, Mrs. O'Connor, to come for the birth, and he promised he would also go for her mother when the time came. But now John was out plowing a field for the spring planting. He would not hear her cries and wasn't expecting to see her until noon when she brought him his tea. She told herself to stay calm, that it was probably nothing yet. She set the pail down on the table and breathed slowly, in and out. Again, the cramp twisted inside her, and she gasped aloud, holding onto a chair. She paced the room then, breathing slowly as she waited for the next wave of pain.

Oh, she wasn't ready to be a mother yet! What did she know of childbirth, taking care of a helpless infant day and night, tied to a baby always needing to suckle? But she'd already fallen in love with this little one, sight unseen. She glanced at herself in the mirror of her wardrobe, and saw her flushed face, her shining eyes, and felt strangely beautiful and strong. She could do this! She was a woman now, just turning seventeen, and she could bring this life into the world. But she'd have to have help. She grabbed her shawl and began walking out to the field. She had to stop every few minutes to bend over and wait for the pain to pass.

John saw her coming from a long way off, and threw down the plow, running toward her.

"It's time," she gasped as he put his arm around her to steady her. Back at the house, he lowered her onto the bed and told her he'd run for the midwife. His face was dark, anxious, and he smelled of sweat. His face was pale as he gasped, "Will you be all right, now?"

"Yes, just go!"

By the time he got back Eileen was drenched in sweat, her body writhing on the bed, her dress awry. Mrs. O'Connor bustled in, clad in a black cloak and black bonnet with bright blue feathers. She shouted, "Now Sullivan, put a kettle of water on to boil and get me some clean towels and sheets!"

She closed the door to their bedroom, and began taking off Eileen's shoes and stockings, pulling her up to a sitting position to remove her dress, chattering all the while. "Ah, girl, those pains are coming fast and hard now, aren't they? That's good. It may not be too long this way. First babies sometimes have a hard time entering this world."

"Tell my husband to go for my mother," Eileen pleaded. "He promised he would."

"Sure, he'll go as soon as we can spare him. We don't really want him around anyway, do we? Men aren't much use now at all, at all," she muttered. Eileen gasped as she felt the woman's cold hands up inside her, checking to see how far along she was. "Sorry, love, I didn't take time to warm my hands." Mrs. O'Connor had not even stopped to remove her bonnet, the blue feathers trembling every time she spoke. Eileen kept her eyes on them, gritting her teeth against the fierce waves of pain, tightening inside her. Those early pangs had been nothing, she realized, like distant thunder before all hell breaks loose in a storm.

The next hours were a blur, just a jumble of voices, orders to push or not push, orders to breathe, breathe, and finally her mother's hands at her shoulders, lifting her up to a half sitting position, rubbing her back until she once more flung herself back into the pillows straining now to push and free herself from this monstrous object struggling to emerge.

A mighty push with searing pain and she heard her mother cry, "There's the head!" Now another push and the waters gushed from her as the tiny thing slipped out into the world, all naked and slick with blood. Both women laughed, shouting in unison, "It's a boy!" Eileen felt only relief. She was barely conscious, lying back on the pillow with her eyes shut as the midwife cut the cord, placing it in a pan of water, waiting for the afterbirth to slither out.

Sometime later, her mother brought the baby to her where she lay half asleep, and she stared down into a perfect round face, rosy cheeks, and long lashes. The child stared up, gazing into her own wondering eyes. She leaned to kiss his cheek, and smelled the scent of a newborn, that fuzzy, milky smell of tender flesh. Then she unwrapped him from the tightly bound cocoon the midwife had coiled him in, examining his perfect little body, the flailing hands and feet, the rounded tummy, the engorged penis. She bent to kiss his chest. She looked up then to see John standing in the doorway, too shy to intrude on the scene.

"Come in and meet your son," she said with a smile.

He moved gingerly over to the bed and sat in the chair nearby. She wrapped the baby loosely in the blanket and handed him to his father. John sat quietly, not daring to speak, just cradling the bundle, and patting it softly as if it might break.

"I'd like to name him Thomas, for my father," he looked at Eileen shyly as he said this. She remembered with a shock that Thomas was the name of his dead child. Was it bad luck to name this child after the dead one?

"Yes, but we'll give him Michael for his middle name." She looked over at her mother, who was beaming down on her little grandson, and saw that stoic Mamie O'Donovan had tears in her eyes as she gazed at the child. Her mother nodded, and then bent to take the baby from Sullivan's arms. She began to croon in Irish, and soon Eileen felt her eyes grow heavy.

"Oh no," cried the midwife. "No sleeping until you've given him suck. We've got to get your milk flowing as soon as possible." She propped the child on a pillow next to Eileen and fumbled to pull down her gown from her shoulders. Eileen struggled to sit up, wincing with pain. She stared down at her breast, not recognizing it as hers, so engorged it was. How would the little one ever get his mouth around her nipple?

She pressed his face to her breast and felt him snuffle and purse his lips, finally tasting the yellowish liquid, making a few feeble attempts at sucking. He soon latched on to her breast firmly and with great determination had his first meal. Eileen could not stop staring at him. When he pulled back, his eyes half closed with exhaustion, she lifted him over her shoulder and patted his back gently.

"That's it," said Mrs. O'Connor, from the other side of the room, taking a pan of water with the cord and the afterbirth in it to the door of the cottage. "Now you can rest, alannah. Your work this day is done."

The weeks that followed were measured now by the baby's

progress: his first smile, the first night he slept all through when she awoke, heart pounding as she saw the dawn through the window, knowing that her baby must have died, rushing over to the crib, leaning in to feel a breath on her cheek, and then the flooding joy of seeing him wave his little fist and give an enormous yawn.

Eileen felt new energy as she moved through her days, cooking, cleaning, washing, and carrying John's lunch out to the fields with the baby swaddled on her back. Her husband seemed to love the little one but paid scant attention to him until after supper each evening, when he sat by the fire and dandled Thomas on his knees, telling him about the cows and the sheep and even the rabbits he had seen in the field that day.

Once a week, usually on Friday, which was market day in Bantry, Eileen packed a bag and set off with the baby to walk the mile and a half into town, looking forward to visiting her mother so the two of them could coo over Thomas's dimples, his fat arms and legs, his searching blue eyes as he lifted his head and took in the new world around him.

But on this Friday, Eileen noticed that her mother seemed pale, somehow shrunken, and the older woman winced when she handed the baby back to her daughter.

"Mammy, what is it? Do you have a pain?"

"It's nothing," her mother said, but the grayness of her face told another story.

"Mammy, don't lie. You are in pain, I can tell."

"Eileen, sit down here and let me catch my breath and look at the wee one for a few minutes." Mrs. O'Donovan pulled up a chair and lifted the bundle from Eileen's back. She unwrapped the baby and peered into his bright eyes, holding her face close and humming softly. Then she sat down, rocking the child, murmuring in Irish. "Sure, it's great joy you've given me, daughter. I never expected to feel such sweetness again holding a baby in my arms."

She looked up at Eileen standing above her. "I'm only sorry that this had to come on you so early in your life."

"Mammy, you're changing the subject. What's wrong with you, for God's sake?"

"For God's sake it's not. I have a lump in my breast, and it's growing."

"Then you should go to the doctor in Cork City. Martin and I will go with you. It may not be what you think. Please, Mammy. I need you right now." Eileen felt tears spring up as she gazed at her mother's gray head bent over little Thomas and watched the calloused hands caressing his face. She didn't remember her mother being so gentle when they were little. She'd seemed always to be ordering everyone around like some kind of general, trying to keep the farm going, hurrying them off to Mass, and never or rarely having time for a soft touch or gentle word. She'd been a woman in charge, a woman forced by widowhood to be both father and mother.

"Eileen, there's a lump in my breast and great pain. I'm only thankful I'm still here to see this one arrive, healthy and strong, so like Michael. . . ." Then she broke off, unable to go on at the thought of her missing son. After a moment in which neither woman spoke, her mother handed the baby back to her. "It's his lunch he's wanting. While you feed him, I'll put on the kettle. You must be famished after your walk this morning."

She stood then and placed the kettle over the fire in the hearth, scurrying around her kitchen to lay out bread, butter, and jam. Eileen put the child to her breast, trying to relax until she felt her milk come down as he began to suck. She rocked him steadily, not knowing what to say to her mother's stubborn dismissal of the idea of a doctor. How could she herself go on, married and now a mother with no guidance, no help? At the thought she realized how selfish she was, only worrying about herself. Michael must know. It would scald her mother's heart not to see her son again. How could she find him? He had to come home before it was too late.

After tea, she kissed her mother goodbye at the door. Her mother wrapped the blanket more securely around Thomas on Eileen's back and then stood in front of her daughter. "Now Eileen, don't bother yourself worrying. We all have to die, and I can rest easy about you at least, all settled in your own home with your beautiful son. I'm not afraid, you know. My rosary in my hand every night, the Blessed Mother herself will be with me, as we say, 'Now and at the hour of our death.'"

Eileen, startled, realized she had never heard her mother talk about her faith. Mamie O'Donovan had gone to Mass every Sunday and holy day of her life, she prayed the rosary on her knees every night, but her religion was private, not to be discussed. Like air, it was the reality she lived in. Eileen wished her own faith were like that. She had trouble even believing in God after her marriage. He had not answered her prayers. What kind of God let a girl be attacked as John Sullivan had attacked her that first night? What kind of Church blessed a marriage that they knew was not freely chosen? And yet, Father Gleason too had been troubled, she knew, by the marriage.

As she walked up the hill toward the farm, the spring sunshine shone weakly through the heavy clouds. She smelled the fields after the rain of the night before, and looking up, a sort of half-prayer, half complaint rose to her lips, "Well, if You are there, dear God, help my mother in her hour of pain. And please find Michael too," she added. The clouds, high above her, sailed across the sky in serene indifference.

Sunday nights in the rectory of St. Finbarr's Church were usually quiet. The housekeeper, Mrs. McCarthy, put out a cold supper before she left, as she always served a big lunch at noon, often with a visiting priest or even at times with Father Gleason's brother over from Galway. After Benediction at six o'clock, Father made his way back to the house in the early dusk, anticipating a quiet supper alone with perhaps a glass or two of whiskey and a cigarette. Then he'd sit by the fire and read last Saturday's *Irish Times,* which never arrived sooner than five or six days after it came out. So, he was startled by the appearance of a dark figure waiting for him at the door of the rectory. He recognized Jim Cronin, the postmaster for Bantry.

"Good evening, Father," the man stepped out of the shadows, doffing his cap.

"Why, hello, Jim," Father said, shaking the man's hand. "Have you come to keep me company and share a glass in front of the fire?"

"Now that sounds very tempting, Father, but my missus will have my hide if I stay out any later. Something came for you in the post yesterday, from London, very peculiar. I decided to bring it over in person rather than give it to one of the carriers." He handed the priest a letter, and in bold letters on the front of the envelope the priest read: Private: Conscience Matter. Cronin stood there, shuffling, waiting for Father to open the letter.

"Why, thanks so much for delivering this in person," Father said, stuffing it casually under his black cloak. "You're sure now that you have to get home?"

He turned to enter the rectory, resting his hand a minute on the brass knob. "Thanks again, Cronin. My best to the missus." Without waiting for a reply, the priest shut the door firmly behind him. He went straight to the bottle of whiskey he kept in the parlor on a shelf under the bookcase, poured himself a full glass, and then settled in the worn easy chair in front of the fire to read.

Dear Father Gleason:

I'll not tell you my whereabouts just in case, but I want you to know I am all right. I had to get out of Bantry because of an incident at the Big House. I'm probably also in trouble with some elements there I got involved with this past year, if you take my meaning. Please get word to my mother and to

Eileen that you've heard from me and I'm doing grand, with
a job and a fine place to stay, all safe. That's all for now but
I will keep in touch. Thanks for all, Father.
M.O. February 2, 1868

February! That was months ago! Father read the letter again
slowly. He knew Michael was lying about the grand and fine part.
He suspected he was hungry and desperate. No return address.
He felt the paper, good quality, and turned over the envelope,
examining the faint smudge of the postmark: *V R*. The Queen's
initials gave his location away: England.

So, he thought, Michael had joined hundreds of other Irishmen in London, hoping to melt into that vast city where it was
easy to be anonymous. The priest stared into the fire and reached
over to pour himself another glass of the beautiful amber liquor.
Ireland was losing her young men to violence, drink, and, of
course, to America.

He himself was impotent, he knew, as far as the struggle.
He could not get involved as a priest although at times he was
badly tempted. The Fenians had decided there was no hope
for Ireland to win independence except through violent tactics:
guerrilla attacks on British barracks, assassinations. . . all evil
acts in God's eyes and in his own. The politicians kept trying
for political solutions, hoping in the good will of Gladstone, but
now the people, especially the young ones, were tired of waiting.

In America, too, the scattered Irish were working and sending money for arms. There were even Irish officers who had
fought in America's Civil War coming back to Ireland prepared
to fight for their own country's independence. The Rising in
the past year had failed, but the flame still burned, he was sure.

Now Michael O'Donovan was caught. What in the hell had
happened at the Big House? Why was he in trouble with the
IRB? Maybe the lad ought to high tail it to America and start
a life there. The priest rested his eyes for a minute; he'd visit

Mamie O'Donovan tomorrow. Slowly the letter fell from his hands as sleep overcame the pastor, worrying over his lost sheep.

After the eight o'clock Mass on Monday morning, the priest ate a quick breakfast and decided to get the task he most dreaded tackled first thing. Visiting Mamie O'Donovan took more courage than being goalkeeper for his old Gaelic football team in Galway, The Ramblers.

"Gleason," the crowd used to chant after each saved goal, "Gleason our goalie!" If the fans had only known how frightened he was every blessed minute of a game as the lads come roaring downfield toward him, ready to strike. It was a guessing game which way to lunge, and it was often pure luck when he guessed right.

Stepping into the fresh morning, the priest swung his walking stick. Life was a whole lot like being a goalkeeper, he thought, pure blind luck when we make the correct choice. Mamie O'Donovan had never forgiven him for that sermon about parents forcing their children into unwanted marriages. Yet, he did not regret at all what he had said. It was a crime to give an innocent child over to a marriage she was repulsed by. He had failed to save Eileen from the marriage. He had seen the hopelessness in her eyes the morning of her wedding. Perhaps if he had refused to perform the ceremony. . . . He sighed, rehearsing just what he would say to Mrs. O'Donovan.

As he approached the cottage, old Queenie came out and raised a halfhearted protective bark before he leaned to pet her. Martin came to the door. With a wide smile, Father Gleason greeted Martin, "Good morning, Martin! May I stop in for a cup of tea this fine day?"

"Of course, Father," Martin looked surprised and a bit worried, glancing over his shoulder at his mother. They were drinking their second cup of tea that morning after the milking.

Mamie rose as the pastor ducked his head and entered the kitchen. "Good morning, Father," she said stiffly. "Come in. Something serious must have made you come all this way."

"Well, Mrs. O'Donovan, if it's all the same to you, how about first pouring me a cup of that tea." He looked into her eyes and was shocked at the change in the widow. She had lost weight, and her hair was almost completely white. She was bent over a bit to one side, shrunken. "Are you well, Mamie?" he asked, his voice gentle.

"I'm fine, Father, just fine. So, here's the tea," she announced as she laid the china cup and saucer in front of him, "and I have some fresh soda bread too, if you are hungry."

"No, thanks kindly." Father watched the woman's face as he began, "I've come with what I hope will be good news. Michael has written to me, but somehow the letter got delayed. He mailed it in February. He wanted me to tell you at once that he's thinking of you all and that he is fine."

Mamie set her cup down hard on the saucer, a bit of tea sloshing on the table. "Oh, thanks be to God! We've been sick with worrying over the boy. Father, can we see the letter?" The woman's eyes were full of tears, her gray face now blooming in a hectic flush.

Father had brought the letter with him, but he'd debated whether to share it with them. Now he felt he had no choice. He handed it to the mother. Tracing the address with her fingers, she then passed it over her shoulder to Martin.

"Read it to me, son," she sighed. "My eyes are failing me too these days."

Martin read the short note in a flat voice, barely keeping the anger out of his voice, the priest noted. There was not much love lost between the brothers, he suspected.

"My God!" cried Mamie. "I knew something had happened over at the House. What has he done?" Her hands moved convulsively over the table.

"Sure, he's mixed up with the feckin' Fenians," snarled Martin. "He's going to bring down the suspicion of the RIC on all of us. Damn him!"

His mother rose and looked at him, and when she spoke her voice was low and menacing. "Martin O'Donovan, if you ever use that language about your brother again you can pack your things and leave this house forever. It's heart-scalded I am to hear you say such evil words about your own brother. Your father's heart would be broken for sure to think his sons had turned against each other."

Martin's face flushed, and he swung away from the table and headed out the door, slamming it behind him. Father sipped his tea and tried not to look at Mamie. She took the cups and saucers to the dishpan and wiped her hands on the towel. "Well Father, it's grateful I am for your kindness in coming here today. At least we know he's alive, even grand," she smiled sadly. "Eileen will be relieved to hear it also."

"How is she?"

"She's over the moon with her baby, little Thomas. Maybe she's forgiven me for forcing her to marry Sullivan." They looked at each other, each afraid to admit what they were both thinking: that she had been handed over, the sacrificial lamb.

CHAPTER ELEVEN

....

Mamie O'Donovan was dying. On the last Sunday in June, Eileen asked Father Gleason to come to her mother's house to give her Extreme Unction after the eight o'clock Mass. Eileen met the priest at the door with the baby in her arms. She'd set up a small table covered with a starched white cloth with two candles and a crucifix near her mother's bed. She led Father to her mother's room and lit the candles.

The priest kissed the purple stole and placed it around his neck, then took out a small enamel cask which contained the oil blessed on Holy Thursday, laying it on the table. He bent to speak to the dying woman, "Would you like to make your confession now, Mrs. O'Donovan?"

The woman gazed up at him, her eyes milky and unfocused. It was too late for that, he saw. She was barely conscious. He leaned down and spoke slowly and loudly into her ear, "Mary O'Donovan, in the name of the Father, and of the Son and of the Holy Ghost, I absolve you from all the sins of your whole life."

He then picked up the cask of oil and anointed her forehead, her breast, her hands and her feet, murmuring the prayers of the dying as he did so. Eileen stood frozen, unable even to say amen. Father stood for a long minute, gazing down at the woman. Finally, he turned to Eileen, "And where is Martin?"

"I don't know, Father. He didn't come home last night. I told John I would sleep in my mother's house these days as her time was close. Oh, Father, you haven't heard any more from Michael, have you?" The priest shook his head. Eileen went on, her voice trembling, "My mother was calling for him so many times this past week. I had to lie and say that he was so busy in London or wherever he is that he couldn't get away, but surely, he would be here soon. He'll be mad with sorrow to have missed seeing her before. . . ." She could not finish.

The priest took Eileen's hand, "May God bless you, Eileen, for the daughter you have been to your mother. I'll see what I can find out about Michael's whereabouts."

As they emerged into the sunshine, they heard hammering coming from the barn. They walked over together, Thomas, wide-eyed and alert, in Eileen's arms. They stopped when they saw Martin inside, hammering newly hewn pieces of wood into a coffin. He looked up when he heard them and rose to greet the priest. Fumes of poteen betrayed his whereabouts the night before.

Martin looked at the priest steadily as he said, "I thought I could do something useful out here for Mammy. But thank you for coming, Father. It's a wake we'll be having now."

A week later Mamie O'Donovan was dead. Martin and Eileen stood over her in the early morning light. *Now we are truly orphans*, Eileen thought. How strange to be barely seventeen and have no parents in the world. She opened the window in the bedroom to let her mother's spirit out of the room. "What do we do now?" she asked, staring at Martin.

"I'll run up to the Big House and then over to tell John." Martin suddenly seemed taller, surer of himself. "Then I'll go to town and notify Father Gleason."

Eileen felt dizzy, glancing at Thomas still sleeping soundly in the crib near his grandmother's body. She should be doing things now, but what? She went to the wardrobe to choose something to dress her mother in for the last time. She chose a white summer dress her mother hadn't worn in years, too delicate for a busy farm woman. After all, it was summer, so nothing heavy like the black one. She'd need help washing and dressing her, and suddenly she remembered they would need a white linen cloth to cover her in the coffin during the wake.

She opened the chest at the foot of the bed, and there was the white linen shroud they'd used for her father all those years ago. Now where was her mother's rosary? She searched helplessly around the room and then thought to look in the bed. She slid her hand under her mother's back, startled at how cold she was. There were the black beads. Eileen broke down, kneeling and sobbing until she heard little Thomas fussing in his crib.

Within an hour, Mrs. Hanrahan from the Big House arrived carrying a basket of food. She entered the house crossing herself, and came over to the bed where Mamie lay, gazing at her friend and coworker of many years lying still at last. Then she busied herself heating the kettle of water as they prepared to wash the body.

Eileen was startled at seeing her mother naked, her once high breasts shrunken, those strong thighs that had carried her to work in the fields alongside her husband and sons now wasted and wrinkled. Tenderly, Mrs. Hanrahan murmured in Irish as she lifted the body, washing each part with delicacy. Then they dressed her in clean linen, pulling the summer dress over her, fastening the high collar, and brushing her long gray hair. Eileen crossed her mother's hands over her heart and threaded the worn black rosary beads through her fingers. Finally, they placed the white linen shroud over her legs, leaving her hands exposed. They stepped back to gaze at the body, then both knelt next to the bed and prayed the rosary, the soft, sibilant words of the Hail Mary filling the room like the summer breeze that blew in through the open window.

That evening it seemed that the whole village crowded into the cottage. Martin, dry-eyed, stood at the door in his only suit, every inch the master of the house now. He shook each person's hand as people entered whispering, "I'm sorry for your trouble, Martin." Chairs lined the room, and women bustled around preparing plates of sandwiches and hot tea, traipsing back and forth outside to the men gathered there, where they were dipping their cups into the bucket of ale Martin had laid in. Once in a while, a shout of laughter would rise from the men, to be shushed quickly by the women.

Eileen made her way through the crowd, stopped at every step by people wanting to embrace her or tell her a story about her mother's kindness to them. None of this was real. She expected Mammy to rise up any minute and start ordering her around, pointing out old Missus O'Connor who could hardly hold her plate of sandwiches on her lap, the poor thing. Many people admired the corpse, *so youthful she looks,* they'd say, or *yes, I remember her wearing that dress, but her hair was dark then.*

The worst moments came for Eileen when people asked, lowering their voices, "And where is Michael this day?" Eileen smiled and raised her chin, murmuring of his work in England and the impossibility of getting home in time. She tried not to notice the raised eyebrows and looks people gave one another, knowing or suspecting that the truth was more complicated. She thought they would never leave.

Finally, near midnight, after Father led the recitation of the rosary, the last neighbor left, stumbling a bit down the dark path away from the house. The priest bent and kissed Eileen on her forehead, shook hands with Martin and John in silence, and stepped out into the summer evening.

The three of them, Eileen, Martin, and John, sank down at the kitchen table in relief. The baby slept nearby in a basket by the hearth, exhausted from being admired all evening. Martin rose then and said, "I'll sleep in the barn tonight so you and John can have the loft. No need to go all the way back to your place in the dark."

"That will be grand, Martin," replied John, looking over at her.

She nodded tiredly. "I guess the black dress I have on will be fine enough for the funeral tomorrow." She looked at Martin, "But I kept hoping tonight that Michael would walk in the door."

Martin's face flushed as he said, "Ha! That one dare not show his face here in Bantry, even for Mammy's funeral. He's gotten himself in a mess, and damn him for breaking his mother's heart these last months. I'm glad he didn't show!"

Eileen did not reply, following John who carried the baby slowly up the steep ladder to the loft her brothers had shared, where they'd tussled and laughed so many nights when they were still friends. How had it happened that they'd grown apart? Martin was proud, fully conscious that he was the oldest and so the heir to his father's house and their position as tenants of the Earl. He despised the Fenians as a bunch of troublemakers that would bring the heel of England down on them harder than ever. He hated politics, wanting only to be left alone to work and slowly add to his property. He showed no interest in women or marriage. He'd become a man on the make, for himself.

Michael was the dreamer, the charmer, Eileen knew, able to get his way with people. Eileen suspected that Michael had been their mother's favorite in spite of his dangerous ways. For this, Martin must have resented his brother. Martin had been the worker, the steady man helping his mother, never putting a foot wrong in Bantry. Why then was Michael the one his mother loved best? Eileen knew there would be no room in this house now for Michael even if he did come home.

In the morning, people arrived at the house for the procession with the body to the church. The beauty of the day mocked sorrow, a day of brilliant sunshine glistening on the waters of an impossibly blue bay, the air soft and fragrant, bees buzzing in the fields now golden with young oats and barley. The wagon Martin had prepared to carry the body was brought out into the yard, the people waiting quietly for the priest to arrive.

At nine o'clock, Father Gleason, garbed in his black vestments, strode up the road with two young acolytes dressed in black cassocks and snow-white surplices hurrying to keep up with him. Martin, John Sullivan, and four other men carried the body of Mamie O'Donovan out of her house for the last time, the house she had come to at her marriage, the house where she bore her three children, and the house where she laid out her own husband's body when he died suddenly at the age of thirty-four. With a last blessing, the priest led the procession, followed by the wagon with the coffin and the family, and the rest of the mourners straggling behind. When they came to St. Finbarr's Church with its steep steps, the men struggled to lift the coffin, shouldering it carefully and making their way one step at a time, groaning under the weight. Eileen was terrified that they would drop her mother's body.

The funeral Mass passed in a blur for Eileen, just as her wedding had. The words of the chant washed over her, *"Dies irae, dies illa, day of wrath, that day!"* But the gospel held her attention. It was the story of Martha lashing out, if gently, at Jesus for not having been there when her brother died. "Lord, if thou hadst been here, my brother had not died!" But then, hedging her bet, she softened, "But now also I know that whatever thou wilt ask of God, God will give thee."

Eileen, too, had thought that God could and thus would do anything one asked in prayer. But He hadn't come through for her when she prayed to be delivered from her marriage, nor when Michael disappeared, and she prayed for him to return before her mother died. She was finding out that God had other answers to her prayers, answers that she did not understand.

After Mass, they made the short walk to the graveyard of St. Finbarr Church. Mamie would be buried alongside her husband. In the silence of a June morning, broken only by a few sparrows in the churchyard, the casket was lowered into the grave that had been dug the night before by Martin, John, and Kathleen's husband. Eileen threw some of her mother's own garden's roses onto the pine box. The first shovelful of dirt thudded in the quiet. When John grasped her arm, Eileen felt faint. Together they walked away, leaving the men to the task of the burial.

Father Gleason waited for her at the door to the church. She shaded her eyes against the sun and looked up into his face. "Thank you, Father, for all your kindness."

The priest held both of her hands in his as he said, "Your mother was a powerful good woman, Eileen. She loved each of you so much although she was not a woman for wearing her heart on her sleeve."

Eileen laughed a bit. "She was powerful when she was mad at you for that sermon, Father!"

"Oh, don't think I wasn't aware of that! It was only at the baptism of little Thomas that she deigned to speak to me at all." He smiled at her, releasing her hands.

"Father," Eileen whispered as he was turning to leave. "How in the world can we get in touch with Michael? He'll be destroyed with the news of Mammy, and I'm afraid of what he'll do in his sorrow."

The priest leaned in to whisper, "I've been trying to reach him for the last two days, but no luck. I'll keep trying though. I have some contacts in London."

John, holding little Thomas in his arms, came to Eileen then, leading her away from the grave, and together they walked toward the gate of the cemetery. She leaned heavily on his arm, her head bowed. Martin had already left. Eileen and John were the last to leave the graveyard on a perfect July day, with the fresh earth smelling of summer covering Mamie O'Donovan at last.

CHAPTER TWELVE

....

On an achingly beautiful, light-filled summer night, with a breeze blowing like a caress off the water, Michael trudged off the London docks, knowing he could not go back to the dank, lonely room this early. His back and shoulders ached with the strain of lifting cargo all day. He headed to the pub nearest the gate, pushed his way to the bar between two tall men and ordered a pint of ale. Lately he'd been thinking and dreaming of home, so when he felt a touch on his arm, he swung round, half expecting to see Quigley or O'Brien from Bantry. A strange lad pressed a note into his hand, and waited a beat, while Michael reached into his pocket for a coin.

"Wait," he called, "Who gave you this note?" But the boy darted out of the pub and was up the street before he could follow him. He fingered the paper, thin but good quality, and pried it open, careful not to tear the envelope.

> *Dear Mr. O'Donovan,*
> *I write to invite you to tea so that I may give you some news of home. Please come by at your earliest possible convenience.*
> *Yours most truly,*
> *Mary Grace O'Brien*
> *13 Gower Street, near the British Museum.*

Who the hell was Mary Grace O'Brien? He paid his bill and began walking. It was barely past six o'clock, surely not too late to make a call. News from home? He felt a knot in his stomach. Who knew where to find him? What could be happening at home?

After walking half an hour, he turned down Gower, a quiet street shaded by sycamore trees. He pulled the brass knocker on the dark green door of number thirteen.

A young girl opened the door. "Good evening, Miss," Michael began, holding his cap in his hand. "I'm Michael O'Donovan, here to see Miss O'Brien."

Opening the door for him to enter, she ushered him into the hall. "You can rest here a second while I call the miss, sure," she said doubtfully, her blue eyes taking in his worn jacket and dirty boots. He thought he detected the west of Ireland in her voice. When she whisked out of the foyer and ran up the stairs, he wet his fingers and tried to smooth down his hair. Too nervous to sit, Michael examined the prints on the wall, and noted that one scene looked like Bantry Bay, with the blue Caha Mountains in the distance.

Hearing a light step, he turned to see a tall, grave young woman descending the stairs, her bright hair pulled back and pinned up, a pair of spectacles swinging from a cord around her neck.

"Mr. O'Donovan, good evening." Her voice was low, firm. Unexpectedly she shook his hand, and her own was dry and warm. "I am Mary Grace O'Brien. Let's go into the parlor."

He followed her into a room lined with portraits and prints, books strewn on every table. A fire burned in the grate although the weather was warm. "Lily will bring us tea in a minute, as I suspect you haven't had yours tonight?" Her voice rose in a question.

He shook his head, embarrassed to admit his hunger, hoping he didn't reek of ale. Suddenly, Michael could not contain the words that tumbled out. "Who are you? How do you know my name? You said in the note you have news. . . ." He was trying to keep panic out of his voice.

"My late mother was cousin to Father Hugh Gleason in Bantry. Father Hugh has been trying to find out where you were and guessed that you were working down on the docks. It didn't take too long for my younger brother, Matthew, to ask around without anyone noticing. But it's bad news, I'm afraid, that Father Hugh has sent." She watched Michael's face, and leaned forward in her chair, their knees almost touching. "Your mother was very ill, and last Thursday, a week ago today, she passed away peacefully in her bed at home." Mary Grace sat back.

Michael kept looking at her face, unable to grasp the strange words: *ill, passed away.* No! His mother was tall and strong; surely there was a mistake.

Miss O'Brien went on, "They had no address for you, so couldn't inform you when she took sick. I am sorry for your troubles, Mr. O'Donovan," she said, softening at last.

He sat still, staring into the fire. He'd never thought of that, of losing his mother to death, his mother a rock, the center that held the family together. He could scarcely remember her ever being sick. She loved him and worried about him, he knew. He knew how much he'd wounded her by leaving with no word, by disappearing all these months.

Just then Lily opened the door to the parlor carrying a tray with the tea and some sandwiches. Miss O'Brien poured him a cup and placed two halves of a sandwich on a plate, saying, "You are in shock now, Michael. You must eat and drink something."

He put the cup to his lips, smelling the strong sweet tea but felt he would choke if he took a sip. Miss O'Brien rose and pulled a bottle of Jameson from the bookcase, half hidden by tall volumes. "Here, take a drink of this first." She poured him a generous splash and watched him down it in two gulps. It burned, but steadied him then. With shaking fingers, he took a sandwich and tried not to wolf it down. He was famished.

Miss O'Brien sipped her tea quietly for a minute, and then asked, "What will you do, Michael? Will you go home now?"

He took a last drink of the whiskey before he answered. "That would be difficult, Miss. I had some trouble there and left in a hurry." He almost laughed at the understatement.

She put down her cup and saucer. "Michael, we in this house support the Fenians. I wrote for the *Irish People* until it was shut down in '66. Father Hugh told me that you had been active in the Rising last year, and I salute you for your bravery in the face of overwhelming odds. The goal now is complete independence. Let the British leave us alone."

Her eyes shone, and Michael saw she was beautiful in a stern, austere way. He smiled at her and shook his head. "Ah, it was a foolish fight going up against the mighty, but still I'm glad I was there." He drank the tea and stared again into the fire.

Miss O'Brien cleared her throat, "Well, what I'm trying to say is that I would be happy to help you sneak back down to Bantry if you wish to go. I know men who drive from Dublin down to Cork each week with supplies for the Fenians, under cover of being farmers, of course. You could ride with one of them dressed as they do, your hat pulled down over your face. You'd have to make your way on down to Bantry from Cork, but it shouldn't be too hard to find a wagon going that way. The tricky part is getting you across the Irish Sea. Do you have any money?"

"Yes, I've been saving what I can." He couldn't tell her that he'd really been saving to go to America. But he knew he had to go home if only to see his sister and his mother's grave. Again, that blow in the pit of his stomach.

Mary Grace went over to a desk and pulled out an envelope. She counted out some notes, and stuffed them into a smaller envelope, handing it to him. Michael started to object when she cut him off. "Don't worry. This is money from America. There are thousands of Irish Americans, true Fenians, sending money to the Cause. There are ladies here in London helping with the Cause, so there's no shame in taking money from the likes of me."

Now her accent sounded more Irish, more like his sister's back home. He took the envelope then and stuffed it deep within the inner lining of his jacket, checking to make sure it was secure.

They both stood at once, awkwardly, and he felt her knee bump his leg as they moved toward the door. In the foyer, she stood facing him, her eyes level with his. "Tomorrow I'll send word about the arrangements to the same pub where the boy found you tonight. Please give Father Hugh my love when you see him. He's a fine man and very sympathetic to our cause although it is dangerous for him to show it."

"I will," he said putting on his cap. "And Miss O'Brien, I don't know how to thank you. You've been more than kind. I felt at home here even though you were telling me the dreadful news."

"Well, it's sorry I am that I had to break it to you. May God keep you safe, Michael O'Donovan," she took his hand. "And in case we never meet again, I'm proud to have met you, an Irishman who's putting himself on the line for Ireland's freedom."

It was still light as he made his way through the streets of Bloomsbury toward his room. His legs felt shaky as he walked, images of his mother swirling before him, his mother baking bread, hurrying across the fields in the rain to help getting the crops in, their quarrel over Eileen's marriage. Maybe his mother had known she was sick even then, he thought. Maybe that's why she wanted to see Eileen settled so soon. He looked up at the clouds in the late summer sky, violet, rose, mauve. Then he thought of Miss O'Brien. He'd never met a young woman like that, educated, refined but passionate! A warrior in her heart, if not in fact. He'd be home soon. With a pang he remembered that his mother would not be there. He'd see Eileen, they'd go to their mother's grave, but then he'd be gone. After that, he was for America.

Two weeks later, Michael sat next to Joseph Cronin, a farmer from Bantry who had been selling his oats in Cork on Market Day. The rickety cart rumbled along, the miles passing slowly as they rounded every treacherous curve. Michael was dressed in old clothes stuffed with rags to give the appearance of a much older, stouter man. He had let his beard grow and darkened his face. The two men were silent, with only the clopping of hooves breaking the peace of the evening. Michael had paid the fellow the last of Miss O'Brien's money, swearing him to secrecy. Cronin knew his family. Michael prayed he'd keep his mouth shut. "What time do you expect to reach town?" he muttered.

"Not before dark."

Perfect. Under cover of night, he had a chance of not being recognized in Bantry. This was the most dangerous part of the journey. Crossing the channel had been surprisingly easy, and he'd hitched a ride with some men from Cork who met him at the pier, all somehow arranged by Miss O'Brien. They'd asked him no questions, and he'd listened silently to their talk of English politics, incredulous to find how little he knew of the big motions for freedom that were bubbling in Parliament these days over the question of Ireland's fate.

He thought of MacDonogh, so fervent and sure of the Cause. He wished he had that passion and dedication. And then there was Mary Grace O'Brien, an impressive, no-nonsense young woman, working tirelessly for independence, not thinking of the risks she ran aiding a fugitive. Their bravery, their patriotism galled him with the sacrifices it demanded. He was sick of the whole thing. He was for America as soon as he said his goodbyes to his sister and prayed at his mother's grave.

It had begun to rain, and the road was slippery as it wound its way south and west, with sheets of rain hitting them in the face. At last, as they reached the peak of yet another hill, they glimpsed a few scattered lights in the distance. Almost home! How small the town looked now that he'd seen London. Still,

Bantry was home, but in the darkness, he remembered: no mother would be there to embrace him.

Michael leaped down, grabbing his sack and staff. "This is where I leave you, my friend. Many thanks for the ride, Joseph. And remember, you have no idea who the old man was that hitched a ride with you. Some beggar, perhaps." In the darkness, Michael grinned up at the farmer, who tipped his hat to him in silence. As he walked into the fields, he heard Cronin call after him, "Be careful lad. Ye and your family are well known here."

Under cover of the rain and the dark, Michael skirted the town, coming around on the other side of St. Finbarr's, walking the last mile home on the familiar road. Suddenly he stopped. Home? Their cottage was now in Martin's hands. He would not go there yet. It was Eileen he wanted to see, so he'd have to walk another two miles to Sullivan's cottage. He doubted that John Sullivan would be any more welcoming than Martin. All was changed.

A single candle flickered in the window of Sullivan's cottage. Michael crept around the back and peered into the kitchen. His sister was sitting in a rocking chair, holding a bundle, and humming quietly. He couldn't see Sullivan. He prayed he was sound asleep. Gently he gave three slight taps on the window, his old signal to Eileen when he had been out late and needed her to open the locked door at home. She looked up with a sharp jerk of her head, and the bundle squirmed in her lap. She had a baby! Their eyes met. Gently, she rose and came to the door. He met her, holding his finger to his lips. "Come outside!"

She nodded, and carefully laid the baby in his cradle, not too close to the hearth. Michael watched her move swiftly to the door, unlatching it slowly, slowly, and then she flew to him and was in his arms.

As Eileen held him, the tears that he'd denied until this day were now flowing freely.

"Oh Michael, aisling, are you a dream?" She wept too, and they stood motionless for a few minutes.

He led her then to the barn, and they sat in the hay, holding hands, and gazing at one another while the rain slackened to a gentle patter, until Eileen said angrily, "We didn't know if you were alive for the longest time. Our mother. . . ." she left off when she saw the pain in his eyes.

"I know, Eileen. Tell me what happened. When did she get sick?"

Eileen tried shortening the story, worried that the child might wake up and cry and alert John. Then she rose, pulling him to his feet. "You can come in, Michael. John will be fine. He's changed these last few months. He loves the baby so and seems happy to have us near him although he and I have little in common other than your nephew, Thomas Michael!"

Michael's eyes shone. He was an uncle! Dear God! What kind of an example was he setting for the wee lad? His own uncle, his father's brother, had been a hard-working farmer, a real grown- up who had taken him for rides on his shoulders, taught him how to fish, who had been there for Martin and him when their own father died. Now Michael was getting ready to flee his family, or what was left of it, leaving his sister and only nephew to the protection of a man she did not love and a brother who was as cold and distant as Neptune.

Michael held her hand as he pleaded, "Why don't I stay in the barn tonight? Then you can feel out John in the morning. He may not want to risk harboring a wanted man in his house. The fewer people that know I'm here the safer it is for me."

Eileen nodded, her heart sinking; *so, he would not be staying.* "I'll bring you a blanket. Are you starving?"

"I can wait until morning for some of your soda bread and hot tea. Go tend to that precious bundle I haven't met yet," he said, kissing her cheek, still streaked with tears. She melted into the darkness, and he lay on the straw, exhausted, feeling the cold comfort of his knife below his heart.

In the morning, Eileen woke, dreading the knowledge that she'd have to tell her husband about Michael. She waited until he had his porridge, even adding a boiled egg and a bit of ham to his plate. As he slurped his tea in the maddening way she'd become accustomed to, she sat down across from him with the baby on her lap. At three months, the child was strong, dark-haired, with a rosy face that broke into a toothless grin when anyone looked at him, sure that he was everyone's darling.

"John, we have a guest with us sleeping in the barn."

Her husband raised his head, his eyes narrowing. "Now who would that be, Eileen?"

"My brother Michael," she said, watching his face which betrayed nothing. "He came late last night when it was almost dark, wanting to see our mother's grave and not even knowing we had a son."

"Damn him! Eileen, you know he is a wanted man. The talk in the town is that he threatened a member of the Earl's family with a gun. He's a Fenian, to be sure. He can't stay here, endangering us all," John's voice rose as he pushed away from the table. He went to the window, gazing out to the barn, and did not look at her as he said, "I'm going out to the fields. I don't want to see him. And when I come home tonight, he'll be gone."

Eileen bit her lip, trying not to show her anger. She'd found it didn't work with John to oppose him directly. He was a slow thinker and liked to believe he was head of the household. She'd learned to manipulate, bide her time, come at him in a subtle way when she wanted something badly enough. Timing was all; a full stomach and a pint or two could work wonders with the man's moods.

She rose from the table and picked up the baby, trying for a reassuring tone, "I'm sure Michael doesn't want to stay long in Bantry. You know he couldn't go to Martin; there's no love lost between the two now that Michael's in trouble. I told him that you would be kind to him in his troubles."

Her husband grunted at that, kissed the baby's forehead, and sat to pull on his boots by the fire. Eileen handed him his lunch, and he left without another word. She watched from the window until she saw him disappear down the hill toward the fields. She'd have to find a way to let Michael stay one more night at least, so he could go to their mother's grave in the cemetery at St. Finbarr's under cover of night. It wasn't safe for him to go out during the day. She made her way swiftly to the barn to tell Michael the coast was clear.

After Michael wolfed down his breakfast, Eileen filled the tub with hot water from the stove and left him alone to bathe in front of the hearth. She took the baby outside with her, carrying him in a sling tied around her neck as she fed her chickens, Thomas laughing at their pecking and clucking. The baby loved being outside, so she'd asked John to fashion a small wagon for him. As soon as he could sit up, she would cart him around with her when she worked in her vegetable garden. He was getting heavy for her to be always carrying him around. John agreed, and now she walked out to the barn to see the half-built little boxy wagon, smelling the pine he had patiently hewn. Nothing was too good for his son, she knew. She glanced over to the corner where her brother had slept. He'd folded the blankets neatly and half hidden them under some straw.

When she went back to the cottage, he was just finishing a second cup of tea, his black hair wet and smoothed back from his forehead. He'd grown up in the months he'd been working in London; his body was firm, his hands calloused, but his eyes were alive, staring out at the world with a blue flame that burned hard. He didn't sit still for long, suddenly getting up and pacing the small room, restless as a caged panther with his black hair and flashing eyes.

"What is it, Michael darling?" she asked, watching him pace.

"I've got to get out of here, Eileen."

"But you've only just come. I thought you were going to the grave of our mother. Surely you can stay one more night with us." She felt more herself with Michael than with anyone else. They had always been close, running free as little ones, cheeks red with wind and rain in all weather, defying their older brother and often their mother too. She didn't want him to leave, leave her alone with this husband they had chosen for her. She saw now how alone she would be when Michael left.

She did not love John. She'd tried and tried to love him, but it was no use. You can't make yourself love someone. Their life together was only tolerable because of their shared love for little Thomas. Living with him was like being in prison. They had little to talk about in the evenings, besides the farm and the child. And this was a life sentence, she feared, according to Holy Mother Church.

"I'm not talking about leaving Bantry only." He looked into her eyes, "I'm talking about leaving this fucking country."

"Michael!"

"Eileen, I can't stand living here. Always looking over my shoulder for the Brits or the IRB to come after me. I've broken the rules of the obedient, smiling, groveling Irish peasant. But I'm no patriot either, as I'm too cowardly to attack the barracks of the Irish Constabulary. I've broken the vow I made to the IRB. So, both sides are after my hide! I'm for America!" He sat down, and his voice quieted. "I had one stroke of luck, Father Gleason's cousin in London, Miss Mary Grace O'Brien."

He told her of the elegant, poised young woman and her no-nonsense kindness to him, her arranging of the trip back here, paid for by funds sent to the IRB from America. "America is where the future for us is, Eileen! There we have a chance, we can work, our children would have freedom to study, to be anything they wanted to be. Why not come with me, aisling? Look at your child and tell me you want him to grow up here struggling on land owned by the Earl, getting our pittance to

work it so he and his family can live in a fine house, educate his children in London or Paris, collect his art from Italy
and Greece."

Eileen knew he spoke the truth, a truth she had learned
bitterly when she was forced to marry Sullivan. She'd been
married off for money. Their lives and welfare depended entirely
on the old corrupt system, and would never change without
terrible violence, a violence she felt coming with the clashes
in the night between the Fenians and the Irish Constabulary.
Michael was already tainted by this violence, now a wanted
man. Did she want Thomas to grow up in this?

"But how will you pay for passage, Michael? I know John
would not help you, and I've only a bit squirreled away from
my egg money."

He rose, "I'm going to talk to Martin. He got everything
when he inherited the rights to the land, and surely, he doesn't
want me around making trouble for him in Bantry where everyone knows everyone else's business. I'll ask for a loan and hope
I can pay it back once I am over there."

"But you can't go out in the daylight!" Eileen gazed at him
sadly, knowing that Martin felt only contempt for the brother
who, in his eyes, had disgraced their family name. Martin needed
to stay in the Earl's good graces, and so perhaps he would be
willing to advance Michael enough money to get far away and
leave him in peace, she thought hopefully.

"I'll go tonight after I've seen our mother's grave." He
crossed himself then, unable to hide the tremor of grief that
shadowed his face.

She nodded. "I'll come with you then," she murmured.
"John can tend the baby for a bit. We'll set out after sunset and
take the long way around to St. Finbarr's."

Michael reached for his sister, tilting her face up to him. "I
wish you'd come to America too, you and John and the baby!
Start over in a new life."

Eileen laughed softly. "John has softened a bit, but I can't imagine him going to America with my renegade brother." Still, as he turned away, a spark was lit. America! Little Thomas would have a future there.

That evening, when the long summer dusk had finally succumbed to darkness, Eileen faced her husband. "I'm going with Michael to our mother's grave, John. We'll be safe this late at night and we'll go around the long way to the church. The baby's been fed and should sleep for several hours now." They glanced as one at his cradle, and she could see the rise and fall of the little back as the child lay tucked beneath a red quilt she had stitched during her pregnancy. His dark hair framed the pudgy face. *Oh, he was beautiful*, Eileen thought, *and growing so well, never sick, the darling.*

John frowned, "Sure, you are asking for trouble, woman, going with Michael at this hour. Can't the man go on his own, for Christ's sake?"

"John, it may be the first and last time I stand with Michael in front of our mother's grave. He's bent on emigrating to America." She raised her chin and looked directly into his eyes, seeing a mixture of anger and hurt there. She flashed on the image of Queenie when someone had kicked her. At times her husband did remind her of a lumbering black dog, slow and inscrutable.

He turned away and took a chair in front of the hearth, not looking at Eileen. She grabbed her shawl and said, "If the baby wakes before I'm back, you can give him some milk. You'll be all right with him, John?"

He nodded, staring into the fire. She found another shawl that had been her mother's and folded it under her own shawl for Michael. In the dark they would look like two old crones, she hoped.

Michael was waiting for her under the tree by the barn. The last light in the west had faded, and the earth smelled of hay from the mowing. A waning moon was rising, and Eileen was grateful it was not full. She covered Michael with the shawl, and they both laughed.

"Sure, it's like old times, sister, with the two of us up to mischief on a summer night," Michael said smiling sadly.

Mischief, she thought, oh no. This was danger, but her heart lifted as they fell in step together scurrying across the hill, making their way around the outskirts of the town to the cemetery next to the black hulk of St. Finbarr's Church. The night was silent, with no bird song, only a few rustlings in the bushes.

Stealthily, Michael lifted the latch of the gate to the cemetery, and they crept between the headstones, picking their way to the corner. Their parents lay side by side, their simple headstones almost touching. When the sliver of moon flashed briefly between clouds, they could make out the names and dates. Eileen made the sign of the cross, and Michael dropped to his knees. He lifted his head free of the shawl, and traced his mother's name in the dark, brushing some scattered dirt from the stone.

"Shouldn't we say a prayer, Michael?" Eileen whispered.

"I'm not sure my prayers are any good these days."

"Hail Mary, full of grace, the Lord is with thee," they recited together, Eileen thinking of all the times after a crushing day of work their mother dropped to her knees to say the rosary, forcing them all to join her before they went to bed. Michael bent to kiss the ground, and with a swift motion grabbed the shawl and rushed out of the cemetery, Eileen racing to keep up with him.

"I should have been here when she died," he muttered. "It's with worry and sorrow she went to her death, and me, the wayward son, not even here." He turned and looked intently at Eileen. "Do you really believe there is an afterlife? Will we see one another again, do you think? I'm having a hard time with God these days. The story seems like a pretty myth to me now with all the evil I see around me. There is no justice for many people in this world, Eileen. Least of all here in Catholic

Ireland!" He kicked a stone savagely and it flew up in front of them.

"I'm having a hard time too, Michael. I prayed to God to spare me from this marriage, but no answer came. And yet, would I not have wanted this treasure that is our son? So, I go on clinging to hope that He is with us at every step of our lives." They walked on in silence, heading back to their old cottage, both dreading the meeting with Martin.

By now, it was late, and the moon glimmered between the fast-moving clouds. As the brother and sister approached the cottage, they saw a lamp burning within. They knocked gently on the door, before pushing it open, to see Martin, his head in his hands, an empty glass in front of him, slumped at the kitchen table. Queenie rose stiffly from her place at the hearth and wagged her tail as she made her way over to greet Eileen and Michael.

Martin woke with a start, "By God, what in the world are yous doing traipsing around in the middle of the night?" He moved toward them, and Eileen reached up to kiss his cheek. She knew they were on a delicate mission, and Martin needed to be handled with tenderness. He stared at Michael.

"So, the prodigal son returns," he finally managed.

Michael extended his hand to his brother, and grinned. "And where is the fatted calf, I might ask?" They clasped arms and Eileen breathed a sigh of relief.

"We've just gone to Mammy's grave. We didn't think it safe to go in the daylight," Eileen said, throwing her shawl on the back of a chair. The room grew silent, each of the children sensing their mother here, half expecting her to bustle in putting the kettle on to boil. Finally, Martin muttered, "May she rest in peace." Michael's eyes glistened with tears, and he made a rough swipe at his eyes.

"Safe, is it?" Martin said coldly as they drew up chairs around the table. Eileen glanced around and saw there was not a bit of food in sight, and the kettle on the hearth was cold over the ashes of the dying fire.

Martin burst out then, "Michael, what in God's name were you thinking to come here like this? You know that you are under suspicion in these parts. Damn it, man, you are finished here in Bantry."

"That's just what I've come to talk to you about. I'm off for America."

"Oh? And how's that going to happen?" Martin sat back in his chair and a brief look of relief passed over his face.

Eileen leaned in and grabbed Martin's hand, "We need to help Michael get away. You said yourself it's not safe here for him."

Michael broke in, "It's five pounds sterling for passage from Queenstown to New York in steerage. The *SS Glendoven* sails from Queenstown next week, and if you could see your way to lending me the money, I'd work and pay you back over time."

"Now where in hell do you think I'd come up with five pounds? It's the middle of harvest season with rains threatening the crops and me working the land alone since you flitted away!" Martin's expression had hardened.

"Martin," she said in a low tone, "if John and I had it I would gladly give it to Michael. But we owe money for grain, and we have nothing to spare, with the little one and all." Her voice trailed off.

Michael rose suddenly and paced the room. "I need to leave Ireland, Martin. I've broken my oath to the IRB for disappearing months ago with no word to them, and the British are hunting me too. Father Gleason's cousin in London, a Miss O'Brien, gave me the money and helped me get over here. She has connections in New York with sympathizers to the Irish cause, and says if I can just get there, they will help me get started with work there. Don't forget, you got the land, and I have nothing." His voice had taken on an edge. Eileen knew it was costing him to be pleading like this. His temper would take over soon.

Martin's voice rose, his face flushed, "Yes, I got the worn-out, measly few acres to farm by myself, with no wife, no child, and little chance of ever having a family I could support. Maybe I'd like to throw everything over and leave too!" Martin got up and paced the room. Eileen felt dizzy with fatigue and fear as she watched her two brothers circle the room. Surely the ghosts of her mother and father were watching them, sorrowful at the Cain and Abel animosity that clung like acrid smoke in their childhood home.

Suddenly Martin faced his brother. "I'll get the money somehow. I've a few pounds saved for emergencies, and I think I can borrow the rest. But give me until Monday, at least." He looked away then. "Sure, it's best that you leave, Michael. You've made your bed, and it will be a hard one to lie in, I'll wager. God knows what awaits you in America."

Michael stood, and his chin rose as he looked into Martin's eyes. "Thank you, Martin. I swear I'll pay you back as soon as I can. As for America, I can't wait to see her shores and feel like a free man. Who knows? Maybe you and Eileen and our little nephew, we might all end up there!" His eyes shone, and he seemed taller and freer, not like a supplicant dog begging for a treat from his master.

Eileen rose and embraced Martin, and in a rare gesture, he kissed his sister on the cheek. "God bless you, Martin. Sure, our mother and father are looking down on you with love and thanks for your help," she said, gathering her shawl around her.

The brothers shook hands, and then all three moved toward the door. Martin stepped aside as Eileen and Michael made their way out into the night to walk back to Sullivan's place. When she looked back, Martin was still standing in the door, with Queenie beside him, watching them go down the path, the lamplight spilling out into the night.

On Monday, Michael packed for the voyage while his sister gathered bedding, a plate, fork, knife, and spoon, all wrapped snugly in his pack along with his few clothes and an old coat that had been John's. Now Michael sat on the floor with his nephew, rolling a toy cart made of wood back and forth to the crowing delight of the baby. Martin had come for tea on Sunday with the money, and the men had toasted one another with poteen far into the afternoon. They'd told jokes and stories and ended up in tears when they sang the old songs:

> *O Father dear, I oft times hear*
> *You speak of Erin's Isle*
> *Her lofty hills, her valleys green*
> *Her mountains rude and wild.*
> *They say she is a lovely land*
> *Wherein a saint may dwell*
> *So why did you abandon her*
> *The reason to me tell.*

By evening, only Eileen was left standing to put Thomas down for the night, her brothers and husband all snoring off the celebration.

Michael would leave town on Cronin's cart under cover of dusk that evening, and there'd be no farewells from anyone else, not even their cousin Kathleen and her family. A poor showing, Eileen thought, trying to hide her tears from Michael.

"It's sorry I am that you are leaving all hugger-mugger in secret, Michael," she said, keeping her tone light. He smiled at her, and she memorized his face, the black hair hanging down over his forehead, the chiseled face, and piercing eyes. "Sure, the girls in New York will be after you soon, I'll wager."

Michael answered with a laugh, "I'm counting on that, sister. I'm tired of celibacy, you know. Speaking of celibacy, I'll get in touch with you through letters to Father Gleason as soon as I get settled in New York. It may be a while, though, until I can write, so don't worry at all." Eileen nodded, unable to speak through the knot in her throat.

When he disappeared into the dusk, silence settled over the cottage. John sat by the fire, smoking, staring into the flames. Even little Thomas was fussy, pushing her away when she tried to feed him. All the light seemed to have gone from the day, and now dark worry and loneliness crept over Eileen, the years of her brother's absence stretching out endlessly before her like the cold Atlantic itself.

CHAPTER THIRTEEN

....

F ifteen months later, Thomas toddled along beside Eileen, chattering away in some ancient language, a mixture of Irish and English and his imagination. At a year and a half, the child was sturdy and bright-eyed, his blue-green eyes so like his mother's. They made their way out to the end of the field where John was digging turf for the coming winter. The scent of peat fire hung in the crisp air. The child wore a blue sweater embroidered with cows and sheep across his chest. Eileen had become quite the seamstress, her needle flying on the long evenings as she mended clothes for John and herself and made new shirts and pants for the growing child. Luckily, she thought, there'd been no more babies. The crops had failed badly for the second year in a row, and John was desperate with worry, spending many nights this past summer sleeping in the barn. Eileen felt secretly relieved on these nights and tried to make up for her relief by making him a soft pallet and light cotton blankets for warmth.

She had no desire for another child. Thomas was all her joy and pride, a child so winning that people stopped her on her way to town to chuck him under the chin and rain blessings in Irish on the little one. Today Eileen carried John's lunch in a sack, and a tin of hot tea swung from her arm as the two made their way through the pasture. Thomas stopped often to examine a hole in the ground, wanting to see if a rabbit was within. Finally, John looked up and saw them coming. Throwing down the shovel, he rubbed his arms to ease the soreness after a morning of digging. He smiled at the little one, running to clasp his daddy's hand in his own, holding out some buttercups he had picked on the way. John lifted him up and put him on his shoulders as they made their way over to the tall tree on the edge of the field.

Thomas was the one strong bond between them, Eileen knew. John adored the child and was surprisingly tender with him. Eileen spread her shawl on the ground and laid out the lunch. They ate quietly, the silence of noonday broken only by the boy's prattle. Eileen saw the weariness in her husband's eyes, the slump of his shoulders, exhausted by his battle to wring turf out of the stony field. After he had eaten, she said lightly, "You look exhausted, John. Sure, we'd be better off in America these days." Her husband looked away.

Michael wrote faithfully once a month, regaling them with tales of his adventures in the grand city of Manhattan, although Eileen suspected he was leaving out the hard parts. Through Miss O'Brien, he'd found lodgings in a place called Hell's Kitchen, which sounded ominous to Eileen, but which he made comical by describing his tiny cold room at the top of a four-story building, the lumpy bed, the porcelain chamber pot, the cracked mirror (seven years bad luck!) over a broken table missing one leg, and the wide window looking out over the slaughterhouses, tanneries, and soap factories with their odors of blood and fat and smoke.

His landlady was a cheerful Mrs. O'Farrell, born in Cork City but with family in Bantry, and therefore she charged him a lower rent than the others, he claimed. He'd found work down on the docks along with many other Irishmen, and on Sundays went to Mass at the newly built church of Holy Cross. The pastor was a grand man from Killarney, one Father McCarthy, who knew Father Gleason from seminary days in Maynooth. They had dances once a week at the parish, and Michael described various lovely girls he had already lost his heart to.

He made it all sound like a lark, but Eileen knew he was hiding the worst of it. So far, he had sent nothing back to Martin to pay off his debt. Somehow, Eileen could not envision taking little Thomas to a place called Hell's Kitchen. Here in Bantry they walked within sight of the sea, feeling the wind in their hair, watching the ever-changing sky, with rain followed by buoyant clouds chased by brilliant sunshine in a single afternoon.

"Sure, Ireland is troubled these days," nodded John, "with the Fenians attacking the barracks, and now two years of bad crops." He paused, and then softly, "Maybe we should look to America. But what in hell would I do there in a city like New York?"

"Well, surely there are farms in America!" Eileen tried to hide her eagerness. That her husband would even consider leaving! "John, you know how to work the land. America is a big, wide country. Maybe we could talk to Father Gleason about our chances over there. Imagine raising our son in a land like America where everyone has a right to be educated? To become somebody, not just a poor tenant to an English landlord." Eileen's eyes shone, the sun glinting on her light brown hair as she nestled the sleepy Thomas in her lap.

John lay back in the grass and closed his eyes, pulling his hat over his face. All around them swallows glided over the hills, down toward Bantry Bay. Yes, the next parish over was America! For the first time, Eileen felt something close to love for her sleeping husband.

Father Gleason sighed as he rose in the dark on Sunday. He'd not slept well the past few nights. Many of the men of his parish were now in the IRB and on the run. People in Bantry were suspicious of each other, the women worried about their sons and husbands. The British Army was beefing up its numbers in Ireland adding to the tense atmosphere. How could he keep preaching the gentle love of Jesus in times like these? The bishops were still forbidding Catholics to take up arms against the British, but more and more of his fellow priests were ignoring the bishops, even getting involved with the Republicans themselves. Terrible times were coming; he could feel it.

He knew that rascal Michael O'Donovan was still involved with the IRB although over in America it was not so dangerous, he told himself. In a separate letter enclosed with the one to his sister, Michael described the meetings down on the docks where he worked with fellow Fenian sympathizers. Miss O'Brien had written to Michael about a new organization fighting for Irish freedom called *Clan na Gael*. He'd gone to a talk by one of their leaders, a young man from Kildare, John Devoy, who'd served five years in a British jail in Ireland for Fenian activity. Michael was fired up by this Devoy. "Devoy is the leader Ireland needs, not these soft politicians over in London pleading the Cause," he wrote.

Father was surprised to hear that his niece, Mary Grace, was writing to Michael. He hadn't seen the girl since she was small, but he remembered her as shy and bookish. The young ones were all caught up in the Cause now.

He sighed as he stepped out into the rainy fall morning to cross the yard to the church for early Mass. What hope had the young people of Ireland for a normal life with marriage and children when the country was simmering with rage and violence? And what was he doing himself in this backwater town to help his country other than hearing the confessions of old ladies and saying Mass for a church full of poor, hard-working farmers, and their wives? He was only forty-five, for God's sake! He could still fight for his country!

He was brought back to reality by the sight of the two altar boys waiting for him in the sacristy, their smiles and jokes lighting up the dark morning. No, he'd made his bed, and a lonely one it was. As he entered the sanctuary clad in the green vestments of ordinary time, he bowed before the crucifix and muttered under his breath, *Lord, you know that I love you, but it's not an easy path you have called me to. Help me not to turn back with my hand on the plow.*

Eileen wrote to Michael on October 18, 1869:

> *Cara,*
>
> *I hope this letter finds you in good health and good spirits. The place you are living sounds cold and hard to me, but I am happy that you are faring well. Do you have enough to eat? Are your wages enough for both rent and food? How I wish I could send you a few loaves of soda bread to have with your tea!*
>
> *We are all in good health here, thanks be to God. You would not recognize little Thomas. He is growing fast and talks more each day. He loves hunting for rabbit holes and running away from me when I take him out to the barn or the fields.*
>
> *Our worry these days is the crop failure. Twice in a row now we have not made enough profit to plant anew and are in debt for last year's grain. John is downhearted and even let slip to me that going to America might be a way out. We could sell the rights to the tenantry here and that would be enough with the house thrown in to pay off our debts and to buy passage to America. What do you think, brother? You know best the conditions in America and whether John could find work there and a place for us to live.*
>
> *The violence here is increasing by both the RIC as well as the Fenians, each claiming vengeance for the wrongs of the other. No one seems to trust anyone, and neighbors are afraid to talk to one another. Sure, all is changed here. Father Gleason*

*tries to preach the love and mercy of Jesus, but it seems to me
no one is listening. Anyway, he secretly sympathizes with the
Fenians, and I am often afraid the RIC or the British Army
will come for him as they suspect everyone now. How can I
raise my son in such a place? I can't imagine him in twenty
years getting involved in the struggle, lost cause that it has
been for hundreds of years.*

*I am afraid, though. To leave Bantry where we have
grown up in sight of the sea, to move to a big noisy city where
we would hardly know anyone, with strange customs, strange
food, no garden, leaving our parents' graves, never to return,
these things haunt me at night, and I lie awake worrying. So,
tell us what you truly think of our chances over there, dear
Michael. I await your reply with loving thoughts flying like
the geese over Bantry Bay to you in New York.*
Eileen
*PS Sending this enclosed in Father Gleason's stationery so it
goes safely to you.*

Eileen slipped the letter to Father Gleason after the eight
o'clock Sunday Mass. The priest smiled at her and tucked it into
his cassock as he bent to pick up Thomas.

"How's my little man?" he roared at Thomas who stared
gravely at the big man in black who was swinging him in the air.
"Och, sure you weigh a ton now, and soon you'll be eating your
mammy out of house and home!" He put the child down gently,
and Thomas hid behind his mother's skirts before he grinned
up at the priest.

"Eileen, I haven't seen John at Mass these past Sundays. Is
he all right now?"

"To tell you the truth, John is afraid and worried about
the crops. He stays out later and later each Saturday night and
drinks himself into a stupor, barely making it home from town.
Then he can't even get up for Mass!" She leaned in to whisper,

"Father, I'm thinking we may be off to America if things don't get better soon."

She saw the priest's face fall. "Sure, I'd miss you and the little one if that comes to pass. Is Michael faring well over there?"

"He says he is, but to tell you the truth, life in Manhattan sounds harsh to me, reading between the lines of his letters. And us with a baby?" she shrugged.

"Well, let me know if you do decide to leave. I have some connections through my niece Mary Grace, and I will ask her advice too. No need to rush into things now, Eileen."

She nodded, and he watched as she turned, striding proudly among the parishioners, nodding to all, Thomas's hand firmly in her own. She'd made the best of her unwanted marriage. He was filled with admiration for such grace in a girl of eighteen. The priest thought of his own fading love for his vocation and squared his shoulders to greet all who awaited him outside of St. Finbarr's. If Eileen O'Donovan could be brave and true to her vows, surely, he, Hugh Gleason of Galway, could serve the Lord. But a woman like that made celibacy all the harder, he thought, amused once more at the power of the flesh.

Later that Sunday, Eileen was delighted to see her cousin Kathleen, three little towheads trailing behind her, coming up the road to their cottage. Sundays dragged for her, with John nursing a hangover, hanging about the house under her feet all day. She ran out to greet the visitors.

"Well, a sight for sore eyes, you are! And just in time for tea. I've made some scones and we'll have them with my own currant jam and a bit of cheese," she said laughingly, clasping arms with her cousin.

Embracing her, Kathleen sighed, and herded the little ones into the house. Thomas squealed with delight to see the big cousins surrounding him, and soon they were all down on the floor playing. Eileen put the kettle on the hearth, and John pulled up another chair to the table.

After they'd fed the four children, John pushed back his chair. "Now who'd like to come with me to see the new piglets I have in the barn?" The children all shouted, and soon were straggling after him out the door, with Thomas enthroned on his shoulders like the little prince he was.

Eileen poured them another cup of steaming tea, and they both reached for the scones, slathering them with butter and jam. It was rare for the cousins to have the chance to talk without the others around. Eileen looked closely at Kathleen and noticed the sprigs of gray in her dark brown hair. Her eyes looked tired and had lost the sparkle of mischief they'd once had.

"Kathleen, what is it? You look tired, alannah."

"Oh, the more fool am I, once more in the family way!" She tried to laugh.

Eileen put her hand on Kathleen's arm, "You are one of the strongest women I know, cousin. You seem to take to being a mother in an easy way. Sure, by now, Brigid will be a help to you, won't she? She's seven and can run and fetch and even mind the new little one if you have to go outside."

"But Eileen, there must be more to being a woman than to be forever bringing children into the world. I adore my brood, but I have no minute of peace any day and fall into bed exhausted. Brian says that we should be happy we have many children, so they can help in the fields and the house, but I wonder how we are going to feed and clothe them, much less send them to school in such dangerous times." Eileen had no answer to that. Kathleen was exactly right. It was a bad time to be bringing another child into the world.

Kathleen looked at her cousin and asked, "How in God's name have you not gotten caught in this past year?"

Eileen sipped her tea for a minute. "John drinks so much on Saturday nights that he comes home staggering and falls dead asleep at once. And to tell you the truth, I am glad that he does. Holding little Thomas is all I desire these days, God help me."

The two women burst into laughter, until tears rolled down their cheeks. When the children came back, they saw their mothers still giggling over their tea and wondered aloud what was so funny. Eileen knew now was not the time to mention her dream of going to America to Kathleen.

As the fall yielded to the Irish winter with rain and howling winds off the Atlantic, John's gloom spread throughout the house. In the evenings, seated next to the hearth, they would talk in low tones about America, weighing the pros and cons of emigrating. When she would argue for it, John would demur, sucking on his pipe and shaking his head about the risk they'd be taking.

"Eileen, where would we live, for God's sake? From Michael's letters, New York must be a cold, busy city." He looked around the cottage, with its cheerful hearth and gleaming pans hanging from the mantle, the picture of the Sacred Heart over it with two brass candlesticks framing a vase of dried heather and sprigs of holly in the middle. Eileen had made his lonely old place a home for the three of them, the table covered with a red cloth she'd sewn, the floors gleaming from their weekly scrubbing, the wooden crib which he himself had carved out of pine, enshrined in the corner of the room, their son sleeping soundly, lulled by their low voices.

Outside, however, in the winds blowing over the Atlantic, the fields lay stripped of grain, the harvest a measly one, its value at market far below his expectations. But they had a kitchen garden, thanks to Eileen, with potatoes, cabbage, onions, turnips, and even a rose bush or two. They would not starve here in Bantry, he assured her, as he and his parents almost had in the Famine. He was old enough to remember those years, the constant anguish of his father and mother when they lived on fish and black bread for three years. His parents had died within months of each other, their eyes dulled by worry and sorrow, and he their only son. Then his mood would shift as he called up the image of his growing son, and he would swear to Eileen that they should leave this godforsaken farm for America. Maybe the farm was cursed, maybe all of Ireland was cursed.

Next Eileen would doubt, wondering aloud what trouble Michael was getting himself into with his talk of meetings with Fenians and Clan na Gael in Manhattan. She knew her brother's restlessness and doubted that he would stay in any one place for long. Could they depend on him to help them? He was barely making it himself despite all the glib talk in his letters about walking down Fifth Avenue and seeing the mansions going up near the park that was being built. And he living in a single room over a tannery!

"No," she'd conclude, "it's too risky to make the long voyage to America. We'll be better off here among our own people."

Their murmurs would end finally when they rose to go to bed, John scattering the ashes so the fire would not go out during the night but keep some little flame alive until the morning.

CHAPTER FOURTEEN

·····················

On Christmas Eve, Eileen carried pine branches from the grounds of Blackthorn House into the cottage. She sat stringing ornaments in various shades of her knitting wool onto a cord: snowy white lambs, horses of deep blue, orange cows and even a couple of pigs made of scarlet wool. Thomas was at her feet playing with one of the blue horses she made for him. John had not yet come into the house for supper. The sharp knock at the door startled her, making Thomas look up, eyes wide. The fire crackled in the hearth.

She opened the door to a slim man dressed in black. He bowed, saying, "Is this the home of the sister of Michael O' Donovan?"

"Yes, it is," Eileen said, hesitantly. "And who may I ask is visiting us on this Christmas Eve with the rain coming down in buckets all over Bantry?"

The man stepped inside before Eileen could object. He took off his cap and stared at Eileen. He held out his hand and said, "I am a friend of your brother Michael. My name is MacDonogh, John MacDonogh. May I come in for a moment to talk to you?" His eyes, blue and cold, looked directly into hers.

"Come and sit by the fire. Let me take your coat and cap; they are dripping all over the floor. I am Mrs. Eileen Sullivan."

She spoke quickly, trying to hide the fear that gripped her. She hoped John would soon be back. "You must be killed with the cold and wet. I'll just make us some tea," she chattered on as she filled the kettle. Thomas toddled over to the stranger, holding out one of the sheep. The stranger bent to the child and took the sheep in his hands, turning it over to admire it, speaking softly in Irish. Eileen watched him as she bustled around with the tea and put some slices of bread on a plate. She poured the steaming tea into a mug and handed it to the man. Her hand trembled. Then she picked up Thomas, holding him close on her lap, facing the stranger.

"I've not long to stay, so I'll make my message brief." Mac-Donogh held the cup with both hands wrapped around it for warmth. "Michael has been gone from these parts over a year now. I wondered if you have any idea where he is." He sat back, waiting.

Eileen's thoughts raced. Who was this man and how much did he know? She fought to keep her voice even and calm. "Now sir, why should I be telling you, a perfect stranger in my house, anything about my brother Michael?"

"Because Michael took an oath as a member of the IRB, and I am his leader. I have a right to know where he is."

"Sir, if you know anything about things in Bantry, you would have heard the gossip about Michael. He had a run-in with someone at the Big House and fled to London. From there we heard he left for America. More than that I can't tell you." She rose from her chair and paced the room. "I knew he was involved with the Fenians. You know that the RIC check the post for Fenian activity, so it's impossible to communicate with a man on the run. Sure, I pray each day for his safety, and if you can tell me anything about his whereabouts, I'd be grateful," she ended, letting a tremor come into her voice.

"Forgive me, ma'am, but I don't believe a word you are saying." MacDonogh rose, setting the mug on the table. In two strides he crossed the room and took up his coat and hat, saying in a low voice, "It's a dangerous game your brother is playing to be hiding from his own fellow soldiers. Don't worry. We'll find him sooner or later." He glanced around the cottage. "Mrs. Sullivan, it's a real home you have here in Bantry. I'd hate for anything to happen to it, and you with a lad as bright as this little one."

Eileen felt a knife-thrust of fear in her womb. Before she could rise, MacDonogh opened the door, disappearing into the driving rain. That had been a threat! She held Thomas in a tight grip, crooning to him as she paced the room. Where in the blazes was John?

That night when John came in, Eileen, her face ashen, told him the story of the stranger. John, horrified, paced the room, "How dare that bastard show up here on my farm on Christmas Eve, barging in on my wife and child!" He filled his mug with whiskey, cursing Michael for a fool to be involved with the Fenians. He railed against the British as he sat finally, getting drunker and drunker, in front of the fire, refusing the supper Eileen tried to get him to eat. Then he stumbled into bed.

Eileen sang Thomas to sleep. He'd been frightened by all the shouting, sobbing in her arms for a long time until sleep overcame him. She laid him in his crib, now almost too small for the toddler, and sat up alone, staring into the flames as they flickered over the woolly toy animals she'd woven among the pine branches. Beneath the hearth next to a basket of Thomas's few toys, including the blue horse she knit for his first Christmas, lay two wrapped packages and an orange for the child. John had carved a toy horse from some fallen elm branches he'd scavenged from the Earl's woods. Eileen's gift was a book of Irish stories for children, telling the legends of Finn and the Fianna. She found it in the wool shop where she bought ends of fabric when she had the money. The slim book was old, but its cover was soft leather, and the gilt letters of the title were still faintly visible. Mr.

O'Malley let her have it for a few pence because, he said, he'd known her family in Bantry for over sixty years.

She pictured the icy blue eyes of the stranger. He'd never raised his voice at all, but she knew for sure that he was threatening her and her family. After Christmas she'd pay a visit to Father Gleason without John. She'd ask for help from his cousin in London to find them a place in America and a possible job for John. Then she'd explain it all to her husband John in a way that would make him feel that going to America was the best solution to their troubles. She'd have to tell Martin, too, and dreaded the thought of his reaction when he heard of MacDonogh's visit. Maybe MacDonogh had already talked to him! Martin had little sympathy for his brother, but Eileen had never told him where Michael was living, and he'd never asked.

Gazing into the dying embers of the hearth, she wept. To think that her family had split apart so since the death of their mother. She pictured Christmases when they were children, gathering on Christmas Eve with cousins and aunts and uncles, linking arms as they skipped down the hill toward St. Finbarr's and Midnight Mass, and then home to drink hot milk flavored with nutmeg and cinnamon, devouring the spice cake her mother made each Christmas. They'd seldom had gifts other than an orange and maybe a ribbon for her and a new pocketknife or toy for her brothers. But her mother had kept them warm and fed and laughing until at last she'd shooed them off to bed, and they'd fallen asleep under the handmade quilts listening to the wind sigh around the eaves of the cottage.

What strange life would they be bringing their little son to in America with only one uncle nearby? *Sweet Mother of God*, she prayed, *help us now in the hour of our need. You too had to flee to a strange place and bring forth your son with only the animals for company.*

They carried Thomas to Mass on Christmas Day, and as Eileen and John greeted Father Gleason outside the church on a sunny frosty morning, the trees glistening with a thin coat of ice after the rains the night before, the priest bent to caress the child wrapped snugly in a blue blanket. The boy twisted and squirmed out of his father's grasp and toddled away trailing the blanket behind him. John ran to catch him, and Eileen whispered quickly, "Father, may I come see you on Friday when I am in town for the market?"

"Of course, Eileen. Just come to the rectory about eleven, and Mrs. O'Malley will let you in. We'll have a cup of tea." He looked at her more closely. "Is everything all right at home?"

She nodded and turned toward John, who had captured the runaway Thomas, now laughing in his arms, quite pleased with himself for his escape. "Mammy, I runned!" he shouted to her.

Together, they made their way back home to prepare dinner for Martin who would be coming that evening. Her brother lived a lonely life with only the dog Queenie by his side in the long winter evenings, so she invited him on Sundays, and he seemed to enjoy their time together. But she'd have to be careful not to mention anything about their plans. He seldom asked about Michael, and Eileen was careful not to share too many details about their brother's activities in America.

When market day came, Eileen left Thomas with her cousin Kathleen, now heavy with the coming baby. When she'd asked her cousin to watch Thomas, Kathleen had laughed and shrugged, "Sure, what's one more with this passel of ruffians I've got? They love the lad and will pull him around in the wagon all morning." Her children crowded around Thomas, vying with one another to hold his hand and lead him outside to the yard.

"I'm going to stop by to see Father Gleason after shopping," Eileen whispered to Kathleen.

"Now what in God's name do you have to confess?" Kathleen laughed.

"It's not confession I'm after. It's advice," Eileen said, turning away, hoping to avoid any more explanation. She wanted no one to know of her plan until it was a reality, not even John.

To her surprise when she walked up the steps to the small house that served as Father's rectory, she saw him bent over some bushes in the side yard, dressed in old brown pants and a rough gray sweater, torn at one elbow. She'd never seen the priest in anything other than his long black cassock or the vestments for Mass. He looked younger somehow, more vigorous, and she thought what a fine husband and father he would have made if God had not called him. She wondered too how hard the life he had chosen must be, how lonely. She called out, "Well, Father, a fine morning you have for playing the gardener!"

"Is it you, Mrs. Eileen Sullivan?" he boomed. "Come over and help me prune these rose bushes before it's too late in the season."

Eileen put down her parcels and hitched her skirt up behind her. He handed her a knife, saying quietly, "I thought it would be better to talk out here in the yard away from Mrs. O'Malley in the kitchen. She does tend to overhear things somehow."

Eileen glanced up at the window of the front parlor, the lace curtain moving slightly as a figure melted away. They worked together in silence for a few minutes, when, finally Eileen said, "Father, I had a visit from an IRB man called MacDonogh on Christmas Eve. He knew I was Michael's sister and wanted to know where Michael was. I told him the bare bones, saying only that Michael had gone to America and I had no idea of his whereabouts. Forgive me the lie," she grinned up at him. "He frightened me so, the way he looked around the house and at Thomas."

"Was John there too?"

"No, he was outside working in the barn before supper. I think the man came when I was alone on purpose. Anyway, I've been thinking, well, John has too, about leaving Ireland."

Father sat back on his heels. Eileen continued, "This visit from the IRB man just made me want to leave more than ever. Our crops have been poor these last two years and we owe money for the grain from last year, so will have no money to plant this year.

We could sell the tenantry and use the money to pay passage for the three of us. But we need a place to go to, not some little hole in the wall like Michael seems to be satisfied with in New York City. John needs work, maybe farming or building. I could help us out with sewing perhaps. And Thomas would be educated."

Straightening up and leaning on his shovel, Father shaded his eyes from the bright winter sunlight and gazed at Eileen. "So, you'll fly away too, after your brother, alannah. I thought I'd have the joy of watching little Thomas grow up." He sighed. "I can't blame you at all, Eileen. Ireland is on the brink of bad times, everyone afraid, not trusting the British to do the right thing, soldiers everywhere, an occupied country still." He threw down his shovel. "I swear, I'd leave too, but my place is here with my poor flock, such as it is."

He walked over to a bench nearby and motioned her to sit with him. "I'll get in touch with my niece in London and ask her where a little family like yours should go. Have you told Michael yet? What about John? Is he up for leaving?"

"No, I've told no one yet. But I think John will be willing after the two bad years we've had here," she said sadly.

Eileen looked into the priest's dark brown eyes. "Father, I've been hateful to you at times, especially about my marriage. But you have been a true friend to me, and I will miss you sorely."

He smiled and looked away, taking her small hand in his large rough one. "And I'll miss you, Mary Eileen O'Donovan Sullivan, mother of Thomas. You've carried on these past two years with great courage. Pray for me as I will for you. God never asks more from us than we can handle. At least he'd better not!" With that, they both rose, and the priest blessed her, whispering, "I'll be in touch."

As Eileen picked up her packages, the lace curtain at the front window trembled slightly again. With a wicked smile, Eileen waved to Mrs. O'Malley in exaggerated friendliness. *Just so you know I saw you watching us, you nosy old biddy!*

The priest turned to his task again, sighing heavily. *And so poor old Ireland loses her young people while we old ones keep digging in this blasted country.* He shoved his foot against the spade, hearing the sharp edge tearing through roots in the earth. He dug and dug until sweat poured from his brow and the wind from the sea did nothing to cool him.

Part 2

···························

THE VOYAGE OVER

CHAPTER FIFTEEN

....

Five months later, John and Eileen Sullivan along with young Thomas Sullivan had tickets in steerage on the steamship *SS Abyssinia*. They would depart from Queenstown for New York on the fifth of May, 1870. The passenger list contained two hundred saloon or first-class passengers and one thousand and fifty passengers in steerage, among whom were listed the following:

JOHN SULLIVAN	42	M	FARMER	IRELAND
MARY EILEEN SULLIVAN	19	F	WIFE	IRELAND
THOMAS MICHAEL SULLIVAN	2	M	CHILD	IRELAND

As the crowd on the dock in Queenstown pressed in around her, Eileen heard the squealing of pigs before she saw them. One by one, pigs, cows, and chickens were being dragged up the gangplank by the crew. A man next to her shouted out above the din, "Sure, we steerage people won't be eating those fine specimens." He spat in the general direction of the gangplank, and Eileen turned away so that Thomas in her arms would not see and try to imitate the man.

The child imitated everything people said and did these days. Now he was twisting in her arms, laughing at the animals, clapping his hands in delight. John stood close to her, lugging the bundles containing all they could bring. Two thin mattresses were folded around the blankets, shawls, and towels she had brought, and another sack held their mess kit, recently bought in Cork: two tin plates, a tin can for water, three tin mugs, two knives, two forks and three spoons, and a small tin basin for, as the merchant said, "When yous get seasick."

They'd sold the few pieces of furniture they had. It hurt Eileen awfully when she could not bring along to America some of her treasures: the mirror her mother had given her, the rocking chair she had nursed Thomas in so many nights and days, the hand-embroidered pillowcases, and even some of the Christmas ornaments she had made for the boy, all left behind except the blue horse Thomas slept with every night.

Luckily, her cousin Kathleen had been happy to get every-thing, promising to return the loved objects to her, "If," she said through tears, "you ever decide to come home again." But hidden in the bundle Eileen carried with their few pieces of clothing were her three most precious treasures: a small bag of dirt from her parents' farm, the single-pearl necklace Michael had given her, and the book she had stolen from Blackthorn House.

Now the crew was sweeping up the traces of the animals in preparation for the cabin passengers who were lined up, chatting happily, awaiting their boarding. Eileen had eaten little breakfast that morning in the boarding house in Queenstown, but she'd saved an egg and some bread for Thomas. She squatted now and held the child on her lap as she fed him bits of food while he gazed in awe at the sailors swinging up on the great masts, the gulls wheeling around them, and in the distance the sea, sparkling in early morning sun. The breeze off the ocean was sharp, and Eileen pulled her plaid shawl around her shoulders, her light brown hair secured tightly in a bun.

She watched the ladies and gentlemen in first class board, the ladies' hats waving with feathers and ribbons, clutching their parasols, their hands covered in soft leather gloves, the silk and muslin dresses sweeping the gangplank. Their servants trailed them, carrying leather trunks, hat boxes, and suitcases. They laughed and chatted as if they were going on a summer picnic, not leaving their homes forever to cross a dangerous ocean for an unknown world.

Finally, after what seemed hours standing around waiting, Eileen saw the gates open for the steerage passengers. John pressed close to her, taking Thomas in his arms now along with the baggage. The child was asleep, his cheeks flushed pink, and his dark hair sweaty from standing in the spring sunshine all morning. They filed up the gangplank, swaying in the dock, and Eileen knew she was stepping away from Ireland itself, perhaps forever. She whispered a quick prayer that, God willing, the next firm land beneath their feet would be America.

People pushed and shoved as they descended a narrow wooden staircase, dimly lit by one oil lamp. Eileen held her skirt up as she went down the steps, grabbing the banister to steady herself. Single men were directed to the left, single women to the right, and families continued down the wide middle of the cavernous dark space. People hurried to find their spots, and for a minute Eileen panicked as she lost sight of John with the child on his shoulders. Then she heard her name, and John was beckoning her on to a cubby hole under the green and white sign numbered three hundred and forty-five that matched the number on their tickets.

A bare wooden plank with one shelf above it would be their home for the next two weeks. It was hot and stuffy with over a thousand people settling into their berths, calling out complaints and jokes about the bloody British who had designed a ship such as this when everyone knew the ship had been built in Ulster by fine Irish craftsmen.

A woman's voice rose over the others, "For the love of God, where is the drinking water?" Someone responded, "And the hell if I know where the lavatory is!" The stewards passed among the people trying to get them settled, pointing the way to the men's and women's lavatories, the water cooler with its one tin cup hanging by a string. So, were they all to drink from a common cup? Eileen vowed she would bring their own cups to the cooler, dreading to think about the coughing and tobacco-spitting passengers who were using the same cup. She would not!

She spread out their mattresses on the plank, covering them with the blankets and shawls she had brought while John took the baby's dirty nappy to the lavatory to rinse it out. Oh God! How would she keep up with the wash? Would there be water enough for all these folks?

"Mammy, the ship's moving!" Thomas cried, his eyes shining. From below came the dull thrum of the engines as the ship, like a great beast, awakened. Cries went up all around them, with people heading upstairs to the deck to watch the ship pulling away from the dock, hoping for their last view of land, perhaps their last view of Ireland.

Eileen shoved their few clothes and belongings into the shelf above the bunk. She smoothed down Thomas's hair and ran her handkerchief over his face. She held him on her lap and hugged him to her, saying, "When Da comes back we'll go up on deck so you can watch the sailors in the tugboats pull us out to sea." He held her tightly as if her own worry and fear entered through her skin touching his. Sometimes she felt they were one being as she gazed at his face with its long lashes shading the blue eyes. "Oh Tommy, my boy, we are doing this for you," she murmured into his soft hair.

John returned and they made their way out onto the deck. Up above the sailors shimmied up the masts, securing the sails. With a huge wrenching, the ship broke loose from the dock, rocking gently in the wake of the tugboats leading them out of the harbor. A cheer went up from people on shore as they waved their handkerchiefs at the departing ones.

With a pang, Eileen knew there was no one there to wave

them off. They'd had their wake the Sunday night before departure at the old farm, with Martin as host. Kathleen and Brian and children, Father Gleason, the Clancys from down the hill, and even Mrs. Hanrahan, the cook at the Big House, and her sister came by to wish them farewell. There were songs and poems, from both Brian and Father, who had a fine tenor voice. The priest had sung the haunting "Rising of the Moon."

And come tell me Sean O'Farrell, tell me why you hurry so,
Hush, bhuachaill, hush and listen and his cheeks were all aglow
I bear orders from the captain, get you ready quick and soon
For the pikes must be together at the rising of the moon.
At the rising of the moon, at the rising of the moon,
For the pikes must be together at the rising of the moon . . .

When he'd finished, Father's cheeks were wet, and he turned away to refill his glass of whiskey. Martin looked bleary-eyed, but Eileen could not tell if from drink or from sadness.

The cottage rang with laughter and jokes, the fire dancing in the old hearth, casting shadows across the room on the late spring evening. Eileen sat at the table, caressing Queenie, now old and arthritic, who lay at her feet. Ghosts crept into the shadows, that of her young handsome father, her mother old, hunched, with curly gray hair, her brother Michael, and the ghosts of the famine that hovered over the town of Bantry, over Cork and Kerry, over the Dingle Peninsula, over all of Ireland. Eileen could not shake her sadness. She too filled her glass once more, trying not to see John, his head on the table, already passed out from the drink. Finally, they'd stumbled home, that evening, she carrying the sleeping Thomas, and John bringing up the rear, mumbling and groaning all the while. Was all that only four days ago?

Now standing on deck, they watched the ship glide smoothly out to sea, the bay tranquil in the early afternoon sun. Thomas crowed in delight to see the tugboats, feeling the rocking motion of the bay beneath them. Eileen prayed they would not become seasick. The bay turned rougher as they passed the entrance to Cork Harbor at Roche's Point, the lighthouse rising above with the blue hills in the distance framing it.

"Hail Mary, full of grace," Eileen murmured as the mainland grew smaller in the distance. Would she ever see Ireland again? What in the world was she doing, dragging John and their little one away from all they had ever known and loved, from the cemetery at St. Finbarr's where her Da and mother rested, from Father Gleason, from the stately, quiet rooms of the Big House, with their filtered light when the rain streamed down the great windows overlooking the gardens, the sea a blur of blue and gray in the distance, Blackthorn House, which she had loved in spite of herself? And for what? An icy feeling came over her as she pictured New York City, its hurly-burly crowds, its strange accents, strangers all, no one she knew or loved there except, maybe, Michael. And how long would he stay close to them?

Her cottage in Bantry seemed ever so dear, its cozy rooms, the way the light streamed into the bedroom at dawn, the cradle beside the hearth, the roses she had planted by the path, the old barn with its scent of hay and cow dung, and always the sea shining in the distance, ringed by the blue hills of Bantry Town. For one wild moment she wanted to shout to the crew, *No! Turn around! I've made a great mistake. Go back! Go back!*

Now the wind from the open mouth of the sea blew her hair around her face, and she handed the boy over to his father. John cradled Thomas in his big arms, bending his face close to the child's, murmuring in Irish. Eileen looked at him, "I'm going to walk a bit, John. Could you take Thomas below and put him down for a nap? Sure, the excitement has done the lad in this day."

"Yes, but don't linger here, Eileen. You'll catch your death up on deck with not even your shawl for warmth," he said, looking back over his shoulder.

The man hardly let her out of his sight, for God's sake! On the voyage they'd be cooped up together for days and nights, no escape. She felt ashamed thinking this, ashamed for the impatience she tried to keep out of her voice when she spoke to her husband. He really wasn't a bad sort. He loved their boy with the same passion she felt in herself, and he never forced himself on her in bed anymore. In fact, his humble, watchful patience drove her wild at times. He was like a great docile dog, trailing around after her, waiting for crumbs of attention. She felt pity for him, but could not say she loved him, not in the way she'd expected to from the novels she still devoured.

Now she paced the deck, ignoring the stares of the other steerage passengers who were joking and chatting in the excitement of finally being at sea. The wind whipped her skirts around her legs, and she pulled the kerchief from her head, wrapping it around her shoulders as a shawl.

Her life was not what she had dreamed of. She should never have read all those books. She could hear her mother's voice, something about a woman's duty. Duty! What did duty have to do with the sweeping flood of desire that she felt sometimes as she thought of some stranger taking her suddenly into his arms, pressing his body all along her own and suddenly bringing her face up to his, then crushing her mouth with his kiss? She stared out to sea, the sun now at an angle along the horizon. She sighed, then lifted her chin and turned back toward the narrow stairs leading to steerage. *Get hold of yourself, girl,* she thought. *You have a darling boy to feed.*

Eileen stumbled on her way down the steep stairs into steerage. A single lantern at the far side of the galley pulsed with a weak glow as her eyes adjusted to the dark space. At last, she found their bunk, relieved to see John snoring quietly on his side, with the boy curled up beside his father, sucking his thumb, gripping the blue horse in his little fist. He gazed up into her eyes as she leaned over him. "Mammy," he whispered, "Da was snoring!"

She smiled and gathered him to her, nestling beside him in the narrow bed. "Hush now, alannah, go to sleep. Mammy is here, and in the morning, we'll go up on deck and watch the sailors as they scramble all over the ship to scrub it clean." She began to hum until she felt the warm little body beside her go slack and watched the thumb fall from his mouth. Beneath her the engine thrummed, and soon the sway of the sea lulled her into a merciful sleep.

By the third day out, Thomas knew the names of most of the sailors working on their deck. A storm had blown up overnight, and now many passengers stayed below deck, felled by nausea and lack of sleep. After a breakfast of watery porridge but good hot coffee, John complained of feeling sick. He lay in their bed with his face turned to the wall, groaning softly. Eileen tried not to nag him about the drink he had taken the night before.

She grabbed her red shawl and tugged two sweaters over Thomas's head, pulled a cap on the lad, and they climbed together onto the deck. A sparkling sea with white-capped waves glistening as far as the eye could see greeted them. The air was crisp and clean, and Thomas began to run, pulling his mother after him looking, as he said, "for all my friends." The sailors nodded and smiled at the pair, and many tipped their caps to Eileen. She'd been surprised at the kindness and good humor of the crew, mostly Englishmen.

The trip had not all been peaceful. There'd been a squabble at the water cooler the day before. Passengers in steerage were allowed no drinking water during the meals, but in the center of the galley stood a cooler of ice water with a porcelain teacup placed on top. This was the cup passengers were to use. However, many women smuggled their own cups and even pots to haul back to their bunks water for washing.

The under-steward, an Englishman named Ronald, had shouted at two women he caught with containers under their shawls: "None of your tricks, now!" he thundered for all to hear.

"You know that water is for drinking only, and that from the cup you see there. You would be emptying the cooler in one hour if everyone brought her own container for other purposes." He glared at the women, daring them to answer back. The women swore in Irish and mumbled a few curses, but the steward stood fast with his arms folded across his chest, guarding the precious supply of fresh water.

Eileen was forced to give Thomas a drink from the common cup many times during the day as the child led her up and down the stairs and all over the deck. All day children ran back and forth to the cooler until the floor sloshed with wasted water.

At night Eileen crept noiselessly to fill her own tin cup when no crew members kept guard. Surely the child would wake in the night crying out for a drink. How she wished she had nursed him longer. She missed the feel of his mouth on her breast, his soft hair brushing her skin, the sweet smell of the lad while she nursed him. She felt love for the child deep inside her body, a sharp stab of love. Nothing had prepared her for the fierceness of this love.

On this day, Eileen and Thomas, hand in hand, walked up and down the almost empty deck, crying out to each other when they glimpsed a bird dive-bombing into the sea. Then, far out, they saw dolphins in elegant play, slipping rhythmically in and out of the water like two dancers, their sleek forms taking turns, appearing, and disappearing, until finally they were swallowed up by the sea. The sun beat down. Eileen pulled off her shawl and pushed up the long sleeves of her blouse.

"Looks like the boyo has gotten his sea legs now!" said Owen, a Welsh youth who looked hardly older than thirteen, his voice still slipping and sliding up and down the register. He'd stopped to talk to them yesterday, confiding to Eileen that this was only his second time at sea and that he missed his mother and little brothers and sisters something terrible!

"But my father said the sea would make a man of me, and besides it was one less mouth to feed. I'm saving my wages so I can go to live in America one day," he'd whispered as if saying this too loud would be a subject of laughter to his mates. Then he'd given Thomas a piece of apple that he'd saved from the mess. Thomas looked up at him now and held out his hand. Eileen laughed and pulled the child away, hoping Owen had not noticed her son's shameless begging. But they'd had no fruit at all since they'd left Bantry. She had some hard candy hidden in her bag and resolved to give the boy a piece when they went back downstairs for his nap.

On day four, the weather turned sullen, with huge gray clouds scudding across the sky and a vicious north wind whipping the deck. The rain began at noon, so after their midday meal of broth with potatoes and few tough pieces of meat, washed down with steaming cups of tea, Eileen and John brought Thomas back to their bunk, and John took out his pocketknife and a piece of wood he was carving into a top for Thomas and began to whittle. The boy watched his father solemnly. Eileen laid him on the bed and began a story that spooled on and on about their farm in Bantry, what the chickens were doing right now, how the piglets had grown. She told of Uncle Martin's old dog, Queenie, how she was missing Thomas and still came to the door every day to watch for him. Eileen felt tears on her own cheeks and smiled to think that she had made herself homesick with her own story.

At last, the child's eyes closed, and Eileen settled back on the one pillow and pulled out her copy of *Wuthering Heights*. Before she'd finished one page her eyes drooped, and the book fell from her hands.

She was awakened deep in the night by Thomas moaning. His little body pressed into hers. She rolled over and sat up. "Hush now, darling," she crooned. Then she lit a candle she had brought against all the rules and examined her child. His face was flushed, and he moved restlessly on the thin mattress. His eyes stared up at her, glassy. Eileen felt his forehead and was startled by its heat. The boy whimpered, "My froat hurts, Mammy, my froat."

"Your throat?" Eileen kept her voice calm. He nodded. "Oh now, darling, open your mouth wide for me and say ah." She held the candle near his mouth.

"Ah," the child croaked.

"John, look. His throat is aflame." John picked up the boy and set him on his lap. He peered into his mouth. Husband and wife stared at each other.

"He's sick with fever," Eileen whispered, cuddling the child. "John, go get him some water and use my cup. Just don't let anyone see you." He nodded and shuffled off, maddeningly slow in Eileen's eyes, slipping their cup under his shirt.

When John returned, Eileen saw that half of the water had spilled from the cup. Thomas tried to sip but pushed the cup away after one swallow. "No, Mammy. It hurts, it hurts."

By morning he had dropped off to sleep once more, but he tossed and turned while Eileen kept watch sitting up, resting her back against the thin board that divided their bunk from the next. Just as she began slipping into sleep, she felt a wetness in the sheets as a foul smell filled the bunk. In the dim light of morning seeping through the cracks in the wood of the ceiling, she saw Thomas's eyes flutter, and she picked him up and held him to her. He tried to smile, and that bravery broke her heart, for the fever still raged in the small, compact body. He bleated, "It hurts, Mammy, it hurts."

"Hush, alannah, now Mammy has to get you cleaned up." She prodded John who slept soundly, his back turned to them. "John! Wake up! The child has dirtied the bed and himself. We need to get the sheet off." Again, she poked her husband until, with an oath, he sat up rubbing his eyes.

"What the devil, Eileen! What's that awful stench?"

"It's your son, John. He is sick. We need a pan of water to clean him. Get up! You must sneak down to the water cooler before anyone else is up and fill our bowls with water. No one can see you." Eileen's lips were dry, and she licked them. She needed to go to the lavatory but could not put the child down.

John leaned over his son and felt his forehead. He murmured to the boy, caressing his hair, and assuring him that he'd finish carving his new top today. Then he stood up, searching for his shoes, and grabbed their bowls, staggering up the aisle among the still sleeping fellow passengers.

Eileen stripped the child of his nightshirt and nappy, trying not to gag at the smell. Then she saw the blood, not a lot, but there was definitely blood mixed in with the child's loose bowels. Her stomach heaved. As soon as it was light, she would demand that the ship's doctor see her child. He was, of course, in first class, but he would see Thomas, she vowed.

She longed for her mother. If only she were here, she would know what to do! She stripped the sheet off the mattress and bundled the child's dirty clothes in it, stuffing it all under the bunk for now. Thomas began shivering, so Eileen laid him on the bare mattress, and with her one clean petticoat, wiped his little body, cursing John under her breath for being so slow with the water. Finally, he was beside her, and she dipped the petticoat in the shallow bowl to finish the task. She dried the child and dressed him quickly, all the while crooning a little ditty about the sheep and the goats in the meadow. Then she poured the bit of water from the second bowl into their cup and gave it to John. "I'm going up to see the steward and ask that the doctor look at Thomas. He's really sick, John. I'm afraid."

"Eileen, I've lost one child in my life, and I'll be damned if I will suffer the loss of another. Do you want me to go?"

She reached for him then, grabbing his hand and bringing it up to her lips. "John, God forgive me for ever doubting you. I know you love Thomas more than life itself. But I'll go. They may have more pity on a heartsick mother." She made her way quickly up the narrow staircase onto the deck. A few sailors were bustling about, sweeping the decks of the debris left by the storm. She went up to one of the older sailors and touched his arm.

"Excuse me, Sir, but my baby is sick with the fever. How can I reach the doctor up in the salon?"

"Now that would not be easy, ma'am. They usually just get one of the crew to take a look at sick people. I doubt the doctor would come down here."

Eileen nodded and pushed past the man. She saw the crew going up and down the stairs that led to the upper deck. If she could just get past them, she could pass herself off as gentry, she knew. She hid in a corner and pulled off the shawl that covered her hair, draping the shawl around her shoulders. Then she reached up and pulled the pins holding her hair up in a bun and combed her long wavy locks with her fingers, rearranging her hair into an elegant chignon just as she had seen her mistress at the Big House wear. She pinched her cheeks and bit her lips to redden them as she darted unseen up the stairs to the upper deck.

Up on the salon deck, couples strolled arm in arm as they made their way to breakfast. A few young men were walking briskly, getting their exercise in before a hearty meal in the dining room. She joined the people headed that way, glancing around for a sympathetic face. She noticed an older couple with a small black dog, strolling arm in arm.

As she passed, she bowed her head and smiled at them. "Oh, the dog is a darling! Would he mind if I pet him?" She tried to speak as her mistress did, with the faintly Irish intonation of the Anglo-Irish. They smiled at her and nodded. As she bent to the dog to caress his silken fur, the woman said, "I don't believe we have met, Miss." She gazed at Eileen keenly.

In a low voice, Eileen replied, "No, you wouldn't have met me. I am Eileen Sullivan, my husband and I and small son are passengers in steerage." She straightened up and looked directly into the woman's eyes. "We are from Bantry, and my family worked for the Earl at Blackthorn House. I need to find a proper doctor for my son, who is terribly ill with fever. Could you possibly tell me where to find the doctor up here?"

The woman looked at her husband. His eyes were kind, somewhat sad. Eileen pleaded, "Sir, I know I am not supposed to be up here. But I am desperate to get help."

The man returned her gaze and bent toward her. "Yes, there is a doctor on board by the name of McGilvrey. He happens to be from our part of Kerry too. I'll see what I can do. Get back down below before someone sees you."

Eileen thought quickly. "I thank you both. The number of our bunk is three hundred and forty-five. May God bless you both for your kindness."

The woman looked around nervously, but the man took Eileen's hand in his own gloved paw. "You are welcome. We lost a little daughter many years ago. God bless and save your little one." Eileen felt tears spring to her eyes as the couple continued down the deck, bowing and smiling at their acquaintances. She edged her way to the staircase used by the crew and waited a few moments until all the men were occupied, then slipped under the chain through the narrow door and down the dark staircase.

Below deck, the steerage passengers were all at breakfast. She stumbled her way to their bunk. Thomas lay motionless, his cheeks pale now, his breathing heavy and labored. John looked at her dully. She tried to smile. "I found a couple who seemed sympathetic. They said they knew the doctor upstairs and would try to get him to see the baby."

He looked up at her without responding. "John, you need to go eat something. I'll stay with Thomas, and you can bring something back for me. Has he taken any water?"

"No. He just turns his head when I try to get him to drink."

"So, go now and eat," she insisted. "I'll stay right here and give him some water." She watched as John made his way up the narrow aisle, his clothes disheveled and his shoulders bent. He looked suddenly old to Eileen. She glanced at Thomas and saw red spots near his neck. Horrified, she gently pulled up his shirt and saw the angry rash covering his belly and upper chest. He opened his eyes then, his blue gaze stabbing her with its trusting sweetness.

"Mammy," he whispered, "I thirsty."

"Good boy," she smiled. "I have a nice cup of cold water for you." She lifted his head and tipped her cup to his lips. To her joy, he managed a few swallows.

He lay back, his gaze still on her. "Where's Da?" he croaked through dry lips.

She dipped her handkerchief in water and moistened his lips as she reassured him, "Da went to get some breakfast for us. Would you like some nice porridge now?"

"No, I was dreaming about Queenie at Uncle Martin's house." Then the child closed his eyes, his forehead hot to her touch.

If only the doctor would come now. Surely, he could save the child, healthy and well-built as he was, with hardly a cold or sniffle in his short life. If he could still swallow, she felt, he might not be so bad. But the rash alarmed her. She saw John threading his way among the people too sick this morning to go up on deck. He carried a tin plate and bowl carefully, not wanting a drop to spill.

"Here's some porridge for Thomas, and an egg and bread for you, Eileen. How's the boy?"

"He drank a little water, but the fever is still high, and now there's a rash. Oh, where in God's name is that doctor?" she moaned. Since Thomas seemed to be in a restless sleep, Eileen devoured the egg and tore the bread savagely with her teeth. The bread was stale, but she was famished and swallowed it quickly. She looked hungrily at the porridge but decided to save it just in case Thomas could eat it when he awoke. She was dying for a cup of tea. John sat next to the boy, humming. He took out his piece of wood and began to whittle. The hours dragged by.

By four in the afternoon Thomas, sweaty and feverish, had soiled himself and the bed once more with a loose, bloody bowel movement. Eileen was afraid she would run out of clean clothes for him. Yesterday's clothes were still damp, hanging from a string over their bunk. As John looked on, she cleaned the child again, telling him a story about the farm as she rinsed his body and dried it with the last clean towel, then quickly slipped on his nightshirt as he shivered on her lap. She brushed back his hair, sticky with sweat, from his high forehead.

He listened to the story and even smiled at times, a brave little smile that scalded her heart. Again, he drank a few sips of water, but pushed away the porridge, now cold and hard, saying, "My tummy hurts, Mammy. I don't want it."

"My, my! What have we here?"

Both John and Eileen looked up, startled at the British accent. There, bent over Thomas, was a white-haired gentleman in a frock coat with a starched white collar that gleamed in the dusky cabin. He carried a leather bag, from which he pulled out his stethoscope.

"Madam, I am Doctor McGilvrey, at your service. My friends, the Connellys, told me of your son. I don't usually see passengers below, that's the ship's first mate's charge, but they were particularly insistent that I see your boy." While he spoke, he pulled up Thomas's shirt, laying his stethoscope against the child's chest. He peered into the boy's throat. Thomas watched him, wide-eyed and serious, fascinated by his instrument. "Has the boy taken any water?" asked the doctor.

"Only a few sips this morning. He's eaten nothing all day," Eileen said.

"That's all right, no need to eat when his stomach is upset, but it is crucial to keep him hydrated." The doctor looked at them quietly. "He's very sick. I am almost sure it is typhoid fever."

He looked around the gloomy quarters. "It's a wonder that more of these poor souls aren't sick with the crowding and the lack of hygiene," he muttered as he took out a snowy white handkerchief and pressed it to his nose. "There's not much to do except to keep pushing fluids on the child, even tea or a bit of beer if the child will take it. I will come back tomorrow morning."

He looked again at Thomas who stared gravely back at him. "He's a beautiful child, Madam." He bent over Eileen's hand as if he would kiss it. She couldn't speak, so she nodded in gratitude.

John rose and shook the doctor's hand. "We thank you, Doctor. He's our only child," he mumbled. The doctor nodded and made his way swiftly out of the bunk toward the light coming from the stairs leading to the upper deck.

Eileen's heart sank. So, the doctor had nothing, no medicine, no assurance that her son would be well. Tomorrow? That was twenty-four hours away. She stared down at her child. *Holy Mother of God,* she prayed, *don't take this child from me.*

Oh God! She should never have left Bantry to drag him across the sea on this cursed ship full of sick people all crowded into a small airless place! It was her fault, her restlessness that had brought them here. She was the one who had talked John into leaving the farm, their beautiful place high above Bantry Bay, where they had family and friends, where Thomas could have grown up healthy and happy, learning the ways of his Da and uncle as they cared for their fields and their animals. *It's my fault, my fault,* she groaned, doubled over now in anguish. *I'm his mother. I should have protected him. Dear God, if you just grant my son life I will never complain again about John or anything!* She wept, trying to stifle her sobs. John looked at her dully.

By midnight the child no longer opened his eyes. His fever rose, and in his restless sleep he muttered and groaned. Eileen lay next to him, her hand on his chest, wiping his sweaty brow and his lips from time to time with a wet cloth. Finally, she could stay awake no longer, and the cloth fell from her hand as she succumbed to sleep, John snoring beside her.

At first light she woke with a start. She turned to the child and was happy to feel his cool forehead. She woke John with a cry, "Why the fever has left, John!" She grabbed the boy up in her arms, "Thomas, wake up, sweetheart! Now you can eat some breakfast with Mammy and Da."

John stared at the child. "Eileen, he's not breathing," he whispered.

"What?" she laughed. "No, he's better!" She began to pull off his shirt, but his body was cold now, cold and there was no flutter of those lashes, no blue gaze from his closed eyes. She felt a vise squeeze her heart.

"No, no, no, no," she screamed. "John, run upstairs and call for the doctor. He said he would come." She rubbed and rubbed the child's back and chest, but he lay stiff and cold in her arms. Two women gathered around their bunk, trying to comfort her with soft whispers and sighs. Eileen shut her eyes and murmured wildly, "No not possible, Thomas is healthy and strong, no, never. . . ."

"Sure, the woman's gone mad in her grief," the older woman sighed. They began to pray, "Hail Mary, full of grace, the Lord is with thee."

In a few minutes John returned, accompanied by an officer from above and trailed by Doctor McGilvrey. The doctor took the child gently from Eileen and laid his body on the cot. He put his stethoscope to the boy's chest. Nothing. He noticed that the rash had faded and nodded in sorrow at John. "He's gone," he said softly. "I am so sorry."

Eileen shut her eyes and covered her ears. The officer looked at John. "We will hold the burial at two this afternoon. It's important to dispose of the body quickly on such a crowded ship. We don't want the sickness to spread," he finished, not looking at the couple now. "I will send a crew member to measure the body for the coffin."

John stared at him in confusion, "But where? Where will he be buried?"

"Why in the sea, of course," the officer said, matter-of-factly. "The chaplain will hold a service with the crew and passengers in attendance, and then we will slip the coffin overboard into the sea."

Eileen became stone. Her eyes wide, she pressed her lips into a line. Suddenly she snatched the boy's body up into her arms and began to rock him and hum to him.

The men stood up, and John thanked the doctor and the officer. The doctor leaned toward John, "Try to get her to eat and drink something. Even a shot of whiskey would be good. She is in shock. Later, you and she can wash the body and dress him and swaddle him in a blanket. I will be back before two to accompany you."

John raised his head, tears streaming down his face. "I do some woodworking myself. Could I help in fashioning the coffin?"

"Of course, man," the officer said. "I'll let our carpenter know that you will be helping." The three men shook hands all around, not daring to look at the mother rocking her dead boy.

Eileen, mute but dry-eyed, with help from the two women next to their bunk, washed the child's body, combed the black hair back from his forehead, and dressed him in a clean white shirt and his one good pair of pants, swaddling him tightly in his favorite blanket, the one he stroked every night as he fell asleep. Eileen slipped her medal of the Virgin Mary under the white shirt. She stared down at the child, his face relaxed and calm, exactly as if he were sleeping. Suddenly she moaned, "But the lad's head will be cold in the icy sea."

Mrs. O'Malley, their next bunk neighbor, put her arm around her. "Now I have just the little cap for him," she said. She slipped away and came back with a knitted wool cap of bright blue. Eileen, unable to speak, nodded her thanks and pulled the cap down over the boy's head. John and the carpenter arrived with the small pine box, the smell of fresh wood filling the cabin. The women lined the coffin with a linen towel. No one spoke. Finally, John picked up his son, kissed his forehead, and laid the child in the pine box. They would leave the coffin open until the last minute.

Then the little group made their way up two flights of steps onto the salon deck. There the crew had assembled with the priest and the captain of the ship, while many steerage passengers crowded around, trying to see over the side of the coffin. John carried it high above, Eileen trailing behind, her hair down around her shoulders blowing wildly in the stiff sea breeze.

The crew placed a table in front of the priest, and someone covered it with a white silk shawl. In deep silence, John placed the small coffin on the table. The only sound was the whistling of the wind and the clanking of the masts in the breeze. Patches of blue appeared and disappeared in the sky as gray clouds hid the sun and then revealed it, as if playing hide and seek.

The chaplain was an old man, his white hair blowing in the wind, his white vestment, worn in honor of the burial of a child, billowing around his tall, gaunt frame. He circled the coffin, sprinkling it with holy water. She watched as he opened his missal and recited:

> *The Lord's are the earth and its fullness, the world and those who dwell in it*
> *For He founded it upon the seas and established it upon the rivers.*
> *Who can ascend the mountain of the Lord? Or who may stand in His holy place?*
> *He whose hands are sinless, whose heart is clean, who desires not what is vain, nor speaks deceitfully to his neighbor.*
> *He shall receive a blessing from the Lord, a reward from God his Savior.*

Sinless? The word echoed in the wind. Eileen almost laughed. Her child had lived in the garden of Eden. Innocent of guile, malice, he'd opened his eyes to a new world every day. He'd gazed in wonder at the sky and the clouds, at the lambs and cows. When his eyes met hers, his red mouth curved in a smile, and his face took on a look of mischief. And what was his reward? To die senselessly on board a ship leading him away from all he knew and loved at home. In exile! She twisted her hands beneath her shawl.

John took Eileen's icy hand in his warm one. She tried to stop the trembling. She watched the priest sprinkle the small casket again and heard the words over the keening of the wind, "Let the little children come unto Me, for theirs is the kingdom of heaven." The priest nodded to Eileen. She felt herself approaching the casket and leaned into the child, pressing her lips on his small cold face. She could not move. From behind she felt her husband take her by the shoulders and pull her back. Then he nodded to the carpenter, who swiftly placed the lid over the casket, and in eight sharp blows nailed it shut. Next the sailor placed the casket in a bag made of sailcloth and weighed it down with two eight-inch cannon balls.

The priest raised his hand once more over the bag for a final prayer. He sprinkled the bag again with holy water. The captain nodded at two crew members who stepped forward and placed the canvas bag with the coffin on a plank and tipped it into the sea. No one heard the splash, but a ray of sunshine gleamed on the roiling waters as the ship steamed ahead on its way to America, Eileen crumpling in a heap on the deck.

Part 3

....

THE NEW WORLD

CHAPTER SIXTEEN

....

Michael skipped Sunday Mass hurrying to get to the dock on time for the arrival of the *SS Abyssinia*. He'd dressed carefully in a clean, pressed white shirt, his only pair of good pants, now somewhat worn but mended at the hem by his landlady for a precious dollar, a dark woolen tie, and a tweed jacket bought second-hand in London. He polished his worn leather boots, the only pair he owned. He combed his hair and examined his face in the mirror, his blue eyes blazing with excitement.

He loved New York in all its chaos and confusion. His work on the docks was brutal, but after work there were the pubs, the meetings with his fellow Irishmen and women who gathered to curse the British and plan how to help the IRB in Ireland. Everything was possible here. No one knew you as you walked down the street, pushing through masses of people shopping, working, people of all classes and nationalities, people on the make, just as he was.

Picturing Bantry some nights right before sliding into sleep, he was glad he had left. There he was a peasant, always made to feel less than the gentry. Images passed before him of that night in the stable when he'd confronted Caroline, the way she'd called him "stable boy." Well, he'd show her, one day returning to Ireland, rich, able to buy land.

Now his sister, and her baby boy, along with her husband, were arriving in New York! He'd keep them for a few days in his own room. He wanted to show them a bit of New York. The surprise he had for them was a letter in his pocket. After hearing from him about Eileen's family's decision to come to America, Miss O'Brien had written from London, suggesting the little family might settle in Holyoke in western Massachusetts, where they needed laborers for the dam they were building as well as on the railroads. There were silk and cotton mills also where Eileen could get a job. Mary Grace O'Brien had contacted the parish priest at St. Jerome's in Holyoke, a Father Dolan, who'd assured her that he would help the Sullivan family find a place to live in his parish down in the Flats of Holyoke, where the Irish settled. Surely, they would feel at home there, in a fertile valley with rich soil and farmland, he thought. Maybe there they could even save enough to buy some land and farm as they had in Bantry. It would suit them much better than the streets of New York.

In his pocket, wrapped carefully in newspaper, was a gift for the nephew he was dying to see again. Little Thomas was two and a half by now, and he'd bought the child a carved wooden horse with a saddle and bridle he'd spied in a shop window on his way to work. It had cost him a day's wages, but since he'd not been home for the baptism of the child, this was the least he could give him. *If only their mother had lived to see this, her first grandson.* Michael grinned to himself at the thought of him giving her any grandchildren. He was determined not to be caught by a pretty face, at least not yet. He was having too much fun with the girls of New York, God forgive him.

And then there was the gathering at which he first heard John Devoy, the firebrand. Devoy was only a few years older than Michael, but he'd done hard time for five years in prison in Dublin for Fenian activity, penal servitude the British called it. Devoy even organized strikes in jail! He was freed on condition that he leave Ireland forever.

Michael had been fired up the first time he'd heard him speak. Devoy wanted the fighting factions among the American Irish to unite to support the cause of Irish independence, so he'd joined the Clan na Gael, the sister branch of the Irish Republican Brotherhood in America, and this first meeting had persuaded Michael to join the confederation. Michael was thrilled to be part of the struggle once more, even though he had to admit to himself how much safer he was fighting for the Cause here in America. Devoy was trying to spread the organization to other cities where the Irish had settled: Boston, Chicago, and even St. Louis. Just last week Devoy had talked to Michael about heading to St. Louis to cooperate with the Fenians there.

But Devoy's suggestion would have to wait for a few weeks now that Eileen and her little family were arriving in New York. He wanted to help them get accustomed to the big city, show them the sights, and get to know his little nephew.

By ten o'clock the sun beat down on the crowds gathered on the pier, but there was still no sign of the *Abyssinia.* Finally at noon the crowd began to murmur and shift as the ship came into view, its bow rising over the horizon leading to Upper New York Bay. Magnificent, stately, the ship steamed into the harbor, surrounded by dozens of tugboats. Michael waved madly, raising his hat, and scanning the multitudes on the lower deck.

An hour later the cabin passengers, already cleared by the health inspectors on board the ship, began to pour into the waiting area. Michael knew it would be several more hours until the steerage passengers were examined at Castle Garden. *As if the rich don't get sick,* he thought. Even here in America he felt the sting of poverty every day. But there were ways to cure that sting here, and he would find them. He'd not throw away his life fighting for Ireland at the expense of his own future. He'd find a way to combine his ambition with love for his country.

Now, he thought, he'd just pop into the pub across the street for a pint. He made his way, pushing and shoving the waiting men at the bar, being cursed at in many languages. The pub was cool and dark, and he looked around as he ordered a beer and a sandwich. He nodded at a fellow sitting alone in the back of the dark room.

"Johnny Hanrahan, isn't it now?" Michael grinned down at the man nursing his drink, his hat pulled down low over his forehead. The man stared up at him, and a slow smile spread over his sallow face. "Why, Jesus, Mary, and Joseph, if it isn't Michael O'Donovan himself." It was Johnny, the son of Mrs. Hanrahan at the Big House, who had disappeared from Bantry several years ago. The man continued to drink, without rising or shaking Michael's hand.

"How's your mother these days, Johnny? She was generous to me many a day when I'd come through her kitchen at the Big House," Michael said as he pulled out a chair and sat without waiting for an invitation.

Johnny stared at him, his expression relaxing, his voice rusty. "Why, I hope to God she is fine. I have not heard from her in the two years I've been here in this godforsaken country." He took a long drag from his drink, his hands trembling. Michael watched the man's face as they both drank. Johnny's eyes were bleary, his face drawn. From his clothes rose a whiff of poverty and shame.

Finally, Johnny looked up and stared at Michael. "And what in God's name brought you here to New York? I thought you and your brother were all set with your mother's place in Bantry."

Michael smiled grimly. "Well, let's just say I got in a spot of trouble with the Brits as well as with the IRB," he muttered, looking around to see if anyone were within earshot. "But today is a fine day since my sister Eileen, her husband, and baby boy are arriving on the *Abyssinia*. You remember Eileen, don't you Johnny?"

Johnny looked away. "I may have seen her as a little girl, the one with light, curly hair, was she?"

Michael nodded. "That's the one. They'll be staying with me for a few days, and then I'm arranging something for them outside of the city." He leaned back, suddenly desperate to get away from this defeated man who'd obviously not found the Promised Land in America.

Johnny's hand shot out and gripped Michael's arm as he rose. "For the love of God, Michael, can you spare a few dollars for your old countryman?" His voice was craven, pleading. "I'm down on my luck these days, as you see."

Michael reached into his pocket and laid a fifty-cent piece on the table. "This is all I can spare, Johnny. God bless," he mumbled, not wanting to look back and see the man gesture to the bar for another drink.

Out in the sunshine of this May afternoon, Michael tried to shake off the sudden dread he'd felt at the encounter. New York was a cruel city for the faint-hearted. He would not be among them, he vowed.

By four o'clock as the shadows along the dock began lengthening, the *Abyssinia* pulled up to the pier. The steerage passengers poured out in waves, lugging their bundles, their faces pale and dazed. Michael scanned the crowd, looking for his sister. In the distance, a man raised his hand and seemed to be signaling him. It was Sullivan! Next to him, her head covered with a black shawl was a tall thin woman. Could it be Eileen? But where was the baby? He pushed and shoved his way through the crowd, finally reaching the couple.

The woman raised her eyes to Michael when she heard his voice, his sister's blue eyes blazing out at him in her pale, gaunt face, the saddest face he had ever seen. "Oh Michael," she sobbed, as she threw herself into his arms, "He's gone, he's gone." Michael stepped back in alarm and looked toward John.

"Where is my nephew, where's the boy?" he tried for a jovial tone.

John lowered his head and stared at Michael. "The child took sick on the voyage. The doctor said it was typhoid fever. He weakened quickly, and then at last. . ." he stopped, unable to say the words, not looking at Eileen.

Michael pushed her back, searching her face. She slumped against him, sobbing, "They put him in the sea, Michael, in that cold dark sea." John and Michael exchanged looks over her head. John nodded; his mouth set in a thin line. Then the three of them made their way down the pier out onto the thronged streets with hawkers crying out to them on all sides.

Back at his tenement on Fortieth Street, they trudged up the three flights of stairs and into Michael's room. He'd washed the walls and scrubbed the floors, put a vase of daffodils in the window where they caught the dim light. He'd even bought a new white bedspread in their honor.

Eileen looked around, taking in the little camp stove with a teapot, and began to heat the water for tea. A smidgen of color had returned to her cheeks. When she went in search of the bathroom down the hall, John and Michael looked at each other. Michael took a bottle out of the cabinet near the stove and poured two glasses of whiskey. He set one in front of John, who downed it in one gulp. He poured him another and put the bottle back.

"She has barely spoken in the week since the burial," John whispered. "But today was the first day I saw her cry." Michael, watching his head droop, realized how exhausted with grief and travel the couple must be.

"Well, we'll have our tea now. I have some ham, bread, and butter and even a small cake to celebrate your arrival. Sure, you must be famished," he said, trying for a cheerful tone. Then he felt the toy horse in his pocket and turned away so that John wouldn't see it. He slipped it into a box he kept by the bed with his clean clothes.

By the time Eileen came back, the two men had spread out the food on the table by the window. Eileen poured the tea, its strong, sweet smell filling the room. She and John sat on two straight back chairs while Michael perched on an over-turned barrel. They ate quickly, hungrily. Eileen leaned back at last and sipped her tea. She tried smiling at Michael and took his hand. "Michael, I've missed you so much. I wanted Thomas to. . . ." She could not finish.

Michael felt his eyes well with tears, and in a low tone he answered, "Eileen, I was so happy waiting to see the lad. Surely, he's in heaven with Mammy and Da."

His sister raised her chin, her voice bitter, "I'm finding it very hard to believe in God these days, Michael. Why would He take a baby, an innocent, from this life in such a cruel, painful way? Who can answer me that?"

John drained his glass quickly. "Hush, Eileen, you're talking crazy. We can't know God's ways."

"Well, I wouldn't want to know a God like that," Eileen retorted, shooting him a glance of disdain as she eyed the empty glass. John began pulling off his boots and soon he lay snoring on the bed, the new bedspread having been turned back carefully.

Michael and Eileen sat together at the table, looking out over the street, now quiet as Sunday drew to a close. Michael pulled out the letter from Mary Grace O'Brien. "Eileen," he said, "I've received some good news for you and John from Father Gleason's cousin in London, Miss O'Brien. I know you don't want to stay here in this crowded city in my small room."

He opened the letter and read:

London, England
April 1, 1870
Dear Mister O'Donovan,

I hope this letter finds you well in the bustling metropolis of New York City. Here in London, we are treated to daily showers and seldom see the sun. Your letter of March 2 reached me on the ninth. I confess, I was surprised that your sister had decided to leave Ireland for America. However, I can imagine that you will be happy to have some of your family there with you. That same week of your letter, I heard

*from my cousin, Father Hugh. He told me of a classmate
of his in the seminary at Maynooth who is the pastor of
St. Jerome's Parish in Holyoke, Massachusetts, a mill town
west of Boston, near Hartford. His name is Father Francis
Dolan, a Kerryman, and Hugh assures me that he is a very
sympathetic supporter of the cause of Irish freedom and
independence. We both think Holyoke might be the perfect
place for your sister and her husband to settle as there are
plenty of jobs available on the railroad as well as the with
the construction of dams along the river there. The woolen
and silk mills employ women also. Holyoke is not too far from
New York City by train, so you would not be very distant
from your family.*

*Michael, I hope this information will be of help as you
guide your family to a safe harbor after what must have been
a most difficult voyage to a strange, new country, far from
home. I remain as ever your friend and colleague in seeking a
glorious freedom for Ireland,*
Mary Grace O'Brien
Erin go Bragh!

When Michael glanced at his sister, he saw that she was
hardly listening. Her eyes were half closed, and she seemed
to sway in her chair. "Ah now, alannah," he murmured, "it's
exhausted you are. Lie down next to your husband while I clean
up the tea things. I'll be going out for a few hours to meet some
of the fellows." As he cleared the table, he watched Eileen sink
down on the far side of the narrow bed, her body held stiffly
away from her husband, her hand grasping a small blue knitted
horse. She turned her face into the pillow and slept.

The girl is barely nineteen, he thought, and has known such
trouble in her life. It all began with that misbegotten marriage!
And now her only joy, her little son Thomas, has been snatched
away from her along with her home and her country.

Well, he'd see them settled in Holyoke and then he'd be off for St. Louis. There was opportunity there, he knew, with Irish gangs who were making money like crazy, money that they then sent over to Ireland to help with the Cause. And some of that money would be for himself and Eileen. By God, he'd not starve and grovel in this country. He'd use the wits God gave him.

That evening Michael made his way to O'Reilly's, a known hang-out for members of an Irish gang called The Wild Geese. They were rumored to be small time thieves and extortionists, connected to some of the rising Irish politicians in the city. Michael was not one of them yet, but he was interested. He wanted nothing to do with violence, but he wouldn't mind getting work in their counterfeiting operations. He'd contacted some members of the group, and they'd promised to get him a meeting with the boss, a man by the name of Flaherty.

Michael, nervous as he entered the smoke-filled tavern, headed straight for the bar. He ordered a Guinness, and stood looking around the crowded, dark room. Several women were seated at a table with a man he didn't know, and their raucous laughter grated.

Seeing his sister today had shocked him: her pure sadness, her dignity, and those fierce, intelligent blue eyes. These women looked cheap, obvious in their sexiness. He'd lost his virginity the first week in America to a prostitute, the experience brutal, leaving him disgusted. Someday he knew he'd meet the right girl, a girl who was strong yet gentle and fine, a girl he could trust. Suddenly the image of Mary Grace O'Brien flashed before his eyes. He swallowed his drink and was asking for another when he felt someone tap him on the shoulder. He swung around to see his mate from the docks, Ryan, who nodded toward a curtained doorway to the left of the bar, and whispered, "Follow me."

Michael took a pull of his drink, wiping his mouth on his sleeve and followed Ryan through the doorway down a long dimly lit hall. Ryan knocked twice on a closed door, and a voice called, "Enter!" Ryan stepped back and let Michael through, closing the door behind him.

Behind a large wooden desk reading a newspaper sat Flaherty, his eyes obscured by wire-rimmed glasses. His black hair, slicked back, shone in the lamplight. He was dressed carefully in a gray suit coat, a gleaming white shirt with a knotted silk tie of deep blue, looking more like a banker than a criminal, Michael thought, as he stood waiting in front of the desk.

Finally, Flaherty raised his eyes to Michael and stood to shake his hand, motioning him to sit. He gazed at Michael a moment before saying in a soft voice, tinged with the notes of the west of Ireland, "So, Michael O'Donovan, the boys tell me you are interested in being a part of our operation. Tell me about yourself." He sat back in his chair, folding his hands on the desk. Michael noticed his fine long fingers, carefully manicured, the hands of a gentleman.

Michael cleared his throat and began, "I'm originally from Bantry, but came over here from London a while ago and have been working down on the docks. In Ireland, I was a member of the IRB, but got myself in a spot of trouble with the landlord's daughter. Not that kind of trouble," he said hurriedly when he noticed a faint look of amusement flit over Flaherty's face. "The problem is I left Ireland without notifying my commander in the IRB, so I've been on the run from both the IRB as well as the Irish police. But lately I've been listening to John Devoy, I've joined the Clan na Gael, and I want to do my part for Ireland."

He looked up to see Flaherty's reaction. Flaherty didn't blink. "Go on," he said.

"Well, Devoy thinks there is fertile ground in St. Louis for raising money for guns to be sent to Ireland with the large Irish population there, but I need some connections to get me in with the people there." Michael looked down, afraid to presume too much. He decided to be honest. "The truth is, Mr. Flaherty, I have no money. I'd need some kind of job, maybe with your organization."

Flaherty's voice was cold, "And exactly what kind of job could you do for us?"

Michael hesitated then ventured, "I have good spelling and writing skills, believe it or not. I was thinking of something in the printing line." He dared not say the word counterfeit.

Flaherty's smile did not reach his eyes. "So, it's keeping your hands clean of the rough stuff, eh, O'Donovan? That's not for the good Catholic boy from Bantry?"

Michael held his breath, not knowing how to respond. Flaherty reminded him of a snake, with the hooded eyes, and his sibilant voice. He felt the icy stare and tried to keep his expression blank. Flaherty rose then and nodded. "We'll be in touch with you, Michael O'Donovan. Someone will let you know when and where."

"Thanks, sir." Michael said, hoping his tone was neutral, not subservient. As he headed toward the door, Flaherty added, "And Michael, take care of yourself. New York is a big city, but the Irish around here are big talkers, not knowing when to keep their mouths shut." Michael nodded and shut the door quietly behind him. As he left O'Reilly's and walked out into the mild spring night, he breathed in deeply. He'd taken a dangerous first step.

After work the next day, Michael met John and Eileen for supper at The Portland Restaurant on Fortieth Street near his room. Afterward they walked for miles through the city. John and Eileen marveled at the number of markets, the abundance of fresh fruit and vegetables, the scent of apples and bananas mingling with the stench of horse manure in the streets, everyone out walking fast, messengers hurrying to offices, street urchins trying to cadge a few coins for shining your shoes or hailing you a horse and carriage. They heard languages from all over, harsh guttural sounds and flowing musical ones too. As night came on, gas lamps burned overhead, casting a golden glow over the streets and buildings, obscuring the ugly corners of the city. At last, they came to Washington Square Park.

Michael noticed Eileen lift her face to the breeze that rustled the new young leaves on the tall sycamore trees and inhale the scent of lilacs bordering the gravel paths. His sister was still quiet and withdrawn, with spasms of grief washing over her face at times, but she was slowly coming back to life. John, shuffling along like an old man, was drinking a lot, but Michael could hardly blame him. He could not imagine losing a child, and now John had lost two of his.

Michael gazed above the trees to faint stars above them in the cool night. How far they were from Bantry! And what lay ahead for them and for him, now getting himself tangled in what could only be trouble? Ah well, he'd been in trouble before. But never had he done something dishonest, something he was ashamed of. He'd join Flaherty's group only for a bit, only until he'd made enough money to establish himself in this new world. He'd be nobody's boy anymore. Like Ireland, someday he would be free.

CHAPTER SEVENTEEN

....

For Eileen, one of the best things about Holyoke was its lending library. She had discovered it by accident one Sunday afternoon after Mass when she and John were out walking. It was a gorgeous October day, the air still and clear with golden and scarlet leaves shimmering beneath the purest blue sky. Eileen thought how everything in America seemed clearer, sharper than in Ireland. In her memory, Ireland was always soft, its colors mauve and green and chartreuse, and pale pink-gray like the inside of a seashell. In Bantry the winter was mild, not like the clear cold nights they'd been having here. America was a place of sharp contrast, everything outlined in vivid hues.

Coming back to the Flats from St. Jerome's Church, they'd crossed Maple Street at Appleton and stopped to admire the newly built Appleton Street School. Red brick, three stories, it was a handsome building worthy to educate the children of Holyoke. Eileen usually tried to avoid seeing children, especially little ones. But today the school was quiet, serene, with no little ones to make her heart stop when any wee dark-haired boy ran by, shouting and laughing. She'd noticed a white placard posted to the one of the double doors.

"John, I'm just going to see what that sign says," she'd called to him, already walking up the front stairs.

LIBRARY OPEN DAILY MONDAY THROUGH
FRIDAYS 8:00 A.M. UNTIL 4:00 P.M.
AND SUNDAY AFTERNOONS FROM 1:00 P.M. UNTIL 4:00 P.M.
MISS SARAH ELY, LIBRARIAN

"John! There is a library inside the school. It's open this afternoon. Let's go in!" Without waiting for his answer, Eileen pushed the heavy door open and stepped into a foyer lit by sunlight streaming in from the glass windows of the door. A sign pointed to the left: Library Open. John entered behind her, and together they walked down the wide terrazzo corridor to the first room on the left and stood in the open door.

A young woman looked up and smiled. "May I help you?" Hesitantly, they approached the desk. Eileen's first thought was that the woman was too young to be a librarian. Somehow, she'd pictured an older, fussy woman.

"Yes, please," stammered Eileen. "We've recently arrived here in Holyoke and were wondering if we could use this library." Eileen gazed around the cheerful room, sunlight streaming in from the two front windows.

The woman smiled and held out her hand to Eileen. "I'm Sarah Ely, the librarian here. Welcome to Holyoke. All we need is the address of your residence, and your place of employment," she said, looking at John.

"Will there be a fee, Miss Ely?" Eileen asked anxiously.

"No, not for newcomers like you and your husband. After a few months if you are enjoying the library, you will be asked to pay one dollar a month. Now let me show you around the room."

Eileen watched Miss Ely's face as she pointed out the reference books with pride, the newspapers hanging on wooden racks, papers from New York, Washington, DC and even the *London Times*. "That one comes weeks late, I'm afraid," she laughed. "But it's still a treasure for all the book reviews and notices of cultural events we are missing here."

In a flash, Eileen knew she would love to work in a library, to spend her days among books and people who loved books, to be able to speak with confidence about new novels appearing, to guide readers to just the right books for their taste. Her marriage had put an end to her education. But what if there were a way she could finish her education?

"Miss Ely," she began, "may I ask what training it took for you to become a librarian?"

"Oh goodness," Miss Ely responded, smiling up at Eileen. "I studied history and English literature at Mount Holyoke Seminary. I never dreamed I would be a librarian. But when Mother died, I had to come home to take care of my father and run the house. So, this past year when a group of men here in town formed a board to establish the new library, they asked me to run it." She lowered her voice then, "To tell you the truth, this position is a godsend. I was bored to tears keeping house," she laughed, and her eyes sparkled.

Eileen wanted to be this woman's friend. Her frank, open way of speaking, her obvious intelligence; oh, she could learn so much from this Sarah Ely! Before she could stop herself, she heard herself babble, "Miss Ely, I would love to come and volunteer here on Sunday afternoons. I work at the Hadley Mill all week, but Sundays are free."

Eileen did not dare look at John to see how he took this. Sunday afternoons were the one time all week they had free time. But she wanted to get to know this woman with her brisk accent who could teach her so much.

"You are welcome to join me anytime you can, Mrs. Sullivan. You can be sure I'll find plenty for you to do," said Miss Ely, looking directly into Eileen's eyes.

They shook hands then, and Eileen grabbed John's arm as he mumbled his farewell. This idea was crazy, Eileen knew. She had so much to do on Sundays after Mass, with the washing and ironing and cleaning of their tiny room. She and John walked in silence for a few minutes when he finally blurted, "What in hell were you thinking, Eileen? You've got enough to do at home without running over here to volunteer."

"John, how dare you complain when I have found something I would love to do! You go to the pub!" she said, her eyes flashing. "I love books. I can learn so much from a lady like Miss Ely. I'm not planning to work in a mill for the rest of my days." John turned away without a word.

Eileen could still smell the books and see the bright eyes of Miss Ely, her dark hair tucked into a neat bun, the fine lace collar on her black silk blouse. In books Eileen escaped from the torment of her thoughts of Thomas both day and night. She kept seeing the small coffin, the black water closing over it as it sank quickly into the depths of the Atlantic Ocean. Books could save her. She didn't care what John thought.

The November dusk fell at five o'clock, so by six-thirty, it was pitch dark. Eileen clutched her shawl around her, vowing to buy herself a proper coat as soon as she'd saved enough money to add to her secret stash in the kitchen cabinet. Her Saturday shift at the silk mill was over, and she hurried through the streets, the fallen leaves crackling beneath her boots. John would be wanting his supper early so he could spend the rest of the evening at the pub. She didn't begrudge him this one night out. His work on the dam was back-breaking, and he came home sore and irritable most nights. And she admitted to herself that she enjoyed the solitude of those long Saturday evenings in front of their wood stove, meager fire that it was. She'd sit with her saved piece of gingerbread and hot tea and bury herself in a book. Tonight, she would finish *Jane Eyre* for the second time, and she was trying to slow down her reading now that Jane had decided to go back to Thornfield to search for her beloved Rochester. Eileen loved the happy ending. Hadn't the poor girl suffered enough? She was glad Jane had thrown over the bloodless St. John Rivers!

Now this Sunday, the sixth of November, would be her first day working in the library with Miss Ely. Eileen hurried, realizing that it was late, and that John would be wanting his supper before he disappeared into the depths of O'Reilly's for the evening. When she entered their room, it was warm with steam rising from the metal tub in one corner. Her husband arose from his bath in full glory, his naked form, hairy and stout, displayed proudly. "So, home at last, Eileen, and me having to heat the water for my bath myself and search out a towel," he grumbled. "You know I like to get to the pub early on Saturday nights, and here is the stove, cold as the moon, with no supper in sight."

Eileen said nothing as she laid her parcels on the table and tied her apron around her waist. She put the kettle on, and as she reached for a plate, she noticed a letter on the table. John watched her as she glanced at the postmark; it was from Michael in New York. It was unopened. "Oh grand!" she cried, trying for a light tone. "Why didn't you open it, John?"

"You'll notice that it is addressed to you, Eileen. I thought it better to wait until you got home."

She glanced at him and decided the letter could wait until he had gone. Now she'd better focus on him to make up for her tardiness. *God! Men were so helpless.* She bustled around the room, chatting all the time about whom she'd seen at Feeley's Market, the price of vegetables and meat, the new trolley which went down Main Street that she'd like to go on soon. By the time John had dressed and brushed his curly, graying hair, she had spread the things for their tea on the blue and white tablecloth. He bent over his plate, wolfing down slices of cold beef and bread steadily without a word. He slurped his tea and dabbed his face with the starched white napkin.

Eileen could hardly wait until he left, but trying to be pleasant, she leaned back in her chair, saying brightly, "So tomorrow afternoon will be my first day working at the library. Sure, I'm a bit nervous."

John looked at her steadily over his cup. "Sometimes, Eileen, I think you look for ways to escape from this house. . . and from me," he finished, looking down.

Eileen was stunned. It was unlike John to say anything personal to her, especially since the death of Thomas. They had not slept together in months, John spending his nights on a thin used mattress on the floor near the stove, while Eileen had the bed to herself. They both knew there would be no more children for them. The wound was too deep.

"And what do you call yourself disappearing for hours every blessed Saturday night to drink and carouse down at O'Reilly's, coming home stumbling drunk?" Her eyes blazing, her voice shrill. She hated herself then for the hypocrisy. She was *glad* he left her alone every Saturday evening. She could breathe and be Eileen O'Donovan then, her true self, free, a girl again, not a wife bound to this man. John rose and pulled on his coat.

She rose too, reaching up to put his wool scarf around his neck. "Let's not fight, John," she looked into his eyes. "We've both been through a horrible time. Let's at least be friends and help each other. Thomas, God bless him, bound us together. . . ." She could not go on.

John nodded, and as he walked to the door, called back over his shoulder, "I'll not be late, alannah. I'll try not to wake you when I come in." He shut the door gently as he left.

Eileen wept as she cleared the table, carefully storing the leftover food away. It was true. She did look for ways to be away from him. She was starved for friends and family, all those she had left behind, so lonely. She washed their dishes and dried her hands, and at last sat down with a fresh cup of tea to read Michael's letter. They had not seen him since they'd left New York, and she was so hoping he'd come visit soon. She ran her hand over the familiar scrawl on the envelope and slit open the letter with a knife.

New York, November 1870

Dear Sister,

   I write to tell you about the news from here, hoping that you and John have settled into your lives in Holyoke. How lucky you both were to find good jobs and a place to live. America is surely the land of opportunity, much as we miss Bantry and home (I know I still do.) But God help me, Eileen, if I would ever go back there it would only be to help Ireland get free of the British, damn them to hell. I am working hard to help that freedom become a reality soon.

   Speaking of work, I have quit my job on the docks and have managed to make some good money by working at a printing job for a Mr. Flaherty here in Manhattan. In these past two months, I have earned enough to make a move to St. Louis, an up-and-coming city in the middle of the country on the Mississippi River. There is a large Irish population there, and Flaherty has connected me with some of his associates. He assures me there is real money to be made there. So, I will be leaving New York on the first of December, making my way to St. Louis by train. There is a branch of the IRB there also, so I can perhaps get back in the good graces of the Brotherhood.

   I wish I had time to come see you and John, but I need to strike while the iron is hot, as they say here in New York. I feel that this opportunity is a once in a lifetime chance. I hope it will not sadden you to have me so far away. Maybe you and John could follow me there once I have made my mark. I'm sick and tired of being poor, of scrounging for money, working at back-breaking jobs for peanuts. In this vast country an Irishman has a chance to be someone!

   Eileen, alannah, I promise I will write and send you my address as soon as I get settled. I hope to God that you are all right, and that the death of that beautiful boy has not

ruined your hope and happiness. How I wish I had known
him better.
God bless, Eileen, I remain your loving brother,
Michael

Eileen put the letter down, troubled. She reached for the tea, now cold. Who was this Flaherty? What did Michael know about printing? And why was he bolting to St. Louis, thousands of miles away from them? All these hints about freeing Ireland and working hard for it gave her a chill. So, Michael was still wanting to be part of the IRB and all their dangerous games! She was afraid for her brother. Now she and John would really be alone.

She stood over the stove, reheating the pot of water to refresh her tea. Then she unwrapped the piece of gingerbread she had hidden from John and picked up *Jane Eyre*. She pulled the one comfortable chair they had up to the stove. She opened the book to her velvet bookmark, to the passage in which Jane comes at last to find her wounded Rochester, and began to read, "*I thought I had taken a wrong direction and lost my way. The darkness of natural as well as sylvan dusk gathered over me; I looked round in search of another road.*" The words began to shimmer before her eyes. She too had taken the wrong road. Would there be another road for her?

CHAPTER EIGHTEEN

....

Michael gazed from the window of the train as the frozen
fields of Pennsylvania, Ohio, Indiana, and Illinois whipped
by. He had hardly slept since he boarded the train in New York,
clutching his coat to him as a blanket, rubbing the steamed-up
windows so he would not miss anything. He'd not been out of
Manhattan since he'd left Ireland and now was astounded at the
vast emptiness of America.

At night the darkness of the land was pierced occasionally
by the lights of a one-street town, and the train would slow,
pulling into a small station to let off a few passengers dragging
their valises into the shocking cold of a December night. During
the day he gazed out at dense forests of bare trees set off by tall
evergreens, fields stubble-filled and frozen. Once in the distance
he glimpsed a barn, a splotch of red against the barren fields next
to a much smaller house, smoke rising from the chimney into the
steel gray sky, and a lone farmer chopping wood.

The countryside stretched on, solitary, lonely. What did it
feel like to live out here, he wondered? Your neighbors would
be miles and miles away, not like in Ireland where you could
walk easily over to the next farm for a drink or a chat. Michael
leaned his head against the glass. Well, damn it, he'd be in a city,
St. Louis, the fourth largest city in the United States, Flaherty

had told him. Not for him the life of a farmer stuck out here in nowhere.

Seeing the farms made him think of Martin back on the farm in Bantry, with only old Queenie for company, all his family gone. Why didn't Martin marry? He felt sad at their distance now, remembering when they were boys getting into mischief around the place, hiding from their father when it was time for chores, sneaking into the kitchen when their mother was busy to steal some freshly baked bread.

They'd grown apart, each keeping his own secrets. Martin was a loner, not even going into the pubs on Saturday night, with no friends that Michael knew of. Finally, politics had really killed whatever sympathy and affection there was between them. Martin despised Michael's involvement with the Brotherhood, mocking him as a fool to think a few farmers' sons could overthrow the British. And Michael felt contempt for his older brother, he who had no passion for the idea of a free Ireland, content to slave away on a tiny farm, at the beck and call of the Earl at the Big House. And now the Atlantic Ocean and this whole huge country lay between them, more separated than ever, orphans, the family in tatters. Michael sighed and closed his eyes, feeling a blessed drowsiness, surrendering to it with relief.

He was awakened by the great lurch of the train and the hiss of steam as it came to a stop. People around him were chattering, gathering their packages, and moving quickly toward the doors of the train car. He gazed out of the window at people streaming by, their faces joyful as they embraced the loved ones greeting them. He stood shakily, grabbing his coat and searching for his lone valise, knowing there'd be no one to greet him, hoping St. Louis would be the beginning of the luck of the Irish for him. He stepped out of the train and into the sunlight of a winter afternoon, glimpsing the curve of a great river, like a wide brown snake, glistening in the light. The Mississippi! These strange names here: Cincinnati, Mississippi, Missouri, places named for the Indians. He half expected to see a tall brave, his face streaked with paint, dressed scantily in skins of a buffalo he had killed. Here he was surely in the New World.

The cold air was bracing after the stuffy train, and the midday sun shone brightly. The crowd hurried off the platform, and Michael was swept along with the other passengers. He felt the gnawing of hunger and knew he had to find a bathroom soon. Once out on the street, he dug in his pocket for the address of the pub Flaherty had given him where he could make contact with some of the boys from New York.

He approached a policeman watching the passengers, swinging his billy club. Tipping his cap, Michael said, "Excuse me, Officer, could you direct me to Egan's saloon on the corner of Broadway and Washington?"

The copper stared at him, unsmiling. "And what in the hell would a young man like you want at that place of ruffians? You'll find nothing but trouble there, boyo."

Michael detected a faint trace of a Dublin accent. He grinned at the man. "Why, it's a powerful thirst I have now, Officer, after that train ride. I'm looking for a job. Is it a Dublin man you are now?"

"That I am, and you must be from somewhere around Cork," the cop looked straight into Michael's eyes with a slight air of amusement. "I'll wager you are fresh off the boat, man, and I'm giving you good advice to stay away from the boys at Egan's if it's honest work you are wanting. But I guess you'll find out that for yourself," he sighed. "Okay, keep straight going north on Broadway for about five blocks until you come to Washington Avenue. Then turn left."

Michael tipped his hat, and as he turned away, said under his breath, "Erin go Braugh!" He didn't turn around to see if the copper heard him.

The corner saloon was dark after the bright sunlight of the streets. Smoke hung in the air. Clumps of men gathered talking quietly over their pints of beer. At the bar, he ordered a pint and asked if he could use the facilities. The bartender, a big, red-faced young man, pointed to the hallway at the left as he dried the glasses. He looked carefully at Michael and said in a low voice, "I haven't seen you in here before."

Michael nodded and stretched out his hand. "I'm Michael O'Donovan, from Bantry, by way of New York City." He smiled at the man, "And Mr. Flaherty in New York recommended your place for giving a warm welcome to someone from the old country."

The man said, quietly, "O'Connor here. You must be hungry too. I'll fix you a sandwich to go with your drink." His expression did not change.

Michael nodded his thanks and headed for the lavatory. When it came, the jab of the knife at his back was barely perceptible through so many layers of shirts and sweaters Michael had dressed in against the cold of the voyage. He put his hands up, and in the small mirror facing the sink saw the two men behind him with their caps pulled down low on their foreheads.

"Who the fuck sent you here?" snarled the shorter of the two.

"Who's askin' me that?" Michael tried to keep the tremor out of his voice. Another jab, this time more insistent.

"I'm asking the questions, boyo."

Michael turned around and faced the two men, his hands still in the air. "I come in peace, gentlemen. Sent here by a friend in New York." They searched him then, patting his body, his jacket, and between his legs.

"Okay, he's clean." The short man removed his cap and slid the knife into a pocket inside his jacket.

Just then, the bartender pushed open the door and stared at the group. Then he barked, "For fuck's sake, Herlihy, let the man alone. Sure, he's famished after his trip, and his pint and grub are waiting for him at the bar. What kind of hospitality are you showing him?" He grabbed Michael's arm, and led him out of the lavatory, leaving the two men staring stupidly at each other.

Michael could barely eat, but he downed the pint swiftly and asked for another. O'Connor winked at him as he finished the second pint. "You'll have to forgive the two numbskulls who jumped you," he laughed, pointing to his head with a circular motion. Yet his eyes shifted back and forth, and Michael was sure the incident had not been a one off. What in God's name had he walked into? The Fenians played rough here too.

As Michael counted out the right amount of change for his lunch, O'Connor leaned in to whisper, "Mr. O'Neill will see you now. Just follow me." They ascended a staircase Michael had not noticed when he'd gone to the bathroom. The bartender knocked lightly on a closed door three times.

The room was shadowy. A tall, middle-aged man rose from the desk, his clean-shaven face full and fleshy, his white hair wavy, cut long on his neck, with all the marks of a once hand-some man whose good looks were failing him. He was in his shirtsleeves, and his snowy white shirt gleamed in the dusky room. John O'Neill reached out to shake Michael's hand with a wide, welcoming gesture. "Sorry about the somewhat icy reception the boys here gave you," he laughed, nodding to the corner.

Michael looked around and saw the two who'd confronted him. He smiled back at O'Neill, keeping his voice even, "I don't blame you for being careful. I am a stranger, after all."

"Well, not quite," O'Neill waved his hand, dismissing the two goons. He motioned for Michael to sit, then settled back in his wide armchair. "We know quite a bit about you, Michael O'Donovan from Bantry. One, that you took part in the 1867 uprising in Cork that was such a fuck-up. Two, that you got into some trouble in Bantry with the daughter of the Earl. Three, that you signed up with the IRB under Captain MacDonogh, went on a reconnaissance mission with him, but then skedaddled for London without notifying him or the Brotherhood."

Michael tried to hide his shock. He had told Flaherty none of this. Flaherty must have checked up on him and sent the news to O'Neill. He nodded at his inquisitor to go on.

"And four, that Flaherty suggested we give you some work here in St. Louis to see if you are serious about the Cause." He sat back, waiting for Michael to respond.

Michael began, "If you mean the cause of Irish freedom from the British, you are correct. The only reason I fled Ireland was that I was a suspect in the eyes of the British for the trouble with the landlord's daughter. She found a pistol I had hidden, and I wrestled it away from her."

O'Neill nodded, leaning back in his chair and putting his fingers together as he stared at Michael. "Somehow, O'Donovan, you look more like an altar boy than a tough guy."

Michael laughed. "Well, it's been some time since I was an altar boy." He leaned in to look the man in the eye. "Look, I admit I've not done any rough stuff for Flaherty or anyone else other than the fuck-up attempt at a Rising in Cork. But I am serious about the IRB and want to help in any way that you could use me. And to tell you the truth, I need money. I heard that there might be a use for someone who was good at, let's say, printing." His voice went up in a question.

O'Neill nodded. "We'll see. Come see me next Monday morning, and we'll see what work I have for you. For now, I have the address of a rooming house you might want to check into. Mrs. Quigley is the owner of the rooming house. Just tell her O'Neill sent you." He scribbled an address on a sheet of paper. He rose and reached across to shake Michael's hand. "I could use a smart lad like you, so don't blab around and fuck up your opportunity, eh?"

Michael thanked him and left the room. As he emerged onto Washington Avenue, he shouldered his pack and picked up his valise to find his way to Mrs. Quigley's rooming house, wondering with each step why he had ever come to this town where he had no clue whom he could trust to be straight with him. He was a long way from Bantry.

The rooming house was on Carr Street, a long ten blocks from Egan's: red brick, two stories, with all the shades drawn. He rang the bell. Nothing. After a few minutes he heard footsteps, and the door swung open to reveal a short, bosomy woman with frizzy gray hair. Michael tipped his cap, "Good afternoon. Michael O'Donovan at your service, ma'am. Mr. O'Neill sent me to you."

The woman peered at him for a few seconds, her eyes, a rheumy blue behind the pince-nez perched on her nose. "Come in, come in, man. You're lettin' in all the cold air." She waved her cane at him, and he followed her down a dark corridor, the smells of cooking mixed with Jeyes cleaning fluid drifting through the drafty hallway.

They entered what he guessed was her own private parlor, and she sank with a sigh into a faded armchair next to the fireplace. She closed her eyes for a second while Michael looked around the room. A statue of the Sacred Heart of Jesus held pride of place on the mantel, with a red votive light in front of it, and a vase of dusty artificial roses beside it. A sofa, one other chair, and a table with pictures of several hulking young men filled the small room. When she opened her eyes and looked again at Michael, she began to laugh. "Well, it's a handsome devil O'Neill has sent me this time." She stared at him, and Michael felt himself blush.

"I've just arrived this day from New York," he stammered.

"I don't hear New York in your voice. I'd guess somewhere near Cork."

"Close enough," he grinned. "I was born and raised in Bantry. May I ask if you are Mrs. Quigley?"

"That I am," the old woman said with a toss of her head. "Mary Margaret Quigley from Kerry, if you please. So, let's get down to business. I have a room for you in the back of the house on the second floor. Breakfast and dinner are included six days a week, but you're on your own on Sundays. Laundry will be done once a week on Mondays."

"That sounds fine, Mrs. Quigley. May I ask the price of the room?"

"Do you have a job yet?" she cocked her head with a faint smile.

"Not quite," he admitted. "But I'm almost certain I'll be working for Mr. O'Neill."

"Then it is a dollar a week for you," she said, struggling to get up from the chair. Michael saw her wince in pain and said hastily, "No need to come up with me, ma'am. Just point the way and I'll get settled in." He watched her make her way slowly to the table and open a wooden box. She handed him the key to his room.

"Supper is served at six sharp. I lock up the house at eleven each night. After a few weeks, when I have gotten to know you, we'll see about giving you a key to the front door." She smiled up at him, clutching her hand over her immense bosom. For an instant Michael glimpsed the mischievous girl from Kerry she'd been, and he smiled back in relief at the warmth of the woman. He tried not to think about how little she would trust him if she knew the kind of work he'd be doing.

"Thank you," he said huskily, "I am grateful to be here with a lady from home."

Again, that laugh, as she said, "Sure, I don't know about the lady part, but you are welcome as the flowers in May, Michael O'Donovan from Bantry."

The room was not bad: a single bed with clean white sheets, a red blanket folded at the foot, a chair next to it, a washstand with a pitcher and basin, an armoire, and one faded easy chair with an oil lamp beside it on a small table. The two windows, not overly clean, overlooked a small backyard with a shed leading to an alley. Michael hung his few clothes in the armoire and laid out his brush, comb, and soap on the washstand. There was a mirror over the washstand, and he gazed at his face, heavy with fatigue. He stripped off his coat, shirt, and pants, and lay on the bed, pulling the blanket over him. As he felt himself sliding into sleep, he pictured his mother in the kitchen at Bantry. What would she say if she knew what he was doing here in St. Louis? Thank God she did not live to see her poor banished children of Eve, as the prayer said.

When he awoke it was dark. He had no watch, but he suspected he had missed supper. He dressed hastily, and made his way downstairs, following the sounds of laughter and men's voices to the dining room. Mrs. Quigley presided at the head of the table, and to her right and left were two men. A young girl scurried around, bringing the platters from the kitchen. They all looked at him as he entered, and he dipped his head, murmuring, "Good evening, all. Sorry for being late. Sleep overtook me, I'm afraid."

"This is our newest lodger, Mr. Michael O'Donovan from Bantry by way of New York City!" Mrs. Quigley had obviously been imbibing from the large mug of beer in front of her. Her face was flushed, her gestures expansive. She motioned to him to sit at the foot of the table. The dark-haired man on her right reached over to shake his hand. "Mike Finn, here. I guess now we have two Michaels in the house."

The man on her left was older, a tall thin man with gray hair, who bowed and said simply, "Willie Barth." Michael noticed that no beer was served to the lodgers, but soon he was devouring the roast, the mashed potatoes, and carrots, trying not to betray how famished he was. The food was delicious, and there was even fresh soda bread and butter to remind him of home.

The conversation was lively. Gradually it came out that that Finn also worked for O'Neill, but it was not clear doing what, and that Barth was a traveling salesman, specializing in ladies' clothes. The meal finished with oranges, the first fruit Michael had eaten since he left New York.

As they rose from the table, Mike Finn invited him to go to a pub for a pint, but Michael begged off, claiming he would need to be up and sharp tomorrow to look around the city, scouting out work opportunities. He did not mention his interview with O'Neill. Mr. Barth retired to his room on the first floor, and Mrs. Quigley had the young girl, Maisie, help her up and carry her mug of beer back to her parlor. Michael climbed the stairs, wondering why he hadn't gone with Finn for a drink. Now the room seemed cold, sterile. For a long time, he gazed out the window at the dark December night.

The next few weeks were tedious for Michael as he made his way early each cold winter morning to the hidden room in the back of an old warehouse on O'Fallon Street near the riverfront. O'Neill was starting him off as a shover, the person who would take the counterfeit bills and try to pass them off at various places around the city, using a large denomination to buy something and then getting the change in real money. Michael realized that he would be the most likely person to be caught if anyone suspected the bills were counterfeit and notified the police. But before sending him out onto the streets, O'Neill wanted him to learn the art of counterfeiting and printing, and so Michael was spending these first days with old Peterson, the artist specializing in drawing and printing the bills. Peterson was German and told Michael stories of having learned his trade in the old country before ending up in St. Louis.

Every morning Michael entered the hidden back room to see Peterson bent over his table, two oil lamps on either side of his drawing board, spectacles perched precariously on his nose, murmuring to himself. On a long table nearby were boxes neatly stacked, filled with the precious paper, finely made in a factory in Holyoke, from which newly minted bills would be printed. In the corner, covered with a blanket, was the small printing press Peterson used. The job had become more difficult in the last few years, Peterson explained, because the Feds were cracking down on every bank printing its own money, so now only federal banks could issue currency.

In their second interview, O'Neill had done a slick job of whitewashing the crimes they were committing with an appeal to Michael's zeal for Irish liberation. "Why man," he'd leaned back in his leather chair, "this work is every bit as important as what you and the lads were doing back in Cork City in attacking the Brits," he smiled faintly, "and far less dangerous."

Michael stared directly into his eyes. "May I ask, Mr. O'Neill, how much of the profits go to the IRB?"

O'Neill's eyes went cold, but his voice remained even. "No, you may not. We'll see about profits as soon as you start working the streets, my boy. After a few weeks I'll have you shadow one of our more experienced men."

Michael nodded, and after a beat he realized that he was dismissed as O'Neill looked down, shuffling the papers on his desk. As he left, Michael felt the chill of doubt and tried to brush it aside. He'd come all this way and he was not going to chicken out now.

As Christmas approached, Michael thought more and more of Eileen. What would his sister think of his work? She'd be horrified, he knew. He sat down one Saturday afternoon to write her a letter, glossing over the exact nature of his job, referring vaguely to working for a Mr. O'Neill in the printing business. He described in great detail the inhabitants of Mrs. Quigley's boarding house; the great thriving city of St. Louis; and the wide, muddy Mississippi flowing swiftly past the waterfront; its crowded banks lined with steamboats; and the rough-and-tumble dock workers, many Irish, loading and unloading goods from all over the continent.

He sent the letter off to Holyoke, hoping that it would reach Eileen and her husband in time for Christmas. It would be a sad one for them, he knew, staring at each other across the barren rooms, trying not to think of the packed-up baby clothes and handmade toys, their first Christmas without Thomas, yet hearing the echo of his prattle everywhere.

On Christmas Eve he made his way with Mike Finn to St. Patrick's Church for midnight Mass. They'd downed a few shots in Egan's with the other rowdies before time for Mass, and Michael was worried that the priest would smell drink on his breath. As they hurried through the streets toward the looming church, wind whipping through his tweed jacket, Michael decided he'd not be approaching the communion table tonight. He remembered Father Gleason's catechism lessons and his careful definition of mortal sin: it must be grave matter, you must know it is grave matter, and you must fully will to do it. He knew his work fulfilled every criterion.

They saw the church from a distance, its windows lit from within, glowing golden in the sleety night. Carriages arrived, but most people were on foot, laughing and chattering, crying out their greetings. They entered through the massive doors of the red brick building, and he and Finn took off their caps, brushing the sleet from their jackets. Michael blessed himself with holy water while Finn leaned over to whisper, "Jesus, Michael, it's many a year since I've crossed the threshold of a church. My mammy would fall down in thanksgiving if she could see me now."

The organist played "Adeste Fidelis," and the two men slipped into a pew toward the back of the long narrow church. The familiar music, the packed heat of so many bodies, the homey beauty of the gilded statues of Mary and Joseph and St. Patrick, so familiar to Michael from childhood, the altar gleaming in the distance, and the empty crib in the center awaiting the placing of the Christ Child, all hit Michael with a dizzying wave of longing. It was cheap to be so moved, he admitted to himself. How could he sit here pretending that he was worshipping when he was breaking every commandment in the book? He was a liar, a fornicator, and a thief. Before long he might well be a murderer.

He looked up at the crucifix hanging high above the crib; the tortured body of the young Galilean looked down at them all, as if to say: *this is the price of love, to lay down your life for your friends.* He knelt and buried his head in his hands.

As they stood for the entrance of the priest and the acolytes from the sacristy, Michael felt a sharp poke in his ribs. Finn whispered, "Well God save us, if it isn't the pious Mr. John O'Neill, our boss!" He pointed toward a silver-haired man a few pews in front of them. Beside him, Michael noticed a tall, slender woman, her black velvet hat adorned with a single red feather. He could not see her face.

"Who's that with him? His wife?"

"No, that's his daughter. His wife died a few years ago. It's just the two of them now, no sons."

Michael found himself distracted throughout the Mass by the red feather on the young woman's hat. She had on a form-fitting black wool coat with a fur collar. When she turned her head, Michael could see the fur brush her cheek. He wished she would turn around.

After Mass, as they made their way to the door, Finn complaining about having a great thirst after all that praying, Michael turned around to see if he could catch a glimpse of the wearer of the hat. O'Neill saw him, and as Michael smiled and lifted his cap, O'Neill shook his head. It was plain that he did not want Michael and Finn to approach him here in the church with his daughter.

Now Michael could see that she was just a girl, but there was something about the way she carried herself, stately, assured, that made him think what a fine woman she would become. He tugged Finn's jacket, "Hey, Finn, let's see if we can bump into the O'Neills accidentally."

Finn stared at him, "You must be nuts, O' Donovan! He won't be wanting his daughter to meet the likes of us. She's a convent schoolgirl!"

But Michael was shoving through the people leaving the church slowly, reaching the holy water font at the same time the O'Neill girl did. He dipped his fingers in only to meet her gloved hand. She laughed and looked up at him. Everything seemed to slow down as Michael gazed into her eyes, a strange blue-green in the dim light, almost like the sea back home. Her hair was black, pulled back from her face, but with wisps escaping from under the hat.

"Excuse me, miss." It was all he could think to say. Then O'Neill was beside him, and Michael hurriedly stammered, "Merry Christmas to you, Mr. O'Neill."

Finn was there too by then, so O'Neill was forced to introduce his daughter to them both. "Rose, I'd like you to meet two young men who do some work for me. This is Mike Finn and the recently arrived Michael O'Donovan. Gentlemen, my daughter, Rose."

Rose smiled at them both and held out her gloved hand to Mike Finn and then to Michael. He shook it, holding onto it a second too long. O'Neill's face reddened, and he took Rose's arm before they could say anything more. He tipped his hat to them as he pulled Rose along, murmuring, "Happy Christmas, fellas."

As the two men walked back toward the rooming house, Michael barely listened to Finn complaining about the length of the Mass, the priest's interminable sermon, and the lack of a place open now to get a drink. Michael could only think of the moment his fingers met Rose's in the holy water. He'd gotten a Christmas gift, after all. The best one ever.

Over the next weeks, Michael pumped Finn for information about O'Neill. What bad luck for him that Rose was his daughter! He knew O'Neill did not want him anywhere near her. He had to see the girl again. Finn told him what a powerful figure John O'Neill was here in Kerry Patch. He made money in bootlegging and the protection racket, which was the part of the business Mike Finn was engaged in, going around each week to all the small businesses on the near north side to collect "fees" from the owners to ensure they were not bothered by the police, half of whom were on O'Neill's payroll anyway.

Finn explained that O'Neill had ambitions to be a political power, not for himself, but to put people in power in Jefferson City and even in DC, politicians who would favor the Irish. With money from the rackets, he'd bought up real estate in the area, hoping to become a legitimate power broker in St. Louis. "In fact," Finn whispered to Michael over his pint as they sat in a dark corner in the saloon one snowy night, "O'Neill owns Mrs. Quigley's place. Did you not know that?"

Michael shook his head, impatient. "So, what about his girl? Does she know what her father is?"

"I have no fuckin' idea, O'Donovan. And you'd be wise to stay away from her!" Finn laughed at the expression on Michael's face. "I doubt that she knows anything, although she may suspect. He's kept her totally away from down here. They live in a mansion on St. Louis Place, with servants and all. She's a day student at the Convent of the Sacred Heart, and she will graduate from there in the spring. She's been raised to be a lady, O'Donovan, not for the likes of you," he snickered and took a long drink.

Michael suddenly flashed on Lady Caroline on that last night in the barn at Blackthorn House. Damn it! Why was he always reaching beyond his station? But wasn't that the point of America? There were no fixed stations. Even a crook like John O'Neill could get ahead and become someone of substance, someone with property, houses, a position in society.

Gradually in the weeks ahead, Michael understood that the path to getting to know Rose was thorny. Would she despise him for working for her father? But every night now, before he fell asleep, it was with the image of Rose's face that he that he said a Hail Mary, praying for a way forward.

CHAPTER NINETEEN

....

The Saint Louis winter settled in hard in January. Every morning Michael had to crack the ice in his wash basin before washing his face, gasping as the water hit him. He hurried into his clothes and went down to breakfast, anxious for the warmth of the dining room. Mrs. Quigley spared no expense in keeping that room and her own parlor cozy with warmth from burning coal. The rest of the tall narrow house was swept by an icy draft at all hours, so the residents wore coats and mufflers until they reached the dining room. Most mornings Michael met Finn, who was already finishing his breakfast, and just sipping the last of his coffee, getting up quickly, "I'm off, my boy! Duty calls."

Michael realized that O'Neill's method was to keep all his men in ignorance of each other's operations. He supposed that was to cut down on squealing. Finn and he were drinking buddies at times, but he had only a vague idea of Finn's duties. And Finn never asked him about his own role in the organization.

The long walk to the warehouse was the best part of his day, with the wind in his face, the smell of smoke, and the bare trees etched against a low gray sky. His training over, according to Peterson, he'd been sent out in the city to pass counterfeit bills now, and he was getting to know the shops all over downtown, even as far west as Grand Avenue. So far, the work was too easy, with no one ever inspecting the five-dollar bills he used to purchase items in bulk for O'Neill's pub, although he had not yet attempted to go into a bank for change, not wanting to tempt fate.

In the evening, about six o'clock, he returned to the warehouse and deposited the cash in a scuffed leather bag, which he carried to O'Neill's. He and O'Neill's right-hand security man, "Big Dutch" Mahon, met in the small outer office upstairs and sat at the table to count the day's take twice. Then Big Dutch would knock softly on O'Neill's door and take the money in to the boss. Michael seldom saw O'Neill. In fact, it wasn't until mid-February that O'Neill came out into the room where Michael waited and motioned for him to come into his office. Michael sat in front of the boss as he slowly lit a cigar and drew on it, the older man's face flushed, his hands trembling.

"So, how's the job going, Michael from Bantry?" O'Neill asked with a trace of sarcasm.

"Very good, sir. No trouble at all, so far." He hesitated, not wanting to be too familiar. "I'm enjoying getting to know the city." He glanced at O'Neill, but could not read his expression, so he kept on, "It was very nice to meet your daughter on Christmas, Eve, sir."

O'Neill did not reply at once. He then leaned back in his chair and sighed, "She's a fine girl, that one. Since her mother died five years ago, I've been trying to be both mother and father." His face brightened. "She's going to graduate this September from the Convent of the Sacred Heart, the most prestigious girls' school in St. Louis. All the bigwigs in St. Louis send their daughters there, so Rose is mixing with the crème de la crème, as they say. The nuns are French, although now they have let quite a few Irish nuns in too. Rose speaks excellent French, they tell me," he said as he got up and paced around the room, lifting and discarding papers on his desk, and puffing on his cigar. "She gets high marks in all her subjects, too."

Michael said nothing, not daring to mention the fact that at least once a week, he strolled slowly by City House, as the school was popularly known, hoping for a glimpse of Rose among the girls at play on the broad field behind the forbidding gray brick building.

As if reading his thoughts, O'Neill sat down and looked squarely at Michael. "The problem is what to do with Rose after she graduates. I'm thinking of sending her to Europe on a long tour around the continent to polish her off. I don't want her around here. She needs to meet suitors of a finer sort, not stay here around the kind of boyos I work with." He glanced at Michael, who kept his face impassive. "That was the whole reason my wife and I sent her to the nuns of the Sacred Heart. We've given her all the advantages. I want a return on that investment."

He stood then, and Michael realized the moment of personal talk was over and that he had been warned off. He shook O'Neill's hand, murmuring his goodbyes. At the door Michael turned, "I want you to know I am grateful for the work. It makes me happy to know the money is going to the Cause. If ever I can do you a favor, please call on me." He shut the door firmly.

Now why did I say that, he thought as he left the building. O'Neill had as good as told him, *stay away from my daughter, you low-life scum.* You haven't a chance. Something rose in Michael, a hot flash of anger and pride. By God, he was as good as O'Neill. O'Neill was no saint! There were rumors of murders when things went bad at his various operations.

Last week a policeman who was on the take but who'd had a change of heart and was starting to sing to the higher ups had been found shot in a back alley off the docks on Broadway. *The Saint Louis Dispatch* had speculated that he was shot interrupting a robbery, but no perpetrators had been traced. In the photo taken at the solemn high Requiem Mass at St. Patrick's, O'Neill appeared in the front row of the mourners, next to the cop's grieving widow and three children. What a hypocrite! Michael wondered again how much Rose knew or suspected about her father.

As he hurried back to the rooming house in the harsh cold, he pictured Rose in the light of the candles on Christmas Eve, her soft rounded cheek, the long dark lashes that framed those eyes, blue-green as the bay at home on a sunny day, her sudden laugh as his fingers met hers, and the frank way she had gazed at him. A girl of spirit, not shy. What did he have to offer a girl like that, a girl who read French, who would go to Europe, to great cities with balls to meet the eldest sons of Earls, a girl who would hold her fan in that flirtatious way, peering over it to see who was admiring her? Damn it! He was getting mad just thinking about the distance between them. And yet, she was the daughter of a gangster in a Midwestern city, a man from Kerry trying to claw his way to a position of power.

Michael left the dining room early after supper, not stopping to smoke and read the day's paper with Finn and Mr. Barth as usual. He wrapped himself in the one blanket from the bed and huddled in the easy chair, the oil lamp burning beside him. He closed his eyes and pictured taking Rose to Ireland, going down to Bantry in a jaunting car, her body swaying toward him at every bump in the road as they made their way south and west toward the sea. Then the coming home to the house where he'd grown up, smoke rising from the chimney, Queenie dashing out to greet them, but there the dream ended. There'd be no family to greet him, or rather only his dour brother Martin, the only O'Donovan left in all of Bantry. And in Bantry he was a wanted man.

Michael, you are the biggest fool, he chided himself. *You've never even spoken to the girl, you dolt. How do you know she's not a cold-hearted snob like Lady Caroline?* He laughed at himself and got up to find the bottle of whiskey he'd bought with his first paycheck. He poured himself three fingers and began to sip, the warmth spreading through him quickly as he stared into the flame that wavered and danced in the draft.

He suspected Rose was a girl he could love. The question was, could she love a man like him? And how in the hell could he get to know her? Soon, drowsy and warm, he heard the sound of needles clicking at the glass panes of the window and looked out to see glittering sleet falling in the light of the gas lamps. He lowered the wick of his own lamp and undressed, falling into bed with the clicking of the sleet to lull him into sleep.

CHAPTER TWENTY

....

By May, Holyoke had blossomed into a leafy, sweet-smelling town, with clear skies most mornings as Eileen made her way to the factory. She could leave their rooms now dressed lightly in a long skirt, blouse, and smock, with only a shawl against the early morning chill. John left for his job on the dam in the dark each morning, but she didn't have to be at the factory until seven. The walk to the factory was a joy as she breathed in the scent of lilacs bursting into bloom in the park near the river.

As she crossed the bridge that led to the Mill, she was joined by scores of women, all chattering loudly as they greeted one another. Eileen had made friends with a few of the girls, one especially from Dublin named Maeve. Maeve was single, supporting her invalid mother and her little brother. At twenty-five, Maeve was someone Eileen admired for her wit and fierce independence. She'd told Eileen how she been educated by the nuns of the Presentation in Dublin before her father was killed in an accident and her family left Ireland. She loved to talk about poetry and novels with Eileen. Eileen knew that Maeve would make something of herself, maybe become a teacher, someone who would not need to depend on a man. Eileen was sorely tempted to confide in Maeve about the loss of Thomas, but so far, she'd shied away from opening herself up to her new friend. They saw one another only at work, and Eileen was afraid she would break down if she began to tell her about the baby.

"Well, if it isn't the fair Eileen from Bantry Bay," a voice called out. Eileen turned around to see Maeve hurrying to catch up with her as they crossed the bridge. They linked arms, and laughing, began running to get to the factory before the second whistle blew. Once inside, the women rushed to their machines, slipping on their smocks, and pulling their hair back in bandannas.

Talking was forbidden once the shift started, so it wasn't until the first break for tea at eleven that she and Maeve could chat. Eileen had told Maeve about her brother Michael, now living in St. Louis, and she'd teasingly suggested that Maeve might be interested in such a handsome scoundrel. Then they would be sisters, a family. Maeve had tossed her head and laughed, but she often asked Eileen if she'd heard from her brother. Now as they sat together during the tea break, Eileen turned to ask Maeve, "So how long are you going to stay on here at the factory wasting your talents?"

Maeve looked down, and then laughing, said, "Until you introduce me to that handsome brother of yours."

Eileen, lowering her voice, started to tell her about his involvement in the IRB when they noticed the foreman, Mr. Wallace, headed toward them.

"Mrs. Sullivan," the foreman said, out of breath, his face flushed, "I am sorry to tell you there has been an accident at the dam. It gave way and many are drowned. They're bringing the survivors to the hospital, so you are free to go and find out about your husband."

Eileen could not move. Maeve helped her rise and led her past all the women staring at them, whispering, all with horrified looks as they passed. Maeve looked at Wallace, "Please, sir, may I have permission to go with her? She's in shock, surely."

Wallace stared at her for a moment. "Well, I'll have to dock your pay for the time you are gone," he huffed.

"Then do it!" Maeve said, shooting the boss a look of contempt as she grabbed Eileen's arm and steadied her. "Where are they taking the wounded?" Maeve screamed at Wallace.

"To the Providence nuns in South Hadley!" Wallace looked at Eileen, who clung to Maeve. "Wait! I'll have Johnny take you there in the cart."

The two women clung to the sides of the work cart as it jostled through the streets toward the nuns' convent and clinic. Nervously, Maeve chattered on, explaining that these nuns had come only a few years before from Canada and were taking in the sick and dying as well as orphans from Holyoke.

By the time the two women reached the plain two-story convent, a crowd was milling around, waiting to hear from the doctors if any bodies had been identified. Maeve asked a man standing next to her what happened at the dam, watching Eileen all the time, and trying not to let her hear the details. Eileen rocked back and forth, with her arms wrapped around her body, her eyes unseeing. She kept whispering in a monotone, "What have I done? What have I done, dear Mother of God?"

"Hush now, alannah! You've done nothing! The dam gave way while a crew was hammering the planks into the stones of the river below, and the men tumbled over the wall and into the raging river. Does your husband know how to swim?" Maeve watched Eileen closely.

"Sure, I don't know. I doubt it, I doubt it!" Eileen's voice rose.

The hours crawled by, and still no one appeared at the door of the nuns' house. Finally, a man dressed in a black suit opened the door and faced the crowd. He clutched a sheaf of papers, and despite the mild, windless day, the papers shook in his hands. The crowd pressed close, straining to hear his voice.

"Ladies and gentlemen," he began, "first I shall read a list of the names of the men who survived and are here being treated. The second list will be the names of the men who drowned, but whose bodies we have recovered and are here. Finally, I will read the names of the men whom we have not located so far."

His voice shaking, he read out the names of six men who were being treated. Shouts and cries of "Thanks be to God!" rose from several women. Then he began the second list. "Bodies recovered: John McCarthy, Edward Fagan, Thomas O'Brien, John Sullivan. . . ."

Eileen stared into Maeve's eyes. "I knew it! I knew he was dead."

All around them women shouted, keening, moaning over and over, "No! No! I don't believe it." There was a rush as people began shoving and pushing their way into the house, demanding to see the bodies. Eileen stood stock still.

Maeve pulled her along gently. "Eileen, darling, let's go into the house and talk to the sisters. They will take you to him." Eileen followed her, clinging to her hand.

They were met at the door by a tiny old nun, her face solemn but calm. "I am Mother Mary Catherine. Please come in, ladies."

"Mother," she whispered. "I am Eileen Sullivan, wife of John Sullivan. His name was on the second list. . . ." Her voice faltered.

"Come this way, dear."

The two women followed the nun into a room to the right of the front door. Six bodies lay beneath sheets. Mother Mary Catherine led them quietly to the last body by a window. There was a tag, neatly printed and pinned to the sheet: John Sullivan.

The nun glanced at Eileen and asked in a low voice, "Are you ready, Mrs. Sullivan?"

"Yes," Eileen breathed.

Gently as a mother uncovering her sleeping infant, the nun pulled back the sheet. Eileen moved to the cot. John was sleeping only, was her first mad thought: his hair brushed, his face clean and peaceful, his hands entwined with a rosary. She bent over him and grasped his hand, cold, so cold. *Like her own heart.* She had never loved the man. Outwardly she had been a good wife, taking care of John, helping with the chores on the farm, making his food, and mending his clothes, all things a servant would have done. When Thomas was born, they'd grown a bit closer in their mutual love for the boy, but after his death they'd grown apart once more. John knew she didn't love him. He'd felt her stiffen at his touch night after night when they were first married until, in this last year, they'd not lain together at all. What had he thought in his last moments as he struggled in the river, knowing he was going to die?

Suddenly Eileen stood up straight, dry-eyed. "Yes, this is my husband. Thank you so much for caring for his body."

Maeve looked at her strangely. Eileen knew she should be showing sorrow, terrible grief, but she plunged on, "Mother, I will make arrangements for John's burial and return when I have someone to help me take the body to St. Jerome's." Her voice was steady as if she were making arrangements for the delivery of some household furniture.

The nun took her arm, pressing it to her side, and Eileen smelled the starched linen, the clean soap smell of all nuns. "You are in shock now, my dear," the sister said kindly. "Go home and rest." She looked at Maeve. "Will you be able to stay with her this evening?"

"Yes, Sister, once I've gone home to check on my mother and brother, I'll spend the night with Eileen. Sure, she has no one else in the world to care for her now except a brother in St. Louis." When they came out into the street, the work cart from the factory was nowhere to be seen, so the two women began the long walk back to Holyoke in silence.

Eileen walked unseeing. In a few moments, John's life had ended, and the horror of it was he had drowned. The black waters had taken him down to death, and now the image of Thomas's body being flung into the sea swept over her. She sobbed, leaning on Maeve, telling her at last the whole story of their child, his sickness on the ship over to America, and the agony of his death. Maeve held her close, trying to soothe her.

When they finally reached Eileen's rooms, Maeve insisted on coming up and fixing the tea. Eileen sat at the table, watching Maeve as she bustled around the room, bringing out the bread, butter, and jam, and slicing the bread in thick pieces for the two of them. Eileen drank the tea, hollow-eyed and silent. She gagged as she tried swallowing a bite of bread and pushed the plate away, rising and looking into Maeve's eyes. "Maeve, I thank you for all your kindness. But you don't have to stay with me. I'll be fine, sure enough."

Maeve started to protest, but something about the set of Eileen's chin and the coldness in her eyes silenced her. She rose and embraced Eileen, "Well, alannah, you know where I live, so send word if you need me for anything. I will tell Mr. Wallace about John. Then I'll go by St. Jerome's to inform Father Dolan. Don't worry at all at all about the funeral arrangements. I'll be here to help you." Eileen nodded, unable to speak. She took Maeve's hand in hers and pressed it silently.

Alone, Eileen stared around the room. She saw John's heavy jacket, left behind on this mild spring morning, hanging on his chair. She walked into the small, cramped bedroom and gazed at the two pillows on the bed. Then she went to the window, and flung it open, the sounds of the street so normal, so usual. The mild air wafted into the room, and she breathed in deeply. Something was struggling to rise in her. She lay on the bed, not on her customary side, but in the middle, stretching out her arms and her legs. She could smell her husband here, his heavy scent of pipe smoke, and a faint trace of his sweat on the sheet.

She'd never in her life been alone. She'd gone from her mother's house to her husband's house, and to this place in America, which could not truly be called her home. She was not yet twenty, and life stretched out before her. Was she wrong to think she might enjoy life once more? Was this rising sense of freedom obscene in the face of her husband's drowning only a few hours earlier? What kind of woman was she? She lay there, taking in deep breaths. As the evening closed in, Eileen slept at last, while the swallows twittered in the early spring dusk, and the sun sank once more behind the blue hills.

Sixteen men had drowned in the accident, the *Springfield Republican* reported. One witness, Dr. Robert Tucker, gave a description in the paper the next day: "I was watching the men at work, pounding the nails into the timber planks that were laid out above the rocks where planks had been bolted securely in place. Suddenly the east end of the newly constructed dam began to give way, and the men lost their balance and were swept into the river rushing into the gap. It was a fearful sight, and the men's desperate cries for help still sound in my ears."

The funerals, most of which were held at St. Jerome's, lasted over a week. Eileen was surprised to see so many mourners at John's Requiem Mass. The front pews were full of men from the dam project, as well as several women from the mill, led there by Maeve. Even the foreman, Mister Wallace, showed up. Eileen, dressed in her Sunday black dress, with her face hidden by a veil that she drew down from her hat, walked into church with Maeve beside her. Was it only three years ago she had made her way toward John in St. Finbarr's Church in Bantry as a reluctant bride? Now she faltered as she walked up the aisle toward the wooden casket covered with a white linen pall. Maeve's strong hand was under her arm. At last, they reached the front pew.

Father Dolan, his deep voice echoing in the half-empty church, read out the gospel, "I am the Resurrection and the

Life: he that believeth in Me, although he be dead, shall live, and everyone who liveth and believeth in Me, shall never die."

But it was not true! Her beloved child had died a cruel, painful death, and now John was gone. How could she believe in this God? He had let the most precious gift of her son be snatched away. She stared up at the life-size image of Christ on the cross, hanging high over the sanctuary. *Even your own Son suffered before He died a horrible death,* she thought angrily. *What kind of Father are you anyway?* Eileen sat through the sermon, unmoving, dry-eyed.

After the burial she stood in the graveyard accepting the condolences of the congregation. She was surprised when she saw Miss Ely from the library approaching her.

"Eileen, I was so sorry to hear that your husband was one of the victims. If there is anything I can do, please let me know," she said gravely. She took Eileen's hand in her own, and her eyes glistened.

"Thank you, Miss Ely," Eileen said, barely able to speak.

"And of course, there is no need to for you to come into the library this weekend. Take all the time you need to recover." Miss Ely looked into Eileen's eyes, searching for grief surely, Eileen thought.

"Oh, but I'd like to come back," Eileen said hurriedly. "The hours alone will drag, I'm sure."

Miss Ely nodded, starting to walk away, when she turned suddenly, "Eileen, have you no family to be with you now? Is there anyone who will be coming to help?"

Eileen said quickly, "I have two brothers, one back in Bantry, and one here in America, in St. Louis. I haven't even written them yet."

Miss Ely nodded, "Well then, I'll look forward to seeing you when you can come back."

Eileen dreaded the thought of sharing the news with her brothers. What could either of them do now? Martin was not coming over here to rescue her, that she knew. And Michael?

She had such an uneasy feeling about his life now, all the vague talk about a printing job, and connections still to the IRB. And yet the thought of staying here in Holyoke, working in the mill, and coming home each night to the empty room. . . .

The day was overcast, a light breeze playing with the women's dark dresses as they walked back to the Flats from St. Jerome's. It smelled like rain, and just as they entered the rooming house, the rain started as a slow patter, then a torrent. Eileen tried not to think of John's body in the casket, the rain drumming on the pine box as the men covered it with dirt.

Maeve bustled around: making the tea, cutting the ham and bread, and laying out a cake the women from the mill had dropped off. There'd been no gathering at her house after the funeral as there would have been in Bantry, nor any wake before the funeral either. It was a meager farewell she'd given John, she knew, but they had few friends here. No family to grieve.

The two women ate slowly with little talk, only a few comments about who had showed up for the funeral, when Eileen stood and embraced Maeve. "Maeve, please take the rest of the cake home to your mother and brother. I cannot ever thank you for your goodness to me. You have been the sister I never had."

"Eileen, darling, no need to thank me. Sure, you and I will be better friends than ever now. You'll spend every Sunday dinner at our house for some good singing before the fire. That little rascal brother of mine loves it when you come and will be expecting the treats you bring." She smiled at Eileen then as she put on her jacket. Eileen wrapped the cake carefully in paper and tied it with a string. The women embraced in silence at the door, and then Maeve clattered down the stairs.

Eileen sat at the table. Every bone in her body ached, but she had to let Michael know about John. If only he were here now, his eyes shining with love and sympathy for her. He knew her better than anyone. Above all, he knew she hadn't loved John, and he had fought hard to prevent the marriage. He was the only one who could really understand the mixture of sorrow and relief she was feeling. How alone she was.

She took paper and dipped her pen in a bottle of ink. *My dear brother,* she began, *it is with sadness that I tell you the terrible news of John's death in an accident. . . ."* When she finished the brief one-page letter, she did not stop to re-read it, just sealed it, and left it propped on the table to mail in the morning. Surely, he would come.

The weeks that followed brought no answer from Michael. Eileen tried to be patient, knowing it took at least twelve days for a letter to reach St. Louis, and then twelve more to arrive in Holyoke even if he had written immediately. The work at the mill deadened her feelings all day. It was only when she came home in the bright spring evenings to the empty rooms that loneliness set in.

Did she miss John? That first surge of freedom had subsided into a dull hollow place in her soul. She was surprised that her nightly escape into reading did not even bring relief. Miss Ely had introduced her to Dickens, and she was deep into *Great Expectations* now. She thought bitterly of her own shattered expectations each evening when she picked up the fat volume.

The one bright spot in the month of June was a letter from Father Gleason in Bantry in answer to her letter with the news about John. She had poured out her doubt and confusion to the priest, telling him how guilty she felt now at her lack of love for John, her coldness, and her refusal to even try to love her husband. His letter was a ray of light, a precious gift. She read it over and over:

> *Cara,*
>
> *It was with great sorrow I read the news of John's death in the accident at the dam. How I wish I could have been there to say the funeral Mass, to help you have a real Irish wake, and to console you after another bitter blow in*

your young life. I immediately walked over to your cousin Kathleen's house to tell her and her husband also, as well as to your brother Martin's house. Everyone here is shocked and sorrowful at John's death. Kathleen said to tell you when I wrote that she misses you sorely and wishes you would "come back to Bantry where you belong." Martin promised he would write soon, and he too, told me he wished you would come home and "keep house for him." Somehow, I can see your face when you read that!

Eileen, let an old celibate priest give you some advice now. You wrote of your guilt at having never really loved John. Sure, you tried to be a good wife in spite of the terrible wrong we here in Bantry did you in not opposing that marriage. I carry the pain of that every day. The Catholic Church forbids anyone to enter marriage against his or her will, and I let that happen. I should have been much more forceful with your dear departed, but quite formidable mother. You have nothing to feel guilty about, my dear.

Now life has given you another chance at true happiness after the terrible sorrow of losing your son. You did your best to be a good wife to John and gave him so much joy in his little son.

But now you are free, Eileen! You are young and strong, and as our Lord says, "I have come that they may have life, and have it in abundance." Seize your life and make it something beautiful. God wills your happiness, Eileen, and you have much to give the world with your youth and energy. My blessing and my prayers are daily for you,
Father Hugh
PS The roses you helped me prune at the rectory that day as we talked are thriving!

Eileen wept every time she read the letter, and the creases became sharp as she folded and unfolded it almost every day. She could picture Father at his dining-room table, his whiskey glass near at hand, bending over the letter as he wrote late at night by the light of the oil lamp. Then the trip to the post office in Bantry the next day to mail it himself so that old Mrs. O'Malley wouldn't be tempted to peek at a letter left lying on the table to be mailed to the States! She had to laugh as she remembered the trembling curtain in the rectory window as Mrs. O had tried to make out what she and the priest were in such earnest conversation about.

One Saturday evening in July, Maeve insisted that Eileen accompany her to the band stand in the park where there was a concert in the long, light-filled evening. The two women sat on a blanket on the grass, sipping the lemonade they bought from a kiosk, and lay back under the trees listening to the Strauss waltzes, the mazurkas.

As the sun set, an old man rose, and intoned a poem in Gaelic. The crowd grew silent. Eileen sat transfixed as his voice rose in the dusk:

> *On some island I long to be,*
> *a rocky promontory, looking on*
> *the coiling surface of the sea.*
> *To see the waves, crest on crest*
> *of the great shining ocean, composing*
> *a hymn to the creator, without rest.*
> *To see without sadness the strand*
> *lined with bright shells, and birds*
> *lamenting overhead, a lonely sound.*
> *To hear the whisper of small waves*
> *against the rocks, the endless sea-*
> *sound, like keening over graves.*
> *To see the shift from ebb tide*
> *to flood and tell my secret name:*
> *"He who set his back on Ireland."*

The words lingered in the air: "He who set his back on Ireland." That's what she had persuaded John to do. . . set their backs on Ireland. No one would remember their secret names with John buried here in a small town in America. Since the day she sailed from Queenstown with the boy in her arms, Eileen had never felt the pull of home as fiercely as she did that night. She could almost smell the sea, its tangy salt air; she could glimpse the town of Bantry from high on the hill over the bay, shimmering in the fading light of a July evening. Maybe she should go home and start again. But where was home now? Back home with Martin, she would be his spinster housekeeper, the widow Sullivan, growing old beside her dour brother.

When Michael's letter finally arrived, she had the answer she'd secretly hoped for. He wrote pleading with her to pack up and head for St. Louis. He had contacts, now, he said, and would find her a place to live and work too. He was sorry about John, but it would be wonderful to have her near him. He enclosed twenty dollars to pay all the expenses in moving, including a train ticket to St. Louis.

She said nothing to Maeve or Miss Ely for a few weeks, trying to decide what to take and what to leave. She'd head west, and it would be better to travel light, she knew. Father Gleason's words sang in her memory, "Seize your life," he had said. Well, she would seize it once more to see what could happen. She had faced the worst things in life; she had little left to lose.

CHAPTER TWENTY-ONE

....

On a hot, sticky morning in St. Louis, Michael walked swiftly through the streets of downtown until he reached Egan's. O'Neill had sent word that morning that he wanted to see him before he reported for work at his job. Michael paced back and forth nervously in the outside room. *Was he being fired?*

O'Neill opened the door himself, welcoming Michael with unusual warmth. "Come in, come in, my boy," he puffed on his cigar, shaking Michael's hand, and indicating a chair in front of his desk. "Just thought I'd check and see how you've been getting on with the work."

"Fine, fine, sir," Michael leaned in, hoping that O'Neill had not heard anything negative about his performance. Truthfully, he'd been bored with the days spent raking in cash from various businesses across town.

O'Neill gazed at him through the smoke, "Not getting tired of this small stuff?"

Michael waited before answering. Where was this leading? O'Neill tilted his chair back, eyeing him closely, "I know you were involved with some dangerous activity back in Ireland, with the Fenians. Some assault on a British garrison that went nowhere?"

Michael swallowed hard, fighting back the temptation to respond with scorn to this overweight, comfortable crook in St.

Louis who seemed to have little interest in what the Irish back home were facing. "That's right," he answered curtly.

O'Neill looked at him for a long minute. As if reading his mind, he leaned back in his chair, puffing slowly on his cigar before he said, "You must think we here in St. Louis neither know nor care about Ireland, that we're just here fattening our own coffers," his face reddened as he coughed, "but I want you to know, boy, that my own mother and father died in the famine years in Kerry, and my brothers and I had nowhere to go, no one to turn to. I'm not even sure where my parents are buried. We fled as stowaways on a boat to England, and when I was a teenager, I was finally able to come over here. So, I have no problem with violence against the fucking British." He sat back, taking a long pull on the cigar. His voice lowered, "I thought you might be interested in a meeting tonight here at Egan's pub. It's the local branch of the Fenians, gathering to hear John Devoy, the leader of the Clan na Gael."

Michael started, "Why, I heard him speak once in New York. He brought down the house that day!"

O'Neill, leaned in, "So if you are interested, Michael O'Donovan, the meeting's at nine o'clock, and the password is Michael Davitt."

Michael knew about Davitt, the IRB hero who was now in Dartmoor Prison for his participation in a raid on Chester Castle to obtain arms for a Fenian uprising. As a fourteen-year-old, Davitt lost his arm working in a British factory after his family was evicted from their home in County Mayo for being behind on the rent. There were rumors that Davitt had been tortured while he was in solitary confinement.

Michael inhaled, "Thank you, sir. I appreciate your telling me about the meeting. I want to be back in the good graces of the Fenians if they'll have me."

O'Neill laughed. "Oh, they'll have you, my boy. Don't worry about that. You're needed for the Cause, man, never forget that."

That night Michael hurried toward Egan's, wondering if he'd misjudged O'Neill. Sure, the man lived in luxury, so he was certainly profiting himself from his criminal activity. He wished he knew how much money O'Neill was raising for the Fenians. The organization had recently been declared illegal in the States, so O'Neill was playing a dangerous game. But if he was truly working for the Cause, then didn't the ends justify the means? He was raising money for arms to be sent to free Ireland from the British.

No, that was not what Father Gleason had drilled into their heads all those years ago in the First Communion classes. It was just the opposite. The ends never justify the means. But then why were half the priests, and even some of the bishops in Ireland, secretly in favor of the Fenians' cause? Well, no use in theological hair-splitting now. He was in it up to his neck, stealing, lying, cheating merchants of their hard-earned money, even cheating the United States government!

Egan's saloon was packed three-deep at the bar, every table and nook crowded with men drinking and waiting to see and hear from the legend, John Devoy. Michael, surprised at the crowd, flashed back to those secret gatherings of the Brotherhood in Bantry under cover of darkness. Here the Brotherhood was illegal, yet every Irishman he'd met in St. Louis seemed to know when and where the meetings were held. The police force was heavily Irish, so they looked the other way. He suspected that many in the crowd were police, just not in uniform.

He caught sight of Mike Finn and nodded as Finn waved him over to his table. He looked around to see if O'Neill was in the room but didn't see him.

"Here he is, the hero of Bantry Bay," Finn called out as Michael approached his table. The other men laughed and Michael shook hands all around. "No, men, I'm serious! This man saw action in '67 in the Rising in Cork."

"A fat lot of good we did," Michael said, his face reddening. That futile attempt still rankled. Suddenly a hush spread throughout the dimly lit room. O'Neill entered, followed by a young man, handsome, dark-haired, with a neatly trimmed beard. A murmur rippled through the crowd. Devoy himself!

O'Neill raised his hands to quiet the crowd. Next to the slight, intense young man, the overweight O'Neill looked aged, with an unhealthy flush to his face. He raised his voice, "Now gentlemen, we have here a hero of our great cause, the founder of Clan na Gael here in America, Mister John Devoy."

Cheers arose and someone began singing, "Old days we are fighting /Head to the place we faced it before/ While there are Irish there's bound to be fighting/ As long as the Saxon remains on our shore!"

Wild clapping followed, with Devoy motionless, a slight smile playing over his face. O'Neill raised his hands again for quiet. "We all know that John has endured a bloody six years in prison, during which he was punished again and again for organizing strikes among the prisoners. On his release, the British exiled him from Ireland forever. That was their big mistake, for now he is among us, we the exiled but still loyal Irish in this great land of opportunity. He is leading the fight over here by raising money for arms, for a fight that must be won!" More cheered. "But now let's listen to our leader, a leader who has sacrificed all to the Cause of freedom and justice for Ireland. Gentlemen, I give you John Devoy, patriot and hero."

As Devoy began speaking in a quiet voice, Michael thought how much more dignified the setting had been in New York last year when he'd heard the great man speak on an autumn afternoon in St. Patrick's. The public had been invited, and in the front pews sat Irish politicians, wealthy businessmen, lawyers, and journalists.

This crowd in St. Louis was rowdy. The bunch of petty criminals, mostly drunk by now, quieted to hear their leader.

Devoy began, "My good fellow Irishmen, I thank you for gathering here tonight in the Cause of Ireland and her freedom.

Like many of you, I know first-hand the cruel injustice of the British who have oppressed us for four centuries. I was born in County Kildare, the grandson on my mother's side of a veteran of the Rising of 1798. When I was ten years old, I refused to sing 'God save the Queen' in school, and was, of course, beaten by the schoolmaster. At age eighteen, I joined the Fenians, convinced by then that passive resistance and political machinations were never going to persuade the British to give us our independence. We would have to take it, *by any means necessary*." His voice rose with the last words.

The men pounded on the tables in a thunderous roar. Michael listened, spellbound, as Devoy laid out the history of the struggle, invoking the names of the leaders from Wolfe Tone to Daniel O'Connell. He ended the rousing speech with a plea for help, his voice rising, saying that now the only way forward was military action to drive the British from the land ". . . by any means necessary!" Once again, the crowd roared. Men banged their fists on the tables and raised their glasses to the hero of the day, John Devoy.

As Michael walked home through the dark, quiet summer night, he missed Ireland sorely. Devoy's passionate speech had summoned up images of his home: the fields softly glowing on late summer nights like this one; the sound of the sea never ceasing as he walked back to the cottage from Blackthorn House; the lamp burning in the window; his mother preparing their tea.

But no, he was romanticizing the past. He was forgetting the incessant reminders every day of his life in Ireland that his fate was not in his own hands, that he was part of a subject people, with no voice in their government, and no chance to go to a university. There was no way not to be made to feel inferior to the gentry, loyal only to England, who owned the land of his ancestors, and who above all, had let millions of Irish people perish when there was plenty of food in Ireland. Only the potato crops failed, but that was all the poor farmers had to live on. All the rest: the grain and the beef, had been shipped to England. The great starvation, or an Gorta Mór, as his mother always called it. No, the ghosts of the dead hovered over Ireland, and they would not be at rest until their land became free. Devoy's speech had ignited his passion for the Cause once more.

For this Cause, he'd become a true outlaw, getting deeper into crime in his new country, a country in which he had hoped to begin a new, a better life. Suddenly in the dark street, the image of Rose was before him. What if he could win her? What if it were possible to have Rose and fight for Ireland at the same time?

He began walking, heading for St. Louis Place, to the O'Neill's Victorian three-story limestone house, just to be near this girl who haunted him. The cicadas called to one another, breaking the stillness of the summer night, and the smell of grass after rain rose about him as he strode, full of hope, down the long blocks. He loved looking into windows at night, lamps glowing in curtained rooms, and a shadow on a curtain of someone sitting at a table or reading a book in an easy chair. On a few front porches, he spied a cigar glowing in the darkness and heard soft murmurings, an occasional laugh.

Finally, he reached the house of the O'Neills. It rose above him, staid and secure, a few windows lit from within, but the heavy curtains were drawn against the night. He looked up to a rounded turret room and wondered if it were Rose's. A lamp still burned, even at this hour, and he pictured her getting ready for bed, unpinning her black hair to let it tumble around her, brushing it over and over as she hummed some song of the day. He stood for long minutes gazing at the window, willing her to come and fling it open and see him standing there.

At last, the lamp went out, and Michael turned, laughing softly to himself, beginning the long walk back to his boarding house with its smells of cabbage and cleaning fluids. What a lovesick calf he was! Once more he was playing the part of the peasant mooning after the princess. But not this time. *I will meet her properly. I will win this Rose.* His steps quickened and he felt a surge of joy. He looked up, and through the broad green leaves of the sycamore trees lining the street, he glimpsed the moon, almost full, as it beckoned him on with its silvery, unearthly light.

A week later, Eileen wrote to Michael thanking him for the money and letting him know she'd arranged her train ticket to St. Louis. If all went well, she would arrive on the fifteenth of July. Michael cursed himself that he could not yet afford a nice little place for the two of them. It would be wonderful to come home to his sister each evening, but how could he explain the odd hours he kept, much less, the true nature of his work for O'Neill? He could not bear the thought of his sister knowing the dirty business he was in, far worse than his involvement with the Fenians in Bantry. At least there, he had not been a thief.

On the Saturday before Eileen's arrival, Michael knocked on Mrs. Quigley's parlor door.

"Ah, Mister O'Donovan," she called from the table where she sat, rustling papers scattered in front of her. "And what can I do for you on this beastly hot morning?" The windows of the parlor were open, but the lace curtains wilted, unmoving. The old woman fanned herself, her blouse open at her throat, gazing at him over her pince-nez.

Michael began, "I told you of my sister's loss of her husband in an accident in Massachusetts recently, I believe, Mrs. Quigley." She nodded, a sorrowful look passing over her face as she made the sign of the cross. He went on, "Well, I've sent for her to come and live here in St. Louis. She'll be arriving on the fifteenth of this month, and I was wondering. . ." He let the request hang in the air, unspoken.

Mrs. Quigley rose from the table stiffly, pushing back her chair. "Now you know, Michael, my dear, that I don't take young women, nor even old women in this house, don't you? I've found that having men and women in the same house only leads to trouble, if you understand." She sat down heavily in her easy chair, motioning for Michael to sit also.

Michael nodded quickly, "Oh no, I wasn't going to ask if she could stay here with me. I thought you might know of a place a respectable young widow could stay. She will need a job too, and I would prefer that she not go into service as a maid. She is a very intelligent young woman. She worked part time in a library in Holyoke as well as at the silk mill."

Mrs. Quigley nodded. "Can she sew?" she asked abruptly.

"Yes, our mother was an excellent seamstress and taught Eileen to sew also." *Or at least I hope so.* He waited.

The old woman rose to her feet laboriously and went over to her desk. She ruffled through her papers and finally found the card she'd been looking for. "There's a fine men's clothing store down on Broadway and Washington Avenue, called Schaeffer's, owned by a German. He makes men's coats, suits, and shirts, and usually hires women to do much of the sewing. You might check and see if he is hiring. The pay is not bad, I understand. As far as lodging, there are lots of rooming houses that cater to women. Sometimes, people even rent a room in their house to a single woman. I think you should check first at Schaeffer's and see if there is a position open. He may even have some employees who could help your sister find a place to live." She smiled up at Michael, "You are a good brother, Michael O'Donovan."

"Thanks so much, Mrs. Q! You've been very kind."

"Well, we Irish have to stick together, don't we? It's not everyone who is happy to give work to the Irish. Sometimes we just have to grab what we can." She looked shrewdly at him then, and Michael realized that she knew a lot about what he and Finn were involved in, and now he understood that she too was in the game in some way.

CHAPTER TWENTY-TWO

....

Fighting back tears, Eileen watched Maeve waving to her as the train pulled away from the station in Holyoke. She'd spent her final night with Maeve, and the two of them had made a visit to John's grave in St. Jerome's Cemetery on that last afternoon. The two women stood beneath the shade of an oak tree, staring down at the simple marker:

JOHN SULLIVAN
B. BANTRY, IRELAND 1827
D. HOLYOKE, MASS. 1871
REQUIESCAT IN PACE

The hastily carved stone plaque revealed little of the life John lived, life that had been cut short by his violent death. He'd lost his first young wife and child, married a girl who never loved him, and suffered the death of his beloved little Thomas. They'd grown closer in the two years of the child's life, and Eileen wondered, if they had not lost the boy, could they finally have been happy together? Now who would remember him, who'd keep his picture with a candle burning in front of it? Who would have masses said for his soul? Well, that would be the least she could do in his honor despite the hard truth that she would not miss him.

At last, Maeve had taken her arm and together the two women strolled in silence through the church cemetery in the late summer afternoon with only the sounds of the sparrows twittering in the elms and oaks that shaded the dead.

Now as the train sped from Holyoke, her heart beat fast. She was going to Michael! She'd never traveled by train, and she sat back facing the window, drinking in the countryside as it rolled swiftly by. With Michael near, she could begin her life again. A letter from Kathleen had arrived the week before her departure, begging her to come back to Bantry. She'd not answered the letter because how could she explain the eagerness she felt to be moving to a new city, the fourth largest in the United States? How could she admit to her cousin that finally through a horrible accident she was free, and that a new life spread out before her, a life with no one to tell her what to do or how to be, maybe even whom to love?

She blushed. What kind of woman was she to be thinking of love with her husband not cold in the ground? Both ladies across from her slept with their mouths hanging open, still clutching their bags to their chests. In her lap, she held the copy of *Wuthering Heights* she had stolen from Blackthorn House. Although she had finished it long ago, the book was a memento from home, a comforting talisman of her life in Bantry.

After days that melted into nights on the jolting, shuddering train, Eileen felt her heart speed up again as the conductor announced they were arriving at the station in St. Louis. Steam hissed as the doors opened, and the first blast of the humidity of July hit her. She dragged her valise down from the overhead compartment and then stopped to help her two companions, whose life histories she now knew after days shut in together.

The two elderly sisters bobbed and nodded to her as they parted, thanking her over and over for her kindness and attentiveness to them on the journey. Maiden ladies, they were returning home to St. Louis after visiting a cousin near Boston. Miss

Nettie Burke, the elder of the two, was frail and distinguished, with white hair pulled back in a chignon, and a beautiful violet traveling suit which somehow had managed to stay unwrinkled throughout the trip. Her younger sister Alice, rotund and cheerful, did not seem bothered by the fact that her brown suit was creased and her hat a bit crooked as she smiled up at Eileen.

"My dear, you really must pay us a visit soon. Here is my card with our address. We are at home every Tuesday afternoon."

Eileen took the card and bent to embrace Miss Alice as she whispered, "Oh, thank you so much. I know I'll be needing friends in this big city." She kept glancing around to see if she could spot Michael amid the throng.

Suddenly Miss Nettie took Eileen's hands in hers. "Eileen, we have a large, empty house that we've been rattling around in ever since my sister and her husband passed away. I don't know what your living arrangements are, but my sister and I discussed the matter last night when you fell asleep, and we decided to offer you room and board in our house." Miss Nettie looked over at her sister, who smiled hopefully at Eileen. "You would be such a bright addition to our household," added Alice, clutching Eileen's arm to her warm bosom.

Eileen stood still, touched by this hospitality. "Oh, you are so kind! But first I must see what my brother is planning for us. He seems to have a very good position working for a Mister John O'Neill here in the city."

The two women looked at each other but said nothing. Finally, Nettie said, "Well, we'll be off then. There's our houseman, Malachy, waiting to take us home in the trap. Will you be all right here on your own until your brother arrives?"

"Yes, I'm sure the scoundrel will have some good excuse for being late. Don't worry about me at all!" Eileen hoped she sounded a lot more confident than she was. Where in the name of God was her brother? As the ladies moved away, Miss Alice called back, "Don't forget about Tuesdays at our house!"

Eileen waved, and as she turned back toward the train, spied Michael running toward her, his smile lighting up the gloomy interior of the station. He grabbed her, lifting her off the ground in a tight embrace. When she pushed him back to look at him, she was surprised to see tears in his eyes.

"Why Michael," she laughed, "I didn't know you were such a soft fellow. I think you've grown taller since I saw you last, and what a beautiful suit you have on! Aren't you the fine gentleman these days!"

He scooped up her valise and tucked her arm into his, hurrying her out into the street, apologizing as they walked, "I'm sorry I'm late, alannah. Are you hungry? Let's stop somewhere and have a bite to eat, shall we?"

Eileen nodded happily, gazing at the tall buildings, granite and red brick, rising above them on all sides. It was not quite New York, but St. Louis looked prosperous: a bustling city with horses trotting smartly in front of fine traps and cabs, and men and women dressed in light summer colors in spite of the dust, everyone walking quickly with a sense of somewhere important to go.

Michael pulled her into the doorway of Miss Holland's Tea Room, and in a minute the waiter seated them at a quiet table in the corner next to a window that looked out onto the street. Eileen watched as Michael smoothly ordered a pot of tea, scrambled eggs with bacon, and two Danish pastries. Her brother was at ease after only six months here in St. Louis, with money to spend without counting his pennies.

Suddenly Michael took her hands in his, gazing at her. "So, my little sister is now a widow. I am so sorry, cara."

"Oh, Michael, it was an awful death for John." She began to tell him of the day, struggling to keep back the tears that surprised her. "And the worst of it is that I never loved him, and he knew that. He went down into those waters just as little Thomas did—" She could not finish.

"Eileen, he probably died quickly, without even knowing what was happening. You were a good wife to him, and you gave him joy in his little son in the short time Thomas lived. And now," he spoke carefully, "you have a chance at a new life."

Eileen shook her head, "But he knew; he felt the lack." She blew her nose and lifted her chin. "I will never marry again unless it is someone I choose." She looked at Michael then, and he dropped his eyes, remembering the days before her wedding in Bantry when he could do nothing to stop the marriage. They sipped their tea in silence for a few minutes.

"So, Eileen," Michael began, with a determined cheerfulness, "it's time to talk about what you are going to do here in St. Louis. My landlady has kindly given permission for you to stay a few days with me in the boarding house, although the dear old biddy refuses to rent rooms to women. But she did give me a lead on work for you." Eileen looked up hopefully. He continued, "I think you can sew, right? Mrs. Quigley suggested you might find work at an expensive men's tailoring shop called Schaeffer's." Michael laughed, "Believe me I could not afford to have a suit made there. But someday I will. Anyway, we could go see Mr. Schaeffer after you get settled in my room for now. I have the whole day off for you!" He called the waitress over and asked her to refill their tea.

Eileen tried not to frown. She'd hoped to find a position as a librarian. But perhaps she was reaching beyond herself. She had no real credentials, just some part time experience at a two-room library in Holyoke. She needed a job right away, as the few savings she had were fast disappearing. She would not want Michael to support her. It was time for her to support herself.

She grasped her brother's hand, "That would be grand, Michael dear. I am so happy to be here with you. Oh! I almost forgot. I may already have a room to rent." Michael looked up in surprise. "Yes, I met two very nice ladies on the train from

Boston, the Misses Burke. They are spinsters, still living in the large family home of their parents, who died, leaving the house to them. As we were saying our goodbyes this morning, they invited me to come and rent a room in their house. So, I guess I passed muster, as they say."

Michael gazed at her, amused. "Why, sister, you are the clever one. I thought you'd be scared to death moving so far away once more, but I see you are fully capable of navigating life in America."

Eileen laughed, "Michael, I'm not your baby sister anymore. I just turned twenty this past May." They left the tearoom and headed for Mrs. Quigley's, arm in arm. Eileen took in the shops and the women they passed on the street, dressed in white, pale blues, and beige, summer colors, their wide hats protecting their complexions from the sun. She felt shabby in her dark traveling dress and the black straw hat of mourning.

When they reached Michael's room, Eileen was surprised by its comfort, the homey touches of books and a few prints Michael had hung on the wall, one a country scene from Ireland.

"Until you are settled in your lodgings, I'll sleep down the hall in a spare room Mrs. Quigley is letting me use. But we can spend our evenings here," Michael said, watching her as she shook out the few skirts and blouses she had brought.

She looked at him then. "Michael, just what is the work you have found here? I never did understand. Wasn't it something about printing?"

Michael rose and pulled down the shade of the window that faced the street, trying to avoid her eyes. How much could he let Eileen know? They had always told each other everything, or almost everything, he thought, suddenly remembering the scene with Lady Caroline in the barn at Blackthorn House. He began, "I'm working for a man called John O'Neill," he began slowly. "He is active in the Clan na Gael. We heard Devoy himself speak here the other night, and Eileen, he was on fire!"

Eileen said nothing, just stood watching Michael as he went on, "O'Neill is engaged in various business ventures to raise money for the Cause of Ireland. He owns a pub—or tavern as they call them here—Egan's, where secret meetings of the Clan na Gael are held. The organization is against the law here in the US, so I guess you could say I am involved in illegal matters." He watched her face, noticing the way her mouth tightened as he spoke.

"Oh Michael," Eileen's voice trembled. "I thought you had left all that Fenian malarkey behind when you came to America. I thought you were starting over."

"Malarkey, is it? Eileen, you can't want me to turn my back on Ireland. I love it here because I am a free man, able to work and make my way in the world. But Ireland is my own country, and I'll not rest until she has the same rights the people of America have, the right to decide her own destiny without the heel of Britain on her throat." He stared at his sister. "You of all people should understand when you think of what Da and Mammy faced in the famine times. Why, Eileen, our mother and Martin married you off to poor Sullivan because we hadn't enough money to survive on the land we worked."

Eileen's voice shook, "Michael, I cannot lose you. Whatever you are doing, I can tell it is dangerous. Please tell me nothing will happen to you."

Michael smiled, "Well, I hope something will happen to me! In fact, Eileen, the real secret I must tell you is I have met a girl."

"Oh, I am glad. Can I meet her?" Eileen's face brightened, noticing the gleam in Michael's eyes.

"Not yet. In fact, I've only met her once by accident. She is my boss's daughter, still a schoolgirl at the Convent of the Sacred Heart. O'Neill wants her to go to Europe and meet the gentry over there. I need you to help me get to know her."

Eileen laughed. "You are the comical one! You don't even know the lass. How do you know she's not a high and mighty snob like a certain Lady Caroline?"

Michael's face turned serious. "Eileen, I saw her on Christmas Eve at Mass. Her name is Rose, and she was so fair I could not look away to follow the Mass. When we met at the holy water font and she smiled up at me, I knew. I knew she was the one."

Eileen went over to where her brother sat at the table. She laid her arm on his shoulder and sighed, "Well, I have never felt that way myself toward any man. So, I guess I will have to trust you to know."

The room began to grow dark as the cicadas' night song rose in the elm trees outside the open window. Anyone looking in would have seen the two heads, one black and one brown, close together in the lamplight, whispering far into the humid July night.

On Tuesday afternoon Eileen studied the crude map Michael had drawn for her the night before. She would go on her own to visit the Misses Burke to see if the invitation to rent a room still held. Perhaps the sisters had already forgotten about the young Irish widow they'd met on the train. She'd noticed their alarmed glance when she mentioned the name of John O'Neill. Maybe they'd decide her brother was too disreputable if he worked for an Irish pub owner.

She counted the blocks from Carr Street to Benton Street on Park Place, the home of the Burkes. Michael had remarked that their house was not far from the O'Neills. Eileen liked a good walk, but she was worried about how she'd look once the heat and humidity wilted her fresh white blouse and curled her hair into frizz. Mrs. Quigley had kindly loaned her a parasol when she saw her in the foyer, but by the time Eileen arrived at Benton Street, she was perspiring; her face flushed with heat.

Number Twenty-Seven rose before her: a red brick mansion of three stories, bay windows on the left side of the front door, a spiked wrought-iron fence warning off the uninvited. Tall elms shaded the house, and deep purple hydrangeas bloomed near the front porch. Eileen smoothed her curls back under the straw hat that shaded her face and slipped through the wrought-iron gate. When she rang the bell, she heard footsteps echoing in the hall. The door was opened by a slender young Black girl, dressed in a gray gown and starched white apron.

"Good morning," said Eileen, smiling at the girl whose black eyes shone solemnly in the dark hall. "Mrs. Eileen Sullivan to see the Misses Burke. I believe they are at home today?"

"Yes, ma'am. Come right this way." Eileen followed the girl to a room on the right and waited while she knocked lightly on the door.

"It's a Mrs. Sullivan to see you," the girl announced, smiling mischievously at Eileen as she stood by to let her enter the room.

Murmuring her thanks, Eileen approached the two sisters who were sitting on a settee facing two other ladies, the sound of silver spoons clinking on teacups mingling with soft voices. Miss Alice rose and gave her hand to Eileen.

"Why, Mrs. Sullivan, we are delighted to see you. We were just telling our neighbors about you."

Miss Nettie looked at her approvingly, and introductions were made all around. After a few minutes the neighbors rose and made their excuses as Miss Alice rang a little bell, calling out, "Bess, would you please see the ladies to the door? And bring us some more cakes, if you please."

Then she turned toward Eileen and, with a smooth gesture, indicated that Eileen should move closer to her. "My dear, she began, "we are so happy you came today. My sister and I were just saying that we hoped you would take us up on the offer of a room. But first tell us how you found your brother." She gazed into Eileen's eyes.

Eileen put her teacup down carefully as she tried to think how much she would tell the ladies. "Michael seems to be doing fine. He lives in a boarding house on Carr Street, a place run by a Mrs. Quigley. Unfortunately, Mrs. Quigley rents rooms only to men. Michael, I should tell you, has joined the Clan na Gael. He was very excited about hearing John Devoy speak the other night." She sat back then and watched the two sisters' faces as they took this in.

"Why, is your brother a Fenian?" Miss Alice leaned forward, her plate with the piece of lemon cake trembling on her ample lap.

Eileen decided to be honest. "That he was, back in Bantry. I know he is passionate about the cause of Irish independence."

"Well, aren't we all," said Miss Nettie icily, "but the question is one of methods. The Fenians are reckless hooligans who are hurting the Cause, not helping. I have studied the papers from London and Dublin carefully, and we believe that the way is through negotiation and parliamentary persuasion rather than violence."

At that, Eileen felt her face redden. Was that remark just a guess?

"And didn't you mention that he was working for John O'Neill?" Miss Alice asked, not looking at Eileen as she brushed some crumbs from her silk dress.

"Yes," Eileen said quickly, "something to do with printing and sales, I believe."

"I see."

Eileen rushed on, "The best news is that I've found a job! Michael took me to meet a Mr. Schaeffer, who owns a men's clothing store on Broadway. Maybe you know the place?"

Both sisters laughed, and the tension in the room dissolved. "Why of course!" exclaimed Miss Alice. "That is where our father had all his suits and shirts made. They do excellent work." She clapped her hands, "Oh, you will enjoy working there, Eileen. All the finest people are their customers."

Eileen smiled, "Sure, it will be a thousand times better than working at the noisy, hot mill in Holyoke!" Both sisters nodded approvingly.

Miss Nettie leaned in then and spoke quietly, "I know you met our girl, Bess, when you rang."

"Oh yes, the servant girl." Eileen nodded.

"No, not exactly. She's more like our ward. But it's a long story, so we'll save that for another time," said Nettie as she rose. "Eileen dear, my sister and I would be so pleased if you would come live with us. We have a room on the second floor that would be perfect for you. Let's go upstairs so you can see it."

On the second floor, Miss Alice opened the door to a room in the back of the house. Filtered light from trees in the back yard entered the room through the venetian blinds, bordered by lace curtains. Eileen gazed at a double bed with a white spread, a chest and mirror with a wash basin, a small desk and chair in the corner, with a lamp beside it, and a rose-patterned wool rug over the polished hardwood floor. She swallowed hard.

"What do you think?" asked the ladies together.

Eileen looked at them, her voice trembling, "Oh, I would love to live here. But I don't know what my wages will be yet, so I am not sure I can afford it."

"Tut, tut, my girl," Alice replied, "we can work that out when you come. I know young Bess will be happy to have you here, someone nearer her age than we two old fuddy-duddies!"

As Eileen was leaving, the sisters followed her into the foyer. Miss Alice embraced her suddenly, hugging her to her ample bosom, "We are so happy you will join us! Come as soon as you can." Miss Nettie took her hand quietly, looked into Eileen's eyes, and smiled as she said, "And please invite your brother to come see us too."

As Eileen made her way past the hydrangeas, she let out a sigh. Her blouse under her arms was damp, and she whispered a prayer of thanks to the Virgin Mary that the sisters had not pursued their curiosity about Michael. She wondered how Bess had become the sisters' ward, and what that meant exactly.

A week later Eileen returned to the Burke's house on Benton Street, valise in hand. Michael came with her to carry her bag but really to meet her new benefactors. The ladies insisted he stay for a cup of tea. Eileen perched nervously on the edge of her chair, but after fifteen minutes her brother had charmed the two ladies so well that they insisted on bringing out a bottle of sherry in honor of Eileen's arrival.

Bess sat with them too, laughing shyly at Michael's sallies. Eileen watched her brother, and how at ease he was in any circle. She prayed that O'Neill's name would not come up. When he rose to leave, the sisters invited him to drop in on any Tuesday or whenever he chose to come visit his sister.

He hugged her at the door, murmuring in her hair, "You've landed on your feet, clever Eileen! They love you already."

She tried to smile up at him as she whispered, "Just don't disgrace us, Michael. Be careful, for my sake, please."

CHAPTER TWENTY-THREE

....

B y August, Michael had advanced in O'Neill's estimation. No longer a "shover" of counterfeit money, he'd been promoted to the black-market liquor business, selling imported whiskey, rum, and gin that had been smuggled into the country from Ireland and England by way of small fishing villages near Boston, and from Santo Domingo and Puerto Rico by way of New Orleans.

He now had his own desk upstairs in O'Neill's saloon, right outside the boss's office. There he kept the books with the orders, the money brought in, and the debts owed, all as neat and tidy as the books of any accountant. He had lists of the names and addresses of every saloon, hotel, and private club on the north side that bought from O'Neill. Michael was relieved that he did not have to do the dirty work of actually delivering the goods; that was left to lads like Finn who did it under cover of darkness late at night. Now when people asked him what he did, he could say he was in sales, as he traveled around the neighborhoods in his one fine suit, calling on his customers.

On a sweltering day in late August, O'Neill called him into his office. He motioned Michael to a chair in front of his desk. "You know, my daughter graduates from the Convent of the Sacred Heart next month," he said, puffing on his cigar.

"I'm thinking of having a big shindig at the house." He looked at Michael then, and for one wild minute Michael thought he was going to invite him to her party. "I'd like you to be there as security, you know, just to be sure we don't have any gate-crashers."

Michael swallowed hard. "Of course, sir. I'm happy to do it."

O'Neill stood then and opened a drawer in the bottom of his desk. He pulled out a small revolver and caressed it, rubbing his spotless handkerchief over the barrel. "Take this now, my boy. It's time you had some protection."

Michael tried disguising his dismay. Somehow, he'd still clung to the belief that he was clean, that the stuff he was doing was petty crime whose only victims were the banks and the US government. He hadn't held a pistol since the night of Eileen's wedding when he'd wrenched it away from Caroline in the barn. Now he took the gun from O'Neill with a sinking heart. O'Neill would never see him as someone fit for his daughter. And how could he ever dare to court Rose knowing that he was her father's hired thug, despite his smooth veneer. He felt O'Neill watching him closely. Michael smiled at him, "I hope I never have to use this, sir."

"Michael, I've come to rely on your discretion, let us say." His eyes were hooded in spite of the friendly words. "The party will be on Saturday, the twenty-fourth of September at eight. Get yourself evening dress. You'll need to be mingling among the guests as just another young man. Wear the pistol, of course." Then, handing Michael a sack heavy with ammunition, he sat down at his desk, and Michael knew he was dismissed.

"Have a good night, sir," he mumbled, the words dying on his lips as he gently closed the door behind him.

The following week, the little bell over the door rang as Michael entered Schaeffer's Tailoring Shop. Eileen looked up from the jacket she was working on in the back of the shop. When she saw him, her face lit up, and she rushed over to greet him. Since Mr. Schaeffer had stepped out, his assistant, Henry, came over to wait on Michael. Eileen introduced him then to the other three women she worked with. They were all aflutter at the arrival of her dashing brother.

"It seems I'll be needing evening dress," he said, smiling at the ladies.

Eileen looked at him strangely, but he said nothing, just stood still so that Henry could take his measurements. They spent a half hour picking out the fabric for the suit and the shirt, Eileen happily showing him his choices. "I'll be doing some of the stitching, and you'll have the finest buttonholes in St. Louis," she laughed up at him.

When Mr. Schaeffer came back, Eileen introduced him to her brother and went swiftly back to the table where she had been working. From her spot, she watched as Michael took out some bills from a wallet and handed them to Schaeffer. *Holy Mother of God! Where does he get all that money?* The gnawing feeling in her stomach whenever she thought about Michael's work returned.

Finally, he left the shop, blowing a kiss and assuring her he'd visit on Sunday. "We'll go to 10 o'clock Mass at Holy Name and then have a picnic in Hyde Park, if the weather is fine." She nodded and watched him as he walked briskly past the windows of the shop, a man about important business, his stride seemed to say.

On Sunday morning Eileen skipped breakfast so she could be fasting and receive Holy Communion. The sisters did not approve of going to Mass so late. "Why Eileen," complained Miss Alice, "Surely, you'll faint away from hunger by the time you and your brother have your picnic!" She ran her gaze over Eileen's slim figure. "You are already nothing but skin and bones!"

Her sister rose to Eileen's defense. "Alice, don't bother the girl. Just because you and I have put on the pounds with the years, doesn't mean Eileen has to lose her girlish figure." Miss Nettie smiled up at Eileen from the breakfast table where the sisters were enjoying their Sunday breakfast of bacon and eggs, and toast and jam, with plenty of hot coffee. There was even a stollen from the German bakery on Grand Avenue. Eileen's mouth watered as the delicious smell of fried bacon mingled with the aroma of coffee. She still was not used to having such rich food every day.

Through the dining-room window she spied Michael coming up the walk, so she kissed each of the ladies on their soft, plump cheeks and hurried to the door before Michael could ring the bell. Bess beat her to the door, and she heard Michael murmur something that made Bess laugh.

"Well, I see my brother has been teasing you, Bess," Eileen laughed. "Don't believe a word this smooth-talking fellow says!"

Eileen had grown very fond of Bess in the past few weeks. The girl was smart and quick, and together they baked in the large cheerful kitchen every Saturday, just as she and her mother had baked every Saturday in Bantry. As they worked, Eileen told Bess stories about Ireland and her childhood, but left out the story of her marriage and the loss of the baby. She'd taught Bess to make Irish soda bread, and Bess had taught her how to bake biscuits, so light and melt-in-your-mouth delicious Eileen could not resist having a second helping.

Bess's status in the household was tricky: she was almost family, much more than a servant. She didn't do the cleaning. That was done by a strong young German woman who came in twice a week. The sisters and Bess did the cooking, and Bess had become quite skilled. Bess took her meals with them in the dining room and sat with the sisters in the parlor every evening, darning socks, or mending, and listening attentively when the one of the sisters read aloud.

On Sundays the sisters went to Mass at Holy Name Parish nearby, while Bess went to the Baptist Church on Grand Avenue. Eileen often heard her humming a hymn in her rich, sweet voice. Eileen had been thinking about taking Bess to the fine new library the Burke sisters had told her about on Broadway. She knew the sisters tutored Bess in reading and arithmetic. According to them, she was proving herself to be an eager pupil. Eileen thought of her own hunger for books at Blackthorn House when she gazed at the beautiful volumes in the library. Surely Bess suffered from this same hunger.

This morning Eileen felt a bit guilty leaving Bess behind as she put on her jacket and hat to accompany Michael to Mass. She glanced at Bess and said, "I'll be back this afternoon, so perhaps we can walk over to Park Place with our books and read."

"Thank you, Miss Eileen, but I'm going to a picnic at my church. I'll be back in time to serve a cold supper," Bess replied, nodding to them both before disappearing down the hall.

Eileen linked her arm with Michael's and the two headed out for the walk to Holy Name Church. "I still don't know the story of how Bess came to be the ladies' ward, as they called her," Eileen said.

Michael frowned. "Have you noticed, Eileen, how separate the Negroes are from the White people here? How Whites talk about them?" He strode more quickly as he spoke. "I know Lincoln freed the slaves, but the way people treat the Negroes here reminds me of the way the English look down on the Irish, with that kind of sneer in their voices, as if they were some sort of backward children who have to be kept in their place."

Eileen nodded. "Yes, and that's why I want Bess to read and learn. I don't want her trapped into marriage too soon. . . ." Her voice trailed off and Michael realized she was thinking of her own life, of the marriage she did not want. He glanced at Eileen, struck by his sister's beauty, etched with a sadness around the eyes that revealed a great loss. He knew she would never fully recover from the death of her little son.

At Mass, Eileen got up to receive Holy Communion. She stared at Michael when he did not go with her, but she resolved not to say anything. After all, Michael was a grown man, so who was she to judge the state of his soul? When she returned to her pew, she sank her head in her hands, and a wave of tremendous love and sorrow hit her. She prayed for her mother and father, her little son, and John. *Dear God, I have lost so much, even my own country. But thank You for bringing me through, thank you for Michael and the dear ladies who have taken me in. Help me to find my way in life.*

As she raised her eyes to the altar, the sight of the great crucifix with the dying Christ struck her. *You know what it is to suffer,* she whispered, *so who am I to complain?* But now, she knew, she was hungry for happiness. She took Michael's hand then, and he squeezed it gently as they knelt together. Rays of sun lit up the stained-glass windows into brilliant mosaics of deep blues and reds, the colors falling on their bowed heads.

After Mass, the two made their way to Hyde Park and found a bench in the shade of a tall elm tree. Michael opened the cloth bag and spread out the lunch of sandwiches, red grapes, and sweet rolls. He spied a fellow with a wagon selling root beer, and soon returned with two ice-cold bottles, and a triumphant smile. They ate in silence, watching a nearby family seated on the grass, their three little ones shouting and laughing as they chased each other in a game of hide and seek. Eileen found herself staring at the smallest boy, a beautiful child with large dark eyes and a head of curly brown hair. Would she ever again be able to watch children without this pang in her breast and her womb?

Michael chattered on about some fellow from Cork he'd met at Egan's, when she turned to him. "You know, I've never understood just what it is you do in your job. It must pay you pretty well, I suspect." She stared into his blue eyes until he looked away.

He sighed, picking grass from his trousers, and fidgeting with his shirt collar. "Eileen, I am still a Fenian, as are many men who work for O'Neill." He glanced around nervously, looking for anyone who could overhear them. "The Fenians are an illegal organization here in the States, so we must be careful to work in secret. When John Devoy spoke a few weeks ago, he fired up that drunken crowd in Egan's. He's given everything for the Cause."

"Yes, Michael, but I want to know what you actually do! I have a feeling it is something dangerous." She reached up and touched his face, forcing him to turn his head to her. "Michael, I can't lose you. You are all that is left to me."

He nodded. "I know, Eileen, but listen." He breathed deeply, "O'Neill is involved in many illegal ways of making money. I'm not going into detail here, Eileen, as it is safer for you to be ignorant of the specifics in case you are ever questioned by the police. What I do right now is collect money from illegal bootleg liquor sales, as well as protection money from our customers. A portion of all the money we make is sent to Ireland by way of the Clan na Gael in New York."

Eileen's stomach lurched. She'd known he was involved in something bad with his canny way of diverting all her questions, the nice suit, and the easy way he spent his money. She looked at him in sorrow. "I don't like it, Michael. It is wrong and you know it, whatever you say about the motive behind it."

His smile disappeared and his eyes grew cold. He looked away from her.

Eileen persisted, "Michael, you're a foreigner here. You can be put in jail; you can be sent back to Ireland in disgrace as a criminal element. You are better than that!" Her voice rose and trembled as she held his arm, forcing him to face her

"Eileen, who are the criminals? What the British have done to Ireland is the biggest crime of all. Our grandparents died in the famine the British allowed to decimate our land, for God's sake! Remember our father, his back bent day after day working for the Earl, eking out our small share of potatoes to feed his family. Then dead at age thirty-eight, surely brought down by heartache." He tore off pieces of bread as he spoke, tossing them in the grass for the birds. "Remember Mammy, she who had so much dignity and strength, having to fawn over Lady Mary whenever they met, trying to make sure that her children had positions at the estate." Michael rose and paced the gravel path before her. "And worst of all, they robbed us of our heritage, our language, our way of governing, and our pride, the bastards! The Irish have become the most pitiable of people, a joke." He looked at her then, his eyes blazing, "So no, I feel little guilt for what I am doing now. I am working for my country, for her freedom and for the honor of my ancestors. To hell with my petty crimes in the face of England's four hundred years of pillage!"

He threw himself on the ground beside her. They sat in silence for a while. Eileen gazed at him sadly. "But Michael, you are in a new world here. America is Ireland's friend, and the things you are doing are against her laws. I thought you were wanting to make a new life here, free from the past."

He took her hand in his. "Eileen, I do want that, with all my heart. I told you that I think I have found the girl I want to spend my life with. But I need to make money for myself as well as for Ireland and working for O'Neill has given me this chance." He smiled at her then, "And as soon as I can, I will break free of this work, maybe even return to Ireland with Rose—"

He had never thought before this minute about returning to Ireland. But now it was clear—one day he'd go back and it would be to fight the British Army when the uprising came. How could he drag Rose into such danger? He had said too much.

Eileen's shoulders relaxed, "And when will I be meeting this Rose who has captured the heart of Michael O'Donovan, may I ask?"

"Ah sure, it's a pipe dream, Eileen. The girl barely knows I exist." He pulled her to her feet then, and they gathered up the remains of their lunch, and arm in arm, strolled out of the park. Michael turned to her then and said, "Just for fun, let me show you where this Rose blooms. Her house isn't far from here."

Together they passed under the elms that lined the streets. The mid-afternoon sun dappled their backs with the shadows of the leaves. The streets were quiet, with people's shades pulled low against the languid Sunday afternoon heat. At last, Michael pointed toward a rambling three-story house made of limestone, with gables and porches, shady and inviting. Rose bushes and wisteria bloomed in a side garden. Michael whispered, "I always think that that bay window on the second floor must be Rose's."

"Glory be, what a fine house," murmured Eileen. "And is Rose an only child?"

"Yes, her mother died when Rose was thirteen, so it's just Rose and the old man, along with the servants, of course.

"Well, still, it's a poor house compared to Blackthorn," Eileen said, hiding a smile, "and bought with ill-gotten gains, I might add."

"And how the hell do you think the Earls of Bantry got their wealth," Michael hissed, "if it wasn't on the backs of generations of Irish who had their lands stolen?"

"Oh Michael, I was just teasing you, surely, I was! You've become a fanatic these days."

She grabbed his hand then and pressed it to her lips. Together, they stared up at the massive house. Not a blind trembled in the silent afternoon.

Slowly they moved away, Eileen tucking her arm into Michael's and breathing a Hail Mary to keep her brother safe. She'd had enough of loss.

When she got back to the house on Benton Street, the ladies were taking a rest, so she went back to the kitchen to look for Bess. The pots and pans gleamed on the shelves and the counter shone in the fading sunlight. Bess was nowhere to be seen. Eileen climbed the stairs to her room, took off her blouse and opened the window to catch what breeze happened to float by. From her dresser she took the blue horse that Thomas had loved, and lay down on her bed, holding the soft worn animal to her breast, trying to catch the scent of her child.

CHAPTER TWENTY-FOUR

....

Michael woke with a start. It was graduation day at City House, the day school of the Religious of the Sacred Heart, and he would see Rose today. The humidity of the summer had finally dissipated with the coming of September, and, as Michael walked to the ceremony, he caught a whiff of fall, the scent of burning leaves mixed with smoke from the smelting plant across the river. O'Neill had invited him to the ceremony as a way of preparing him for the security job that night. He was to observe the hundred or so guests that would crowd into the O'Neill's house for the celebration of his daughter's graduation and entrance into St. Louis society, as her father hoped. O'Neill wanted to be sure Michael recognized Rose and her friends.

Little did O'Neill know, Michael thought, how often this spring he had made his way to City House on the corner of Broadway and Convent Avenue, smelling the early May lilacs that hung over the convent wall and hearing the laughter of the girls at handball, hoping to recognize the sound of Rose's laughter since the wall was too high for him to catch a glimpse of her. Somehow it brought him closer to her to know she was there, just behind that wall, safely waiting for him. Then he laughed to himself. What a poor show he was, skulking about after a schoolgirl who barely knew he was alive.

As he entered the chapel, he removed his hat and handed his invitation to the nun at the door. He bowed, "Michael O'Donovan, Sister. I'm a guest of Mr. O'Neill, the father of Rose O'Neill." The tall nun smiled and wordlessly glanced at his invitation, waving him in. Michael sat in the second-to-last pew, close to the aisle so he would have a good view of Rose as the graduates processed in.

The chapel was all white marble, the altar banked with two vases of deep red roses, stained-glass windows glowing fiery red and deep blue in the morning sunlight. The nun playing the organ began the processional, and all rose to watch as twenty-four young women dressed in long white gowns, each with a blue sash across her breast, carrying an armload of red roses, filed gracefully up the aisle. There she was! Rose passed so close to him he could have reached out and touched her; radiant she was, with her dark hair pulled up into a white flowered headband. Michael willed her to look at him, but she passed him swiftly, staring straight ahead.

After Mass, the girls sat to listen to Mother Marie Therese, the head of school, give the graduates her parting words. Her voice, with a hint of a French accent, rang out clearly in the chapel.

"Dearest children of the Sacred Heart, it is with profound pride and love but also a tender sadness that I gaze at you today. We have always demanded the best of each of you, urging you to excellence. We trust we are sending you out into the world armed with the best education we could give you. Over these last years you have studied English, French, arithmetic, both sacred and profane history, geography, mythology, poetry, rhetoric, natural philosophy, domestic economy, painting, drama. You have worked hard, as the ribbons you wear attest.

Above all, we hope that we have prepared you as women who will live their Catholic faith in whatever life you choose, whether as wives and mothers, artists, writers, musicians, scientists, teachers. Dare we hope a few of you will join us as Religious of the Sacred Heart? In whatever life you choose, remember we are all called to follow Christ, a man for the poor and needy. The greatest virtue is love, love for all of God's creation. May our Lord and the Virgin Mary bless you with good health and a joyous life as educated daughters of the Sacred Heart."

Mother Marie Therese stepped from behind the lectern as the girls rose to applaud. Michael watched carefully as each girl approached the nun to receive her diploma, curtsying deeply as they had been taught. What privileged girls, Michael thought. He envied them their studies, although he knew he never had the discipline such a school would have demanded. But then he thought of Eileen. She would have devoured such an education.

Now the girls were filing out, bowing and smiling to their parents and friends in the congregation. As Rose passed him, their eyes met, and smiling broadly, he winked at her. She blushed and walked on without acknowledging him. *What a damn fool,* Michael cursed himself. *Now why did I wink? I couldn't help it!* She looked so solemn, almost sad. Maybe he could apologize at the party. He slipped out of the chapel before O'Neill passed by.

The party on St. Louis Place was to begin at eight. O'Neill had asked him to be there by 7:15 and to station himself inside the foyer, near the receiving line, mingling with the guests, so that it was not obvious he was security. The day before, O'Neill had given him a copy of the guest list. He had seemed unusually agitated and nervous.

"Are you expecting trouble, Boss?" Michael asked.

O'Neill chewed on his cigar, pacing the room, flicking papers on his desk as he passed. "Yeah. There are a couple of guys in this city who are after our business. Hogan over on the north side has been making threats to our guys who do business downtown. They are a bunch of low-life hoodlums, just in it for themselves and willing to use every dirty trick in the book." His fingers trembled as he held his cigar. "A couple of nights lately we've had prowlers in the back yard. They know where I live, and they know about the big party tonight. They would love to disgrace me when I have the Bishop here as well as the bigwigs in the Democratic Party. Watch me all night and I will signal you if I sense trouble. Your job is to ease any uninvited guests out with no one actually noticing anything. What you do with them outside is your business." He stared at Michael then until Michael nodded.

Now Michael inspected himself in the mirror before setting out. His new evening clothes were the most elegant he'd ever worn. Eileen had seen to all the details herself: the sewing around the collar of the coat, the buttonholes, and the silk lining. It fit his slender frame perfectly. He brushed his dark hair back until it shone in the gas lamp. Whatever else happened tonight, he would say a few words to Rose. He was tired of mooning about. He hated to think he'd be carrying a pistol. If she knew that, she'd cut him dead.

O'Neill had sent a carriage for him so that he would look like any other guest arriving. Michael tipped the driver, who whispered as he got out, "Sure, you'll enjoy yourself tonight, O'Donovan! You look like the gentry, begod."

Michael looked at him closely, recognizing Herlihy, O'Neill's henchman, the one who'd pulled a knife on him that first day in Egan's.

People were already arriving, laughing and chattering as they went up the steps of the porch where they were greeted by a footman in uniform. The foyer was lit by hundreds of candles, their flickering light reflected in gold-framed mirrors lining the room. *By God,* Michael thought, *O'Neill is pulling out all the stops.* Even a small orchestra for dancing later.

At a quarter past eight, a trumpet blared a fanfare, and all eyes turned toward Rose as she made her way down the staircase. Michael stared. She wore a deep-red velvet gown with her shoulders bare, and he saw that the folds of the dress were gathered on one side in the shape of a rose. Her dark hair was pulled back and laced with pearls, her face pale, and her chin held high. When she reached the foyer, her friends surrounded her, and her laugh rang out above the rest. Now her eyes sparkled and her color rose. He could not keep his eyes off her.

O'Neill formed a receiving line, and slowly people made their way to greet father and daughter. Michael joined the line, feeling the perspiration on his face, relieved he had thought to bring a handkerchief. *He was some tough guy letting this chit of a girl cause him so much trouble.*

When Michael reached the couple, O'Neill shook his hand and reminded Rose, "Darling, I think you will remember my associate, Mister Michael O'Donovan. You met him at church on Christmas Eve."

Michael bowed over her hand, but when he looked into her eyes, her face flushed. She turned away from her father and whispered to Michael, "You have a lot of nerve showing up today at graduation. I know why you're here tonight, to be my father's hired bodyguard." Michael pressed her hand hard but said nothing, just smiled as if she had said something witty.

The rest of the night was a blur. Michael drank, trying not to let O'Neill see how many times he refilled his glass with the boss's Irish whiskey. Several times O'Neill caught his eye and frowned. He was being watched.

It wasn't until past midnight as the guests were leaving, with O'Neill still in the living room huddled with a few politicians, that Michael saw his chance. Rose had slipped into the library alone. He followed her, shutting the door firmly. She turned around, and he noticed she did not look shocked.

"Rose, please, let me explain why I've come."

"I know why you've come," she said evenly. "You work for my father, and he hired you to be sure there'd be no trouble. I'm not an innocent, Mister O'Donovan."

Michael edged closer, hoping he would not startle her. "It's true I work for your father. But this night has given me the chance to see you, something I've been longing to do since Christmas

Eve. I have not ceased to think about you, Rose. I've even walked by your school many times hoping to catch a glimpse of you." He watched her carefully as if she were a fawn who might dart away.

But the girl surprised him by walking toward him. She stared into his eyes, searching and saying nothing. Michael could bear it no longer.

"Rose, is there a chance I could see you sometime? I'd like to explain why I left Ireland and why I'm working for the Cause here. Maybe we could meet in the park one day."

"Do you think that my father would approve of that?"

"No. He would not. But I have the feeling that you are your own person, Miss Rose O'Neill."

At that, she smiled. "Well, if you are not afraid, I have a music lesson every Friday at City House at two o'clock, and I walk home through the park a little after three. Perhaps we could bump into one another one afternoon, accidentally, of course." The hint of a smile played around her lips.

"I'll be there this Friday. Thank you, Rose!" He bowed, not trusting himself to say more, and left the room, glancing around to see if anyone had seen him. O'Neill was still deep in conversation with the men in the living room, so Michael walked out into the foyer and then onto the porch.

He let out a shaky breath into the damp night air and lit a cigarette. Staring into the dark garden, he looked up through the trees until he glimpsed the moon shining high above, bathing the garden in silver. His heartbeat slowed. The girl had spirit and grit. She was not the timid schoolgirl at all. But he knew the game he was playing was a dangerous one. O'Neill had eyes all over the city, and he had made it clear that he had grand plans for Rose. Those plans did not include an Irishman fresh off the boat, much less an employee doing dirty work for the IRB.

He walked around the back yard, checking all the shadows under the trees and bushes. Nothing. He would bid good night to O'Neill, trying not to think that he was betraying him in the worst way of all by wooing his daughter.

The days after the party dragged. By Friday Michael could think of nothing else. He tried to be cool and offhand while O'Neill kept coming and going through the outer office. He bent over the accounts, avoiding the boss's eyes. It was as if the old man suspected something. He had not dared to comment on Rose when O'Neill thanked him gruffly after the graduation party, stuffing an envelope with cash into his jacket.

When O'Neill stopped at Michael's desk at noon, he looked up, trying not to show alarm. O'Neill looked over Michael's shoulder to see what he was working on. He was silent for a few seconds before he said, "I'm off to a meeting out at Hogan's place in the county. Everything okay here?"

"Yes, sir. I'm almost finished with this month's numbers. I'll wait until Finn comes by with the last collection of this week to tally the whole amount. I may slip out for lunch after a bit." He waited a second, holding his breath.

O'Neill grunted as he put on his suit coat and grabbed his hat. "See you tomorrow then," he called over his shoulder as he left the room.

Perfect! Michael could not believe his luck. He'd spent a good part of the morning planning the lie he would tell the boss when he left at 2:30. He'd brought a sandwich for lunch just in case he'd have to eat at his desk. Now the office was empty, and from the open window that looked out over the street, the sounds of carriages and wagons mingled with the shouts of newsboys selling the *St. Louis Dispatch.* Michael unwrapped the sandwich and pulled a chair up to the window to watch the action in the street. He hated being cooped up in an office these days. September's crisp fall weather had brought a blessed relief from the wet sticky heat of August. He would not arrive bathed in sweat when he met Rose.

He still marveled at the girl's pluck. And no chaperone to contend with either. Then it struck him. What if O'Neill had her followed whenever she was out alone? He wouldn't put it past him, but her father would have to be so careful that Rose did not observe the man. He knew she would be furious to think she was being followed. He'd have to have his wits about him in the park. He was tempted to go downstairs to the saloon for a pint but dared not show up with beer on his breath.

At two o'clock he checked his hair in the mirror and pulled on his best jacket. His new white shirt gleamed, and the dark green tie added just the right note of color against the somber black of his suit. He clattered down the steps to the saloon, nodding to Patrick, the bartender, "I'm off for a bit of lunch, but I'll be back in an hour or so to meet Finn with the drop."

He did not stop to chat, but as he reached the door, Pat called to him, "Sure, you're looking dapper this day, Michael O'Donovan! What's the big occasion?" Michael laughed but did not reply. Damn! His eagerness must be written all over his face.

He walked swiftly up Broadway, turning west at Cass Avenue. Now it was a good ten blocks to St. Louis Place. When he got to the park, he realized he had no idea at which entrance Rose would appear. He sat on a bench near the Market Street entrance, watching mothers pushing their prams, hoping to lull the babies to sleep in the early afternoon air. He wondered if Rose wanted children. She was barely more than a girl herself. The thought of supporting a family chilled him.

At last, he glimpsed a tall, dark-haired girl clutching a sheaf of papers walking slowly toward him. She came closer, laughing and said, "A penny for your thoughts, sir!"

Michael hoped she had no way of reading his mind. This girl may turn out to be a witch! He rose, taking off his hat, and took her hand. "Why, if it isn't Miss Rose O'Neill on this fine afternoon." They gazed at each other for a minute.

Rose began walking, holding her music to her chest, and said, "There's a lake nearby where I look for my favorite white heron. Maybe she'll show up today if you don't scare her."

As they strolled together, Michael felt her skirt brush his leg once or twice. She was almost as tall as he was, and he marveled at her coolness, her ease at this arranged tryst. He couldn't think of a thing to say for once in his life.

"Mister O'Donovan," she began.

"Call me Michael, please."

"Michael, why are you working for my father?" She stared ahead, not looking at him.

Michael didn't answer at once. How could he explain? He took a deep breath. "Rose, I came to America because I got in trouble in Ireland. There is group there called the Irish Republican Brotherhood. They are trying to get the British out of Ireland, using any means necessary. The politicians do nothing but talk." He looked at her then to see if she understood. She nodded, so he went on, "I took the oath of the Brotherhood and even participated in one unsuccessful action in Cork. But I ran into trouble when the daughter of the Earl my family worked for found a gun I had hidden. It's a long story, but I had to leave Ireland in a hurry and could tell no one in the IRB." He told her then of the back-breaking work on the docks in London, the lonely life there, and finally his decision to leave for America.

"I've come to America to make my way here, but I'm still committed to the cause of Irish freedom, as is your father. Your father, among other things, is raising money for the freedom of the Irish." He stopped then, knowing how weak this last part would sound to a girl educated in morality by the nuns. They walked on in silence, circling the small lake in the center of the park.

Rose surprised him by changing the subject. "Tell me about Ireland! I've begged my father to take me there, but instead he wants me to tour the rest of Europe. He says the time isn't right to visit Ireland yet."

Michael tried to make her see Bantry on the edge of the Atlantic, with its wide harbor glistening in the sun and the purple hills in the distance, to make her smell the hay in spring and the burning peat fires in winter. He described Blackthorn House and told her about his mother and father, his brother Martin now alone on their farm, and the dog, Queenie. "And best of all, Rose, I have a sister named Eileen. She's recently arrived in St. Louis. She's living only a few blocks from here with the Misses Burke on Benton Street."

"Why, Michael, I'd like to meet her." She gazed at him then, a direct, frank gaze with none of the sly coquetry he remembered in Lady Caroline.

Gently he took the papers from her arms. They stood under a tall sweet-gum tree, its leaves just beginning to darken into copper. "Rose, there's nothing I'd like better," he said, looking away. "But I don't see now how it can happen. Your father would kill me if he knew where I was this minute." Seeing her face, he hurried to explain, "That's just an expression, Rose."

She faced him then, looking into his eyes, her eyes the deep blue green of the sea. He was drowning.

The laughter was gone, and her voice was low. "Michael, I don't understand how you can be working for him. I know what he does. I doubt very much that he is working for Ireland. I hate what he's doing."

"Rose, he is working in his own twisted ways for the liberation of Ireland. You know the Irish were not welcomed here in America when they arrived in droves to New York during the famine. They couldn't get work! By God, there are still signs in New York saying 'NO IRISH NEED APPLY.' Much of the money your father is making goes to John Devoy, who is raising money for the overthrow of the British in Ireland.

"So, you are saying that the ends justify the means? That cheating and stealing and pressuring storeowners to pay protection money here in the St. Louis are not wrong? That's not what I was taught in Father Flavin's theology class!" She began to walk away quickly, her steps keeping pace with the urgency of her voice.

He followed, muttering in a low voice, "Ah, what the hell do the priests know in their comfortable rectories drinking the best whiskey?"

He was suddenly horrified that on this first day together they were quarreling. The worst of it was that the girl was right. Michael had no real proof that the money was going to Ireland. He also knew that O'Neill's "business" was more dangerous every day, that they were taking more and more chances, and that any day they could all be caught. He watched her stare out at the lake, its waters still and mirror-like, reflecting the golden and russet leaves of the surrounding trees.

"Michael, I am afraid every day of my life for my father. And now you are enmeshed in his crimes." She turned to face him.

"Rose, I am thinking of going back to Ireland. If I thought I had a chance in hell with you…." He stopped then, afraid to scare her off.

"Not so fast, Mister O'Donovan." She was laughing now, her eyes sparkling. "This is our first conversation and we have mostly spent it arguing. Is this the way you court a lady?"

He was relieved that she could laugh. He had played his cards badly, he knew, but she wasn't giving up on him. This girl was going to be a challenge in every way. She waved to him then and strode quickly to the other side of the park.

He shouted, "So next Friday then?" He wasn't sure she had heard him. He walked rapidly in the other direction, sure that he'd been gone over an hour. He passed a man sitting on a bench near the exit, reading a newspaper. Michael had the queer feeling he'd seen him somewhere before but could not quite place him.

CHAPTER TWENTY-FIVE

....

"**B**ess, I was thinking of taking a nice long walk this afternoon to the Mercantile Library. Would you like to come along? I'm sure the Misses won't mind," Eileen said as the two worked side by side cleaning the kitchen after baking all morning. Eileen was eager to see the library that Miss Nettie told her about, one that was open to visitors in the main reading room. You had to be a member and pay an annual subscription fee if you wanted to actually check out any books. She could not afford the fee yet, but she wanted Bess to see this place too, wanted the girl to see the wide world that would be open to her if she could continue her schooling. Eileen thought sadly that she herself was too old to go to school now.

"Why, Eileen, they'll never let me in," Bess said, shaking her head.

Eileen looked at her. At fourteen, Bess was a tall, slender young woman. Eileen had noticed how avidly Bess listened to the ladies reading aloud in the evenings. "For heaven's sake, Bess, I certainly think they will let us both in," she added, hoping she was right.

Bess looked at her doubtfully, and Eileen said a quick prayer that her confidence would be rewarded. She dreaded a scene in which Bess would be humiliated. Eileen had seen the slights the girl faced every day as she shopped at the market for her mistresses, making her way through the streets of St. Louis. She'd seen the way the ladies who visited the Misses Burke swept by her with barely a murmured greeting, handing her their gloves or umbrellas as they entered the parlor.

Back in Ireland, Eileen thought, she'd felt that same sense of being less than the gentry and having to resort to groveling just to survive. She'd believed that in America everyone was equal, but now she saw the truth. Even though the Confederacy had been defeated, and the slaves were free, Bess and her people were second class citizens, still dependent on their old masters, working as tenant farmers in the countryside or in cities, living in their own shabby part of town, and worshipping in their own churches, not welcome in any restaurant or store. Worst of all, there were few schools for Negro children. Bess was lucky in her mistresses who insisted on teaching her to read and write and do her numbers. Like Eileen, Bess loved stories, so Eileen had spent a precious dollar to buy a new book that had just come out: *Little Women.* They were reading it aloud together, taking turns after dinner each night, and the Misses Burke were delighted with it also.

Seeing a fine library could only intensify Bess's thirst for reading. Eileen was determined. She decided not to tell the ladies the purpose of their excursion today. She'd say they were going shopping for Bess, which in a way was true, she rationalized, scarcely admitting to herself that they might not approve of this visit to the Mercantile Library.

After lunch, Eileen and Bess put on their bonnets, and Eileen grabbed the parasol she kept in the foyer. Miss Alice accompanied them to the door, fussing about the heat of the afternoon, wanting to know why they were going shopping in such heat. "I could get Malachy to bring the carriage around for you two," she wheedled.

Eileen laughed, "Sure, I am needing some exercise these days, Miss Alice. We'll be fine."

Away from the house, Bess glanced around. As they walked, Eileen linked arms with Bess, telling her about her job in the library in Holyoke, the way that anyone could just come in and sign out a book and keep it for two weeks.

Bess laughed at that, then looked doubtful. "But what would happen if somebody just kept the book and never took it back?"

"They would charge you a penny a day for each day it was late," Eileen assured her. Bess just shook her head, still not convinced that such a system would work. Gradually she relaxed, and the two chattered on as they made their way downtown, stopping to look in shop windows. Eileen pretended not to notice the stares that shot their way. A few men muttered things that Eileen pretended not to hear, but she was sure that Bess heard every word.

When they arrived at a solid three-story brick building, the Mercantile Library Hall, Bess stopped. "I . . . I'm not sure I should go in there with you, Miss Eileen." Bess looked down, not meeting Eileen's eyes.

For a moment Eileen hesitated. Did she really want to chance putting Bess in the position of being refused entrance because of her color? This situation felt familiar to Eileen, and suddenly she recognized it. She'd felt exactly the same many times in Bantry in the Earl's house. She was more than welcome to clean there, but she never would have been invited as a guest, worthy to sit at table in the grand dining room. Why should Bess have to feel this way in America because of the color of her skin? Wasn't this supposed to be a country in which all are created equal?

She turned to face Bess. "I know what you are thinking, Bess, but let's march in together as if we are confident that we have the right to be there! I'm only an immigrant, but you are a free woman now."

Bess looked at her doubtfully, but she linked arms with Eileen as they entered the hushed cool stillness of the grand foyer. The marble floor, carpeted in red, lead to a long wooden desk. Gas lamps lit the hall, casting shadows on the walls. Two elderly men sat at the desk, peering over their glasses at the two young women before them.

"Good afternoon, sirs. I am Mrs. Eileen Sullivan, and this is my friend Miss Bess Jackson. We would very much appreciate seeing your reading room if that would be possible."

The men looked at one another. "Are you a member of the Library, Mrs. Sullivan?" They carefully avoided looking at Bess.

"No sir, I am not. We are living with the Misses Burke of Benton Place, and they assured me that anyone was welcome to look around the reading room. They are both members of the Library."

"Yes, we know Miss Nettie and Miss Alice. They joined several years ago and often come to meetings here." The older of the two men coughed. Now he stared at Bess for a long moment. Once again, the two men looked at one another.

Finally, the younger man raised his eyes to Eileen. "Miss, I am afraid that your servant is not permitted to enter here. She may wait outside while you look around." He held Eileen's gaze as she felt her face flush.

"Miss Jackson is not my servant. She is my friend." Eileen's cheeks burned.

"I am sorry then, but you may not enter with her." The two men looked down at their papers, shuffling them, trying to ignore the two young women standing before them.

Eileen felt Bess pulling her arm, murmuring softly, "Come on, Eileen."

Eileen turned away, but stopped suddenly, looking back over her shoulder, raising her voice as it echoed in the great hall, "I thought in America all people were created equal. Sure, that's what we all thought in Ireland, and that's why so many of us have come here. I see the news has not reached you here in the fair city of St. Louis."

Back in the street, the two women walked fast, Eileen burning with fury and shame. She should never have presumed to take Bess there to suffer such a scene. Her own white skin had protected her. Bess, born a free person in this country, was not welcome in this library solely because of the color of her skin. How little she understood America, thinking the two of them could just waltz in and be welcomed. The War had saved the Union, but here in Missouri it had not changed the hearts of the people. She, who had fled Ireland because of the poverty caused by the injustice of the British rulers, should not have been so naive.

Bess walked on, head high, saying nothing. Finally, at the corner of Benton Street, Eileen faced Bess. She took her hand, saying, "Bess, you were right. I should have listened to you. I am so sorry. . . ."

Before she could finish, Bess looked at her gravely. "Don't worry, Eileen. Those two sorry old men can't stop me from reading. In fact, I was thinking that I could become a teacher myself somehow. So now I want you to show me what books I should be reading!" A smile began to play around her mouth as she added, "And I wager those two old white fellows are still twittering on about that saucy Irish girl and the bold colored girl who dared to disturb the dust in that place!"

Eileen vowed to talk to the Misses Burke and suggest that Bess have the daily paper as soon as they were finished with it. The ladies also had bookshelves full of novels and biographies, encouraging Eileen to help herself to what she wanted. Why in the world hadn't they extended the same generosity to Bess? Perhaps they didn't think she'd be interested in their books, or even worse, maybe didn't think her capable of understanding them.

Eileen, stung, remembered how it felt to realize that people did not think you were smart just because you were poor. She pictured Lady Caroline at Bantry House, leaving her clothes on the floor for Eileen to put away, speaking so coldly to her, the same girl she used to love to play with as a child until Lady Mary had made it clear that they would not be friends.

Bess had spoken so fiercely! Two fuddy-duddy old white men weren't going to stand in her way. Eileen felt a flush of shame as she understood now that in America her white skin would let her escape the prejudice against the Irish, at least as soon as she lost her accent, but that Bess could never escape the color of her skin.

CHAPTER TWENTY-SIX

....

T he heat returned one night in September, with people coming out on their porches, dragging mattresses to upper balconies to sleep outside, hoping to catch a wisp of moving air. But at night the mosquitoes came out, too, and sitting outside in the late evening after the sun set, swinging on the porch glider, Eileen found her arms and ankles covered with bites, large red welts that itched and kept her awake.

Was she happy? she wondered. Not happy exactly, but for now, content. She felt as if something were coming. She found herself remembering Thomas in a shadowy, hazy way, the smell of his soft hair, the way his lashes, long and full, rested on his cheek when she caught a glimpse of him from the side, how his little back felt so straight and thin under her hands when she stroked him to sleep at night. The pain still stabbed at her at unexpected moments, but now there was a sweetness, too, as she lingered among her memories. Every night she prayed, knowing he was safe in heaven with her mother and father and, she hastily added to herself, his Da, John. Surely heaven meant being happy with our loved ones. She could not bear the thought of her child wandering alone in some vague afterlife.

By the third week of September, Eileen noticed a hint of coolness in the air. With leaves turning yellow, she loved the walk to Schaeffer's in the early morning hours. Bess packed a lunch for her, sometimes leaving a note in her bag telling her what book she was reading. They had become closer, united by their love of books, with long discussions about characters as they washed the dishes and tidied the kitchen every night.

Sometimes Bess asked her about the news in the paper, and she was especially curious about life in Ireland. Eileen found herself trying to explain what the English had done to the Irish over the centuries but realized that it was Michael who should be tutoring Bess on Irish history. Bess begged her to tell stories about Bantry and Blackthorn House. But for some reason, Eileen had still not told her anything about her marriage, nor about her son. No one in St. Louis except Michael and the Misses Burke knew her whole story. She wasn't sure why she hadn't told Bess about this part of her life.

When she entered the shop on Monday morning, Miss Schneider, the chief seamstress, looked up in relief. "Oh, thank God!" she puffed, her face flushed. "We already have a customer this morning, and I was hoping you'd be here in time to take his measurements, as I am working on the wedding suit for Mr. Mahoney." She rattled on, "Now that fall is here, the orders will be picking up."

Eileen scanned the shop. "Where is the gentleman?"

Before Miss Schneider could answer, Eileen heard a deep baritone, "Now who in heaven's name is accusing me of being a gentleman?"

Eileen stared. A tall, lanky young man, blond, with a friendly grin, bowed to Eileen. "Mister Delancey Jordan, at your service, ma'am." Eileen said nothing, distracted by the way the man's grin lit up the dusky shop. She turned away to gather her measuring tape and the pin cushion she used in taking measurements. Usually old Mister Horst did this, but he'd been sick now for several days. She was surprised to feel her hands shaking as she pulled the tape around her neck.

"This way, if you please, Mister Jordan. Just stand on this stool for me and stay very still."

"Yes, ma'am," he said lightly, "I won't argue with a lady armed with a spiky pin cushion."

Eileen began with measuring for the pants: first the waist, then the length and then the inseam. She felt her cheeks burning as she worked, with Delancey humming happily, raising his arms meekly when asked to, turning at her command as she jotted down the numbers. She hoped she could read her jottings afterward. Her handwriting was shaky.

Now for the jacket. "If you'd step off now, sir," she mumbled, "so I can measure for the suit coat." When he faced her, she realized how tall he was, her forehead facing his chest. She stepped up on the stool he'd abandoned, and found herself gazing into lively brown eyes, which held hers longer than she liked. As she leaned into him, he murmured, "By God if I don't smell roses in here, Miss." He was laughing at her, she knew, and she tried to keep herself from smiling back.

"Now what should I call you?" he asked suddenly.

"I am Mrs. Eileen Sullivan."

"Oh, I didn't see a ring."

"I'm a widow," she answered softly, wondering why she was telling him this. The fellow was fresh, but she found herself liking him in spite of it. Finally, she was done, and he headed over to the counter to arrange the next fitting with Miss Schneider. Eileen heard them laughing, but their voices dropped, so she could not make out their conversation. Eileen went into the back room for some fabric and glanced at herself in the mirror over the bolts of cloth. Her eyes were bright, her cheeks flushed. She felt sparked by some energy she had not felt since she was a girl climbing trees at home. When she emerged, she felt Miss Schneider looking at her. Eileen desperately wanted to ask her about Delancey Jordan, but her interest would be too obvious. They worked the rest of the morning in silence.

That evening after supper, the ladies invited her to join them in the parlor to play cards, but Eileen pleaded off, saying she was tired after a long day. Bess had gone to choir practice at her church, so after doing the dishes, Eileen slipped into the back yard into the fast-approaching dusk. The air was balmy, the smell of earth mingling with smoke from the kitchen chimney.

Eileen paced round and round the garden, slipping through shadows, her thoughts circling wildly, scattered as the leaves rustling around her. She remembered nights like this in Bantry, she just a girl, restless and moony, longing for something she could not name. Somehow that young man she met in the shop today made her feel like a girl again, with everything before her. Just thinking of him and his ridiculous name, Delancey, for heaven's sake, made her laugh to herself. She'd thought her heart had closed shop. Now she was not so sure.

The week passed slowly, until finally on the following Thursday, Eileen heard Mr. Horst tell Miss Schneider that the suit was ready for Mr. Jordan's next fitting. The messenger boy, Peter, took the message with the address, repeating it to Miss Schneider. Eileen looked up from the buttonhole she was stitching to listen: 1005 Lucas Avenue.

When Peter left, Miss Schneider looked over and said, "That Mr. Jordan is a charmer, isn't he?"

"Yes, and well he knows it himself," laughed Eileen, trying to hide her confusion. Why did just the mention of his name make her giddy? She was being a fool!

"He's a young man who works hard as a supervisor at Joseph Ward Painting Company." Miss Schneider continued, "For someone from up north, he's amazingly polite." She looked over at Eileen, who did not meet her gaze, continuing, "A young lady could do far worse." Then they both broke into a laugh, and Eileen spent the rest of the morning wondering when this paragon of manhood would appear. She was startled at the drop in her mood when Delancey Jordan did not show up.

Two weeks passed slowly, and October came, the nights chillier, and the trees all a burst of scarlet, yellow, flaming orange, lit by the afternoon sunlight. Eileen walked home slowly each late afternoon to take in the smell of burning leaves, the slanting light illumining each tree. She felt leaves landing softly on her hair, her shoulders, like so many butterflies. Everything seemed heightened, more vivid.

The fact that it was raining on the morning when she heard the bell chime as someone entered the shop did not even squelch the hopeful humming in her veins. She knew who it was without looking up.

Delancey Jordan pulled off his dripping cap, ducking his head in greeting to Miss Schneider at the desk, "What a fine morning to be walking," he laughed.

Finally, he looked over at Eileen, and her breath quickened. She fought the impulse to say something, just nodded her head, not trusting her voice to be steady. *This is ridiculous.* She was a grown woman with a past, not a green girl to be swept by fantasies.

Delancey hung his coat on the rack and went into the dressing room for the final fitting of his suit. When he came out, both Mr. Schaeffer and Miss Schneider examined him carefully, murmuring about the fine stitching, the excellent fit, how it showed off his shoulders and slender frame. It was perfect!

"Well, I guess this means I'll have to settle up now. The boss wanted me to have a good suit made for the times I have to call on some of the contractors in town to get the bid on a paint job. There are tall buildings going up all over, even some a distance away from downtown. St. Louis is expanding fast," he chattered on, fiddling with his wallet. Eileen could see him pulling the bills from it, counting them carefully. Well, he wouldn't be coming back. He was not a rich man who could afford the fine tailoring that the shop provided for the wealthy men of St. Louis. She'd never see him again.

"Eileen, could you wrap up this suit for Mr. Jordan. It needs to be well wrapped so the rain doesn't get to it." Miss Schneider glanced meaningfully at Eileen, who hurried over to the counter. Mr. Schaeffer retired to his office, and Miss Schneider disappeared into the fabric room.

"I was hoping you'd be here, Mrs. Sullivan," Delancey said quietly, all his cocky sunniness suddenly turned into shyness. Eileen looked up, trying not to smile, but when their eyes met, they stared at each other in silence. Then he said quickly, "I was hoping I could call on you at your residence." She could not think of what to say. He hurried on, "I work six days a week, but I have Sundays free."

Eileen was carefully tying string around the package, then tying a double knot to secure it. She looked up. "My name is Eileen."

Relief flooded Delancey's face. "And you can call me Lance. All my friends do." He held out a card. "Please write your address on this. Would three o'clock next Sunday be convenient?"

"Yes. I live in the home of the Misses Burke, and you're welcome to join us for tea next Sunday." She tucked a loose bit of hair back into the low bun she was wearing and smoothed down her work apron. He stood watching her as she bent over to write the address carefully, until, to break the silence, she said, "I hope you get back home before it starts to rain again. We wouldn't want your fine new suit to get wet!"

He moved to the door then, grabbed his cap, and with the package tucked under his coat, turned once more to look at her. "It will be a long time till Sunday, Eileen. Thank you." She heard the rumble of wagons splashing through the puddles in the street as he closed the door behind him. The rain had stopped, and the trees glimmered, the autumn leaves shot through with sunshine mirroring her joy.

CHAPTER TWENTY-SEVEN

....

On the following Sunday afternoon Lance sat stiffly with Eileen, Miss Nettie, and Miss Alice in the front parlor, sipping tea from a translucent china cup, trying not to drop the crumbs from the yellow layer cake with caramel icing Bess had baked especially for the occasion. Miss Nettie's poodle, Pansy, growled at Lance when he entered but was now perched at his feet, slyly begging crumbs from the hand that was stroking her soft, taffy-colored coat absentmindedly.

The ladies skillfully grilled him about himself, and so Eileen learned that he had grown up in Wisconsin, Fond Du Lac, to be exact, and that his mother had died when Lance was fourteen; at this the ladies murmured sorrowfully. His father was a farmer who had built a house in town, turning over the farm to his tenants, and he'd wanted his only son to study law. Lance had two sisters, one of whom was married and living in South Bend, Indiana.

As Eileen listened to him, she realized she needed a map of the United States. She had never heard of Fond Du Lac or South Bend! He said that he had been raised as a Methodist, but somewhat shamefacedly added, "I haven't been a very good Methodist since I came to St. Louis."

Eileen's heart plummeted. Lance was a Protestant! Then Miss Alice asked, "And may I ask why you did not study law and instead landed here in St. Louis?"

"Well, ma'am, I was restless in Wisconsin. I had never been anywhere except one visit to Madison to see the new college there. I was nineteen, and I wanted to see the world. When I left to go out west, my father cut me off, telling me I'd have to earn my own living if I were going to pass up his offer to pay for an education as a lawyer. So, I hitched a ride on a wagon to St. Louis, thinking I'd go out west to be a rancher or something." He laughed softly then, looking down, and added, "I never made it farther than St. Louis, where I lost the little money I'd saved in a card game at a saloon down on the riverfront."

The ladies glanced at each other, and Eileen got up to serve everyone another cup of tea. She smiled at Lance encouragingly, "But now you have a good position at Ward's, isn't that right?"

"Yes, one day I was downtown when I noticed a sign in a shop saying, "Painter Wanted." I applied for the job, and old Mister Ward hired me on the spot. Said I looked like a strapping fellow who could last on this job. After two years, he made me foreman, and now I supervise the men, and go out and get bids for more jobs." Lance sat back and gazed at Eileen.

Eileen wished they were alone, walking together in the park. The room was stifling with the fire crackling in the grate even though the day outside was bright and sunny, inviting.

As he rose to go, Miss Alice said, "Eileen, will you see Mr. Jordan out?"

In the dim foyer, Lance stood close to her, turning his hat round and round. For a moment he said nothing. Then he whispered, "Eileen, it will be forever until next Sunday. Can't we walk together somewhere then? Alone?"

"Oh, I think that could be arranged," she smiled up at him, but he did not smile back, just stood there, looking into her eyes. Suddenly he took her hand and brought it to his mouth.

His blond mustache swept her hand, his lips warm on her skin. Then he was gone.

The week dragged by for Eileen, but finally Sunday arrived, a slippery, silver-hued fall day with the sun fading in and out, brief bursts of showers in between. Eileen had casually mentioned at breakfast that she and Mr. Jordan would be taking a picnic to the park that afternoon.

"Oh dear, I'm afraid it will be too wet, and you'll catch cold sitting on the ground," Miss Alice rattled on. Miss Nettie said nothing. Eileen had noticed the slight downturn of her mouth when Nettie heard the plan, but Eileen was not asking for permission. After Lance's first visit, the ladies both said they liked Mr. Jordan very much, that he was engaging and quite handsome, but, as Miss Nettie said gravely, "You never know about strange men from up North."

Eileen had been careful not to mention his name all week, afraid she would reveal too clearly how often he was in her thoughts. After all, she barely knew him. She had to be sensible. What if this man were only playing with her? She would talk to Michael, somehow have them meet. She trusted Michael's judgment more than anyone else's. After Mass, she wrote a quick note to Michael:

> *My Dear Brother,*
> *It has been three weeks since I've seen you. I wish to talk to you about someone I have met. His name is Delancey Jordan, and he works for Joseph Ward Painting Company. I find that I like him very much. Do you have time to meet somewhere for lunch next Saturday?*
> *Your loving sister,*
> *Eileen*

She sealed the letter and put it on the hall table to go out on Monday morning. She placed the picnic basket under the table and entered the parlor where the ladies were reading, getting up twice to check her dress in the long, gilt-framed mirror in the foyer and re-tying the ribbon of her bonnet. The two ladies peered at her over their spectacles, pretending to be engrossed in their scripture readings. Finally, she heard Lance's step on the front veranda. When she kissed their cheeks in farewell hurriedly, Miss Nettie said, "Oh heavens, Eileen! Aren't you going to invite Mr. Jordan in?"

"No, I'm afraid we'll get caught in a shower if we don't take our lunch to the park right now. The sun has broken through just this minute," she said hurriedly. She turned at the door, "I'll tell Mr. Jordan you asked after him." She grabbed the basket, opening the door before he could ring the bell.

When she saw him with the raindrops still glistening on his dark coat, his hair combed carefully back from his forehead, and his eyes shining with happiness, she felt suddenly calm. *Oh, God help me, I'm lost now.* Never had any man looked at her like this. And never since Thomas died had she felt such a surge of joy as when he clasped her hand and murmured, "Eileen! I thought Sunday would never come."

Together they walked down the street toward the park beneath the dripping autumn leaves, shot through now with sun, the basket swinging between them, both laughing softly as she told him of Miss Nettie's disappointment that he was not coming in.

They found a spot in the park nearby under a large tree, its branches bending so low that the two could spread out the cloth in the grass and sit together with no curious eyes observing them. Lance ran his hands down the tree's bark, examining the almost purple leaves and declared, "I'm pretty sure this is a copper beech tree. We had a few of these at home in Wisconsin."

Eileen smiled up at him, "I always forget that you are a country boy, Lance. You seem so sure of yourself here in the big city."

"And you, Eileen, aren't you a country girl too?" He gazed at her and his face turned serious. "Eileen, I know you were married, but you have told me nothing about that part of your life."

She shuddered, taking a deep breath. This day had to come if they were to become true friends, but she dreaded telling him. She began slowly, her voice low, "Lance, it was not a happy marriage. I never loved John. I was sixteen when my mother and brother told me that I would marry him, a forty-year-old farmer whose land lay next to our small tenant farm. I didn't even know him." She felt Lance's gaze and heard the sharp intake of breath. Without meeting his eyes, she went on, "He was not a cruel man, just morose and slow. Of course, he could tell I did not love him." She stopped then, and with a tremor, "There was a child born, a darling boy whom we named Thomas. He died of the fever on the trip over. He was just two." She stopped, unable to go on.

Lance took her hand. "Eileen, you don't have to tell me any more if it is too painful."

"No, I want you to know this," she said. She held on to his hand as she went on, describing her desperate grief, the landing in New York, having to tell Michael, the move to Holyoke, John's drinking, their growing estrangement and finally, John's death in the accident, and her guilt and sorrow. The picnic lunch lay forgotten on the cloth. When she finished, they sat in silence.

Lance began to gather up the things as thunder rumbled in the distance. "We'd better get you home, Eileen, before the storm breaks."

She watched him, noticing he did not meet her eyes. But on the way back to the Misses Burkes' house, he slipped his arm around her waist and held her close to him under the umbrella as the rain pelted down, lashing their bodies with sudden fury.

After spending Saturday morning at O'Neill's finishing up his accounts, Michael hurried toward Miss Holland's Café to meet Eileen. He'd been rattled by her note telling him about this Delancey fellow. Somehow, he'd pictured Eileen waiting a long time before she'd even think about getting involved with another man. And what kind of a man had a name like Delancey?

So, he'd made a point on Wednesday afternoon to stop by the painting company where the fellow worked, although it was far up north on Union Avenue. He pretended to be scouting out companies to paint Egan's saloon, joking around with the elderly Irishman behind the counter. "Now, do I hear the lovely tones of Galway?" he smiled at the man.

"Not far away, lad. Oughterard was my home. Still is, I guess, but all my people are gone now. Famine times, you know. Been here in St. Louis for almost twenty years now."

They chatted on for a while, Michael telling the man stories about Bantry, when he casually asked, "I hear you have a man working here by name of Jordan."

The older man brightened. "Yes, he's the supervisor of the men. A fine bright lad. Mr. Ward thinks the world of him, youngster that he is. A real straight shooter! Too bad he's a Protestant," he laughed, "or the old man might have made him his heir." Then he looked more closely at Michael. "May I tell him you called here? I didn't catch your name."

"Just tell him someone from Egan's was in asking about getting an estimate for a big paint job," Michael smiled. "I'll try to come by when he's in." He thanked the man and strode quickly to the door, not wanting to linger in case this Jordan fellow turned up. Eileen would kill him if she knew he came by to check Jordan out.

A Protestant! He hadn't bargained on Eileen stepping so far out of the family's ways. What would their mother and father have thought about that? Of course, he had to admit to himself, what would they have thought about his own current occupation? Things were getting hot at O'Neill's these days. A rival group, some were even calling it a gang, the Hogans, had started making raids on their various businesses.

O'Neill was furious because they were Irish also. "Bad enough," he'd thundered, "that the Dagos and Negroes are horning in on our operations, but to have the Irish!" He was setting up a meeting with Hogan and his men, somewhere far out in the country. No one, not even the cops on the take, were to know of this secret meeting.

And then there was Rose. They'd met on several Fridays, and Michael felt he was making progress. Sure, didn't she laugh at all his jokes and tell him stories about the nuns at her school, and about her friends with their plans for a grand tour of Europe in the coming summer.

His heart had almost stopped last week when Rose had turned to him and said, "Michael, I don't want to go to Europe. I'd rather go to Ireland," then she added softly so that he had to bend down to catch it, "with you."

He loved her for her frankness. There was nothing coy about Rose. Her feelings shone in her eyes, and it was all he could do to keep his hands off her. He was caught for sure. They loved each other, he knew, though neither of them had said those words, the shadow of Rose's father looming between them. He could not see a way forward.

Now, lost in his worries, he did not see Eileen until she was right in front of him. She laughed, "Why, Michael O'Donovan! What a welcome for your darling sister whom you've not seen in forever!"

"Cara," he said, pulling her toward him in an embrace. He held her away from him, examining her carefully. "Why, Eileen! You look wonderful!" Her eyes were bright, and the dark green of her dress set off her light brown hair streaked with blond. "You've even gained some weight! We'll have to be careful in

Miss Hollands. I know you love her lemon layer cake." He took her arm and tucked it in his own as they entered the café.

After they'd finished, both seemingly famished from the way they attacked their roast beef with carrots and potatoes, Michael leaned back in his chair. Eileen sipped her tea, looking at him now and then over her cup, watching him enjoy every bite of the cake. She'd passed up dessert, a bit stung by his comment on her weight.

"All right, Eileen. So, tell me about this Delancey fellow," Michael sighed, sitting back. She leaned toward him, telling him how they'd met, how much the Burke sisters liked him, and of his important position at the paint company. She stopped then. When she looked up, Michael saw her eyes were full of tears. "Michael, I love him. I know it's sudden, but I knew almost from the beginning that he was the one. I'm not a green girl. I have been married, had a child, lost both child and husband, but I have never felt so whole, so myself as when I am with Lance," her voice trembling as she said his name.

Michael took her hand in his. "Eileen, is he a good man? Does he know you've been married and had a child?"

"Yes, I told him the whole story last week. I think he was surprised, and somewhat downcast after I told him. He was quiet on the walk back to the house. Then two days later I received this letter from him, the first one he's written to me."

She pulled it from her bag and spread it out so Michael could read it. The handwriting was bold, firm.

Dearest Eileen,

Forgive me for taking so long to respond to all the things you told me last Sunday, but I needed to think things over. I knew you were a widow, but I admit it was a shock to me to hear about your little son. I can barely imagine the pain and sorrow you have been through. You seem far too young to me to have been through such suffering. Also, I admit, the

thought of you being forced to marry a man like Sullivan,
someone you did not love, made me furious and jealous at
the same time. I suppose every man wants to be the first and
only for the girl he marries. To my shame, I have had other
women. But somehow, and I know it's not fair, the thought
of you with that man . . . well, I could not get that image
out of my mind.

So that night I did not go home after our meeting. I
walked until long into the night all the way down to the river,
trying to become calm and think things through. Finally, I
went home and fell into bed, still wrestling with my feelings
and doubts. But the strangest thing happened the next morning.
When I awoke, it was later than usual. The sun was shining
through the shade over my open window, and I could hear the
birds calling to one another. Then I pictured you, your smiling
eyes, your laughter, and the touch of your lips on my cheek,
and I knew that all the past was nothing. I am the luckiest
man in the world to have found you, and nothing can keep
me from you, if you will have me.

Can you forgive me for doubting even for one night? I love
you, Eileen, and it is I who do not deserve a woman like you.
Yours,
Lance

Michael folded the letter carefully and handed it back to
Eileen. He looked at her for a moment. "Well, the man was
certainly honest with you, cara. He sounds smitten, indeed."

"Oh Michael, I love him so much. I cannot believe the good
luck that was mine the day he walked into the shop, and I heard
his voice."

"But Eileen, what about his religion? He says nothing about
that, but to me that's the stumbling block, for sure. A Protestant!
What would Mam and Da say to that?"

She stared at him. "How did you know Lance was a Protestant?"

He glanced away from her. "I went to Ward's Painting Company to investigate this lad. I talked to an old fellow there from near Galway." Her eyes were cold, her mouth drawn, unsmiling. He rushed on, "I know I have no right to lecture you, what with the things I have gotten involved in." He was grateful that she did not respond. Then he looked at her hopefully. "I don't suppose he would consider becoming a Catholic?"

"I doubt it, Michael." Eileen looked glum.

"I know!" Michael looked up, eagerly. "You can write to Father Gleason and ask him what you should do. He is very fond of you, Eileen, and maybe he could help you convince this fellow to become a Catholic."

Eileen looked up at him, her eyes blazing. "Michael O'Donovan, I will do no such thing. Sure, isn't it my whole life that others have been telling me what I must do? What if Father says I should not marry him? No! Lance can be whatever religion he wants to be, and so shall I. We will work it out! I'm not asking anyone's permission to do what my heart tells me. I made that mistake when I was sixteen, but I've grown up now. I will choose my own life." Her voice had risen, and several people in the café looked over at the pair.

Michael began to laugh, shaking his head. "By God, Eileen, you sounded just like Mammy now. Not that she would agree with you!"

CHAPTER TWENTY-EIGHT

....

O ctober faded into November with rainy, gusty mornings, the leaves, golden, scarlet, brown showering down, crumpling on slick pavement as Michael walked to Egan's every morning. Late on a Thursday afternoon as Michael was finishing the daily accounts, O'Neill opened the door of his office and beckoned to him.

An oil lamp burned on the boss's desk, the rest of the room in shadow. O'Neill gestured toward a chair in front of his desk, "Sit down, Michael. I've a job for you." Michael waited. O'Neill reached for a cigar, spending several minutes trimming it, lighting it, and taking several slow draws. For one wild moment, Michael thought, *he's found out about Rose and me. Oh God!*

Michael broke the silence first, "What's up, boss? Everything all right?"

"No, it's not. But I've arranged a meeting—very secret— with Hogan and two of his top men. I'd like you to go along with me. No one else." He gazed at Michael through the haze of cigar smoke.

"Sure, Mr. O'Neill. When's the meeting?"

"Tomorrow night at nine. It's out of town, at a tavern north of the city called The Green Room. Finn will drive us out there and wait in the carriage."

"May I ask the purpose of the meeting?"

"Yeah. I'd like to come to some kind of agreement on the division of our respective operations. I want Hogan's people to restrict their activities to the near southeast side of the city, and we'll have the downtown and near northeastern side."

Michael hesitated, then asked, "Do you think they'll go for it?"

O'Neill grunted. He rose and paced around the room. "They'd better. We were here first. I intend to keep my customers. Hogan's people have no interest in the Cause. They're a bunch of hoodlums, low class." He spit. "They even have Dagoes like Cammalini in their gang." He drew on his cigar and let out a cloud of smoke.

Then he turned and looked straight at Michael. "Hogan knows I have some pretty high contacts in the police force who would appreciate a tip from me on his gang. A word from me, and they'll come down like the fires of hell on Hogan and his people. I think he'll deal."

"Will I need my gun?"

"Of course, boy. You needn't ask." He sat down heavily, not looking at Michael. When he nodded, Michael knew he was dismissed. As Michael turned to leave, O'Neill added without looking up, "Meet me here tomorrow night at eight. Finn will drive us." As he left the room, Michael felt O'Neill's gaze on him.

Once outside in the dark November night, Michael's initial feeling of relief that the boss had not discovered his meetings with Rose faded fast. *Something about this meeting sounds off.* Michael walked home beneath the dripping trees, glancing up at the clouds scuttling across the sky, revealing a slice of silver moon. It was odd that O'Neill had picked him as his only security. Usually, meetings took place on their own turf, like Egan's pub, where they could put a closed sign on the door and only the invited could enter. Meeting in a strange place, late at night, was dangerous. What if Hogan had more protection hiding in the darkness? Worse, what if this was a set up? But he knew he

was going anyway, for Rose's sake, if for no other. She loved her
father, in spite of what she knew about him. Once home and in
bed, sleep would not come as Michael tossed and turned until
the first pale light showed through the window.

The next day, the hours dragged as Michael pretended to be
busy with the accounts at Egan's. O'Neill's door was shut, and
finally at noon, Michael pushed away from his desk, grabbing
his coat, and heading for the door, when the boss's door swung
open, and he peered at Michael. "Take the rest of the day off,"
O'Neill examined his face for a minute. "You've been slaving
away." He lowered his voice. "See you at eight."

Michael nodded, and clambered down the stairs, striding
quickly through the dim pub, where two dark shapes huddled
over their pints at the bar. As he stepped outside into the damp
air of noonday, he inhaled. If only he could see Rose. How would
she look at him if she knew what was planned for this night? Well,
it was for her that he was going through with this meeting. Her
father was in danger; he could feel it as sure as he'd felt danger
all those times in Bantry when he'd been with MacDonogh. Both
men gave off a scent of some held-back anger beneath their cool
exterior. If O'Neill suspected his feelings for Rose, or worse, their
secret meetings, this night could be a trap for him.

He imagined the scene: O'Neill would turn and face him at
the door of the empty shack. There would be no Hogan people,
just the two of them with Finn waiting in the carriage, hidden
in the trees. Then the cold steel of the revolver in his ribs, right
before he'd hear the crack! And then darkness.

Michael realized his hands were shaking. A drink, by God!
He ducked into the pub on the corner.

By eight o'clock, he and Finn arrived at Egan's, smoking
nervously beneath the awning as they waited for O'Neill. Finn
pumped Michael as they waited, asking, "What the hell are
we doing, going off half-cocked like this to some out-of-the
way dive?"

Michael kept his mouth shut, remembering O'Neill's crack about Irishmen who talked too much. Finally, O'Neill appeared with his long dark coat shielding him from a vicious wind, and his tall hat pulled down over his eyes.

"Good evening, gentlemen," he nodded, gesturing to the coach in front of the tavern as two black horses bobbed their heads, steam rising from their nostrils. Finn got up in front and took the reins. After instructing Finn on the route they would take, O'Neill motioned to Michael to get in the cab with him, and soon they were trotting smartly through the deserted streets of the city, heading north.

O'Neill's cigar tip was the only light in the cab. Michael gazed out the window as the familiar streets disappeared and the coach headed onto a lonely road through farmland, far outside Michael's usual trips around downtown St. Louis. There was no moon, but the clouds flowing across the sky sometimes revealed fields of stubble, and Michael could smell those wet fields carrying him back to Bantry and the farm. Oh, what a long way he was from that.

Suddenly, O'Neill turned to Michael, his voice cutting through the silence. "What the hell are you doing, O'Donovan, meeting my daughter?"

Michael went cold. *The man on the bench in the park. O'Neill had Rose followed.* What a fool he'd been. He turned to face O'Neill, half hidden in the dark interior of the carriage, only his eyes glittering fitfully when he puffed on his cigar.

"Boss, ever since I first saw her on Christmas Eve, I haven't been able to get her out of my mind." Michael waited.

"You're nuts, boy. Rose is not going to end up with some two-bit Irish lad with no money." O'Neill's cigar bloomed in the darkness as he inhaled deeply.

So now I know, Michael thought. *I'm only the two-bit Irish lad in O'Neill's mind.* "Sir, I swear to you that I would never hurt Rose. But I love her, and," his voice shook, "I believe she returns my feelings."

O'Neill grunted, "Feelings, is it? I hate to break it to you, O'Donovan, but life isn't about feelings. The girl will do what she's told. She's going to Europe in a few weeks, and you are to stop messing around with her. I mean it. One more slip-up, and you're out. Now shut up."

They rode on in silence, the only sound the horses' hooves clopping along in the dark. Finally, Michael felt the coach slow as they bumped along a lane until he heard Finn whistle with a soft "whoa." O'Neill stubbed out the cigar, but the smell of smoke lingered on both men as they emerged from the cab. O'Neill looked up at Finn, and whispered, "Move the coach over beyond the trees there, and wait. If you hear two sharp whistles, come in blazing, you understand?" Finn nodded, his face pale in the dim light.

O'Neill and Michael stood together in the sharp wind, the trees swaying, and watched the coach disappear beyond the edge of the woods. O'Neill nodded at Michael, gesturing for him to go around to the back of the tavern to be sure they were alone. Michael crouched, moving fast, trying not to step on any branches. He saw nothing, the only sound the whistling of the wind in the woods surrounding them. He nodded at O'Neill, and muttered, "All clear."

O'Neill pushed open the door beneath a faded sign, The Green Room. Inside he lit an oil lamp that stood on the table and looked at Michael, his eyes hooded. "It's a shame, kid. I liked you. I even saw something. . . ."

With a sharp crack, the back door swung open, and four shapes rushed in, firing at O'Neill. Michael dropped to the floor, crouching behind a table as he struggled to get his gun out of the deep inside pocket of his coat. Then a searing pain in his ankle, and he fell backward. He struggled to reach his gun, but before he could even aim, the four shapes disappeared, and he heard the crack of twigs and branches beneath their feet as they fled through the woods.

He whistled twice for Finn, and dragged himself over to O'Neill, who lay face up, his blue eyes open, staring at the ceiling. Blood trickled from a wound in the side of his head. Michael bent and put his ear to the man's chest but could hear nothing. He brushed his hands over the man's eyes in the gentle motion of a child stroking a bird. Then he traced the sign of the cross on O'Neill's forehead and mumbled a Hail Mary. He lay beside him until he heard Finn at the door swearing softly.

"My God, Michael," he hissed. "I heard nothing until the shots rang out. What happened?" With a jolt, Michael realized that he himself could be the suspect here. Only he had seen what happened. Finn had to believe him.

"There were four of them. They burst in the back door, took shots at O'Neill before I could even reach my gun. Look! I didn't even get a shot off." He lifted the revolver to show Finn, opening the chamber so he could see the fully loaded cylinder.

"Is he dead?"

"Yes."

"Fuck. You're bleeding!"

"They got me in the ankle. I don't think I can walk." Michael felt an icy calm descend. "God knows where they hid their coach or how they even got here. But they are long gone. Bring the coach around. Somehow, we have to get his body in the cab. I'll ride up front with you in case there's any trouble."

With Michael hobbling, his wound bleeding through the scarf he'd wrapped around his lower leg, they dragged O'Neill's lifeless body out into the yard. Finn ran to pull the coach up to the door, and Michael trembled now, trying not to look at O'Neill's face.

On the long way back, Michael's thoughts raced as he fought off the pain is his ankle. The Hogans had double-crossed them. With O'Neill out of the way, their men could take over all the operations in the city for the Irish. O'Neill had not trained anyone to be in charge. Michael knew he was out now. The game had turned deadly. But what about the rest of the men who'd been part of O'Neill's operation? Would they go over to the Hogans? What had O'Neill called them? Hoodlums. And what were he and the others? No better.

He thought of Rose then and groaned. He would have to be the one to tell her. He had not been able to protect her father. What she feared had happened, and he had been right there, helpless.

Finn's voice broke the silence between them. "So, what's the plan, now?"

"We go to the police."

"Are you mad? We need to get you to a doctor."

"No. The police. We go with the truth. We tell them we had a meeting scheduled with the Hogans to talk over some business, and O'Neill was gunned down in the dimness in front of me. They got me, too, which makes the whole thing more believable. I didn't see their faces, but it had to be Hogan's gang. "

"Michael, that's crazy."

"No, O'Neill has connections with the police force in the city. Lots of them are on the take too, so they'll be sure to go after the Hogans. But, Finn, I'm out. For good."

"What the hell I am supposed to do?" Finn cried.

"That, my boy, is up to you." They went on in silence through the gusty night.

After bringing the body to the police station, Michael and Finn were separated and questioned for hours, but the local precinct cops seemed halfhearted about the whole process. O'Neill was a well-known figure in the precinct, so it didn't take long for the police to label the killing a turf war. Michael and Finn gave the police the address of their boarding house, and the sergeant in charge made it clear that they were to be ready for further questioning as needed, and under no circumstances were they to leave the city.

"Any family member who can come and identify the body?" Detective Ward asked Michael.

"Yes, sir. He has a daughter. But I am Mr. O'Neill's employee, so I can assure you that is O'Neill," Michael said softly.

"Employee, is it? And just what in the hell are you employed to do, I wonder, Mr. Michael O'Donovan?" Michael felt the contempt of the man as clearly as if he'd spit in his face. The detective motioned to his leg. "Better get that wound looked at. You're still bleeding."

When Michael and Finn were finally let go, they came out to see O'Neill's body being loaded into the cart that would take it down to the city morgue for evidence. It was well past midnight by then, but Michael knew he had to be the one to tell Rose before she heard it from anyone else. Exhausted, grimy with perspiration, his body going cold with shock and pain, he looked at Finn. "One more favor, Finn. I've got to get to O'Neill's house to tell Rose. I can't walk. I need you to drive me there and wait."

"Fuck, man. I'm not a taxi service," he grumbled, putting his arm under Michael's shoulder so he could rest on him. His face pale, Finn helped Michael into the carriage, and they headed toward St. Louis Place.

The house was dark. Finn helped Michael up to the porch, and then retreated to the carriage. On the dark veranda, Michael stopped and took a deep breath before ringing the doorbell. The sound echoed in the foyer. After what seemed like an eternity, lamps began to come on, first in the hallway and then he saw a light in Rose's window. He leaned forward so she could see him. He heard a window thrown open above him, and then Rose's voice, full of laughter, "Why Michael O'Donovan, are you drunk, showing up at this hour?"

"No, Rose. But I need to talk to you." He waited, not wanting to alarm her yet.

"Michael, my father will see you! Go away, please."

Just then, Cronin opened the front door and peered out at Michael. "For God's sake, man," he began, shuffling in his robe and slippers, the candle in his hand trembling, "you have a great nerve banging around here at this time of night."

"Mr. Cronin, please. It's Michael O'Donovan, Mr. O'Neill's employee. There's been an—accident. I need to talk to Miss Rose."

The old man stared, looking down at Michael's leg, the blood-soaked scarf. Finally, he helped Michael come in. "Is Mr. O'Neill all right?"

"No, he's not. Please, fetch Miss Rose for me, will you?" He looked directly at Cronin, and the man turned and made his way haltingly up the broad front staircase. In a few moments Michael heard light footsteps running down the hall, and Rose flew down the stairs, her long dark hair tumbling around her shoulders, her flowered kimono billowing out behind her as she descended.

"Michael, what is it?" Then she saw the blood. She brought her hand up to her mouth, staring.

"Rose, let's go into the library." She led the way and lit the oil lamp on O'Neill's wide mahogany desk. Michael came toward her, taking her hands in his. "Rose, darling, it's so hard to have to say this. There's been an accident, and I'm afraid your father. . . ." He found he could not say the word.

Rose stood motionless. Her face was closed and set. "Just say it, Michael, he's dead, isn't he?"

"Yes."

"What happened?"

He drew her to him then, leading her over to the sofa. She caught hold of him as he faltered, and gently pulled him down beside her. Michael moaned, "Rose, I'll get blood on the sofa."

"Just tell me."

He held her while he told her the story of that night, how her father had known about their meetings, how angry he was, and then, how he had not been able to protect him when the killers had burst in the door. He waited, frightened by her frozen face. She said nothing for a long time, just sat there shuddering in his arms.

Suddenly with a furious movement she rose and began pacing back and forth, her voice crackling with anger, "I knew it. I knew this would happen. All that talk of his business, his connections to the high and mighty in the city, his hopes to rise in politics, when all the time he was a gangster involved in cheating and stealing other's people's money. A great shakedown artist." He let her rave, watching as tears streamed down her face.

Then when she stopped, exhausted, he said quietly, "Rose, that's not all he was. He was a father who loved you and was dearly proud of you. He was a patriot of Ireland, trying to help free his people from the British in the country of his birth."

She raised her eyes to him then, her gaze as cold as the sea. "And what of you, Michael O'Donovan? You are hurt. You could have died too!" Her eyes were wild, unseeing. "What has he turned you into? You too could be sprawled on the floor of an empty tavern, lying dead in a pool of your own blood."

He looked away from her then. In a low, strangled voice, he began, "Rose, everything you say is true. I came to America to be free, to become someone. And what I've become is someone I am not proud of. Someone who is afraid of getting caught every moment of the day, afraid of causing grief to my beloved sister, and now, above all, to you. Rose, I am done with that life. It was a wrong turn."

She looked at him then, and he was heart-scalded by the doubt he saw in her eyes. He had nothing to offer her.

They sat in silence holding hands as the clock ticked the minutes, until finally it rang the hour, four o'clock. He tried to rise.

Rose grabbed his arm, "No, I'm sending for our doctor, Dr. White. You need to have that wound taken care of." Her voice was cold, and he didn't dare object.

An hour later, Dr. White was examining the leg. "Well, my boy, it seems you have a severed Achilles tendon." He probed the wound as he spoke, his face grim. "You were damn lucky, O'Donovan. The bullet grazed your ankle and came out the other side. But I fear you will be walking with a limp, probably for the rest of your life."

The doctor turned to Rose then, "I'm so sorry for your troubles, Rose. I've known your father for a long time and liked him. But I can't say. . . well, good night," he finished lamely.

Rose saw him out, and when she returned to the library, Michael was hobbling toward her. As she hurried to help him, she hissed, "You fool!" Then she pulled him toward her, lifting her face to his. He kissed her then, her mouth cold but urgent, and they stood embracing for long minutes, Michael wondering at how love and sorrow could feel the same. As he turned to go, she whispered, "Michael, thank God you were with him."

The next day, the St. Louis Dispatch *led* with the story above the fold:

JOHN PATRICK O'NEILL, BUSINESSMAN,
PHILANTHROPIST, AND SUSPECTED CRIME BOSS,
GUNNED DOWN OUTSIDE THE CITY!

The Hogan gang were listed in the article as prime suspects. Once he had been seen by the doctor, who quickly cleaned the wound and bound his ankle tightly, Michael and Finn had spent the day after O'Neill's murder being grilled once more by two older detectives, Ward and Fagin. They separated the two of them and called Michael in first as the only eyewitness.

Over and over, he repeated his story of what happened. No, he did not get a good look at their faces. He had been shot too, trying to reach for his gun. No, he had not fired a shot. They could dig up his gun which he had buried in the woods behind the tavern to check it. When the officers veered too close to questioning him about the business they were supposed to discuss with Hogan's people, he admitted only to the bootlegging side of the operation. He was shocked that the two men did not pursue this line of questioning. When the detective finally told Michael he could go for now, he understood. *They were not going to investigate the business.* It would only expose a web of corruption that the police themselves were caught in. They let him go with a warning to stick around in case they needed him as a witness.

Michael, the day after the shooting, rang the bell at the Burkes' house, dreading the meeting with Eileen. He tried hiding the cane behind his back so it wouldn't be the first thing she saw. When Eileen flung open the door and saw Michael, she grabbed him close, almost toppling him over. Once in the ladies' parlor, she shut the door. They sat facing each other, neither saying a word. Finally, Eileen wept. "What is wrong with you, Michael? You are crippled! You've brought sorrow and shame to us now."

Michael sat, head bowed. She continued, "I warned you, I told you that you were involved with bad business." Michael said nothing, still not looking at her. She raved on, "First the IRB in Bantry, now this shady business that has ended in murder!"

At that he looked up. "Well, I'm done with it now, Eileen. It's over. I just pray Rose will still have me, a cripple, who couldn't even protect her father." He could not tell her then with her anger flaring, what happened the night of O'Neill's death, that O'Neill knew he was seeing Rose, and that her father had dismissed him as a two-bit Irish fool to think he could win Rose.

Three days later, on Monday, the thirteenth of November, the funeral of John Patrick O'Neill was held at St. Patrick's Church on Sixth and Biddle. Monsignor William Burke, a native of Tipperary, celebrated the solemn Requiem Mass. Various priests from the city attended, but the Bishop was noticeably absent. The Religious of the Sacred Heart, who had been Rose's teachers, gathered in two front pews on the left side, their voices rising like silver as they sang the Gregorian chants of the Requiem Mass. Rose, veiled in black, sat in the front pew, with only her Aunt Margaret, her mother's sister from Chicago, beside her.

Michael with Eileen and Lance sat two pews behind Rose and her aunt. He spied Finn and the other men who'd worked for O'Neill scattered throughout the church, seated far away from the politicians who sat toward the front of the church.

After the burial at Calvary Cemetery, Michael, on crutches, and Eileen, with Lance hanging back shyly, greeted Rose. Her face pale beneath the black net of her wide hat, Rose was shivering in spite of the unusually mild day. Michael introduced his sister and Lance to Rose and her aunt, who gazed curiously at him when he took Rose's hand in his own and held on to it through the introductions.

Afterward, the O'Donovans and Lance headed for the carriage Michael had hired for the funeral. Eileen was quiet as they headed back into the heart of the city. She was heartsick to watch her brother hobbling along, her swift strong brother who could have been gunned down that night. She felt the sting of scandal now since her brother's name had been in the newspaper, listed as an associate of Mr. O'Neill who had witnessed the shooting. She wondered if Lance might be having second thoughts about loving a woman whose brother was involved in crime.

Eileen suspected that everyone in that church knew who and what John O'Neill was. The Misses Burke had been horrified when the news of O'Neill's operations had come out in the paper, and several Congressmen had suggested a federal investigation into the activities of Irish immigrants in St. Louis, even into the activities of the highly popular Ancient Order of Hibernians.

Michael said suddenly, "Why don't we stop somewhere for a bite to eat. I'm famished."

"Yes," Eileen sighed, "the funeral was so cold. Everyone there knew what he was." She looked at Michael, with a mixture of scorn and pity. But she was happy that Lance agreed to come along this morning. She'd been wanting the two men she loved most in the world to meet, maybe even to get to like each other, in spite of the trouble her brother had gotten himself in.

When they settled into a booth in Miss Holland's Café, they each ordered a hearty breakfast with strong hot tea. Outside the windows of the café, the trees were bare, but it was an unusually mild, sunlit day for November. Eileen watched as her brother and Lance tried to make conversation, carefully avoiding any reference to the horror of a few nights ago.

Lance looked up hesitantly and said, "There's something I don't understand about the Catholic Church. How could they have allowed such a grand funeral with the priests and nuns all there when everyone knew what a terrible fellow this O'Neill was?" He looked at them both anxiously.

"Why Lance," Eileen tried to smile. "Surely all of us are sinners. The Church isn't only for the saints, you know."

He looked at her, still dubious. "I guess I have a lot to learn about your religion, Eileen."

Michael grimaced, shaking his head at his sister's quick explanation. He wasn't as sure in his expectation of God's compassion as his sister was. He had a lot to be forgiven.

Finally, Eileen put down her cup and looked at her brother. "Michael, love, what in God's name are you going to do now?"

He stared at her, his face flushing. For a minute he said nothing, then burst out, "Eileen, I'm going back to Ireland."

"What?" She looked up, "You are joking, surely?"

"No, I'm dead serious. I'm going to ask Rose to marry me, and we will go back home, at least back to my home," he faltered.

"Have you asked her yet?" Eileen tried to keep the doubt out of her voice.

"No." The waitress brought them the check, and Michael

and Lance tussled a minute, with Michael finally ceding the bill to Lance. Outside, Eileen embraced her brother, and the two men shook hands. Michael, leaning on the crutches that were a bit short for him, made his way carefully down the street.

Eileen took Lance's arm, and they fell into step. He was the first to break the silence. He frowned and said hesitantly, "Well, your brother seems like a fine fellow, Eileen. But I cannot understand why he got mixed up in the business with O'Neill and his crew."

Eileen said nothing. How could she explain to this hardworking, confident American the feeling of being a stranger in a new land, with no money, no family to support you, hungry to get ahead. And then to find a group of Irishmen who were raking in money for Ireland, or at least that's what you hoped, and drawn in by your own need of money, love for the country of your birth, and the illusion that you were helping Ireland by shaking down storekeepers in St. Louis, you silenced your conscience in the same way you'd done back in Ireland when you entertained the thought of attacking the barracks of the British soldiers and stealing their weapons. No, it was useless to try to explain all this to Lance, as useless as it would be to explain what led her mother and brother to have, in truth, sold her to a man she did not love.

"Getting involved with O'Neill was a mistake, love. And to my brother's great good fortune he's survived a shooting before what happened to O'Neill happened to him. I've lived in dread every day since I caught on to what he was doing. I hope you'll come to know the Michael who has been a rock to me my whole life." She stopped, and faced Lance, "I hope that Michael's involvement in this awful business doesn't change how you feel about me."

Lance took both her hands in his as he pulled her to him, "Eileen, nothing in the world could change what I feel for you. This may not be the right time to say this, but I can't wait. You know I love you. I want to marry you, and I don't want to wait any longer. So, would you do me the honor of becoming my wife?"

Eileen looked into his eyes, so clear and honest in the afternoon light. Here was the man she had dreamed of meeting, one so straight and kind, yet sure of himself and his place in the world. He walked with a swing in his step, he laughed easily and often, confident in his ability to navigate whatever came his way, so American. Then she saw the way his lips trembled and knew that he was vulnerable too.

"My God, Lance, I thought you would never ask!" She gazed at him laughingly, dazzled by the love and joy that broke out on his face. And right there on Benton Street in the middle of a November afternoon, passersby saw a tall young man pick up a young woman in a dark dress and kiss her while swinging her around until they were both dizzy, dizzy with love.

CHAPTER TWENTY-NINE

....

A month later Eileen and Lance's wedding plans were in motion. The wedding on Christmas Day was to be a small affair, Eileen decided, and Lance agreed. They would be married at noon by Father Fitzgerald at St. Patrick's Church, but in front of the altar railing, not in the sanctuary, since Lance was not a Catholic, Eileen explained to Lance, who nodded uncertainly. It would not be a Mass, but rather a brief ceremony with the readings from scripture, a short homily, and then the exchange of vows. Michael would give Eileen away, and the Misses Burke and Bess would sit with him in the front pew, along with Rose. Rose had invited a few of the nuns from City House, one of whom would play the grand pipe organ, with Bach's tender *Air on a G String* as Eileen came down the aisle. The people from Schaeffer's Tailoring Shop would be there also, wanting to see the bridal gown they fashioned for their newest employee.

No one from Lance's far-away family would attend, but his father sent a telegram congratulating them and inviting Lance and his bride to visit them in Wisconsin as soon as they could. On the groom's side of the church would be his boss, old Mr. Ward with his wife Margaret, an O'Flaherty from Oughterard, as well as several of the men who worked with Lance at the painting company. After the wedding they would all crowd into the Misses Burkes' house for a splendid luncheon prepared by Bess and Eileen days before, with a grand wedding cake from Miss Holland's Café.

Eileen was worried about the dress. Since she was a widow, she wanted it to be simple. And yet, she wanted to be beautiful for Delancey. His kisses and embraces, his mouth on her neck and even on her breasts a few times, aroused her more each day. Little by little all the old shame and fear about sex fell away from her. Now her body would be a gift to Lance, just as his would be for her. She had sewn her own trousseau with its silk nightgowns and negligees, new satin undergarments in ivory and pale pink blush. Imagining their wedding night, she wanted him so much it shocked her. She tried not to remember John Sullivan and their miserable wedding night.

One evening three weeks before the wedding, Miss Alice, huffing from her climb upstairs to Eileen's room, knocked on the door and entered, laying a carefully wrapped package in scented tissue paper on the bed. When she caught her breath, she began, "Eileen, I've saved this fine lace made by nuns in France for many years, waiting for just the right occasion. If you think it would be suitable for your wedding dress, it is yours."

Eileen opened the package, and yards of ivory lace spilled out, with the faint smell of lavender wafting from its folds. "Oh, Miss Alice! It's beautiful! But are you sure you have no use for it?"

"No, my dear. Any hopes I had for being a bride faded years ago. It would give Nettie and me great joy to see you walk down the aisle in it." The old woman's cheeks were pink, her eyes misty.

"Miss Alice, was there ever anyone you wanted to marry?"

"Why, Eileen, I had so many suitors down in New Madrid that the young men had to take turns courting me on Sunday afternoons," she laughed, heading for the door. Eileen realized she had not really answered her question.

Christmas Day dawned bright, the sun gleaming on a landscape lightly dusted with snow that had fallen silently during the long night. Eileen woke thinking of her mother. Oh, if only she could be here with her now. How much her mother would have loved seeing her this happy with Lance. She remembered waking up on that other wedding day in Bantry, gazing at the blue dress her mother had so painstakingly made for her, hoping somehow to make up to her for that dreaded marriage.

Now she jumped out of bed and rushed to the dresser where she kept her wooden box of treasures. She picked up a felt pouch of dark blue, blue as Thomas's eyes and lifted out a lock of her son's hair, inhaling his faint scent. She would sew the lock of hair inside her wedding dress, so that a trace of the child would lie close to her heart on this happy day, balm for the sorrow that rose in her daily when the memories hit her. She searched through the trinkets until she came to the necklace of a single pearl on a silver chain that Michael had given her on that day in Bantry. She'd wear the necklace today. After all, she didn't need much adornment, since the night before Lance had pressed into her hand a small package.

"Should I open it now or save it for after the wedding?" she'd asked shyly. Eileen felt as if she were dreaming. Was this all really happening?

"Open it now. I hoped maybe it was something you could wear tomorrow." He tapped his foot, impatient at her delay. Inside the black box, nestled in pale blue satin, was a pair of silver filigree earrings, with single pearls dangling. "Oh," she began, but he stepped toward her and gathered her in his arms, kissing her deeply.

"Eileen O'Donovan," he whispered, "if you don't hurry up and marry me, I'm going to have to carry you off over my shoulder. I can't wait another night!"

"Well, Delancey Jordan, you are going to have to wait one more night in spite of this most extravagant and beautiful gift. I shall wear the earrings tomorrow until you take me to bed." She blushed at her own words while the little dog Pansy ran round and round the couple, barking at them as they kissed once more.

The scent of evergreen branches adorning the high altar filled St. Patrick's Church on the morning of the wedding. The stained-glass windows refracted the sun's rays into shafts of blue, scarlet and green. As Eileen walked down the aisle, her hand lightly resting on Michael's arm, the lace dress clinging to her body, she held her head high, her light brown hair pinned up and fastened in place by a wreath of white roses. She clutched a small bouquet of violets, and with each step their scent mingled with the odor of incense, left over from the Christmas High Mass celebrated earlier that morning. It was a special favor to have the wedding on this day, she knew. Somehow her brother's persuasive talents had convinced the young pastor at St. Patrick's Parish, Father Thomas O'Shea, to allow this brief ceremony to take place on Christmas. Lance turned to watch her, and her shoulders relaxed as she walked toward him.

The reception at the Burkes was festive, but during the breakfast and the interminable champagne toasts, she and Lance kept gazing at each other, wanting to be away. Lance had booked a room in the Planter's Hotel, the second finest hotel in the city. He'd been so proud to tell Eileen that Mr. Ward had given him a raise and a bonus in honor of his marriage. Now they could start their life together in a small but elegant apartment on Union Boulevard, not far from the Ward Painting Company. For the first time since they met, they would be alone together.

Finally, Lance rose from his seat at the long dining-room table, and cleared his throat, waiting for silence. A laughing murmur ran through the company, as jokes were made about the couple's impatience to be off.

"I'm not much for making speeches," Lance began, "but I want to thank everyone for being with us on a most wonderful day. Meeting Eileen was the luck of the Irish for me, and I'm not even Irish. But getting to know her brother Michael, Miss Alice and Miss Nettie, Miss Rose, and Miss Bess," and at that he smiled over at Bess, who was wiping her eyes and trying to smile back at him, "I see that Eileen was loved and welcomed into this city and this country by all who met her. I can only say thanks to each of you for letting her go, and yet, we'll not be far away, so we look forward to welcoming all of you into our home as soon as we get settled." At that, he lifted his glass, "Now let's all raise our glasses to my beautiful bride, Mrs. Delancey Jordan, the belle of Bantry Bay." Amid laughter and tears, Eileen gazed around in love at the smiling faces shining down at her.

The newlyweds made their getaway soon after the last toast. Eileen had changed into a long fitted gray traveling dress, with a saucy blue feathered hat cocked sideways on her head. The silver earrings dangled and caught the sun's light as she jumped nimbly into the carriage. She felt Lance's arm encircle her and hoped he could not hear the mad beating of her heart.

Later, as night fell over the city and the gas lamps winked on, the couple stood together at the window of their hotel room on the eighth floor overlooking the great Mississippi River. Arms entwined, they gazed for a long time at the steamers and tug-boats making their way through patches of ice that glistened in the setting sun. Tomorrow they would be boarding the steamer *Natchez* on their honeymoon to New Orleans.

Finally, Eileen turned to face Lance, "If you'll excuse me, I'll go change now." She stared into his eyes, and he caught her hands in his and raised them to his lips. "Eileen, you're a woman who constantly surprises."

In the bathroom her fingers trembled as she undressed and pulled on the delicate satin nightgown Rose had surprised her with. Then Eileen let her hair fall around her shoulders, but she kept on the earrings Lance had given her.

When she opened the door, Lance had lit two oil lamps, one beside the bed and one on the table by the window. The room was in shadow now, but the golden light of the lamps pooled richly on the polished tables. He was sitting on the bed, in his shirtsleeves. He said nothing, watching her as she walked toward him, then suddenly he rose and took her in his arms with a groan, lifting her across the few feet to the bed, and laying her down as he bent over her. Swiftly, he pulled her nightgown over her head and tossed it to the foot of the bed. She gasped as his hands and mouth began to caress her neck, then her breasts, moving gently but surely down her legs, until he touched her there, where she had wanted him so. After she could bear it no more, she opened herself to him. A thousand stars exploded in her, down to her toes.

Later, Lance lay sleeping beside her. She loved lying here, nestled into him, watching him as he slept. He looked so young and innocent, a boy almost, his blond hair tumbled over his forehead. *So, this is what the all the books were on about,* she smiled to herself. For a moment a dark memory hovered in the still air, as images rose before her of that first wedding night, Sullivan, rough, with whiskey on his breath, and her bitter tears on the pillowcase in the musty farmhouse. She'd come out on the other side of life. But she'd had to go through a dark time for this joy: the loss of Thomas. *My son, my son.*

She brushed the tears away. Well, God had given her another chance at happiness. She vowed she would love and cherish this man and hoped she would give him sons and daughters too. As she felt sleep coming on, she turned on her side, dreaming, half-awake, of a baby girl with small round cheeks and wispy fair hair.

CHAPTER THIRTY

....

I n the late afternoon of Eileen's wedding, Michael walked Rose
home. It had been six weeks since the shooting, and he still
limped. Rose slipped on her boots for the walk through the snowy
streets and sidewalks, carrying her good shoes. Rose, muffled
in her cape of dark red with its fur collar pulled up in front
of her face, was radiant, Michael thought. Finally, she had lost
that haunted look of the last few weeks. She chattered on about
the ceremony, Eileen's dress, the delicious food, but Michael's
thoughts were somber. He and Rose had talked about marriage
in the weeks following her father's death. But Michael knew he
had nothing to offer her, no money, no job, no future, really.

Rose had blithely brushed aside his worries, saying she was
inheriting some money from her mother's estate. Her Aunt Margaret was staying with her for the time being, and they were
meeting with the executor of her mother's estate in the coming
week. She vowed not to touch any of her father's money, which
was tied up in the courts with the police and the lawyers, the
case fated to drag on for years. But Michael was not reassured.
How in the hell could he marry Rose under this cloud? He'd be
seen as a gold-digger for sure, and in fact, her formidable Aunt
Margaret seemed to give off that suspicion beneath her carefully
polite manner.

As they reached the front door, Rose lifted her face to Michael for a kiss, and Michael held her face between his hands, and sighed, "Rose, you are so beautiful. How I envy my sister and Lance this night." He kissed her then, and her mouth was warm and soft, lingering on his. "I'm headed home now before Mrs. Quigley locks me out for the night. Ever since the... events, she's taken my key away."

"See you tomorrow then?" Her eyes shone in the fast-falling dusk.

"Yes." But Michael was not going home. He limped on painfully, heading south toward Cass Avenue, then east toward the river. He met no one on this Christmas night but gazed at the lighted windows of the houses he passed, many with Christmas trees still lit with candles illuminating the darkness. His breath rose in the frosty air. Finally, he reached the river, its great width dark, with few vessels on this night.

He had to think, to plan. Going back to Ireland would be hard, a defeat. Martin certainly would not welcome him with a new wife back at the farm in Bantry. Of course, he wanted to show Rose where he'd grown up, the farm, Blackthorn House, the wild Atlantic in all its changeable moods, but Bantry was not the place for them to settle down.

They'd settle in Dublin. In *The Freeman's Journal* these past few months, Michael read of a young politician named Parnell. Although Parnell was a Protestant, he stood up for Catholic Ireland against the bloody British. Maybe there was hope for a peaceful solution. He'd write to the editor of *The Freeman's Journal*; perhaps there was work available at the paper, even on the printing side. He'd not be needing a gun working at a newspaper. He laughed grimly to himself wondering how he could explain his background in printing press work, gained at the hands of old Peterson, the forger. He lit a cigar he had saved from the wedding, the smoke dissolving quickly in the cold air.

Then there was the problem of his allegiance to the Irish

Republican Brotherhood. Technically he was still a member, although he doubted that he was in good standing. He thought of the ominous visit MacDonogh had paid to Eileen that night in Bantry, the not-so-veiled threats when he'd asked her about his whereabouts. But he still believed in the Cause.

As he turned back toward the boarding house on Cass Avenue, he felt a surge of hope. He and Rose would go to Ireland. Rose, with her curious mind and impetuous spirit, would be at his side, and, he admitted to himself, her money would start them out, paying for the voyage and for a place to live until he could find work. He'd not be too proud to accept that. He'd vowed to the slain O'Neill that he'd let his girl come to no harm! He'd write to both Father Gleason in Bantry and Miss O'Brien in London to tell them he was returning to Ireland. But first he had to marry the lass.

Rose and Aunt Margaret waited for the lawyer in the parlor of the O'Neill house on the second Monday of January. He was from the firm of Bailey and White, a firm her father had retained for many years. It's odd, Rose thought, that Geoffrey Bailey was not Irish, but rather from an old St. Louis society family, a member of Christ Episcopal Church. He was, Rose knew, everything her father wished he could be, in spite of his professed loyalty to the cause of Irish freedom. Above all, her father had craved respectability, and what bitter irony it was that not fame but infamy came in a rain of bullets. Stifling the tears that came at the image seared in her mind, she turned to watch Aunt Margaret.

Margaret Keane, a handsome woman of about fifty, living with her friend, a Miss Godwin, in a townhouse in Chicago, was her mother's younger sister, and the two had been close, or so her father had told her. The problem was her aunt could not stand Rose's father, so she'd had little to do with them over the years.

Over these last few days Rose had come to admire her aunt, an educated, strongly opinioned woman who was working for women's suffrage.

Both Margaret and her mother had been taught by the Religious of the Sacred Heart, as Rose had been, and the nuns had trained the girls to think and to reason as well as to play the piano and speak French. But at this moment Rose wasn't sure her aunt approved of Michael. She'd told her aunt that she was in love with him, and that they wished to marry, but her aunt had just looked at her for a few minutes in silence.

Now as they waited for Mr. Bailey, the lawyer, Margaret cleared her throat. "Rose, you've had a great shock. I know you think you are in love with Mr. O'Donovan, and I certainly see his charm. But I believe it is too soon to make such an adult decision." Margaret rose and walked to the window, gazing out at the bare trees. Then she turned to look at Rose, "Rose, I was thinking maybe you'd like to come to spend some time with me in Chicago. The city is very exciting these days, with all the beautiful stores opening on Michigan Avenue, the lake, the opera and symphony." She paused, waiting for some response. When Rose said nothing, she added, "I've talked it over with my friend, Miss Godwin, and she has agreed that you would be very welcome."

Rose felt the color rising in her face. She tried to keep her voice low and steady. She took a deep breath, "Aunt Margaret, I have been in love with Michael for months. He has been a perfect gentleman all this time and the only barrier between us was his position working for my father. I really believe. . . ." Just then the door swung open, and Mr. Bailey hurried into the room.

"My apologies, ladies, for the late arrival." He bowed to both of them, and they seated themselves once more. Rose leaned forward during the lawyer's reading of the terms of the trust, listening carefully, trying to grasp the foreign language of banking, trusts, capital, and interest, language that the nuns at City House had neglected to impart. But when Bailey read out the sum of fifty thousand dollars, "payable to said female child, Rose O'Neill, upon reaching her eighteenth birthday."

Rose stifled a gasp. This was far more than she'd expected, and it would come to her much earlier than she'd hoped.

"Rose, do you have any questions about the inheritance?" Mr. Bailey peered over his glasses at her.

Rose shook her head. "No, sir, I believe that it is very clear what my mother intended." There was silence in the long parlor for a moment, and Rose saw Bailey and her aunt exchange glances.

"Now, Miss Rose, I know your father would have preferred that I handle the money for you and put it into safe investments. So, I will be drawing up a list of. . ."

"Excuse me, Mr. Bailey. But your help will not be needed. I am going to take the money in cash as soon as the bank advises me that it is available. I shall be going abroad shortly." Rose closed her lips firmly, and Bailey waited a moment for her to explain, but it was soon evident that no explanation would be coming. He frowned in the direction of her Aunt Margaret, but to Rose's surprise, Margaret rose to her feet, thanking Mr. Bailey for his administration of the trust over the past eighteen years, and assuring him that her niece would be a careful steward of the inheritance. Gracefully, she ushered the bewildered lawyer to the door, and again they were alone.

"Well, my girl," Aunt Margaret smiled, "How does it feel to be an heiress?"

"I'm not sure, Aunt. How did you and my mother inherit such an amount of money? I know very little about my grandparents."

Margaret sighed and began to pace the room, her arms folded. "Your grandparents, Thomas and Katherine Keane, came over from Galway during famine times. They had inherited a small farm there on the death of my grandparents. You understand that it was very unusual for Irish Catholics to own land in Ireland. But after the marriage, they could see that there was no future for them in Galway, so they sold the farm at a fairly good price to a wealthy landlord in the area, and came to the States, settling in Chicago. My father, who had been educated by the Christian Brothers, got into the railroad business there, and worked his way up in the Illinois Central Railroad."

Margaret began to pace around the room, touching the lilies in a tall vase absent- mindedly. "Your mother, Mary Katherine, was born first, and I followed two years later. Our parents sent us to school in Chicago at the Convent of the Sacred Heart, and luckily for us, we received a fine education, as did you. When your mother came down to St. Louis for a visit with a friend from school whose parents lived here, she met your father at a dance at St. Patrick's, where many Irish came on Friday nights."

Rose looked up then. "What did your parents think of my father when they met him?"

"They thought he was a charming scoundrel." Her aunt came and sat beside Rose. She took her hand, "Rose, I don't want to speak ill of the dead, but we all were worried that summer when your mother came home engaged to a person we thought. . . not really worthy of her. There were awful scenes, tears, and threats, for weeks."

Rose looked down, wishing with all her heart that she had known her mother as a young, impetuous girl. Margaret hesitated before she spoke again, "Well, nothing could stop your mother from marrying, so my father put money in a trust for both of us, just to ensure our future, no matter what happened. As you see, I have never married, and the money has given me the independence to live my life exactly as I choose." She turned Rose's face to her then and added softly, "Rose, it would break my heart and your mother's heart to see you repeat the terrible mistake of marrying the wrong man."

"Aunt, I can see how Michael seems to you. He has no money, no prospects, and was involved in the crimes of my father. But he is a fine man, and he is dedicated to the cause of freedom for Ireland." She got up then, smiling down at her aunt although her eyes were full of tears. "Besides, it's too late. I love him and have thrown in my lot with him, for better or worse."

On New Year's Eve, Michael sat at the table in his room at Mrs. Quigley's trying to write a letter to Father Gleason. He had scratched out several versions, not knowing how much to confess to the priest of the events of the past year. How could he admit that he had wasted the opportunities coming to the States offered him, in his haste to make money by getting involved with O'Neill; that he's been involved in shady activities, downright crimes? That he'd watched his boss being gunned down in a gang turf war and had been wounded and maimed himself? All the money he'd made had been from crime. And then his old involvement in the IRB, that had been a fiasco too.

What he would tell Father Gleason is that he was returning to Ireland a chastened but hopeful man. Above all, he had found the woman who made him want to be better. He would explain how Rose O'Neill and the love she had for him gave him the courage to change his life, and that it was a life he was longing to live in Ireland. He would tell Father of his plan to get work at *The Freeman's Journal* in some capacity and ask if he had any connections in Dublin who would help them find a place to live.

When he looked up from the final draft, he saw snow falling gently past the dark window and heard the soft click of the flakes on the pane. It was a new year! 1872. His heart beat fast when he thought of Rose and the new life that beckoned. For the first time in forever he felt at peace, a feeling that he was headed in the right direction on the journey, a journey in which he would not be alone.

CHAPTER THIRTY-ONE

....

The wedding of Miss Rose O'Neill of St. Louis, Missouri, and Mister Michael O'Donovan, lately of Bantry, Ireland, took place on Saturday, March 17, 1872, on the feast of St. Patrick, in the chapel of The Convent of the Sacred Heart on Church Street, where Rose had gone to school.

It was a small affair, attended only by family and a few close friends. Because of the violent circumstances of the death of Rose's father, the last thing Michael and Rose wanted was notoriety in the press. So, the banns of marriage supposed to be announced in St. Patrick's Parish on three consecutive Sundays had been waived by special permission of the Bishop, due to the persuasive powers of Aunt Margaret.

Michael had teased Rose often about eloping, but they'd decided that three months had gone by since her father's death, so a small ceremony would not be disrespectful. Rose would wear the same dress her mother had been married in after slight alterations for her height. Aunt Margaret found the dress in her mother's closet, carefully wrapped in tissue. Rose was moved at the simplicity of the organdy dress, as light and airy as early spring.

Michael had been surprised when Rose told him that she had asked her Aunt Margaret to walk her down the aisle. "But isn't some man supposed to give you away?" he asked with a smile.

"I'll not be given away by anyone, Michael. I'm giving myself away!" Rose said, her eyes blazing.

Michael came and kissed her lightly, saying, "Ah, that's the girl. Sure, and I'm marrying a woman a lot like my sister Eileen for spirit." Secretly he was pleased. It would be boring to marry a stiff, proper girl, and Rose would need all the fight in the world to make a life with the likes of him.

Father Gleason's letter was pessimistic about Michael's plan to his return to Ireland, claiming that things had not improved since Michael left Ireland. The IRB had gone underground, but they were still active, especially in the west of Ireland. Times were harder than ever in Bantry, with several years of crop failures. Michael wrote back, telling Father that he would explain more of his circumstances when they were reunited in Bantry, and that he was looking forward to introducing Father to his Rose.

Now as Michael entered the chapel on this chilly spring morning, the scent of narcissus and jonquils filled the air. He'd asked Lance as his new brother-in-law to be his best man, and Eileen was to serve as matron of honor for Rose. As Michael walked out slowly from the sanctuary before the nuptial Mass, he faced a sea of black and white. Nuns filled the pews of the chapel, delighted to be included in Rose's happiness.

When the music began, he watched Eileen as matron of honor walk down the aisle, radiant and assured. Then he saw Rose coming toward him, carrying a bouquet of lilies-of-the-valley, and at her side, her Aunt Margaret in a pale gray gown. Rose's face was hidden by the veil, but she moved like a young princess with her head held high.

She faced him then, and Margaret lifted the veil from her face. Rose was pale, her lips trembling. He took her hand in his and tried to warm it as he gazed at her. Then her face lit up, and she answered his smile with blue eyes full of tears. Together they turned to Father O'Shea as he began the words of the Mass, "Introibo ad altare Dei...."

Michael lifted his eyes to the crucifix and breathed a swift prayer to the Savior: *"I know I don't deserve her, Lord. Help me to be worthy of her. A thousand thanks."*

Two months later, on the last Sunday in May, Michael and Rose headed for Union Station downtown to catch the train to New York. They were booked on the vessel *SS Wyoming* in second class. Michael, still clinging to the habit of frugality, had declined Rose's suggestion of going in first class. Since they weren't scheduled to depart from the port of New York until the third of June, they would have a few days to see the city while they rested for the long ocean voyage to Queenstown.

Summer had set in, the trees lush and full, the days hot but not yet unbearable as they would be in August. Eileen and Lance hired a cab to take them to the station to see her brother and Rose off. Eileen fanned herself as the horse plodded through the dusty streets. It was Sunday, the city quiet except for the bells ringing out the call to worship. She had gone to Mass alone in the early morning. She and Lance had worked out a compromise about religion: Eileen would not try to convert him, and he would occasionally accompany her to church when the weather was especially bad. Eileen often entertained him at lunch on Sunday with any particularly amusing bits of the priest's sermon.

"You're awfully quiet this morning, Eileen," Lance glanced sideways at her, keeping his eyes on the street.

"Oh, Lance, I'm so going to miss Michael, and Rose too. It's been lovely having them close by. And what in the world is Michael going to do in Dublin? Then I start thinking and wonder if I will ever see my brother again in this life." She stopped then, not wanting to say what she most feared: that

Michael would become involved again with the IRB. The cold-eyed MacDonogh's visit to her back home was etched in her memory. These were serious men, men who would not hesitate to punish someone they thought had betrayed his oath of loyalty.

"Eileen, I think your Michael has learned a painful lesson during these past months. Besides, isn't he planning to work at a newspaper there?"

"I hope so," Eileen murmured. She stared out at the deserted streets, unseeing. There was something else on her mind. She suspected she was pregnant. She'd said nothing to Lance yet, trying to tamp down the joy she was feeling, not wanting to jinx her hopes.

"What is it, Eileen? You're as fidgety as a cat today!" Lance looked at her anxiously.

"Nothing in this blessed world is wrong when I have you at my side," she smiled at him, and took his arm pressing it to her side. They arrived at the train station near the river, surprised at the size of the crowd swarming the riverfront. Lance grabbed her arm, and they pushed their way through the people milling about, saying their farewells, steam hissing from the rumbling bowels of the train.

"Eileen! Lance! We're over here," Michael's voice rose above the din, and relieved, they ran toward the little knot of people gathered at the door of one of the last cars on the train. Aunt Margaret and a few young women, friends of Rose, were gathered around the newlyweds.

"My God, Eileen, I thought you'd miss us," Michael laughed. "I never knew my sister to be on time in her life." Eileen shoved him then, trying to hide her sudden tears. Rose embraced her, and the two women held each other for a moment.

"Rose, take care of my brother," Eileen whispered. "Don't let him go off half-cocked when you get to Dublin."

Rose laughed. "I'll do my best, Eileen. But you know your brother. He's not one to take advice kindly." Eileen saw how young she was, so innocent of what might lie ahead for her in a new country, with no family, no friends, just this handsome, impetuous brother of hers who had swept into her life.

Then Michael grabbed Eileen and crushed her to him, whispering, "Eileen, God bless and keep you. Be happy! You deserve it!"

Finally, the porter blew the whistle, and the couple boarded the train. Michael turned and waved one last time, his smile wide, excited. He looked at Eileen, blew her a kiss, and disappeared into the train behind Rose. Eileen held her smile until he was inside the train and then turned away, shutting her eyes to fix forever the image of her brother as he was that morning.

In silence, Eileen and Lance strolled, arms linked, along the Mississippi, the river wending its way languidly along. They gazed out at the wide expanse of water, blue sky overhead blooming with clouds, tugboats and barges churning up-river like toys, while the great city on their left thrummed with life. Eileen felt the child stir within her. This child would be an American, born of one who had turned her back on Ireland, but one who would carry within her forever the fields and skies of Bantry, its towering white clouds blowing over the sea, the smell of the turf, the sound of the sea lashing the shore, her green island of sorrow and beauty.

Acknowledgments

....

"Story is our only boat for sailing on the river of time," says a character in Ursula LeGuin's novel *A Fisherman of the Sea*. This novel, *Out of Ireland*, is my attempt to imagine the life of my great-grandmother, Ellen Hickey Sullivan Jewett. My mother, Margaret Ward O'Shea, knew her well and told me stories of her. I also have two letters from my grandmother, Nettie Marie Jewett Ward, and her sister, Alice Jewett Hurd, from the 1960s, in which they shared with each other their scant knowledge of their mother's life in Ireland. So, this story is "sailing on the river of time."

I am grateful to my six brothers and sisters: Dan, Katie, Ellen, Tim, Mary Grace, and Matt, for reading the manuscript and giving me their comments and suggestions. I owe much gratitude to Herta Feely and Niki Gonji of Chrysalis Editorial for their careful reading of the manuscript, and their detailed notes which made it a much better novel. I thank my dear friends, Peg Wallace and Karen Sirmans, who read an early draft of the novel, for their support and suggestions.

I owe a big debt of gratitude to Oliver O'Hanlon—a PhD candidate in history at University College Cork and a writer for the *Irish Times*—for his meticulous examination of the manuscript for historical and cultural accuracy. His comments were invaluable. I am also grateful to Claire McCarthy, former Consul General of Ireland in Austin, for her enthusiasm and support. Jeannie Burke O'Fallon of St. Louis helped me with the history of the Religious of the Sacred Heart and their role in education in St. Louis. I owe a huge debt of gratitude to my amazing publisher, Brooke Warner of She Writes Press; my kind and patient project manager, Shannon Green; and to the talented cover designer, Mimi Bark, for the beautiful cover design. I have the luck of the Irish in getting author and literary advocate Caitlin Hamilton Summie as a publicist.

My three children and their spouses: Kristin and husband Max Benitez; Tim Wernicke and wife Sarah; and John Wernicke, have been the best cheerleaders, encouraging their mother to follow her dream of being a writer and helping her achieve it. Finally, I can never thank enough my beloved husband, Michael, for his great patience, his careful proofreading, and his steady belief in my work. His love and care sustain me always.

About the Author

Born and raised in an Irish Catholic family in St. Louis, Missouri, Marian O'Shea Wernicke is the author of the novel *Toward That Which Is Beautiful*, a finalist in both Literary Fiction and Romance Fiction in the 2021 Independent Book Awards, and a finalist in Multicultural Fiction in the 2021 American Fiction Awards. The 2021 Catholic Press Association awarded the novel Honorable Mention in Fiction. She is also the author of a memoir about her father, *Tom O'Shea: A Twentieth Century Man*. A nun for eleven years, Wernicke worked in Lima, Peru, for three years. After leaving the convent, Wernicke taught English as a second language in Madrid, and later was a professor of English and creative writing for twenty-five years at Pensacola State College, where she edited the literary magazine, *The Hurricane Review*. Marian is married to Michael Wernicke, and they are the parents of three adult children. After years of living in Pensacola, Florida, Marian and her husband Michael live in Austin, Texas, where they enjoy being near their children and grandson.

Author photo © Matthew O'Shea Photography

SELECTED TITLES FROM SHE WRITES PRESS

She Writes Press is an independent publishing
company founded to serve women writers everywhere.
Visit us at www.shewritespress.com.

Toward that Which is Beautiful by Marian O'Shea
Wernicke. $16.95, 978-1-63152-759-3. In June of 1964 in a
small town in the Altiplano of Peru, Sister Mary Katherine—a
young American nun afraid of her love for an Irish priest with
whom she has been working—slips away from her convent with
no money and no destination. Over the next eight days, she
encounters both friendly and dangerous characters and travels
an interior journey of memory and desire that leads her, finally,
to a startling destination.

Estelle by Linda Stewart Henley. $16.95, 978-1-63152-791-3.
From 1872 to '73, renowned artist Edgar Degas called New
Orleans home. Here, the narratives of two women—Estelle, his
Creole cousin and sister-in-law, and Anne Gautier, who in 1970
finds a journal written by a relative who knew Degas—intersect
. . . and a painting Degas made of Estelle spells trouble.

Eliza Waite by Ashley Sweeney. $16.95, 978-1-63152-058-
7. When Eliza Waite chooses to leave a stagnant life in rural
Washington State and join the masses traveling north to Alaska
in 1898 during the tumultuous Klondike Gold Rush, she
encounters challenges and successes in both business and love.

The Green Lace Corset by Jill G. Hall. $16.95, 978-1-63152-769-2. An artist buys a corset in a Flagstaff resale boutique and is forced to make the biggest decision of her life. A young midwestern woman is kidnapped on a train in 1885 and taken to the Wild West. Both women find the strength to overcome their fears and discover the true meaning of family—with a little push from a green lace corset.

The House on the Forgotten Coast by Ruth Coe Chambers. $16.95, 978-1-63152-300-7. The spirit of Annelise Lovett Morgan, who suffered a tragic death on her wedding day in 1897, returns in 1987 and asks seventeen-year-old Elise Foster to help her clear the name of her true love, Seth.

The Vintner's Daughter by Kristen Harnisch. $16.95, 978-1-63152-929-0. Set against the sweeping canvas of French and California vineyard life in the late 1890s, this is the compelling tale of one woman's struggle to reclaim her family's Loire Valley vineyard—and her life.

Printed in the USA
CPSIA information can be obtained
at www.ICGtesting.com
JSHW021435111023
49859JS00003BA/3